Morris, Alive

A Novel by Joel Bowman

ISBN: 978-1-7368381-1-2 (Paperback)
ISBN: 978-1-7368381-2-9 (Hardcover)
ISBN: 978-1-7368381-0-5 (Ebook)

This is a work of fiction. Names, characters, places, and incidents either are the product of the author's imagination or are used fictitiously, and any resemblance to actual persons, living or dead, events, or locales is entirely coincidental.

Front cover image by Alejandro Baigorri.
Layout and design by Muhammad Faizan Altaf.

Printed by IngramSpark, Inc., in the United States of America.

First printing edition 2021.

www.joelbowmanbooks.com

CONTENTS

For Anya

~~~

Afoot and light-hearted I take to the open road,
Healthy, free, the world before me,
The long brown path before me leading wherever I choose.

~ Walt Whitman

~~~

Morris, Alive

PART I

Chapter I

Floreat Romance

Morris came to America in a trance. A grungy blonde with sand between his toes, he traveled not directly from his native *terra australis*, but by way of that common colonizing ancestor. And though England in general, and London in particular, had helped him sever the umbilical thread of his childhood, there existed a peculiar, unspoken allure in America that no other place could quite match. Not then and, in many ways, not since.

Standing there alone, on the cusp of a new and tumultuous century, the streets of New York City throbbing just a few miles away, indifferent to his presence and yet somehow expecting him, Morris felt a flush of adrenaline course through his wiry frame. He was not yet in his twenty-first year but he sensed, with the unassailable confidence so breezily familiar to youth, that this coming decade would make of him something remarkable, something thoroughly, wholly unique. As he imbibed of the atmosphere around him, wintry and luculent, he knew that this was the place to be, the setting against which his own narrative could begin to take shape.

As for history, Morris hadn't a great deal to speak of…at least, not much he recalled at that very instant. If prompted, he might have remembered a soft, raven beauty who had stood with him on the beach near his parent's house on the eve of his departure and the deep, oceanic longing in her eyes as she foretold of his future diverging from hers.

"You're not coming back, are you." It was not a question. "You *want* to get lost. No, you want to *be* lost."

There were other moments, too, lingering just beyond the event horizon of his own recollection. Occasionally they would well up from deep within, morphing into vaguely familiar shapes or colors or sounds; a murmuring of conversation, sunlight painting the waves in rippling dawn hues, the scent of burned sugarcane suffused in the warm evening air.

But none of this occurred to him just now, for it was not the past that brought him to this moment as much as it was a desire to crystallize his own nascent reflection in the future. And so, not for the first time, a trembling soul focused on what lay before it and sought resolve on those shores of infinite possibility.

Yes, he repeated to himself. This was the place to *be*. Lost…or otherwise.

Unknown to those born in the United States, there exists a curious momentum in America apparent only to her visitors. In the widened eyes of these newcomers, the country appears to be hurtling forward in time at blistering, maniacal pace, her citizens unconsciously bound to a collective destiny of grand, mythological proportions, a mishmash of waiters and engineers and hookers and playwrights and teachers, of slick and desperate criminals and orange-hued T.V. evangelists, of frat boys and southern belles and Marlborough men and block-jawed G.I.s, of cowboys and surfers and poets and junkies, all marching arm in arm along a great concrete road that hasn't quite set.

Morris felt it now in his chest, this dizzying speed. Standing outside the terminal at JFK, he smoked a cigarette, then another, acutely aware of his newfound anonymity. He was a nameless figure in a strange and unfamiliar place, an invisible actor who had wandered onto a set where everyone else knew their lines, their cues, their positions. Around him the hectic brotherhood of a raw and original New World landscape raced, their accents, regional dialects as yet indistinguishable to him one from the other, chorused in his ear. He stood, shivering a little though entirely transfixed, as planeloads of strangers teemed from the main building, carry-on rollers in tow, sleek attaché cases slung over winter coats, breath heavy in the young morning air. They hurried along, pouring into their waiting taxis and town cars, a loosely attired assembly of trench coats and baseball caps and shocking pink tracksuit pants, wave after wave of people who didn't know his past and couldn't guess his future.

For the first time in a long time, Morris felt calm. Not a sense of calm, merely, but a warm and deliciously numbing silence emanating from within, a private cavern of solace and comfort, halcyon in the eye of a human hurricane. He was a glorious nobody to nobody in particular.

Of course, there was one person here who knew him. At least, she knew as much as he had confided in his letters.

#

Katelyn had traveled to London to visit a friend of a friend. Or rather, she had ventured to Cambridge to do so, but serendipitously dislocated from the college town click to pass a day in the capital, feeding pigeons at Viscount Nelson's feet, wandering amid the Parthenon's transplanted fragments and surrendering a mid-afternoon's eternity to Vermeer's extravagant pigments and masterful brush-strokes. It was a heady time for the eager young Marylander who, just a few months older than Morris, had until this very trip never before met the need to present her passport. So

London came alive to her, in museum scenes both indoors and out. As she walked the sites of her art and history textbooks, letting the works and days of bygone centuries wash over her, she felt a welling of self-satisfaction for having decided to make the trip after all. It seemed only yesterday she had been staring blankly at the submission forms for the coming school term, wondering where her life was going so fast without her and how on earth she had become so numbly estranged from it.

She was determined, however, not to let her mind dwell, to sink into the familiar, brooding comfort that she knew so well. Feeling accomplished after a full and independent day touring the city, she decided a celebratory libation was in order. One of those infamously warm ales, perhaps.

A half dozen blocks to the southeast, a wanderlusting antipodean was laboring through the late shift; the only one his habitual evening revelry would reasonably permit him to perform. When at 4pm that Thursday afternoon a satisfied young American strolled into his bar with a beaming smile that asked, in those chipper, Mid-Atlantic tones, for "a pint of something local, something you would drink on a triumphant afternoon," Morris was already starting to feel the legacy of the previous night's excesses fading away.

"Well, I'm not exactly local." He paused to let his own accent linger for a second, exotically backlit (so he reckoned) against the monotonous hum of Estuary English otherwise filling the room. "But I'm sure we can find you something for the occasion."

Katelyn smiled, first with her eyes then, as she watched the expression returned from across the bar, her whole being. Morris noted her posture, her confidence. With a ballerina's poise, she rose to just above average height, her thinnish carriage moving gracefully under a ripple of maple gold hair, fastened now with a dragonfly clip. Her deep green eyes flickered intelligently whenever she spoke.

"You might just be the cheeriest bartender in all of London," she remarked when he returned, still grinning, with her pint.

"Oh no," he protested from under a raised eyebrow. "I'm as surly as they come."

"I somehow find that hard to believe." She raised her glass and took a satisfying sip.

Acknowledging a threesome of regulars entering through the side doors, Morris started on a fresh round. "Oh yeah," he glanced back toward the smiling foreigner. "Ask anyone here. I'm a right bore. Stubborn. Moody. Well, ordinarily I am, anyway."

"Ordinarily?"

He nodded as if to say "I'm afraid so," but his continuing smile betrayed this guilty plea.

"So what's different about today, then?" she pressed coyly, sensing herself somewhere in the answer. "Why so chipper now?"

Morris topped the pints off and, taking them three in hand, ferried the glasses the length of the bar to where the regulars were taking their familiar seats.

"Maybe it's not 'what's' different," he said when he returned. "Maybe it's 'who.'"

She smiled again, this time all at once.

In between patrons Morris and Katelyn joked about the English weather and the warm beer, and about the patrons themselves. Playfully mocking the airs and pomp of the Old World around them, they fell easily into a silly, flirtatious banter.

"You see that woman over there," Morris nodded with pseudo seriousness toward a dowdy, septuagenarian tea-drinker by the door, her beige pinafore scant protection against the lurking urges of their sophomoric humor. "I used the 'Down Under' line on her just last week. She's been in here every day since, poor dear. I haven't the heart to tell her it's not on…"

Katelyn drew her hand to her mouth just in time to muffle an involuntary gasp, equal parts horror and exhilaration. Then, wearing a mischievous expression of her own that seemed perfectly tailored for the occasion, she dove headlong into the repartee.

"Would you like me to have a word?" Her widened eyes teased at Morris' attention when she continued. "I can tell her you're spoken for, if you think that's best. A pretty young American traveler has stolen your heart. Or," she made to roll her cashmere sleeves up over a pair of delicate, softly downed arms, "I could just put the fear of God in her right this moment."

"Hmm… as tempting as that is," Morris drew his lips back over clenched teeth and shook his head slowly," there's a darned lot of paperwork to be done whenever there's a death in the pub. If she drops from sheer shock, you know, on account of your ferocious threat, I'll have to stay back after work and fill in a mountain of forms. Awfully tedious, as the Brits would say."

"It seems there's nothing else for it, then," Katelyn's softened expression surrendered to the pitiful impotence of defeat. "I'll just have to give in. And you, you'll have to make good on your 'Down Under' promise, then marry the dear old woman and move into her flat. I bet she's got a fascinating doily collection. And you'll get used to the early bird menus and the sponge baths in no time at all."

"Oh, I don't mind an early dinner. Nor a good sponge bath given the right company. Although," he teetered on the edge of a thought, "I'd just as soon go with that pretty young American you were talking about a moment ago."

"Oh, I doubt your lady friend there is open to polyamorous arrangements," Katelyn sighed. "You know that generation, such…" and she finished the sentence by tracing the proverbial parallelogram in the quickening air between them.

"Right, I was afraid you'd say that. And here I was imagining the possibility of dining this evening with you both."

"Well, I'm not much one for sharing either." Her gaze was drunk with unmistakable intent. "I guess you'll just have to choose."

#

And so the whirlwind gathered its first surge of energy, frenetic from the start, then intensifying exponentially, hurtling its contents toward an unknown destiny sensed, but not understood, by them both. Giddily they spilled out of Morris' pub during his half hour break shortly thereafter, instinctively clasping hands as they crossed the street to grab a one-way coach ride, Victoria-Cambridge.

"Now I'm going to get to know all about you, Morris…?" her question lingered.

"Just Morris," he smiled.

"I see. Well, you'll have precious few secrets left by the end of my expert examination."

"No, we'll talk about you," he insisted. "Then, if you're lucky, I'll relent and reveal to you how this story of ours ends."

"Like you know!" She raised her eyebrows in playful defiance. Pulling her scarf up against the chill, she smiled into the plush argyle.

Morris arranged to take the seat next to hers, promising the spotty ticket clerk a free pint next he wandered into the

King's Head. The ride was scheduled to depart in a few hours, before his shift even ended.

"I'd ask if this kind of romantic impulse was a force of habit to you," Katelyn half probed, "but I'm afraid I don't want to know the answer."

Around them the streets hummed their old London tune. Day trippers alighted from foggy black taxis and red buses and emerged, bleary eyed, from that iconic subterranean network.

"What will you do about your work?" Katelyn queried as a group of young professionals filed past them, en route to some distant world of drab, romance-free responsibility.

"Ah, someone will cover for me," Morris assured her. "Davo, probably. Well, hopefully. And I'll find my way back to London tomorrow, I reckon. Or the day after..."

Morris was convincing, without being presumptuous. His blithe manner intrigued Katelyn and stirred in her something vaguely recalling the days before she had gone off to college, that summer when the world laid itself out before her like a grand feast to which she was welcomed as honorary guest. She accepted his happy-go-lucky disposition with a gleeful demeanor all of her own.

Looking at him now, in the open air outside the pub, moving freely against the staid surroundings of the city, she noticed for the first time his impressive stature. He was tall, over six feet she guessed, though his movements were easy and unencumbered, as with an athlete of some discipline; tennis, perhaps. Or swimming. His shoulders were broad, but he was not bulky, unlike the football players she had disregarded as mental infants back at college. It was clear, too, from his felicity of wit that he was no such dope. When he spoke, his eyes did the talking, his mouth following later as a kind of wily understudy, delivering words when his gaze either locked with her own or drifted abstractedly to some point far-off in the distance, as it often did. He was unlike her classmates, those unworldly, small town folks. In fact, now that she thought of it, he was unlike anyone she'd ever met.

Katelyn and Morris walked for his entire break, stopping only once to buy two cans of cider - "roadies," he had called them, to her amusement - and once more when they encountered his workmate, Davo, a block from the pub.

Of course he'd cover the evening shift, Davo assured them with a bowing wave of affected chivalry. Their encounter was brief, but warm.

"You kids have fun now," he jogged off to sneak in an all-day breakfast at the café next door before his now-extended commitment behind the bar.

"Your friend is very generous," observed Katelyn. "A pretty girl saunters into your bar and he's diving on shifts for you."

"He knows I'd do the same," Morris replied in earnest, "except pretty girls never come in the bar asking for Davo."

"You're evil!" she castigated him with a smiling shake of her head as they clasped hands once more.

Davo was, in fact, Morris' closest friend. They had traveled together from Australia, though their ambitions were rather independent. Within a year, Davo would be back home, courting a beautiful woman that would become his devoted wife and mother of his children. Morris, however, had no such plans.

Immediately Katelyn and he were back at the pub, Morris shot off to the living quarters upstairs to pack his bag. She wondered, on seeing him return not five minutes later, what he could possibly have bothered to throw in his overnighter in such short time and, faintly, whether it had been readily prepared all along, an optimistic duffle waiting by his bedside table for just the right moment to escape. She did not spoil the moment with inquiry, but greeted him excitedly when he dropped it lightly by her feet and ordered a six pack of ciders for the journey.

"Thanks, Davo," he nodded as they left his mate behind the bar. "And, if ever a beauty should find her way in here asking after you…"

"I'll know exactly who to stick the shift with," Davo finished the sentence as he watched the rapturous pair breeze out the door and into a world of their own.

#

The roughly two hours between Victoria coach station and the Old Schools passed between Morris and Katelyn in an exalted kaleidoscope of confessions, quirks and coincidences. Everything happened so quickly, as if they were living each decision before it had firmly been made, existing in the vertiginous, unformed moment immediately preceding reality. Between them, an unspoken acknowledgement propelled them forth while the superficial chitchat regarding bizarre colloquialisms and other such banality soon gave way to unguarded moments of real honesty and contemplation.

She told him, with a frankness of detail that both impressed him and stung vaguely at his bravado, about the prompt unraveling of her last relationship; how she had returned, taken ill, to her dorm room midway through class, only to uncover her boyfriend lustily entwined with a sweaty little sophomore scamp of deservedly wayward repute. She recalled the vixen to mind with a detached laugh, as if by giving words to the incident for the first time, she only now comprehended its utter insignificance. Pausing to give the event one last thought, she allowed it to pleasantly, peacefully extinguish from her mind.

"It might never have happened," she mused. "That was all so long ago. At least it seems that way now, here with you, on this random bus ride in the middle of a foreign country."

"Maybe it's not random at all," Morris shrugged. "Maybe this is just where we're supposed to be. Where we've always meant to be. You. Me. All of us."

"And what about him?" she motioned toward a derelict two seats over, slumped over and snoring intermittently in his chair, his tenuous grasp on a torn paper bag threatening at any moment to give way and free the liquid contents all over his soiled clothes.

"Well, not everyone has such lofty fates," Morris observed. "Who are we to argue with the universal order?"

"Ah right, the Universal Order," she was serious for a moment. "That, or we're just the culmination of arbitrary, unordered happenstance. A collection of lives inhabited by individuals who could just as easily have set off on infinite paths, unending possibilities. Sometimes I wonder what it's all for, this hot blazing second. There's more to it than that, of course, but that's the wedge. The beginning of a thought."

"We've got all night for philosophizing," he encouraged.

"We'll barely scratch the surface," she turned her gaze out the window. "There's more to understand than we'll ever really grasp."

"Beauty is truth, truth beauty…" he began.

"Yes, but is that all we on earth need to know? Alas," turning to him, she sighed with a sincerity he hadn't seen before, in her or anyone else, "Keats, right? Alas, my dear Morris, this is no century for poets."

Morris drank her in. Her words. Her presence. Her reflection in the glass, transposed over the quickening past as it flashed by outside. She had smooth, broad cheeks set above a wide and generous 'All American' smile which, he would come to discover, was equally adept at relieving tension as it was underscoring the sudden bursts of euphoria to which she was frequently given over. As for her eyes, he knew the moment he met them that their mysterious, sea green glimmer would be with him always.

Her unusual beauty notwithstanding, there was something else about Katelyn that most captivated Morris; an unaffected self-assuredness that derived from somewhere beyond her knowledge of quotable couplets and music references and scientific theories. There was, behind her ready smile and flickering eyes, an inexplicable calm about her that Morris couldn't quite capture, an elevated quality that drew him nearer, that held him enraptured when she spoke and aroused in him a need to know more about her than he had ever known about anyone else in his life.

Their conversation flowed along the motorway, streetlights in yellow and brilliant white streaming across the windows and stretching out into the unrelenting darkness of the miles covered. At the depot, they left the man with the brown paper bag and alighted to search for a taxi to take them the rest of the way. As usual, the atmosphere was draped in that faint mist that hangs like stretched cotton over the middle of England whenever it is not positively down pouring.

At last, they were deposited at a sparsely appointed student flop in an old stone two-story walkup, whereupon Katelyn introduced Morris to a pair of young ladies, both of them garrulous and, as the violet rings around their lips attested, already tipsy on red wine. Amy and Sarah were known to Katelyn through an intricately, pedantically explained social web, promptly forgotten by Morris.

"Which brings us finally, and lastly-but-not-leastly," Amy nodded toward her first guest, the viscous words coagulating like mercury in her mouth, "to Sarah. Sarah and the connection-to-Katelyn, who we see-you've-already-met…"

"Yes, Katelyn," Sarah added, then somewhat redundantly, "We see you've already met Morris."

The girls rambled messily, spilling wine on the linoleum floor as they emphasized this or that point with wild gesticulation, voices shrilly raised to overcome the electronic music emanating in thudding bursts from a room somewhere down the hall. Morris nodded encouragingly and smiled, gladly accepting their cask cabernet while Katelyn shot him flirtatious looks of mock reproach.

"Morris here is a regular romantic," Katelyn conveyed to the girls as the glasses were filled again. "If you're not on your guard, you're liable to find yourself in a rowboat with him before long, drifting down a quaint little country stream somewhere sunny while he recites Keats' Odes to you under the falling leaves."

"I'm not entirely to blame here," confessed Morris, arms raised in a farcical stance of conditional surrender, "some women are simply impossible to resist."

Then, indulging the crowd, he leaned to bended knee in Katelyn's direction…

> *Pale were the lips I kiss'd, and fair the form*
> *I floated with, about that melancholy storm…*

"Melancholy story?" whooped Amy riotously. "Tell us another one, Romeo."

"The impertinence of our curious man," whispered a playful Katelyn to her Morris as he laughingly regained his footing.

"And does this romantic have any friends to whom he might introduce us?" ventured the other happy lush. "We might have a regular petting party on our hands. Ha! Ha!"

When Amy and Sarah were very drunk and the newcomers not far behind, the little band made for a nearby club where one of the girls knew the DJ. Inside it was loud and humid and smelled of undergraduate desperation. Shortly after arrival, their hosts having vanished into the flickering, amorphous mass of sweat and booze on the dance floor, Katelyn took Morris by the hand and led him away from the crowd. Her lips were warm against his, their embrace long overdue. Soon they were back at the flat, smoking cigarettes out the top floor window, watching the exhaled clouds comingle in the stillness around them and drift away under the scattered morning stars. Even London seemed an eternity away.

A few hours later, Katelyn found herself on a plane, her forehead pressed gently against the cool glass somewhere over the Atlantic. Morris spent the day at a drab student pub near the coach station, waiting for a standby ticket between slow and solitary pints.

#

It was Morris who wrote first.

"Not a moment forgotten to me... to think you 'chanced' on this place... all the pubs in London!... could just as easily have missed me... Euclidian parallels and all that...

I imagine you here every day... winter sunlight at your back... corner table, by our poor and pinafored lover (who, by the way, sends her regards. 'To the victor,' she crowed when I told her you'd fled)...

Streaming lights on the coach ride... fading into cheap cabernet and that delicate, lingering moment before your lips were on mine...

I half expect you to walk through the door and change my life again... Perhaps, someday... Affectionately, Morris."

Her reply, though slower in arriving than he had wished, brought him no end of joy. He read it so many times he found himself reciting it while alone, rolling the sentences over deliciously in his mind, envisioning her pen on the paper, wondering at her mood as she composed her jutty Rs, her childlike, irregular Gs, the cramping, slanting font, struggling to squeeze in the lower right corners of the pages before blossoming outward again overleaf.

"Over 7,000 pubs in London... Amy checked the guide... says the odds are miniscule, so it must be Providence at work... she approves of you, for sure... Sarah too, from what she can remember...

"I can see you working behind the bar, shooting me cheeky, knowing looks... your blonde hair, unkempt then and on my shoulder by morning...

"It's strange here now I'm back... something changed for me, within me... looking from the window on the flight home... the unfathomable ocean between us... I imagined you standing at the station, as I was carried away at a thousand miles an hour...

Yes, someday. But someday soon. Tenderly, Katelyn.

P.S. Meanwhile, enjoy your decrepit floozy. I don't need to tell her, I've got time on my hands. K

Over the next few letters, with a cheesy Big Ben postcard (his) and some kitschy lipstick seals (hers) thrown into the mix, the narratives began to merge and a wide-eyed romance arose to beckon them onward.

Wrote she...

"These last few weeks have been so impossibly long, our 'gloomy days and o'er shadowed ways'...

"But if I knew for certain you were somewhere in the future, I could bear it...

'yes, in spite of all,
Some shape of beauty moves away the pall
From our dark spirits.'

"I don't know about the Land of Milk and Honey, but there's plenty here for you... in America, and in my arms.

Devotedly, K

And from his pen too...

"The century of poets is coming to pass, My Dear. Behold! Katelyn is moved to Keats! Floreat romance!

"Yes, I've heard a little something about your great land of opportunity. And who isn't tired and poor and yearning to breathe free? So what do you say? Shall we meet by 'the air-bridged harbor that twin cities frame?'

You see now, it's not only the Nightingale calling us forth.

"P.S. *Remember the Sonnets too, for 'there is a budding morrow in the midnight.'*

"P.P.S. *I've confessed this love to our retiree friend. Results were, sadly, as predicted. Now I've got a mountain of paperwork to file before getting to your next letter. All the same...*

Yearningly, M.

So their correspondence increased both in frequency and urgency, and some comedy too. Before long, Katelyn found herself penning letters every other evening. She wrote about her college, her neighborhood, her deepest grievances and loftiest aspirations. It seemed as though she were writing to herself in a way, a diary that existed not on the page but that came to validation only upon his reading and confirming it.

Meanwhile, each new fragment of information she divulged became for Morris one more piece of an abstract collage gradually taking shape before his eyes. His mind searched to fill in the picture. He imagined the street on which she played as a child... the Sycamores and White Oaks and great American Lindens swaying gently in the breeze... the parents calling her inside from a wide and friendly porch when it rained on late summer afternoons... the family sedan, idle in the driveway... a shingled garage, full of American junk, out the back.

Morris saw himself in front of that house, a taxicab driving off down the road, his worn leather bag in one hand, wildflowers in the other, just like in the movies. He imagined it so clearly he began to see it as a kind of dreamscape before him, something he could conjure, *they* could conjure, from an atmospheric realm of unwritten impossibility.

Days and weeks passed by thusly, Morris and Katelyn composing and awaiting letters, reading, reciting, rewording passages of a conversation stretched over time and space, until it became a permanent fixture in their lives, an intoxicating soundtrack overlaying their ordinary daily activities. Then suddenly, on an otherwise unimportant afternoon, Morris received a shock that jolted their shared mirage from the page and into three bold dimensions.

#

His back to the entrance of the pub, Morris glanced with an absent mind into the unpolished mirror behind the King's Head bar. He was half way through pouring out a double measure of gin, one he wished was his first of the day and not the waiting patrons' fifth or sixth. The afternoon had been unusually busy in that, even though the crowd was relatively thin, it was a troublesome one. A few of the mouthier lads had had to be evicted, owing as much as their general state of inebriation as to the obscenities they had shot over the bar. It was sometimes like this, especially when the coaches came in from some of the rougher parts up north and the lads had little else to do on the ride but bury into their brown paper bags.

Morris drifted in idle contemplation, thinking about Sycamores and Lynchburg lemonades on the porch when, in the slow motion that sometimes accompanies reverie in reflection, he saw a shadowy figure emerge in the doorway. The sinister shadow lurched unsteadily, baring something of evidently considerable weight above its growing frame. The image grew larger as it stumbled toward the bar, where

Morris glimpsed in the man's oddly familiar face the anger of a crazed lunatic.

Turning, Morris extended and flexed his right arm in just enough time to deflect the searching projectile, an iron roadwork sign of unwieldy proportions, he later learned, before it crashed with a terrific explosion of glass and liquor into the bottles and the mirror behind him.

Faintly, he was aware of the twinkling shards raining around him as he watched the man briskly tackled to the ground. There the attacker rolled and struggled until Davo's knee became firmly planted in his back. A dull pain dragged on Morris' left arm and presently he noticed it was bleeding. There he stood, in an absent daze behind the bar, while time collapsed around him.

The raving figure, refused service by his intended victim not an hour earlier, was summarily dragged from the pub, all the while screaming nationalistic obscenities as the startled onlookers gaped.

Morris turned his back again to the door and saw himself, shattered amongst the needles of broken mirror still clinging to the wall.

Any other day, he might have been content to pass the violation off. Just another certifiable nut, he would explain to his workmates, an urchin swinging madly from the gutter, clasping at the bootstraps of anyone who happened to be passing by. But something in him was stirred that afternoon, a curdling fear no amount of willful denial could silence.

That night Morris hardly slept, and the few moments he could snatch from the murky pool beneath his consciousness were violently recaptured by the presence of the man's snarled and contorted face. It carried an expression at once demonic and yet absurdly placid; indifferent, as if its owner was merely carrying out an order handed down from some unknown minister of the damned, an immovable snatcher of souls.

Next morning, while the forenoon shift dispensed teas and scones to the sweet brigade of pensioners and the jukebox sang out Neil Diamond's "Sweet Caroline" as if nothing had happened, there came word from upstairs that management had received a security threat at the coach station next door. Such occasion was not uncommon in those days, despite the Irish question having being largely settled.

"Another Glaswegian in 'is cups forgott'n 'is bag, mos' likely," mumbled the old governor, himself a transplant from the Emerald Isle, down the intercom. "Bes' run the lads through the drill jus' the same."

The staff of the King's Head convened at the unofficial meeting point, a drab little café not two blocks away, and ordered Dr. Peppers into which each infused his preferred liquid anodyne. A few familiar faces from nearby pubs waved from across the street.

So, a quarter hour passed in loose chitchat; about the bomb scare, about the nationalist front, about the previous day when Morris very nearly had his head taken off. At that moment Davo, looking around, realized the latter had not bothered to follow the drill. Knowing his good mate's penchant for truancy, owing as much to his dreamy absentmindedness as to any conscious neglect of his post, he assumed Morris must still be asleep.

"He wasn't like himself last night," Davo recalled to nobody in particular.

"Might've been a bit shaken after all."

On a hunch, he sent one of the fresher South African lads back to see if Morris was in his room. The youngster returned a few minutes later, alone, but brandishing a note.

Reading it to himself slowly, Davo learned his wandering companion had on the previous afternoon cashed in his return ticket to Australia and, together with the decent stash he'd managed to save hawking Polish cigarettes from under the bar and a few bob he'd borrowed, and promised to return, from Davo's tip jar, booked a flight to America for that very evening, with enough to spare for an adventure of modest appetites.

The note ended in a P.S.

Debt to be repaid in crisp, American greenbacks, redeemable on your expected arrival Stateside.

Davo noted with a smile that one, English pounds were stronger than American dollars and, two, he had no intention of ever traveling 'Stateside.' So, he smiled and raised his own Dr. Pepper, with no small tot of rum mixed therein.

"Off you go, you crazy bastard," he said, again to nobody present. "And good luck to ya!"

#

The remainder of his time in England, those receding hours before the tube spirited him, heart in mouth, out to Heathrow International, Morris spent retracing the steps Katelyn had described to him on the day they met. He followed her scent through the lighted dust falling heavy on ancient sarcophagi; envisioned through her emerald eyes Nelson's victory off Cape Trafalgar, silhouetted now against the leaden sky overhead, and finally felt the Rokeby Venus, by the great Velasquez, stir in him memories of their impromptu nocturnal sojourn. These images flickered before him later in brilliant staccato projection as slumber washed over his brow 30,000 feet above the New Brunswick coastline.

Customs and immigration were a blur. The somnambulant alien was ushered from post to carousel, stamped and processed and harried along corridors of fluorescent, emergency theater lighting, and eventually ejected from the other end.

Now, bracing himself against the icy wind as it rushed across the parking lot, Morris came to a rude state of alertness. He recalled the last 24 hours as a dipsomaniac pieces together the disparate components of his lost years. Confusedly and with no apparent respect for chronology, he saw a labyrinth of Egyptian tombs, city doves taken to flight against the English sky and, in the reflective shards behind the King's Head bar, the relentless drive of a maniacal, demented patriot who might kill him without another thought. In a desperate, bewildered moment, Morris wondered what he was doing here then, more urgently, whether Katelyn would arrive to meet him after all or whether, as seemed suddenly, absurdly possible, he had invented her, a whole cloth fabrication of his mind, a catalyst to spur himself on, further and further from his home and deeper into the unknown world that hung faintly but assuredly beyond his grasp.

And then he saw her, the shimmering in her sea green eyes, a dragonfly gliding across the crowd as she ran through the space between them.

"You look like death," she gasped, falling into his embrace. The cold air rushed from his lungs and he felt her warmth pressed against his body.

"And yet, I've never felt so alive."

#

Chapter II

Penn to Penn

New York City wore winter like a great fur coat the year Morris came to meet her. From the gleaming lights of her towering office buildings to the full, immoveable weight of her bedrock, she flaunted her elegance with a dangerous confidence that Morris perceived at once calmly majestic and yet utterly, frenetically intoxicating. Here was the city of Parker's Algonquin, of Fitzgerald's Ritz and Biltmore and Plaza, of Salinger's haunted, seedier dives, Miller's air-conditioned nightmares and Thomas' soused and dying light. Before him, rising up in blackened gothic spires, in needles of reinforced steel and shimmering glass, a jagged edge cutting into the infinite night sky, was a city against which history's leading figures had cast their indelible stories.

But all that jazz, as they say, would have to wait; the fast martinis over unhurried lunches, pretentious sidecars in bright, gilded lobbies, tables for two beneath sparkling chandeliers at Balthazar, test-tubed vodka flights at Pravda and Dean & Deluca caviar on Seaport terraces with uninterrupted 4th of July views over the Brooklyn Bridge; all that would hold for the men who would show him the City and the dazzling women with whom he would, in turn, share its epizootic splendor. For now, Morris had to content himself with being innocently awestruck by the banal, halted in stupefied reverence before all that which locals regard as 'commonplace' and 'natural' in the sanguine fashion only people born in the world's great cities can convincingly effect. The birthright of cool, casual indifference. He'd sensed a shade of it in London, of course, a kind of latent cocksureness, but there it had been tempered by the vicissitudes of time and so now cast a rather haughty hue.

Looking out the window at the passing scene, Morris tugged at a thought about national mythology, something tied to imagined realities and symbols and collective consciousness, then abruptly lost his leash on it as the taxi surged forward in response to an impatient driver behind. He was suddenly back in the moment and, with a rush of dizzying euphoria he found difficult to repress, the young Australian visitor regarded his very American guide, brought to supple flesh and seated, implausibly, impossibly, beside him. For almost two months he had relied on pitiful, assembly line memory to fill in her form. Now she was here, real, her sweet-scented presence rendering the crude doppelganger of his imagination instantly obsolete. How he had longed to look at her!

For perhaps the first time ever, he marveled unrushed at the fluent elegance of her profile. Fine and slightly upturned, her delicately freckled nose contrasted with a soft fullness that he had not recalled in her mouth. Her smile she deployed even before she knew there was a witty turn afoot, a habit made visible in the tiny curves at the edge of her lips and which, in concert with her seemingly infinite wellspring of patience, endeared her to even the dullest storyteller. Her chin, pointed but ornately so, ceded to a confident jawline that traced gracefully back to the golden waves presently at play about her ears. Wide set, her brilliant green eyes shone against the smooth, opalescent complexion on which they were set, a ménage so effortlessly complimentary she seldom had cause to use paint or brush.

Morris was considering the thinness of her lilywhite neck when Katelyn sensed his gaze. She turned to face him and, realizing his unguarded captivation, fought a smile that crept regardless across her exquisite features. Her eyes flashed a striking emerald, refracting the glare of the snow falling outside in their aqueous shimmer.

"Truthfully, you're…beautiful," he declared, helplessly, at last.

"Oh, you poor, poor romantic," she blushed and turned her exhilarated composure back toward the window.

Their cab was bound for Harlem, somewhere between Malcolm X and Frederick Douglas Boulevards; so he remembered marking it on the handy and compact map he forgot, after all, to pack. Katelyn had arranged the room - "Standard Belle View economy. Yes, smoking is fine." – in nervous anticipation of his arrival just last week. Countless times she had imagined them in that room, together, alone, time and space collapsed between them. She considered her decision now with quickened pulse and wondered whether she shouldn't have chosen something a little more comfortable. Then again, she had no idea for how long they'd be staying. More than a week or two in anything above a three star and she'd have to phone her parents for a wire transfer or head back to Maryland, perhaps alone. No, the Harlem flop would suit them just fine.

The current plan, though subject to change (as they repeatedly agreed), was to spend a short, unfixed while in the city, a spell to luxuriate in their reunion, then, and only if they felt like it, to take the train down to visit Katelyn's family home in Baltimore.

"It's a straight shot, Penn Station to Penn Station," she explained with a willing smile, "but they're worlds apart. I mean, Baltimore is nothing like this place, and that's both good and bad. It's…" and here she paused, unsure of where to begin before finally resting on the quietly leading, "Well, you'll see."

"Good, good," Morris nodded along, the scenes of the city outside overpowering the creeping weariness of the journey. "No, great. I mean, yes. I want to see and feel it all."

From his vantage point in the back of the cab he followed their iconic yellow reflection as it splashed across enormous department store windows. Choking, sputtering buses, metal containers brimming with the tired and the bored, perforated the vista. One by one he counted the city blocks as they inched through uptown traffic. Fatigue was setting in, but his mind raced across the island unperturbed, down the canyons of her broad and gusty avenues, fervently probing the tiniest nooks and alleys, breezing through cafés warm with familiar conversation and bars where the regulars' names appeared on little bronze plaques by their smoothed wooden stools, in and out of dusty bookstores battling mildew's unrelenting assault and through steaming Chinese laundries, where sweating old women with hair growing from unsightly moles swore in discordant tones at frightened, undocumented girls named Lin.

There's so much to feel, he repeated silently. His attention drifted along Madison Avenue, ambled through the snow falling on Marcus Garvey Park, boarded a train to Baltimore, reclined for a brief moment's respite in Belgrave Square Garden and finally washed ashore the yellow chalk beaches of his hometown, another world away and already on tomorrow's clock.

Katelyn woke him when they arrived.

#

Later that afternoon, after Morris had slept for what felt like a million lifetimes, his thoughts returned vaguely to "the plan." It had a weight all of its own and he found himself pushing it toward the fringe of his mind, or sidestepping it altogether.

"You know, it's strange to say it," his mitted hand attended a nervous itch somewhere on the back of his neck, "but I really can't imagine anything in the future. It's as if my entire mental capacity is absorbed by the fullness of the moment, in this place, here with you. Like there's nothing before or after." Then, turning to face her in full, "Just the bliss of now."

They were smoking tax free tobacco on a miserly little balcony overlooking the building's internal courtyard. Katelyn studied the amber tip of her cigarette, smiling now and then as the chilled eddies set it aglow in her fingers. Below them the breeze stole pages from a discarded newspaper and sent them whirling around the variegated air conditioning units. It was a hovel, no doubt about it. But it was their hovel, at least for now.

"You're waxing romantic again," she chided, exhaling a large plume of smoke and frosted breath. "But it won't work, you know. You're that boy I once knew on a night bus between London and Cambridge."

"And now you know me in New York City, too."

Katelyn considered for a moment that, postcard bridges aside, their physical relationship was barely two days old and yet seemed much deeper. He'd grown older since London, she noticed. The straw blonde hair, though still unruly and pronounced against the grey cinderblock of the hotel interior, had grown long enough to sweep behind his ears, as he now wore it. His face, consequently revealed in fuller profile, was more angular than she remembered, though the boyish enthusiasm in his dark brown eyes remained a source of comforting familiarity.

"Yes, here too, I guess," she replied at length. Then, her appetite suddenly gnawing from within, "Where do you want to go for dinner? Let's do something to celebrate… something bold and crazy."

Morris flicked his cigarette into the windswept square below and they watched it tossed across the icy concrete, its vital energy dissipating in a miniature pyrotechnical display before an audience of two. "Let's just walk and see where we end up."

At last they left the hotel and rode the subway downtown with no particular destination in mind. On board, a procession of passengers talked in pairs and threes, some in shrill, unguarded excitement, others in hushed, vaguely furtive tones. A few rode solo, distant and detached, their minds absorbed by newspapers and cheap, pulpy paperbacks. Scrawled across advertisements for free legal advice and night time English courses, a hieroglyphic graffiti alphabet declared indecipherably who was here and when. Overhead, the handles swayed in unison against the jerky motion of the train. The smell of steel and damp rushed in through the cracked windows. On the whole, the scene appeared to Morris as if it had been lifted from a motion picture set so that, at any moment, a portly man with a cigar clenched between coffee-yellowed teeth might step into view and exclaim, "Cut!," dispersing the surrounding actors from their positions in a chorus of hemming and accusatory scowls.

Morris was about to remark on the calm authenticity of it all when, at either 103rd or 96th street, Katelyn indicated to him a short black figure in perhaps his middle twenties that had just boarded the train. Over the man's head a loose, fur-lined hood stole his face from view, but the crowd registered his presence as if by instinct. Confidently he strode toward the center of the carriage where he deposited a scuffed, rectangular speaker of about knee-height. Within an instant the little box burst forth a noise of such immense volume Morris at first thought it must be an emergency announcement. With a violent spasm the man sprung to movement, contorting his body under the oversized parker, jolting and convulsing in time with the beat as it shattered all surrounding conversation. The passengers clapped along in unison, urging the man on, magnifying his action in their vibrant cheers and howls. Behind him, Morris heard a group of women shriek in delight and he turned to see the man throw back his jacket, the blue black skin covering his intensely muscular frame ablaze with perspiration under the carriage's flickering lights.

The applause reached crescendo when, in what seemed to Morris a direct challenge to the laws of physics, the coiled busker executed a standing backflip with the ease expected of a fat man eating a cupcake.

"Yeeoooww!" cried the women behind him in unbridled, orgiastic elation. "Yeeeeooooooooow!"

The entire display lasted less than five minutes and by the next stop, having collected a few crumpled bills and a handful of warm silver shrapnel, the man had vanished into the tunnels, to another show, another audience, another world altogether.

Not for the first time that day, Morris found himself perfectly enthralled, an alien joyously adrift in another sublime reality. He breathed deeply and extended his arm around Katelyn's shoulder, feeling her slender form lean in toward him as the train hauled its load around a gradual bend in the track. They would ride another few stops, she suggested, then find a midtown restaurant with a greasy menu and a full bar.

"We'll start with wings," she insisted, "just as hot as you like 'em."

She pressed her hand in his as their carriage tumbled through the darkness. High and noisy above the subterranean madness, supremely indifferent to the enchanted presence of Morris and the beaming girl at his side, the great city hurtled itself into the starry winter sky.

#

For nearly a fortnight Morris and Katelyn set their internal clock against the beating heart of Manhattan. They woke lazily when the sharp, interloping shriek of honking traffic distinguished itself from the softness of their entwined slumber. Together they dressed and bathed and smoked the day's first and last cigarettes. They took aimless subway rides, sometimes for hours at a time, and wandered under snow-filled canopy through vast, leafless sections of Central Park, until the icy winds ushered them into nondescript Irish bars or the lobbies of unnamed hotels, where they would drink in the amber warmth until it made them drunk and slurred their words.

One night in that second week they found themselves in such a place, seated at the bar alongside regulars and tourists alike. The crowd was thin but steady, the mood fit for an unimportant, midweek afternoon. Behind the bar, silenced by the hum of dive bar rock, beautifully muted news anchors mouthed the latest about an upcoming presidential election from unwatched television sets. Between plumes of backlit smoke, Morris saw the desperately pleading faces of an over-sincere insurance salesman and a doe-eyed imbecile and decided, without further consideration, that he favored neither man for the office.

"Don't get dad started on that circus." Katelyn followed Morris' eye to the offending screen. "He's unfailingly polite, of course. It's part of his deep southern charm. But that's where he gets his politics, too. Which is not necessarily a bad thing, *per se...*"

She leaned over the table, her green eyes rippling in the depth of numerous postprandial cocktails. "Dad's what they call a 'die-hard confederate.' And he's always looking for fresh converts with a sympathetic mind for the cause."

"You're not accusing me of loose sympathies, surely?" Well into his third stinger, Morris found himself in a jovial mood.

"Hey, it's your neck," she shrugged, "but don't say you weren't warned."

Katelyn indicated another round to the waitress, whose blonde ponytail and immodest uniform teased the attention of a few old soaks leaning against the bar as she strutted its length to mix two fresh libations. Morris surveyed their frontline faces, grey and sallow, etched with the creases of a merriment long since surrendered.

"Maybe I'll chide him a bit," he snapped to with fresh enthusiasm, "accuse him of being a closet Yankee. From a strictly antipodean standpoint, you're all yellow-bellied northerners to me."

Katelyn let out an inspired shriek. "Let me know when you try that one, would you? I want to be seated nearby with a stiff drink in hand."

"So, he could go either way then, you reckon?"

"Try you it and just we'll see."

A few brazen but otherwise innocuous leers followed the pretty young maid when she returned with the drinks. Morris considered her for a moment as the swinging door admitted, between uneasy stragglers, a rush of cold night air. "Christine," as the nametag astride her breast pocket fibbed, dealt in the fast currency of flirty smiles and suggestive innuendo. Her look was wholesome; the All-American cheerleader, but with a sidearm banter she drew quick and kept ready. Ah, the undignified pick-up lines she must've heard! Morris winced at the thought. He wondered whence she came and what she had left behind; a destiny strewn with fleeting treasures; the empty tire swing in her parents' front yard; a sincere, cross-my-heart-hope-to-die proclamation carved into the trunk of some ancient, leafy oak; the solitary, late night yearning of a poor, deserted adolescent who had watched her car pull away on an otherwise romantic spring afternoon, the untouched ring left burning in his blue jeans pocket.

Or maybe she's from Brooklyn, Morris backtracked, working a shift while daddy puts the twins to bed. His mind drifted…

"Team *Morlyn Monroe*?" a thick, bearded voice announced the next game of pool.

Katelyn very nearly leapt from her seat. "We're up!"

They commanded a respectable run of the table, owing largely to the facility with which Katelyn distracted the mostly male opposition from their shots, all while executing an impressive array of her own. Morris watched, somewhat flat-footed, as she danced her amber curls around the felt before each carefully considered shot, rewarding all but the bawdiest table comment with an impish giggle. Barstools rocked with riveted attention, the regulars' palms set aglow with rapt applause. Her every stroke, lithe body bent suggestively over the rail, sent a flare through Morris' veins and he was secretly glad when they at last ceded the table to a foursome of visiting Minnesotans who wished to play pairs.

A few days later, in the circuitous fashion know to females harboring accusations of all stripes, Katelyn revealed the inspiration behind her magnificent display.

"I felt sorry for that bartender the other night. Didn't you?"

"Which one?" Morris replied, his brow knitted behind the steam of the morning's first coffee. "What bartender?"

She ignored his attempts to stall for time. "I thought she was rather comely, even squeezed into such an unforgiving outfit. Still," her mouth pinched to one side, "all those men gawking at her from behind the bar. It can't have been at all comfortable for the poor girl."

Morris started to say something, then thought better of it.

Sometime afterward, they found themselves crunching peanut shells underfoot in the very same bar. Christine, Morris could not fail to notice, was off duty and, in her place a dull brunette of unremarkable proportions captured nobody's attention. Morris and Katelyn drank ciders, linked cigarettes in a mile-long chain and became generally lost in each other's conversation. At last, the name above *Morlyn Monroe* was dusted from the chalkboard and the bearded voice announced their invitation to the waiting crowd.

Inexplicably, and to the disappointment of all but one man, Katelyn appeared to have lost her magical touch.

"That's alright," she whispered to Morris after they lost early to an impromptu duo of crestfallen regulars. "I'm not in the mood for games anyway. At least, none we'd want to play here."

#

On an unusually still day during their second week, Morris suggested they wander into the Plaza Hotel for a midafternoon bracer.

"If we hurry, we might just be in time to catch Mr. Ellington in the Rose Club," he enthused.

"Sure! And afterward you'll surprise me with the keys to a corner suite overlooking the park, where we'll spend the rest of our time here."

"You never know."

"Well, I'd love to...but it's not really our *scene*, Morris," Katelyn laughed, haughtily emphasizing the word for effect. "But we can go in for a look, if you really want to."

The next block or two passed in silence until they came upon that corner of the park clipped by Sherman's monument. There Morris wondered aloud, "What, exactly, is our *scene*?"

"You know what I mean, Morris."

"No, I don't." His tone was unusually curt.

"Look at what you're wearing," Katelyn was suddenly the picture of indignation. "Look at what *I'm* wearing."

Morris shrugged and with hands upturned shot back a glance that both exclaimed and underscored, "*and…?*"

"You're being obtuse," she demurred. "That," pointing now to the iconic edifice at their right, "is not exactly in our budget."

"Who said we have to buy the place? Just a drink is all."

Katelyn turned to face him, but Morris was already cutting across the square. She found him standing at the bar overlooking the lobby when, after brooding over a solitary cigarette on the sidewalk, she finally determined to enter.

"What'll you have this fine day, my sweet and darling angel face?" Morris affected a loud and pompous accent that cast a spotlight in her direction as she approached the hallowed oak.

"You're an idiot," she declared, looking around in obvious embarrassment.

"Yes, quite," he bowed. "At your service, m'dear."

"You're an idiot," she repeated, more slowly this time.

"And you appear both smart and casual, perfectly attired for such a festive occasion."

Katelyn considered him coldly for a moment. He was stubborn when he wanted to be. It ate at her that, even in his worn chords and secondhand cardigan, he didn't look entirely out of place here.

"Fine. If you want to make some stupid point, you're an idiot who can stand me a kir royal," she said at last.

When the pale violet flute arrived shortly thereafter, Katelyn drank it down quickly and snapped her fingers for another. "On him," she shot Morris a triumphant stare.

Morris nodded toward the bartender who, looking him over, inquired as to whether "The gentleman would care to start a tab? We accept all major cards, of course."

"Cash will be fine, Jeeves," Morris grinned.

"Better yet on my tab," a sonorous voice carried from somewhere over Morris' shoulder.

The tab, as well as the cigar baritone, belonged to a middle-aged man in an impeccable, charcoal three-piece, one of a dozen near identical suits hanging in a closet ten floors above where he presently stood. His slate grey eyes and colorless hair added to the monochromatic palette so that he looked as though he might have stepped directly out of a black and white film. A thin, unalloyed silver mustache completed the effect.

"Now where are you from, young man?" he turned his attention to Morris. "And don't say 'out of town.' I know that already. Left the island for a few minutes in the 70's. Plenty enough to see the outside world."

"Originally from Australia," Morris began then, not quite knowing why, added, "but I was in England for a spell before here."

"I see. You're on vacation, then?"

"Well, I'm not quite sure yet." Morris became acutely aware of Katelyn's presence beside him.

"And what about your lady here?" the man followed.

"His lady is from Baltimore," Katelyn interjected. "And we're happy to buy our own drinks, thank you all the same."

"No need," the man said and downed the rest of his own glass in one. He nodded to the barman as he rose to leave. "That's all for me, Harry. Be sure to get these two whatever they want." Turning to Morris, he added, "I admire a young upstart, however rough around the edges he might be. Reminds me of myself in a way. Well, good luck to ya."

They watched as the man strode casually across the foyer and disappeared beyond the revolving door. Morris could feel the bartender's eyes fixed on him. Katelyn's, too. For a moment, he considered ordering a bottle of the finest champagne on the menu, but found his thirst had quietly disappeared.

The walk back uptown was long and the silence humbling.

#

Morris didn't often think about his friends in London or his family in Australia during those initial days and weeks in America, but standing atop the Empire State Building one clear and melancholy afternoon, the sheet glass atmosphere stretching out before him in all directions, he thought of them, scattered over distant horizons, with a feeling he imagined might be nostalgia's fraternal twin.

"Do you miss them?" Katelyn asked. She had developed, with apparent ease, moreover, a mildly unsettling ability to guess his thoughts.

"Not really."

"Not really...but not not-at-all?"

The comment irritated him. "Look, they're not dead," he remarked with rather more emotion than he'd intended to conscript. "Only," he trailed off…

She weighed his expression against the crystalline firmament; pale, hardened forehead drawn tight about the brow, eyes squinted against the relentless gale whipping across the Hudson, cheeks flushed a dry red in the frigid air. His chin, coarse and defiant, jutted out as he drew breath through semi-clenched teeth. She considered relieving the silence, but shied.

"Only… they're living their own lives, off in another queen's land," he relinquished after a slow pause and, turning to her appended in vaguely apologetic tones, "but I'm here with you, discovering your home, and that's what's important to me now."

His foreign past remained a kind of innocuous phantasm, about which they wouldn't speak again during their time in the city, though it would come in time to bear on their relationship in a way neither Katelyn nor Morris could ever properly comprehend.

Morris ran a mitted hand along the barricade's intersecting diamond bars, feeling their chill fight its way in through the tingling wool. Together they drifted toward the building's southerly aspect. Cutting a line west to east, Morris followed Broadway down the island, marveling as it dissected those magnificent avenues, teaming with traffic and flesh and dreams, with a lofty arrogance all of its own.

"So many lives…" he began, then faded…

"You can't live them all, you realize," Katelyn immediately regretted her presumption.

From the ledge a pigeon casually alighted and Morris felt for a moment his stomach going over with it. He watched the creature drop, then disappear against the slate grey of hardened concrete below. She was right, of course, but not in the way she thought.

"It's not that," he replied. "It's not the weight of the infinite possibilities unlived…"

"Then…?"

He muttered something about "names written in water," then broke off again, his thoughts strewn elsewhere... in a dive bar downtown, perhaps, talking to a jabbering stockbroker or a pretty Latina waitress or a bum who'd wandered in out of the cold to snatch a few peanuts before an iron-heart manager shooed him back into the fray.

They left the subject up on the 86th floor and walked toward the park in silence. When a cold wind whipped around the corner of Columbus Circle, they descended the subway stairs and rode the No. 3 train the half dozen stops back to the hotel.

That night, and over the harried few that followed, Morris and Katelyn imbibed more heavily than usual, frantically, almost. Before them, a giant question mark loomed. Somewhere in the midst of that heady ebullience, neither would recall exactly when, they conjured up a day after tomorrow…then a week to follow the next. Gradually, stealthily the future edged itself into their dialogue, lingering at first on the edge of suggestion, an uncertain hint or acknowledgment, then fully, starkly at its center, as if there had never been a word said between them without a path to infinity laid out before it. When they finally determined to go to Baltimore, it was as much for lack of anything else to do than part of a definite plan. Inertia carried them onward.

"The lease on my apartment is good for another three months," Katelyn said, "but obviously we're not tied into anything."

"And we can always come back to New York," Morris acquiesced, yet even as the words escaped, something inside him fell away. There the city remained, anchored firmly in its place, that hardened Manhattan schist, sure and permanent beneath the hollow, peripatetic feet that were fast carrying him away. So, two roads began to diverge.

"*I* could always come back," he soliloquized as guilt and relief washed over him in equal measure. A fissure had appeared in his resolve, through which a faint, almost imperceptible light shone to reveal the dense organic mass of doubt at his core.

Katelyn was standing by the window, one folded leg lost beneath the threadbare hem of his favorite undershirt. Surveying her now in that familiar setting, Morris saw in her kind and loving eyes all the naked vulnerability that attends hope and faith. He wondered if she had perceived his silent confession, his momentous doubt.

"Sure we can," she nodded to him. "We can return whenever we want."

For a burning second he yearned to cut the alliteration with an atomic *I*, but quicker still he shuttered the vision and watched as the soft light disappeared.

"Right, then. Baltimore it is."

#

Chapter III

The More He Saw

Winter dug itself into long, deep trenches that first year, the smog of America's rustbelt cities captured in the falling snow and packed tightly against the hard, frozen earth. Asphalt streets and windswept parking lots in places like Wilmington and Trenton and Philadelphia cracked and split along creeping hairlines, their subsequent depressions sinking into unseen potholes lurking beneath the ashen slush. A motorcar accident on one such road, a forlorn stretch between Pittsburg and Titusville, left a young mother of three widowed and her husband, a drunkard and a philanderer on his last chance, ejected from this world through the shattering windscreen of her Oldsmobile clunker. Notification of the incident dissolved over the phone, left to hang lifelessly at the end of its hallway cord, as the woman shuffled to the fridge and, removing the unpaid registration bill from the straining magnet, let it fall into the trashcan with the rest of the day's news. She would tell the children after dinner, she supposed, when their favorite television show would be on to distract their attention.

Elsewhere, things were not quite so bleak.

When not losing hands of gin rummy to the flirty, green-eyed shark seated in cross-legged repose opposite him (K – 11; M – 3), Morris spent the duration of their straight shot between Penn Stations staring vacantly out the train window.

Between the steel and reinforced concrete of indifferent cities, long and somber stretches of deciduous sterility yielded to expansive valleys strewn with mist and cut deep by old grey rivers. Cleaving to the banks and set astride the time-softened hilltops, farmhouses stood in humble, red and white defiance of the eternal elements. Morris imagined their inhabitants; hardscrabble, salt of the earth types, probably, whose sons had for generations ploughed the fields alongside their fathers, whose daughters had learned to knit and bake and refuse in puritanical earnest the well-intentioned advances of boys at the local fare; clichés of a bygone era, in other words, long since adulterated by the relentless vagaries of modern convenience and the collective quest for hackneyed uniformity.

This was essentially Republican country, Katelyn's father would later insist through the confident haze of innumerable rye tumblers. The problem, he would expand from the comfort of his front porch rocker, was that such honest land was perforated by what he considered the "Yale blue stain" of its metropolitan centers. Many such discussions were to come, featuring characters he was yet to meet and subjects he was still to learn, but Morris wasn't thinking of politics as their Amtrak All Stops chipped its way along the icy northeast corridor toward the nation's capital. All that would come later.

"A-a-a-nd, that makes twelve," Katelyn declared, unfurling a heartless treble of sixes and a ransomed king with an ill-repressed air of satisfaction.

"A-a-a-nd that's too good for me." Morris returned half the deck to the crowing victor and his interrupted attention to the world outside their train car.

"What are you thinking about, when you look out there?" She squinted at him. "Some less traveled road, bent in the undergrowth?"

"Just looking," he shook his head, ignoring her playful jab. "Just…thinking."

He knew these vague, non-committal responses irritated Katelyn but, somehow, he couldn't marshal the concentration to paint for her a fuller, brighter picture. His mood became suffused with the indecisive palette rushing by his window, a yawning blur in varying shades of white.

"I see," she replied, flatly.

His tone was, itself, helplessly absent. "What do you want?" he shook his head and returned his gaze to somewhere off in the middle distance.

Around them the silence grew. Eventually, a clumsy passenger dragged the faint stench of stale tobacco down the aisle and into the next car.

Katelyn sighed. "Well, I'm going to the bar car," she announced at last with a vague air of annoyance. Then, with widened eyes darting back and forth in conspiratorial seriousness, she whispered, "Don't get too lost out there, hey, lest any of these delinquents run off with our priceless artifacts."

Morris watched as she drifted down the aisle, her delicate form counter swaying gently against the curves of the track, tawny waves trailing playfully behind. Approaching the door, a tall man in a beige trench coat coming from the other direction doffed a plaid trilby and, with exaggerated maneuver, stepped aside to allow Katelyn through. His predictable gaze turned and followed her young shape as it disappeared into the darkness between the cars and beyond. Morris knew exactly the smile with which she had returned the man's faux chivalry, the kind that at once dared and reproached his furtive leers. He had seen this look before, learned it as he had learned a hundred other such nuanced expressions. With the cock of an eyebrow, Katelyn could transform joyful abandon into cavernous incredulity;

skepticism gave way to distant melancholy with the pout of her lower lip.

So Morris let his thoughts linger amidst the various forms of her emotional registry. Immediately she was gone, though, he regretted not having joined her. Jousting pettily with Katelyn was, after all, infinitely preferable to enduring her outright absence. Now he was marooned with their collected luggage, three motley suitcases plus a grocery bag full of snacks and magazines they'd picked up at the station. It was too much for him to squeeze between the rocking seats by himself. Absently, he withdrew one of the glossies and flipped listlessly through the pictures; frail models lying about in a sprawl of plaintive, half drugged inaction, their puckered lips suggestively agape, eyes doll-like and transfixed on some point far behind the camera, remnants of the soft grunge, heroin chic movements popularized in the mid-90s. Whether white, black or Asian, short or long haired, standing, seated or strewn across velvet armoires or bearskin rugs, the women appeared to have been cut and measured in the same factory, an endless assembly line of non-uniqueness, each haughty specimen identical to the last.

Morris reflected on the value of true individuality and then, without consciously apprehending the connection, wondered how long Katelyn planned on spending at the bar. Surely not the rest of the trip, he hypothesized in prickly agitation. What if he needed to use the restroom or get up and stretch his legs? Hey! What if he desired to go to the bar himself? He fidgeted restlessly. Was she bringing drinks back, or just lounging up there, the very picture of en-ticement, flirting with whoever happened to park himself handsomely by her side?

After fifteen minutes that seemed like an hour, Morris decided he would head to the bar to order a beverage of his own. If she protested that he wasn't keeping eye on their luggage, he would remind her that he had nothing of worth in his solitary suitcase anyway and that, if she wanted an obedient minder for her own things, she might have at least brought him a thoughtful quencher. The point having thus been firmly established, he would return, triumphantly, to his gin and tonic and await her humbled apology.

Even before Morris reached the glass and steel gates separating his own lifeless carriage from the imagined, orgiastic festivities of the grand gala car beyond, he sensed Katelyn's presence on the other side so that, when the doors slid open to reveal her gleaming surprise, he could do nothing but relieve from her grasp the considerately arranged tray-for-two and follow her gratefully back to their abandoned seats, drinks in hand.

It was well after dark when they finally arrived.

#

While the brave and confident New York City rushed headlong into the new millennium skyscrapers first, Baltimore, now haggard and worn, shot through with raging gang violence, syphilitic and degenerate and drug addled to the point of despair, pined for her fast-receding glory days as an aging siren yearns for the promise of her squandered youth. Here and there, peering beyond the decrepit, boarded up row homes and sprawling slums foul with the stench of bigotry and neglect, one might catch a fleeting glimpse of that elusive and former grace; the elegant, 19th century mansions bejeweling the parks around the Washington Monument; the neoclassical basilica rising up on Mulberry Street; the Owl Bar tribute to Edgar Allen in the lobby of the stubbornly majestic Belvedere. A narrow but sturdy spinal column running up Charles and down St. Paul, extending from the Inner Harbor, itself a tawdry trap appealing to domestic visitors of even more domestic sensibilities, to just beyond the Meyerhoff Symphony Hall (but certainly no further than the Charles Theatre), attested to more prosperous times. Stray a few wayward blocks along those sinewy side streets, however, down West Fayette or East Lombard or along Edmondson, and Baltimore's infamous underbelly soon reminded the terrified interloper that these were not welcome parts.

For decades had Charm City's fortune and population been in steady, tandem decline. The reasons for this were many, varied and doggedly argued, though the result was simply that Baltimore was a weary old city, ground down by time's inexorable march.

Cracked and calloused union hands, for their part, clung like scared orphans to the popular rustbelt narrative; factory lines and hydraulic presses, once the molten lifeblood of a heavily industrialized northeast, had been slowly usurped by automation and cheaper labor abroad, so that once-secure jobs were effectively 'shipped oversees,' invariably to the lowest bidders. This Great Hollowing Out had left entire communities without means or purpose, chaff in the winds of ruthless, capitalistic progress.

Suburban whites, from the cheap and roomy comfort of their eyesore McMansions, harbored a much darker re-sentment; black men, they asserted in grave and impassive tones, were incarcerated at such a rate as lack of education or opportunity were no longer sufficient to explain. The resultant breakdown of the Afro-American nuclear family, Mr. White continued, exacerbated by the black man's tendency to moral depravity of all kinds, sexual promiscuity, proclivity for hardcore drug use and its attendant violence, plus 'things you and I can't even imagine,' had turned 'our once vibrant metropolis' into a decaying wasteland of broken windows and shattered glass pipes.

The truth, as is usually the case, was infinitely more complex than even the most ardent bigot or willfully illiterate armchair economist could ever hope to conceive. A million discrete occurrences, infinitesimal and irrelevant on their own but tidal in concert, had colluded over time and space unknown to grind the city into its present, attenuated form. Nor was the impact uniformly felt; in some areas, poverty weighed like an anvil on the residents' collapsing chests; in others, a thirsty coven of community organizers gorged itself healthily on public funds, none of which actually went to alleviate the root cause of the general malaise, but instead enriched those who, with immaculate conscience, dealt in the self-congratulatory business of dividing up precious resources on behalf of people with whom they hoped never to have to pass any time.

For Morris, the spirit of the moment would be forever encapsulated, like an insect in amber, by the image of a homeless man asleep on a park bench, the city's hollow motto, "BELIEVE," branded absurdly into the wooden backrest against which he shivered under an apathetic new moon.

#

"I can bring a blanket and pillow down there if you'd prefer to rough it on the stoop?" Katelyn called from atop the stairs leading to her fourth-floor walkup. Her silhouette was propped against a glass door. The soft, yellow light from the lobby poured onto the sidewalk below. Lingering curbside, Morris peered up at the red brick edifice before him, a scuffed suitcase hanging at the end of each arm.

"That would be a real, authentic Baltimore experience," continued Katelyn from her perch. "Just be sure to tell the crack heads you're a guest in the city. Or better still, say you're a weirdo Australian who's not used to sleeping indoors but who, like all your countrymen, carries a large knife whenever you venture into the urban American jungle."

"I'm sorry," Morris gave a laugh and shook the ghost of déjà vu from his expression. "It's just that I've seen this building so many times before. I've seen you standing there, in fact, in that very spot. It's bizarre to be here, that's all."

Physically, structurally, Katelyn's apartment was just as she'd described it; a narrow, galley style kitchen opened onto a largish lounge room in the front of the building while a thin hallway led to the two bedrooms, one with *en suite*, the other used presently as a kind of office-cum-hobby studio, in the rear. Double overhead ceilings more than compensated for what might otherwise have been a slightly cramped floor plan and two generously proportioned windows in the living room admitted ample afternoon light, so that guests were obliged to feel they were in more spacious settings than was actually the case. A working fireplace and elaborate, if peeling, cornice work conspired to round out the effect. The walls were uniformly painted a dull, rental white. In the bathrooms a pool of Mediterranean blue tiles filled the space to about shoulder height before surrendering to an ambitiously chosen pear green.

Morris set the bags down in the tiny entranceway and, for a frozen moment, had no idea what to do next. Katelyn relieved her visiting statue from the burden of guessing.

"Shoes go on the rack, there." She motioned to a knee-high shelf displaying a half dozen pairs of her own seasonal footwear, all a solemn, wintery black. "Coats on the hangers, there. If you need the bathroom, it's all the way in the back, at the end of the hall. You can just leave all the rest of that stuff there. We'll get to it later. First, though, I'll grab us a bottle of something. Red ok?"

He nodded while untying his dampened boots. "Smoking?"

"The landlord hates me for it, but he's a sweetie and I tell him I get chills standing out in the weather." She handed him an ashtray, a bottle of wine and a corkscrew "Glasses are up there, second cupboard on the right. Just make yourself comfortable in the living room and I'll be through in a minute."

Katelyn disappeared down the hallway, leaving Morris to inspect his new surroundings, to run his finger along the spines on the bookshelf, wonder at the trinkets and curios on the mantelpiece, puzzle over the nameless faces smiling cheerily, absently at him from the photos adorning her walls. Rather than be caught midway through a staring match with some ex-boyfriend, grinning supremely from an antique frame, Morris decided instead to take his place on the sofa and to fill the musty air with cigarette smoke.

"I took the place in a wild fit of independence," Katelyn announced when she emerged a short while later in a burst of shower steam and fresh clothes. Her wetted hair hung loose about her shoulders while she searched for her brush. "I signed on for six months, with an option to make it twelve if I liked the place. All the furniture is mine," she swept her arm gloriously across the room as if showcasing the priceless items at a Sotheby's auction. "Some of it's from bulk trash night, other pieces are hand-me-downs from concerned relatives, and still others the hopeful offerings sent to me from a string of lovers I keep in a perplexed state of desperation back on the continent." She winked and, having abandoned her search for the brush, lit a cigarette of her own.

Surveying her now, in her natural surroundings, Morris sensed that a renewed calm had come over the woman before him. For the first time in the almost three weeks, they had spent together, he felt she had finally let him close to her, invited him to her innermost sanctum, where she kept all the things that mattered in her private estimation of the world. The rest was peanut shells on barroom floors.

"This little guy," she rescued a diminutive lama wedged in a hardback ravine, Wilde on the one side, Poe on the other, "was a gift from my baby brother. He picked it up on a hiking trip through Patagonia and carried it all the way back for his favorite sister. And this fatty," a jade Buddha of about the same size, plucked from beneath a Homeric lean-to, "his second favorite sister brought to me from her trip to Viet Nam last year."

She offered it to him for examination. The light from the fire imbued the figurine's smoothed stone edges with a soft and fuzzy nimbus.

"Ain't siblings sweet?" she affected a yokel accent, exhaling into the light.

"Especially when you say so in that southern drawl," he replied, returning to her the tubby keepsake. "Where are they now? Your bro and sis."

"Mike's in Colombia somewhere, supposedly working on his Spanish. We all suspect he has a thing for the Latin ladies."

"I see," Morris concurred. "Well, that'd be the place to go then. Clever lad. And what about…"

"Chloe? She's here, in Baltimore. But only for a few more months. She's doing an exchange semester in Seville next year. It'll be her second stint abroad. The other she spent at some little arts college in the Hungarian capital, on the Pest side, I think."

"So, matadors and turncoats? She too have a lust for *los extranjeros*?"

Katelyn's eyes widened behind her cigarette. "God, no! Mom would kill her if she ever brought some aspiring foreign suitor home."

They were silent for a moment. Morris refilled their glasses and leaned back again into the couch. Katelyn drifted over to the window.

"And what about you?" he asked her at last.

"I told you, they won't mind." She lifted the wooden frame slightly ajar. "I'm the oldest. Besides, dad hated my ex. All of them, actually. Turns out with good reason."

"No, no. Not that," Morris began. "I mean, I hope they like me and all. It's easier that way, though not essential. But I'm talking about traveling. Sounds like your brother and sister are all over the map, and good for them, but England was your first time out of the States."

"Ah, that. I'm just efficient, you see." She took a final drag on her cigarette then flicked the emptied shell into the fireplace. "I picked up everything I needed on my first trip."

"No longing for Andalusian adventure, then? Some distant, Latin love?" Morris lit another link in their endless chain.

"When it comes to peripatetic wanderlusts, I prefer the Greeks. And," she replaced the little Learned One beneath his makeshift Odyssean shelter, "I've got all I need right here."

That night, and many more thereafter, Morris and Katelyn passed in her great front room, lost in conversation and each other, while the flames climbed gently up the walls around them and the silken moonlight spilled in through the frosted windowpanes.

#

Without any warning, Katelyn rose before noon one Monday morning and, turning to a dozing Morris, whispered airily in his ear, "Sleep as long as you like, my sweet. I've got to get ready for work."

Morris fought groggily through slumber's sticky membrane and, calling out over the gushing showerhead, consolidated his question into a bewildered, monosyllabic exclamation. "Work?!"

Presently submerged, Katelyn did not answer.

With gradual, Herculean effort, Morris salvaged a fragment of conversation buried deep in the boozy squall of the preceding weekend. Was it Friday night they had kicked off? Or Thursday? He recalled a few of Katelyn's friends and acquaintances, stippled faces lingering nebulously between this bar and that. There was Ben, the witty, self-deprecating Presbyterian with the ebbing hairline and the hyphenated surname. He was there with - who was it? Jen? Jane? Jamie? The pretty redhead, in any case. The one in the billowy white blouse and vertiginous heals, who they had to practically carry to the taxicab after the sidewalks had frozen over.

"Remember, Ben and Joni are coming by later," Katelyn leant over to kiss his forehead, her movements the very essence of sobriety and virtue against his stale, pungent indolence. In silken movements she dressed her porcelain figure. Morris rubbed his eyes against the early morning light. "You three can have a drink or two here then come by work afterward," she added. "I finish at nine."

The mere thought of imbibing alcohol rushed to Morris' temples a fresh round of dull, thudding pain. Gingerly, he reached for a bedside cigarette.

"Christine said she might join us, too. You haven't met her yet, but you'll like her. She's a real firecracker." Seated by a full-length mirror, Katelyn glided a pair of stockings up her legs. Standing to complete the action, she turned her attention to Morris. "Only, don't get her and Ben started on religion. He's a perfectly reasonable agnostic, except when she's on one of her atheist rants; then he starts trotting out all kinds of doctrinal nonsense. I once suffered through three straight hours while the two of them went through the Book of Confessions, line for line. I had the Nicene Creed rattling around my head for weeks, like that song you hate so much...."

"What, *Lullaby*?"

"*Everything's gonna be all right...Rock-a-bye, rock-a-bye.*"

Morris propped himself on one elbow and, admiring Katelyn's slender reflection in the full-length mirror hanging from the back of the bathroom door, reflexively blockaded that terminally insipid ditty from his own fragile skull.

"Ugh!" he uttered at last. "That sounds hellish!"

"No! That's just the kind of comment that could set them off," her maple locks darted around the corner. "I'm serious. That or anything about the Book of Confessions or Calvin or the whole ecumenical movement question."

"Ah yes," he was still shaking the tune from his head, "the dreaded 'ecumenical movement slip.' I'll try to remember."

"Please do, or they won't let you forget it. Trust me. *We believe in one God, the Father Almighty, Maker of all things visible and invisible...*" her teasing monotone disappeared down the hallway from where, shortly thereafter, the palliative waft of fresh coffee retraced her steps.

Moments later and Morris was slowly coming to, the brain fog of the foregoing binge evaporating into the shower's thick cotton steam. Celebrations had indeed commenced the previous Friday afternoon when Ben and Joni (Ah! That was her name!) dropped by after work, something to do with PR or advertising or marketing, he could never remember the difference.

At first blush Joni had appeared jarringly attractive by Ben's chubby side, so much so that Morris wondered if one of them harbored some extraordinary characteristic that clandestinely leveled the field; he a wealthy uncle nearing the end, say; she a rare and undiagnosed mental disorder. Only later, watching the Ben & Joni Show in its full, vibrant swing, did he come to understand that it was their very togetherness, replete with overlapping sentences and shared history and interwoven subtexts, that they so cherished in one and other. Under Joni's doe-eyed gaze, Ben transformed from a short, paunchy Everyman with poor skin and no keen eye for fashion, into a towering, razor-tongued *bon vivant* of impeccable pedigree. And by appending her otherwise unremarkable comments to the end of Ben's quirky and ever-insightful observations, Joni's ordinarily pale con-versation was elevated to a daring level from which she was frightened of descending. It was for precisely this reason that enterprising admirers of both partners discovered, having pealed their object of desire away for an intimate powwow on the fringes of some broken conversation, that in the other's absence either her chemistry was irretrievably diluted or his wit insufferably dulled. Better together, then.

Dried and dressing leisurely, Morris recounted, piece-meal, the remains of the weekend. After Friday's cocktail hour had grown into two and "one last round" doubled back for a thirsty encore, the foursome tottered off to a nearby bar, on Charles Street, he figured, for "something to warm the belly."

It was the first stop on their escapade, but the last Morris could recall with any real clarity. Next came a late dinner in Little Italy; he could see the red, green and white lights draped between telegraph poles at the barrio's entrance but not resurrect the trattoria's interior beyond the starched napkins and chilled Chianti served from a shabby wicker basket. After that, a hip, literary pub of some kind, The Poe or maybe The Joyce?, followed by, in no sure chronology, a smoky Midtown boat club, a brick cellar with craft brews and dim candles and, possibly, bacon and eggs back in their front room as the sun thawed the horizon. Saturday and Sunday followed much the same path, though were all the more discombobulating for having begun with mid-morning brunches rather than in the comparatively subdued, postprandial fashion.

"Ok, I'm off," Katelyn slung a canvas tote over her shoulder and reached for her parker.

Morris thumbed her collar gently then, remembering a flash of conversation from the sodden weekend, blurted, "Katelyn, dear. You're an actress."

"Very good, Morris," she laughed, as if at some private joke. "But today, I'm still a waitress. And, I'm late."

She kissed him hurriedly and made to leave but he pulled her close again and drew her lips tenderly to his own.

"Until tonight, Katelyn Louise Hayes."

She simpered, despite herself. "Don't be late."

#

Whatever awkwardness Morris felt in admitting to Katelyn's home two of her closest friends, pals who had likely lazed there dozens of times before his name even registered in the vast and sentimental orbit of their conversation, was instantly dissolved in Ben's toxic winter punch.

"It's delish, darling," Joni gloated after their first cheers. "He makes it this time every year. To me, it just tastes like the holidays." She pranced from the kitchen and into the front room; thither the two men followed.

"You don't need a waxed mustache and an old-time rocking chair," Ben announced, dropping himself into a familiar corner of the couch, "but you do need a certain small batch bourbon, I can't divulge which one, and my homemade honey syrup."

Morris hoped the soothing syrup might protect his stomach against the noxious magma now splashing around inside it. The hope soon passed, in vain.

"You two have been together for a while, then," he managed to conceal the fiery wheeze in his voice with an all-purpose groan as he took his own chair near the window.

"Six years this spring," Joni started.

"A-n-n-n-d, I'm sure Morris doesn't need to hear the whole story again, Joni. We must've bored him half to death with it the other night."

Morris searched his memory for any clues of the narrative, but came up empty. He thought vaguely how the three of them, Katelyn and these two friends, employed the same elongated a-a-a-and at the beginning of their sentences.

"A-a-a-and, I hope to hear it many more times to come," he parried, and before he could retract it, discovered his own glass carried forward in salutary enthusiasm.

"I'll drink to that," the happy couple chorused, raising theirs for the familiar clink.

And with that, they were off.

Entering the Belvedere's Owl Bar in high spirits a short while later, Morris and his companions might have been mistaken for old buddies. Coats checked, they proceeded directly to the bar where Morris ordered a round of ciders.

"So any place at all?" Joni brought the conversation in from outside.

"I reckon so," replied Morris. "I mean, for a while at least."

"What about Iran?" inquired Ben, "Or Russia?"

"Are you kidding? Those are two places I'd actually love to live. I thought you were going to nominate some obscure destination, like Chad or Bhutan or…"

56

"I hear Bhutan is just sublime this time of year," Joni chided.

"Well I like it just fine here in Baltimore," Ben affirmed his place of birth as if he, personally, had chosen it from a carefully whittled list of possibilities. "Four distinct seasons. A flourishing arts scene. And we've got plenty of pretty birds," he nodded to a slightly ruffled Joni. "Ravens, owls and oriels... Who would want to live anywhere else?"

"I don't know," Joni ventured, somewhat wistfully. "I'd like to visit Australia someday."

"It's a fine place," agreed Morris. "I spent eighteen years there once."

"Too many deadly animals for my blood," Ben shuddered. "No offense, mate."

"None taken."

"Aw!" Joni was tugging at Ben's shirtsleeve, an ingrate child beseeching her unyielding parent. "Don't you want to see the cute little Koa-a-a-alas?"

"Actually, they're the most deadly of all," Ben needled. "Viscous little critters. Unsuspecting tourists lose fingers and toes to them all the time."

"Wait, toes? Well anyway, I don't care." Joni folded her arms in firm protest. "I like Morris' idea. Any place on earth, for a little while. Except India, of course. My stomach's too sensitive. And for the same reason I could leave China out too. And most of Asia, I guess."

"That's a third of the world's population stricken from your to-go list," Ben's tone carried more than a trace of triumph. "And here I was just beginning to think you were about to pack your bags and join our new friend Morris here as some kind of perpetual drifter."

"There's still plenty to see," rejoined Joni.

"The more he saw, the less he spoke," Morris read aloud the epigram cut into the stained glass above the bar. The Ben

& Joni Show looked at him and then, in unison, gave out a duet of laughter. So the banter continued so until a shrill voice pitched itself above the low, convivial hum of the barroom.

"That'll be Christine," Ben affected his happiest McHappy face.

"No religion tonight," Joni pre-scolded then, turning to Morris, "He's still smarting from their last run in."

Morris watched as a platinum shock parted the sea of diners between them. With sweeping theatrical graces she kissed Joni on both cheeks. Her exclamations of "darlings!" and "m'dears'" drew notice from more than a few tables.

"And no sulking from you tonight, Benjamin James," she eyed her recent foe with playful derision. "Or else I'll have to put you back in your place again."

Christine repeated her salutation on each of his flushed jowls before turning to the one unfamiliar face in the group. "And you must be the famous Morris. Katelyn's told me a-a-a-all about you."

If her suggestive emphasis on the totality of her knowledge was supposed to unnerve Morris, she didn't notice its failure to do so.

"Now, when's that girl of yours coming, anyway?"

"She finishes her shift at nine," Morris remembered aloud. "Should be over shortly after that."

"Any luck with the auditions?" Christine continued and then, without waiting for an answer, "You know, I was the one who told her she should try acting in the first place. Such a pretty thing. I hope my advice doesn't prove to have been given in error."

Morris made to grab the bartender's attention only to find Baltimore Ben already hard on the case. The consequent round arrived just as Katelyn did and the remainder of the evening dissolved, as so many before and after, into the flickering hours crowding the morning side of midnight.

#

During the winter days, while Katelyn worked her long shifts for short pay, Morris remained cocooned indoors. On frigid afternoons, when he could scarcely have blamed the sun for failing to make an appearance at all, he poured over her bookshelf, imbibing of the collective American canon all that his own, prescribed education had overlooked in favor of sentimental, quota-conscious, homegrown nonsense. He found himself suitably awed by Miller and Bellow, troubled by Kerouac and Burroughs, transported by Hemingway and Fitzgerald and restored in turn by Frost, Eliot and Cummings.

American authors, it seemed to Morris, appeared either unable or unwilling to divest themselves fully of their country of birth. Whether these writers remained within its fifty states or expatriated to the world at large made scant difference; shades of their Americanism, if that's what it was to be called, were irrepressible; as if, having drank of the water, it had permeated something beyond mere physiology. This tendency he found particularly well steeped in those who harbored passionate, even zealous opposition to the prevailing American status quo, arrested and imperfect as it might have been in any given moment in history.

Having nothing much else to do, Morris read non-fiction too. And here he noticed the same habit; the unapologetic Americanism of those who most took their country to task, highlighted her shortcomings, pointed at her blemishes and fallibility. At their finest, it was men the likes of Spooner and Thoreau and Charm City's own H.L. Mencken who stood for Morris as the towering exemplars of critical thinking, reasoned dissention and civil disobedience he had so admired in what, bereft of a sharpened phrase, he had always referred to privately as the *American Spirit*. Gradually, guided by their essays, Morris began to consider the concept of America as an idea, abstracted from the pageantry and infantile trappings of mere patriotism, far greater than what might be contained within the imagined borders on any map, drawn and redrawn by men whose own lives had come to but handfuls of dust.

He floated the notion, still inchoate, amorphous, to Ben over whisky sours one night at the Owl.

"No borders? You've been visiting that commie café again," Ben laughed off his friend's bumbled précis. He slapped Morris on the shoulder affectionately. "All those anarcho-syndicalists with their 'free trade' coffee and 'ethically sourced' food," he made the sign for italics, universally understood to convey derision or irony, around the appropriate buzzwords. "They'll have you handing out pamphlets on icy street corners if you're not careful."

"No, no," Morris rejoined. "I mean, yes, I sit there when I begin peeling the paint at Katelyn's. And it's true, they serve good, strong morning brew...whether 'fairly' traded or not."

Ben gave an affectionate, almost apologetic look of skepticism.

His friend continued. "But it's not for their political bent that I go there. If anything, they're driving me in the opposite direction. I mean, it's great that they question the accepted wisdom and all. Slaughter the sacred cows – democracy, say, or the role of the state in man's life – but they have some very confused ideas about private property and the role of capital in general."

Morris could sense Ben's interest wavering but, with the gust of a third highball firmly in his sails, he pressed the point.

"Look, it's not that the borders don't exist. Clearly, they do, and there are severe consequences for anyone who doesn't observe that fact. I'm only saying that this reality is an imagined one, reckoned into existence by mere men. Men, Benjamin, no more human than you or I or that guy in the corner." Morris slaked his thirst while Ben considered the unmistakable humanity of a mustachioed dipsomaniac swaying gently against the wall.

Draining his own glass, he carried on. "Political borders are not part of the cosmic firmament, Ben. They're as man made as the Twin Towers or the rules of Monopoly or those weird marshmallow-biscuit-things you insist on toasting over every available open flame…"

"Hey now! Call into question the political fabric of this great republic all you like," Ben raised a hand to his heart and cast a solemn gaze upon an unseen spot in the distance, "but you go startin' on s'mores and we're gonna have problems."

Morris pretended not to hear. Somewhere through his groggy mind the ghost of a point was wandering. "It's just ritual, ceremony written in smoke. The idea of America, Ben, the core I keep coming back to, is that of man not beholden to anyone but himself. That includes any majority calling themselves church or state, or any other group claiming authority over his individual sovereignty."

"Ok, Ok. So, there are no borders in the world." Ben sensed this was a conversation his young friend needed to have. "You've snapped your fingers and now anyone can go anywhere and do whatever it is he or she wants. It's chaos, Morris. Anarchy. Alright then. So, what's to stop some random nutcase from wandering in this very bar and shooting us all to high heaven?"

"What's stopping him now?" Morris' eyes widened. "You honestly think a lunatic with psychopathic tendencies pauses to consider whether he's violating one of God's commandments, much less some unholy line in Man's own criminal code? I sincerely hope there's more standing between me and the next guy on the street than myth and fiction, that the only thing holding you back from going postal in this bar is not the alleged existence of an ancient stone tablet or the agreed-upon validity of some scrap of parchment sitting in a government basement."

Morris peered at his friend then, suddenly aware of his conspicuous vim, glanced down sheepishly into his empty whisky. After a generous pause, Ben took up the reigns once more.

"It's more than that, Morris," he began, calmly. "What you're talking about is the entire edifice of western civilization; the accumulated knowledge of our collective experience; rules and laws that were developed over time and in accordance with our commonly shared values."

"I know, I know," Morris had composed himself, but the thought burned at him nonetheless. "Look, I'm not suggesting we throw any of that out. Quite the opposite, in fact. Of course it's important to recognize where we've come from and how we got to this point. Standing on the shoulders of giants and all that. I'm really talking about the institutions that administer those values. That mandate an unquestioning patriotism, say. Or demand unquestioning obedience. Look, here we are, peering over the lip of a new century, a shiny new millennium. Ideas about how society is to be ordered, or if it should be ordered at all, at least in the traditional sense, are going to be reexamined."

"So... so the New Order is No Order?" That familiar, confident tone had crept back into Ben's voice.

"Not the kind of order that's imposed by the force of a select few," Morris replied. "I'm imagining something more horizontal. Where each individual is responsible for his own life and the consequences, good and bad, of his actions. Not an absence of rules," he concluded, "more like an absence of rulers."

"But where would we be without their deft guidance?" Ben pointed to a television behind the bar. On it, a confused and misty-eyed mammal was repeating the words fed to him.

"I, George Walker Bush, do solemnly swear ... that I will faithfully execute the office of the president of the United States ... and will to the best of my ability ... preserve protect and defend the constitution of the United States ... so help me God."

Morris turned to Ben and, each reading the other's thoughts, the pair let free a laugh so hearty it might well have carried them through the rest of their days as friends.

#

Chapter IV

The Less He Wrote

Morris barely perceived the slow advances of spring until, emerging from a friendly bar down in Fells Point late one afternoon, he noticed the cobblestone streets still dappled in the sun's lingering haze. Drawing a cigarette to his lips and feeling the air fresh and young on his face, he ambled contentedly toward Harbor East. From there, he would be able to watch the day fade gently into the skies over old Federal Hill. Puzzling the northern hemisphere seasons out in his head as he walked, Morris noted with no particular interest that his birthday was due the following week. He briefly considered mentioning it to Katelyn then, for reasons he couldn't quite understand, chose not to.

Though they spent most evenings together and enjoyed immensely the days when she was free, Morris and Katelyn had gradually come to occupy worlds of faintly differing color and tone. Hers revolved around a series of floating shifts at the restaurant, punctuated by auditions for minor roles she did not exactly need and for which she was not ultimately suited. She told herself and Morris, truthfully, that these setbacks were of no real concern and that she was enjoying her first year out of college just bumming around. A break would come along by summer and, if not, she could always go back to school and turn her fine arts degree into something her father might call "marketable." For the moment, she had income enough to accommodate her modest needs, a comfortable, if cozy apartment in trendy Mt. Vernon and a kindred soul with whom to while away the star filled nights.

For Morris, Katelyn's late morning departures marked the hour he would begin the day's reading, either in the immediate warmth of the front room or, if he were feeling restless, in one of the innumerable cafes he'd come to know around town. He had no set curriculum in mind but, instead, found one author invariably led him onto the next either by direct reference or, and this was particularly the case with the so-called Lost Generation who had expatriated to Paris after the Great War, because they occupied a similar "space and time." Like Katelyn, Morris couldn't feel any pressing desire to alter what was, after all, a perfectly satisfactory arrangement. He cared deeply for Katelyn and sometimes wondered, usually during the serene glow of their nocturnal excitations, whether he might not even love her.

A few days after the vernal equinox gave the budding season its official stamp, Katelyn broached again the subject of dinner at her parent's house. They had planned to go there on numerous occasions but, owing to a series of last-minute cancelations on both ends, dates were shelved until weather and schedules cleared up. Morris agreed the time had probably come and proposed they bring a bottle of her father's preferred drink to celebrate the occasion. He was thinking as much of his own thirst as anyone else's, for the evening had lingered at the edge of his thoughts in the place where niggling obligations tend to congregate. Katelyn complimented his courteousness just the same and set a weekend date to which all parties looked forward with a mixture of intrigue and enthusiasm tempered by a mild, latent apprehension.

#

So faithful was the reality of Katelyn's home address to the one he'd imagined while reading her letters that, for a brief moment, Morris wondered whether he hadn't traced these exact steps before. Approaching the place now on foot, for the taxi had dropped them at the liquor store at the bottom of the hill, he recalled the feeling that had passed over him when first they arrived at her apartment a foggy month and some weeks earlier. The scene comprised of neatly trimmed front lawns and star-spangled balustrades. Newly waxed SUVs occupied the driveways and, just as he'd envisioned, white oaks and umbrageous lindens bordered the long, doglegged street as it inclined gently to her door. It was all so very familiar. Maybe, he pondered, slightly out of breath on nearing the top of the slope, all of this has happened before. The visit to this house. To her apartment. The coach ride to Cambridge. Maybe there really was no such thing as self-determination in this world, nothing new under the sun, only the distant recognition of all that has already gone before. Perhaps we're all just actors, Morris' concentration drifted, minor roles reading from a script written before we were born, that contains our birth and death and the fortunes between, one that will continue on long after we pass. Maybe...

Katelyn's house was not obviously dissimilar from any other on the block, except that it was the only place in which, to Morris' mind, she could conceivably have lived out her childhood days. Nothing in the construction itself gave him this impression, but he knew the moment they came upon the Hayes residence that this modest, two-story abode of red weatherboard under pitched, asphalt shingles, was the place she had called "home." The air seemed even to smell faintly of her...or was it the other way around? Either way, Katelyn was a part of this house, this street, this neighborhood and of the gentle spring breeze that, rustling the leaves of the great trees, passed through this time of year.

As if to confirm his very intuition, an elegant, middle-aged Katelyn in a blue and white maxi dress appeared at the front door and, calling across the garden path, welcomed the young adults both familiar and foreign into her domain.

"I was beginning to worry we'd said something wrong," she exclaimed, embracing her daughter with one arm and accepting her husband's rye with the other.

"Your dad will appreciate the effort."

"Thanks, mom. It was Morris' idea, actually."

"That's lovely," she said, turning to him now. "And how are you, Morris? We've all been waiting for Katelyn to let you 'round to see the family."

Morris regarded the earlier model as all young men do their sweetheart's mothers: with a heady blend of trepidation and curiosity. He was, naturally, eager to learn what the future might hold for his own Katelyn, still very much in the flush of her youth. But he was also a little wary of meeting that face a day sooner than absolutely necessary. Mrs. Hayes was the picture of country-club charm, with a poise that suggested many a long, unhurried afternoon with the tennis coach. Her coloring, in hair, eyes and skin, was virtually identical to Katelyn's, so much so that an amateur portrait artist might have covered their twin canvasses without once altering his palate. At first blush, Mrs. Hayes only added to Katelyn's own account.

"I'm very grateful for the invitation, Ma'am," Morris remarked at last.

"Nonsense," she quacked cheerily in return, sending unknown ripples over his calm waters. "Delighted you could make it. We're always curious to see what our little Katelyn's been up to."

Morris followed the ladies of the house inside, cringing ever so slightly in their steps.

#

The spacious front room was arranged with a meticulousness that might have belonged to a depression-era hoarder petrified of discarding a single lace doyly, lest the day arrive when the global inventory finally depleted and coffee circles were left to rule unchecked. Either that or a lepidopterist with obsessive-compulsive disorder had been conscripted as interior designer. Morris couldn't decide. He stood for a second, surveying the floor to ceiling picture frames of no immediately discernable theme that crowded the walls. Trinkets and bric-a-brac competed to fill every available inch of shelf space and stacks of books were piled aside the already straining cedar cases. Even the stairs, off to the left and winding up toward a dusty shaft of light emanating from somewhere inside the second story, found themselves exhibiting an endless procession of records, vases, encyclopedias and unopened FedEx boxes. It was a kind of organized mess with a million stories to tell.

Entering the room now, Morris became aware of a corpulent figure sunk deep into a chesterfield armchair near the far wall. Motionless as a statue and spotlighted, rather dramatically, Morris thought, by a single reading lamp, he nevertheless exuded an air of importance that seemed to dare anyone to break the silence laid out before him. As the ladies quieted their chatter and the shadow of receding conversation grew long across the room, the man raised slowly the extended pointer of his right hand and, at length, looked up from his book.

"Darling," his eyes settled fondly on Katelyn. "Your mother didn't mention we were expecting anyone. What a wonderful surprise!"

"I must've told you twenty-five times since yesterday," Mrs. Hayes protested, though her husband, a fellow of no meager proportions, was already panting his way across the room.

Morris watched as Mr. Hayes turned from a normal, if slightly ruddy complexion to a deep, hypertensive crimson during the course of the fifteen feet journey. The sheer effort spent liberating his unsteady mass from that cushiony leather membrane seemed testament enough to the affection the old boy must have felt for his daughter. Morris got the impression that, in some shape or form, he had been in that chair since perhaps his late twenties, when his tennis playing, yoga stretching wife had finally despaired of turning her husband into anything that might be proudly displayed in a swimsuit or, for that matter, any suit.

"Daddy!" a childlike voice cried out from somewhere within the fleshy embrace then, stumbling back a step and drawing breath again, "I'd like you to meet my friend, Morris."

"Oh yes, yes. Morris," the giant man took the younger's hand in his own and shook it vigorously. "Very good, very good."

Mr. Hayes had a tendency to repeat himself, as if confirming in his own mind that his initial proclamation was, indeed, what he had intended to venture.

"Welcome, welcome." His jowls shook heartily. "Welcome to our happy home."

At that point Mrs. Hayes, who had disappeared unnoticed from the room, returned with a salver of hors d'oeuvres, into the center of which her husband casually plunged. Before another round of pleasantries could be repeated, the assiduous hen had circled back from the kitchen, this time with a tray of champagne flutes in one hand and a silver ice bucket in the other.

"We'll get to your father's rye after dinner, darling," she cast a cautionary glance in Katelyn's direction. "But he needs to take it easy. You can feel his heart thudding away from across the room." Then, shaking her head with closed eyes and raised brows, she added, "Not exactly the picture of health, our Norman."

Mr. Hayes, *Norman*, swatted his wife's reproach with a dismissive wave of his oven mitt paws and let out a laugh that began somewhere deep inside his cavernous torso and ended, to his mild annoyance, with a coughing fit he struggled to quell. Innumerable years had passed since he ceased to care what his wife said about him, either in private or, as was the case now, before new acquaintances. Once, long ago, their marriage had been a mark of pride in his world, something about which his friends spoke in admiring tones and which he, confidently, held up as an example for others to emulate. Sometime during the past two decades, when the children were young and underfoot, that love had dissolved and, in its place, a thick fog of miscommunication had descended until, after a period of epic breakdowns and shrieking threats of divorce, mostly from her, they had signed an unwritten truce and agreed to a loveless cohabitation, each satisfied in the knowledge that they were at least standing as obstacle to the other's happiness elsewhere.

"Don't listen to her fussing, sweetie," Mr. Hayes denied his wife the eye contact she craved. "You know how she is. We'll get to what we want when we want. It was a lovely gesture."

The phone rang from a distant room and Mrs. Hayes, excusing herself in a fluster, disappeared once again. With some effort, the giant man retook his position in the corner chair. Cushion and owner chorused a long wheeze as they became one again.

"Sit down here, you two." He motioned to the sofa opposite him. "Now, how did you two meet? And where? Morris, do I detect a British accent?"

"Of a sort," came the reply. "Descended of British convicts, actually. But arrived in your country by way of Ol' Blighty, yes."

"Convict ancestors, you say?" then, turning to his daughter, he gave a look that seemed to say, "I see this could go either way."

#

Though he anticipated a frigid dinner conversation, Morris was pleased to find nothing of the sort awaited him at the Hayes supper table. In fact, it was almost comical the way the married couple never once addressed each other directly. Instead, they communicated entirely through the third parties at the table via a series of amusing verbal jabs and parries.

"Your father used to be friends with a group of expatriates from somewhere in the Commonwealth," Katelyn's mother ventured sometime between her third and fifth half-glass of Chablis. "South Africans, I think. Of course, that was before you were born."

"New Zealanders they were, Katelyn," the large man corrected. "Kiwis, as Morris here would have them. And I met them after your mother had your brother. You would've been about seven or eight, I suppose. Anyway, a few of the guys from the club were trying to talk sense into them about the proper role of government in man's affairs. Namely, that there should be none. They were stubborn bastards, though.

71

Kept on about their welfare programs. Just imagine; all that magical free stuff, and nobody paying a damned cent for any of it. Huh!"

Mrs. Hayes stiffened in her chair. "And that's just the kind of language he used to bring home from the bar when their little troop of political vigilantes got into their whisky," she demurred.

"Needless to say," Mr. Hayes continued as if his wife had said nothing at all, "we didn't go to the bars in those days. Had all our meetings at the club headquarters."

"Club headquarters being what your father and his buddies called the bars downtown."

Mr. Hayes breathed deeply. "Any place for a young man to discover a little peace and quiet, Katelyn, away from life's many and mixed distractions. They come in all forms, as you see."

And with that, his wife suddenly recalled to mind an apple pie, hopelessly abandoned to the fiery perils of an unwatched oven. Out she flittered once more. Katelyn shot Morris an apologetic glance which he caught, assuaged and returned in the form of a poorly concealed chuckle.

The old fellow either missed this little interchange or chose to ignore it and, instead, took the opportunity to cast a line into Morris' own political millpond.

"I'm afraid I've not given the matter sufficient thought, sir," Morris replied regarding his own position.

The inquisitor leaned back in his chair, grinning like a fisherman who had just witnessed a gaping carp leap into his canoe.

"Come now, Morris," he smiled. "Mrs. Hayes has her pretty head deep in the oven recovering a pie. You're amongst friends at this table now. Please, feel free to speak your mind."

From the corner of his eye, Morris thought he saw the fisherman's daughter grinning ever so slightly. She's seen this all before, he realized.

"Well," Morris braced himself for a moment then continued, "hearing the candidates in this past election espouse knowledge and solutions on virtually every conceivable subject, I'd have to conclude either that these people comprise an elite class of pure, unadulterated genius, in which case I'd have to wonder why they weren't busy finding cures for orphan diseases or improving on the work of Keats..."

"Or?" the old man interrupted, nostrils leading his full moon face in an involuntary forward advance that seemed to conscript his body from the waist up.

"Or," Morris paused, tilting his head so as to peer down the empty hall into which Mrs. Hayes had earlier disappeared then, seeing it clear, added, "If you'll pardon the expression, Sir, they're all full of shit."

Mr. Hayes, *Norman*, halted the onward lean that had begun sometime between rare ailments and the late English romantic and, with some effort, returned himself to the upright position. Daughter Hayes, Katelyn, held her wineglass by the stem, motionless and equidistant from the lace doyly and her still, open mouth. Only her eyes moved, first to her father's stone face, and then down to the gravy-mopped plate in front of his straining shirt buttons. There it remained, on notice...

#

"Oh, Morris!" Katelyn shrieked through tears of her own much later that evening. "I haven't seen him laugh that hard in years. And the look on mom's face when she came running in with the pie! Like the Holy Ghost had visited her

73

in the dead of the night, only to tell her the whole thing was a sham after all!"

Morris motioned to the bartender for another round. "Part confusion, part terror," he smiled out the side of his whisky glass.

"Part indignation that she'd missed a burst of emotion from him, the likes of which she may never see again!" Katelyn added between fits of laughter. "Really, Morris. That was priceless."

"You know, I thought for a moment he was going to flatten me. Just reach out with those bear fists of his and slug me one right in the nose."

Katelyn let out another howl. "Believe me, your face said as much and more. Oh, if I could only have a recording of the whole event. Mike and Chloe will never believe me. Not in a thousand years."

"Ah, Katelyn," Morris sighed at last, taking her open hand in his. "I'm going to remember this evening. I'm going to remember it for a long time."

"Me too, Morris" she agreed from behind glazed green eyes. "Me too."

That night they slept in the great front room by the hearth, warm and content in each other's embrace. It was the last time they lit the fire that year and, though neither of them could have imagined it, the last evening they would pass together in its flickering glow. Outside on the streets below, through the parks and crate-filled alleyways and over the shimmering argent harbor, the atmosphere around the city was quietly expanding, pregnant with the nascent pledge of spring.

#

Plans were made to call on Katelyn's parents for dinner again though, save for a handful of afternoon visits, when conversation was mostly constrained to the front porch and Mrs. Hayes was nowhere to be seen, the dates passed largely unfulfilled. One of those cocktail hour occasions, during which Mr. Hayes poured generously from his small batch gift until the bottle was dry, remained with Morris long after the white oaks and lindens and waxed SUVs lining the street had faded from memory.

The conversation washed along an enjoyable enough path, from the historical to the political, the philosophical to the existential, the faintly sentimental to, eventually and with plenty of sweet bourbon in its britches, the outright farcical. Mr. Hayes, as he was accustomed to doing, held forth with unrestrained brio on a wide range of subjects.

"Ginsberg? Now there's a hack, plain and simple. If Whitman were only alive to see what followed him. *The poets, orators, singers and musicians to come*! Ah, poor ol' Walt…"

"See, in Harding you had the resolve of a man fit for office. It's thanks to his courageous inaction that school children today aren't learning all about the Great Depression that began in 1920-21 …"

"Sure, we were all in it together in 'Nam, but I never heard a Yankee voice coming down the line when we radioed for help. Always some southern boy. 'Hang tight, fellas,' he'd growl. 'We're cummin' a gicha'…"

Morris conscripted an endless infantry of hand-rolled cigarettes, cheap and strong, as he listened to the old man opine on this topic and that. A warm breeze blew in across the verandah, carrying his smoke and the smoke from the storyteller's pipe off down the hill. Katelyn, he couldn't avoid noticing, neither drank much nor, stranger still, smoked at all. Casual in flannel and denim, she perched gracefully on the front railing, right leg bent at the knee, back propped against the corner post. There she listened to the two men ramble and watched absently as the green-grey storm clouds gathered themselves up in the distance.

Sometime between Bob Dylan and "what passes for music today," the first drops fell, plump and sweet and in the afternoon light. The smell of fresh cut grass soon filled the air and a fine, ambrosial mist suffused the scene.

"I'm still listening," Morris removed his cardigan and, stepping down onto the lower stair in t-shirt and threadbare jeans, he kicked off his shoes. A puddle formed at his feet and soon the path leading in from the road was inundated. There he stood for half a minute or so longer, watching the downpour intensify. Drenching torrents quickly displaced the soft mist and soon it was impossible even to see the houses immediately across the street.

Morris felt a tingling in his wrists and down the back of his neck. Breathing deeply, he closed his eyes and, without turning around, strode in slow, deliberate steps to the middle of the Hayes' front lawn. There he stood, blind, alone, not a little drunk, and with arms outstretched. Minutes or hours later, he noticed Katelyn's hands in his. How long had she been there, in front of him? Morris opened his eyes. Through the rain he saw in her unflinching expression a tranquility that seemed to transcend the moment. It was as if she had glimpsed something beyond his understanding and, more than that, made peace with it too. He could feel her breathing heavily, the shudders of a post-sob retraction, when the body attempts to quell an emotion dredged from deep within.

Impulsively, instinctually, Morris moved forward to kiss her. He felt his lips on hers, wet with rain and salt, before she drew away and rested her head on his chest, the heavens pouring down upon them.

"C'mon!" she shouted at last, shaking him to attention. "Dance with me, Morris! You've come all this way! Dance with me now, before you forget!"

Young lovers on the verge of everything and nothing at all, the two swung around the yard in a state of dizzying exaltation. Not even Mrs. Hayes, who watched from the window of her daughter's childhood room on the second floor, could suppress a smile.

Later that same week, over a lunch of Brie and crackers and cheap rosé, Morris made the suggestion Katelyn knew was coming.

"Let's take a road trip someplace, Katey. Get out and see the country a bit."

"Where would you like to go, Morris?"

"I don't know, really. Anywhere. Everywhere. Your dad was talking about his 'Yale blue' metropolises again the other day. Maybe we could go to Philadelphia. Or someplace out west. Chicago or… I don't care. Anywhere. There's plenty to explore, you know?"

"Yeah, I know, Morris," she smiled and took a long drag of her cigarette. "And you want to see it all."

"I knew you'd understand, Katey," he replied absently.

"I do, Morris. I do."

#

On a clear sky afternoon filled with birdsong and the sweet scent of lilac and hyacinth, Katelyn met with her sister for a respectably sober coffee at a downtown beanery, one known to both to serve excellent sangria. As the caffeine gave way to the grape and tongues loosened in turn, the pair discovered, to their mutual shame and modest embarrassment, the impromptu catch-up had in fact come at the behest of their perennially concerned mother who, not for the first or last time, had played both sides of the schedule.

"Go talk to your sister!" they chorused in mocking tones, laughing over the clinking glasses.

The pair watched as a gaggle of tourists peeled around their outdoor table-for-two and passed on down the cobblestoned street toward the harbor. The cool afternoon breeze still had a lingering freshness to it, though the winter bite was all but gone. Chloe was the first to speak, as she always did on those not-quite-spontaneous rendezvous.

"She hates him, you know." Her delivery was flat, intended neither to incite pain nor anger. She was like that, Chloe. No frills.

Katelyn channeled all her available equanimity. "You didn't need to tell me that, you know."

"I'm your sister, Katelyn. I'd tell you anything."

"No, I mean I already guessed as much. It was plain from the moment she met him," she exhaled a deep violet plume into the sidewalk air with practiced insouciance.

"Did she tell you about dad's laughing fit and how she nearly launched the apple pie all over the table that first night?" then, without waiting for a reply, "You should've seen the way she came bolting in from the kitchen, Chlo. She looked just like a plucked hen."

The two sisters interwove a girlish giggle fetched from their teenage years.

"Yeah. Dad told me," Chloe managed, recovering herself. "Twice."

"And the two of them together, Chlo. You know, I think dad might actually like him."

"Like as in, not want to shoot him?"

"Maybe even that much. Maybe."

"Well, if dad likes him mom's practically bound not to," Chloe raised a single, obstinately unplucked eyebrow.

She was beautiful in her own way, Katelyn thought. Her tussled, earthy hair and pale, unblemished skin; her quietly European dress; the way she held a stare for longer than was comfortable, as if issuing a silent challenge to the world. She was rough. Unruly. But not in the way other kids her age were. There was something nonchalant about her, sure. Something that said she honestly didn't care about the crowd's opinion. Maybe Morris was onto something; maybe it would take a matador to tame her after all. Katelyn noticed a sudden and deep affection for the young woman in front of her. Why didn't they talk like this more often, she wondered?

"And what about you?" Chloe withdrew a cigarette from her sister's pack. "These things will kill you, you know?"

"I know, I know."

"Well?"

"Well what?"

"Well…what about him? What about this Morris of yours?"

Katelyn took a long sip of her bloodred sangria. "Yeah, he's a lot of fun," she said and, after a pause, "He makes me smile."

"And…"

"Ok, he makes me smile a lot. He's fun."

"You mentioned that."

"OK. Well, he's attractive. I mean, you wouldn't think so, probably. But to me… And he's kind, in his own way," Katelyn felt a strange tightness creep in under her ribs. She reached for another cigarette, then realized she had one already lit.

"Ka-a-a-a-te?" Chloe's eyebrows were now working in unison to assume the kind but incredulous arc known to fibbing sisters throughout the ages.

"It's just that," she paused. "Oh, I don't know…" Katelyn replaced her faded sentence with another sip of sangria. "He's just very 'in the moment,' you know? Like, sometimes I don't know what he's going to do next week or next month. Or where he'll be. I'm not even sure he knows...or cares."

Chloe reached over with a napkin to dry her sister's cheek. Until that moment, Katelyn hadn't realized she was crying.

"Oh, what am I saying?" she made a lunge at composure but fell embarrassingly short. "I'm sorry, Chlo. I honestly don't know why I'm crying. It's nothing at all. Oh, how stupid."

"Have you talked to him about it?"

"About what?"

"About this," Chloe motioned toward her sister with palms upturned, "whatever 'this' is? Something's obviously bothering you."

"No, no. I'm sorry, Chlo. It's probably something else. I've got a ton of auditions coming up and I'm just feeling a little... I don't know. Unanchored, I guess."

"Hey, I get that," Chloe surveyed her sister's expression and decided it best to revisit the subject another time. This would take more than a sidewalk sangria to resolve.

"Look, if anyone knows about unanchored, it's this gal right here," she thumbed her striped turtleneck accusingly.

"You know the Spain thing fell through. I haven't told mom and dad yet..."

"Oh, Chlo! You were so excited! What are you gonna do?"

The familiar sororal order momentarily restored, Katelyn wiped her eyes and embraced her sister's dilemma with all the gushing enthusiasm of someone trying desperately to ignore their own.

#

One of the afternoons Morris and Katelyn didn't go to Chicago, or Philadelphia, or even so far as Annapolis, the great and nebulous subject of "the future" visited them right at home. Returning from her morning shift at the cafe, Katelyn found Morris in a state of lurking inebriation, slouched in what was now his regular chair by the window. Beside him, a stack of books leaned in precariously over a stained-glass ashtray piled high with discarded butts. Morris didn't look up at once when she entered, but dawdled along with the text in hand, ambling over the page and coming to rest, eventually, at the end of the passage, roughly a third of the way down the next page. Here he placed his finger and, allowing his eyes to adjust to the new distance, raised his gaze toward the figure in the doorway.

"Sorry," he offered, shaking his head confusedly. "I was just getting to a stopping point." Morris placed his book, open and face down, on the stack next to him. "What about your day?"

It didn't sound to her much like a question, at last one he was genuinely interested in hearing answered. Katelyn surveyed her sandy blonde border through the heavy silence. He was unshaven and ruddy about the cheeks, flushed with the afternoon's drink. His clothes, the grungy maroon cardigan and olive corduroys, were as unchanged as the furniture with which he seemed to be gradually assimilating. The air hung dank and stale, arrantly contrasted against the nectarous currents swirling around the streets below.

"I'm fine, Morris." Katelyn's voice cut a slightly higher register than her normal, loquacious tones. "How about you? What have you been doing around here?"

Unsure as to what proportion of the question was accusation, Morris found himself wary of responding in a way that might invite further scrutiny.

"Hello? Morris," Katelyn snapped in before he could venture a reply. "I asked how your day was. Did you even make it outside?"

"Right, right," he scrambled, realizing he was, indeed, under fire. "I thought about going out in a bit, actually. What's the time? Can't be after two..."

"It's five. Thirty."

"Ah, well then…" though his conscious mind pondered the next move, Morris was vaguely aware that the subconscious processes had already determined the appropriate course of action, or at least a course of action.

"Should we head over to the Owl for a few drinks then?" he heard himself say before he could snatch the words from the air.

Katelyn, having waited long enough for an answer, had already disappeared into the kitchen, from where a cacophony of disturbed pots and rummaged Tupperware could be heard jolting in discordant annoyance.

Morris sensed that his indolence, or rather what she mistook for indolence, was gnawing at Katelyn's nerves. The clamoring continued from the other room. How could someone look so loudly for something? He made to tidy the side table but settled, on seeing the ashen meniscus peering hopelessly over the lip of the blue and orange glass, on lighting another cigarette. He was in the middle of considering the plight of poor Sisyphus when, rounding the corner with the absconded saucer firmly in hand, Katelyn shot him a glance of unalloyed reproach.

"The Owl Bar?" she mouthed in conspicuous astonishment. "What on earth are you talking about? Ben and Joni are supposed to be here any minute!"

Morris searched his mental archives for a snippet of the conversation he saw presently forming on Katelyn's lips. Had they discussed something about this?

"The planning meeting?" she goaded, hands motioning in a kind of empty cycling gesture at her front. His eyes were blank.

"The trip?" she repeated.

Still nothing.

"Your Goddamn road trip, Morris!"

Her weakened timbre skimmed across the words like a stone across a pond, then promptly sunk when it eventually found his name. Save for the welcomed purview of gleeful abandon, a state that appeared woefully distant at this juncture, it was the first time he had heard Katelyn's voice strained in such a way.

"I know, I know," he searched vainly for something of more substance. "There's no need to worry about it now, though." Suddenly he became aware of how absurd this must have looked, his attempting to mollify her from a comfortable, seated position as she stood fuming in her work attire. He wanted to leap to his feet, to stride across the room defiantly and take her by the arms, to shake her and tell her everything would be just fine, but something held him staid.

"Look, I just... I forgot," he finally offered. "No big deal."

"No big deal? This was your idea, Morris," she shook her head hopelessly, arms surrendered to her side. "I'm trying to listen to what you want, to help you do whatever it is you want to do. You say 'road trip' and I attempt to organize something. Company. Transport. Logistics."

"Who said we need any of that stuff?" Morris blurted out with a force that took them both a little off guard. His eyes fixed on Katelyn, whose thin frame appeared upright and rigid on the threshold, as if poised for a duel.

"Look, I appreciate what you're doing," he continued in noticeably calmer tones. "I really do. And I know your heart is in the right place, but you're missing the whole point of the exercise."

"And what's that, Morris? Please, enlighten me." Katelyn's expression indicated to him that, where the road forked at compromise and combat, she had opted for the latter route. Her folded arms completed the effect, even if the saucepan, still dangling from her grasp like some kind of gnome's shield, did appear a little ridiculous.

"It's about spontaneity, Katelyn. Sometimes it's best not to plan these things, but to just...go!"

"You know what, Morris..." but she broke off.

"Go on, Katelyn." He was on his feet now, feeling strangely like an unknown character in a scene they hadn't properly rehearsed. "Something's obviously on your mind. What is it?"

"I just want to know what you're doing. You talk about traveling and getting to know America. You go on and on about living in the moment and being spontaneous, like you're some kind of bohemian wanderer. But all you do, as far as I can tell, is sit inside all day and drink..."

"I've had one glass today," he shot back, reflexively.

"I don't care, Morris! It wouldn't bother me that you'd had ten already, if you were out there actually doing something."

"One, Katelyn. One glass." He held up an empty tumbler as if it contained unassailable proof of his testimony. "And I told you what I'm doing. I'm working up some ideas..."

"For your novel." It was not a question, but a statement laced with incredulity. Morris tried to conceal his wounded ego.

"So, you were paying attention." He reached for his packet of cigarettes, only to find them infuriatingly empty.

"You talk and talk about writing," her voice came from over his shoulder, "but all you've done since you arrived here is vegetate in my living room. I haven't seen a pen in your hands yet."

"I'm reading, Katelyn. It's part of the process, part of... You know what, never mind." Sensing the ground shaky beneath his feet, Morris turned to attack. "What about you, then. Huh? Since we're in the nasty business of doling out unsolicited advice. You talk about wanting to do something more than work in that cafe. OK, great! So how's your acting going? You haven't been to an audition in weeks."

He could see the tears welling up behind her eyes, but rather than ease up, he pressed his advantage. "You don't hear me harping on you about it, do you? I don't even bring the subject up."

"No, Morris. You don't mention it at all. And neither do I."

"Exactly."

"Of course, if you did care to check in from time to time, you'd know I did get a part. A lead, actually. Last week."

Though he couldn't remember exhaling, Morris watched the smoke drift out of his lungs to fill the silence between them. It seemed to emit from another body entirely; from someone else in the room, perhaps, someone who was keeping score. Advantage, Katelyn.

"Katey, that's... I mean…" He was scrambling, unable to locate a departure point for his next exclamation. "Why didn't you..."

"I didn't want to harp on about it."

Morris checked the emotional composition of his gut. The unmistakably sour aftertaste of embarrassment. The bitterness of wounded pride. The bilious mixture of shame, impotence and, he had to admit, niggling jealousy. As he felt the strange concoction churn inside him, a tower bell rang out in his ears, shaking him to a rude but welcomed state of alertness.

"That's the door, Morris." He heard Katelyn utter with plangent matter-of-factness.

"Don't you trouble yourself, though. I'll get it."

#

Chapter V

Tableaux Baltimoreans

"I'm going for some smokes."

Morris heard the words trail off above him. He took the stairs two, three, five at a time, spiraling down the building's internal drain, bounding from one platform to the next in a whirlpool of muddied doormats, frayed carpet and his own threadbare nerves. The scene back in the apartment - the whitewashed walls, Ben and Joni's startled faces as he pushed by them at the threshold, Katelyn's expression, vacant and painfully distant, the jade Buddha grinning arrogantly from the bookshelf - flashed through his mind in a randomly ordered series of polaroid snapshots. Descending, the steps disappeared beneath his feet in a vertiginous blur. He took the landing in a half dozen thudding, off balance paces before bursting onto the concrete sidewalk, feeling the cool air rush at his face. North along St. Paul he ran as the frosted glass door of Katelyn's lobby shrieked away on its hinges somewhere in the fast-fading afternoon behind him.

A few blocks later, Morris braked first to a jog, then a wheezing, panting walk that drew the attention of some curious though unconcerned pedestrians. Eventually he came to a stop near a bench on which "BELIE_E" was painted across the backrest, the "V" having long ago surrendered to the elements. By now almost doubled over,

Morris half collapsed on the seat. Elbows propped on corduroys, he hung his head between trembling legs for a few deep, reviving breaths then, leaning back against the abbreviated slogan, waited for his thoughts to catch up with him.

It was still early in the evening and rush hour's impartial crowd was beginning to thin at the edges. Cars and taxis honked and sputtered their way down toward the harbor, a one-way ribbon of undulating metal clunkers, all headed for the drink. Morris closed his eyes for a few seconds then, shaking his head, opened them again with a start. That the same scene presented itself, brown, mottled and humid, he found oddly discomforting. For no reason he could explain, Morris felt suddenly and abruptly alone in this strange city, as if Katelyn's private, unshared success had drawn her away from him. With a growing pulse of anxiety, he began to wonder where he was, and why.

The idea of the peripatetic wanderer had always presented Morris with a sense of indefinable poeticism, but could he really ascribe such lofty attributes to his own experiences and motivations? Perhaps Katelyn was right. What, after all, had he achieved these past few months? Nothing worth writing down, it seemed to him. His days and nights oscillated between thick, late morning lethargy and the cheap, early evening jubilance that kicked in around cocktail number five or six. More and more it seemed to Morris that he was slowing down, becoming fixed in, and fixated on, a kind of permanent, horizonless boredom. Where was all this going?

Leaning back against the bench, Morris imagined the city around him from an aerial perspective. Zooming out from his central coordinates, he widened the scope so that it included first the suburbs encircling the downtown traffic, the beltway spokes of grey-shingled roofs and nine-to-five commuter vehicles and kitchens with preheated ovens and crudely jig-sawed spice racks. Further out, the patchwork farmland of the neighboring counties came into view, Towson, Bowie, Hagerstown and more in browns and greens of varying hues and saturations. Wider still, he imagined the Assateague coastline, devoid of his footsteps, and the aged nubs of the equally mysterious Shenandoah range to the vast and pleading west. Between them sprawled uncountable convenience stores and gas stations, concrete overpasses and high school football fields and letterboxes stuffed with yard sale fliers and discounted takeout menus. America in bits and snatches. Wider still the frame drew, until he pinned to the unfurling map the nation's cast iron Capitol, a modern-day pantheon posing as ancient stone and wisdom. Next came Philadelphia, rusted and weary at the confluence of the Delaware and Schuylkill, one time stand-in for Washington, star of the Revolutionary War. And at last, with a curious sense of expectation and foreboding, Morris glimpsed the distant, gloriously immovable New York City, Lazarus' New Colossus beckoning him forward into the night. Here the animation paused, a flickering reel in burned sepia tones, suspended in a moment of infinite repetition.

Faintly at first, Morris heard Ben's voice approaching. It was even, characteristically self-assured.

"We'll grab a quick one at The Owl," he intoned, patting Morris on the back as he strolled on behind the bench without bending his gait.

Morris watched his pudgy figure move toward the Chase Street intersection. What had Katelyn told them? Did they already know about her big role? Was he the only one in the dark? Pitiful, fragile Morris, ego of glass. He waited until Ben's white polo shirt turned the corner, then rose gingerly to his feet and made his way along the now familiar path.

#

"They're not expecting us back for a while," Ben announced when Morris finally dragged himself onto the barstool beside him. A couple of rocks glasses stood in wait.

"Look," he started, taking a sip and surveying his friend's wan expression, "I don't know what's going on with you two...or you, or...whatever. It's really none of my business."

Morris wondered what exactly Ben did know, but fought the urge to ask. Instead, he said nothing. *The less he spoke...* Morris recalled the words above and a faint smile appeared at the corners of his mouth.

"Anyway, I wanted to tell you," Ben rescued the conversation from the threat of silence. "I was speaking with one of Joni's colleagues the other day - nice guy, actually, Jimmy-something-or-other. Anyway, he mentioned they have an opening that I thought might interest you."

"A job, you mean?"

The suggestion was not one Morris had foreseen, though he had to admit, it dovetailed well enough with the afternoon's general motif; something about idle hands in need of occupation or, at the very least, suddenly self-conscious boredom seeking distraction.

"No, no. Not just a job, Morris. Think of it more as," Ben paused for effect then, with wide-eyed salesmanship, "a unique opportunity to travel across America, Sea to Shining Sea, from the Great Plains to the Great Lakes, the Rockies to the Prairies, the wetlands to the badlands. You'll get to meet people from all over. And," he drum-rolled his chubby knuckles, P.T. Barnum-style, on the bar, "You get paid handsomely to do it!"

Morris let slip a clipped chortle. With an incredulous expression he goaded at the fine print.

"Sounds pretty amazing," he said. "Except?"

"What do you mean 'except?'"

"I mean, what's the exception, Ben? The 'but.' The 'only.' The '*caveat emptor*.' The..."

"OK...OK...OK." Ben, grinning cheekily, took a long, bracing sip from the fiery liquid before him. "If there *had* to be something, I guess you wouldn't *actually* be traveling, at least not physically. For that part, you'd mostly have to use your imagination."

"Mostly?"

"OK, entirely."

"So, no travel." Morris wore a flat smile. "Fine. What else?"

"What else?" Ben threw up his hands in a show of mock innocence. "Morris, I'm shocked that you would even insinuate... Alright, alright! So, the pay's not actually that handsome either. In fact, it's downright ugly."

Morris thought of his own fast dwindling stack of British pounds and how, were it not for their present strength against the greenback, he'd have depleted them entirely weeks ago. In fact, he wasn't sure even they would last him the rest of the month.

"Well, sometimes ugly is the prettiest option," he conceded. "What about the 'meeting people from all over' part? I suppose that's not quite the truth, either?"

"Actually, that part I did not embellish. Only..."

"Ahem..."

"Only, you wouldn't so much as 'meet' them as you would talk to them over the phone.

"Ah, I see," Morris stroked his chin. "So it's one of those 'unlimited earning potential, be your own boss' type of things, is it?" He had seen the A4 printouts taped to telegraph poles and power boxes, their tabs seldom removed. Probably with good reason, he assumed.

"Nope," replied Ben in the self-satisfied manner of someone who has had time to prepare for the most banal questions before they're inevitably posed.

"This one comes replete with a boss. Better still, you get a desk too, so you can complain about life in a cubicle as much as you like. The humdrum of monotony, how routine killed the artist, all that Nietzschean quackery you rogues like to press on about. And it's close by, too. You could even walk home for lunch. Or swing by the Owl for a quick pint."

Drinking on the job? It was a nice touch. Morris had to admit, Ben had thought of all the outs. "Did you mention anything to...anyone else?" Morris had only one 'anyone' in mind.

"You mean, did I mention anything to Katelyn?"

Morris let his silence answer in the affirmative.

"No. I thought you might want to hear about this privately. Decide for yourself. Look," Ben turned to his friend, "Meet with one of the HR girls in Joni's department and see if it's something you're interested in. If so, great. If not, no big deal. You can return to your renegade coffee shops and midday drinking without having missed a shot. Maybe you'll even find something to put in your book. What's it all about, anyway?"

Morris was suddenly bolt upright, the picture of affected indignation. "Why Ben, it's the *Great American Novel*, of course."

"Right, right. Stupid me. And written by an ingrate non-American, no less."

"Who better for the task?"

"*Touché*!" Ben doffed an imaginary cap at the only non-American he really knew. Strange bird, he thought to himself. "So, how about the job? Want me to ask Joni?"

92

Morris hesitated for just long enough to hide the true extent of his enthusiasm, then raised his glass and nodded in sincere gratitude.

"Do me a favor, though?"

"What, another one? So soon?" Ben chuckled. "Don't worry, Morris. I won't mention it to... to *anyone*."

They brought their glasses together, just in time for a familiar shock of platinum hair to appear itself between them.

"I see you boys have resolved today's great barroom debate without me," Christine's tone was florid. Her voice carried scents from the springtime air outside.

"Ah, I'm afraid you're too late, Ms. Christine," Uttered Ben as he made to take her jacket. "I think Morris and I have most of the big issues out of the way, don't we?"

"I'd say so, yes," agreed Morris. "I mean, since we've been sitting here at the bar we've unwound that needless mess in the Middle East, cleared up most of the outstanding algebraic conjecture..."

"And hummed a nice little ditty to round out Schubert's unfinished eighth," capped Ben. "So you see, purposeful conversation has officially drawn to a close. From here on out, it's light banter, tomfoolery and drunken gibberish only."

"Well, that's no fun. Apart from the drunken part," Christine made a pouty face that was decidedly more vamp than simper. "Of course, I'd do my best to inject a little controversy, some *gravitas*," her blonde waves danced about her shoulders as she unfurled a plush cream stole, "but the other ladies will be in any moment and you know how they hate it when I steal the spotlight. Especially now that we have a bona-fide starlet in our midst, am-I-right?"

Ben glanced at Morris, who was in the process of ordering another round from the bar keeper. "Better make it five," he signaled.

"The anarchist and the actress!" shrieked the blonde, glaring at the grungy bearer of whiskeys. "My, my! What a pair you two make!"

#

A mid-month cold snap ambushed spring's chipper advance, forcing much of the city's burgeoning social activity back indoors. Against the general vex and chagrin of the crowd, Morris was glad for the temporary chill. Not that his routine would be drastically impacted, but the cooler air seemed to hold in place for Morris something he'd lately sensed was thawing in the city's gathering heat; the peaceful calm of detachment, perhaps, of gentle, anonymous solitude.

Drifting for a moment from his American curriculum, Morris found himself carrying about a dog-eared collection of Charles Baudelaire's poems and essays. The Frenchman had written a favorable critique of Baltimore's own master of the macabre, Poe, (was that how it got here, he wondered, thumbing the pages in his jacket pocket?) and even translated to great acclaim some of the latter's works. But it was the poet's curious take on aristocracy as the only "rational and assured" form of government, and his corollary disdain for the childish pursuit of monarchies and republics, based on "feeble" democracy, that first interested Morris. For Baudelaire, only the offices of priest, warrior and poet were worthy of respect. "To know, to kill and to create." The rest of society, he concluded, were born "for the stable."

Peering over the rim of the coffee-scented cover and mulling one or another of the *Tableaux Parisiens* contained within, Morris surveyed the scene laid out before him early one evening. Huddled around the bended brass taps, a dozen or so professionals were chattering in the upstairs section of the popular Brewer's Art lounge on North Charles. Though mostly overweight, they were stiff about the limbs, a fleshy jumble of poorly fitted synthetic suits in navy blues and khakis and charcoal greys. The conversation they kept at a mercifully low burble, although a wearied clause occasionally escaped the morass, only to suffocate in the stale air surrounding the group.

"... and *then* you'll be billing at three-fifty an hour..."

"... caught in a vicious short squeeze just as the thing popped..."

"... won't see another pass like that all season..."

As far as he could tell, there were no prostitutes in the crowd. No artists. No beggars or gamblers or would-be flaneurs. Nothing for the aspiring decadent or the eroticist, nothing to dislodge the howling vacancy of bleak, post-Romantic modernity. Morris lamented. A century and a half ago, in a rundown Parisian tavern, someone would at least have been smoking a pipe or urinating on the floor.

At the high tables to his right, framed by floor-to-ceiling windows that faced out onto the street, another ten or twelve bodies idled away the faint, crepuscular moments before dark. Morris considered their neatly checkered oxfords and pleated chinos and the soft, inoffensive hum rising above them and, draining the rest of his pint in one, made for the stairs leading to the building's cellar bar.

It took a few moments for his vision to adjust to the candlelight as it struggled through the subterranean darkness. Pungent jabs of garlic and yeast and malted vinegar suffused the atmosphere. Morris saw a procession of faces and bodies, lit with emotion against the void, stark figures from one of Caravaggio's canvases. But the scene was a lively one; not funerary. From the bar, opposite the stairs where he stood, the sounds of gaiety and music and general abandon echoed around the space. A Dionysian ruckus. Ah, more like it, he thought.

Stuffing his book deep into his pocket, Morris sidestepped his way across the uneven stone floor. The crowd was thick and steamy and full of breath. In a vacant pocket, over near the street entrance, Morris found room to maneuver an elbow, which he used to wedge his way up to the smoothed wooden counter. He ordered one of the house specialties, a red ale of considerable potency, and examined the faces animating the crowd.

Across from him, three young men, no older than himself, Morris guessed, were slapping each other on the backs and laughing heartily. Their drinks splashed on the ground and sometimes on their shirts, but they neither noticed nor seemed to care. They all three wore beards of similar length, black, stringy and with beer foam at the lips. Morris thought for a second about his spell in London, about the times he'd stood awkwardly in all-male groups at the bar while someone told jokes and the others laughed. He shook his head, confusedly, then continued his scan. Beside the bearded ones, to the right, a porcelain-skinned woman with raven, gothic black hair was leaning over the rich cherry wood attempting to catch the barkeeper's attention. Her dress, velveteen and swanning from the jugular notch, left her breast more exposed than she seemed aware. Morris looked instinctively to his right, where two men at the end of the counter were enjoying the oblivious starlet's exposé.

At the opposite corner, a mixed group of perhaps five or six thespian types were hotly debating some topic of interest when Morris noticed among them Katelyn's unmistakable countenance, refulgent against the dancing shadows behind. She was stunning. Luminous. Alive. Morris' first impulse was to hide, to duck behind the bar, or maybe throw down a note and steal away altogether out the side exit. But movement wouldn't come to his legs. Or the rest of his body. Instead, he stood there, staring at the woman he'd followed across the Atlantic, with whom he currently lived and once shared a bed, whose front room he would return to this very evening, to sleep alone. He watched her laugh and extemporize in confident, silken gestures. Her eyes, crystalline in the near absence of light, carried the coversation, arresting the others in her group and conveying to them the true depth and meaning of whatever it was she was saying. They were captivated. He, Morris, was captivated.

The bartender signaled to him for another drink and, reading the responding gesture, brought him the bill instead. Morris finished, unhurriedly, his strong red ale. For a blissful moment, he observed Katelyn in her natural state. A beauty belonging to the past.

#

The anarchist and the actress didn't much speak during those few weeks, except to trade awkward pleasantries in the hall and between rooms of Katelyn's suddenly very tiny apartment. There were the unavoidable exchanges, of course, in which Morris apologized for his apish behavior and Katelyn, in turn, played contrite for some shortcoming of her own, usually something manufactured to assuage moments of despondency on his side. This conversation they had in a series of varying shades and tones, but always in the same, foreboding color.

Besides their mutual aversion to confrontation, busy schedules conspired to waylay the creeping, delicate subject hanging between them: the soft decay of their relationship. Still, it peered from the bookshelves, leered from the coatrack, lingered over the wet towels and unwashed dishes just the same, until it came to permeate the entire indoor space.

Though a single honest, direct word might have sufficed to dissolve the miasma, neither, it seemed, had the time nor inclination to offer it. After work at the cafe, Katelyn spent most of her time in rehearsal. Often, and with growing frequency, these sessions crept later into the evening. On those occasions, it was easier for her to simply eat with the cast, and for Morris to grab something, or not, at one of the bars. The arrangement or, rather, lack thereof, meant it was not uncommon for days to pass on end without the cohabitants seeing each other at all.

Sometimes these periods of isolation seemed to drag on into eternity. They were drawn into the same hemisphere, same state, same red-bricked square footage, but could see no intersection in sight. Euclidian vessels crossing the vast, unending plane. Then, a chance brush in the hall...the jangling of keys on the other side of the threshold...a snippet of dialogue over the last half of a rushed coffee, lost words and plans and promises trailing her departing curls, and Morris leaning out the front room window to watch his American girl vanish into a city all of her own.

In his more sanguine moments, Morris tried not to fret the break. It would do them good to focus on their own interests for a while, he told himself. Katelyn had her acting and, according to Christine and others whom he ran into now and then downtown, things were going well for her. There was even talk of her signing a proper contact, a multi-performance gig of some sort with a theatre company of sound repute. Either way, he didn't press Katelyn for details. Nor did he sense his approach was altogether welcome. He had felt a hardening of Katelyn's exterior of late, a cool change in her demeanor, a new metallic glint in her once soft and unguarded stare. A strategy for emotional self-preservation? he wondered. Or, more likely, she was simply moving on, in her own way. Embracing the constancy of change. It wasn't just the river that ebbed and flowed. They, too, were different.

Eventually, Morris came to think of her time at the theater, with her troop, her kin, absent from him, as something redemptive. At the same time, his own sphere of interest was developing. At Ben's behest, he met with an HR representative from Joni's to inquire of the mysterious position available at their firm. He was neither nervous nor expectant, but curious just the same.

"Morris, right?" The woman rose jauntily from her chair in a trendy Midtown cafe and, to Morris' surprise, met him almost eye to eye. "I'm Rachel," she announced, tossing her red hair about her shoulders in a way that somehow managed to look both overconfident and unnatural. "Would you like something to drink? Coffee? Tea? They make an excellent lemonade with fresh ginger..."

In three words, Morris ordered a triple espresso from the approaching waiter and took a seat. With an exaggerated sigh, Rachel thumbed a sheaf of papers, then set them aside with a satisfied little pat-pat.

"There," she pronounced, definitively, as if Morris ought somehow to be aware of the cosmic importance contained within the stack. "On to you. Joni told me you were interested in the Account Manager position. To be blunt, it's not exactly brain science, or whatever. We just need someone responsible who can talk to our subscribers when they call in with problems. And they do. Call in, I mean. All day. Between you and me," she leant over conspiratorially, very nearly unsettling her lemonade from the table as she did so, "a lot of them are just old and confused. They forget their passwords or their usernames. Or both! You'd have to guide them through their account information, troubleshoot, remind them what subscriptions they have with us, that kind of thing."

Morris nodded. Rachel didn't seem like the kind of person who needed an active interlocutor in order to enjoy a perfectly satisfactory conversation. Rather, he got the impression that anything he said was likely to detract from her favorable impression of their neat little meeting.

"Anyway," her eyes widened and her Midwestern accent scrambled up an octave, "tell me a bit more about yourself. Like, what would you say is your biggest weakness?"

"Sloth," Morris replied, without thinking. "Well, sloth or gluttony."

He paused for a second, drawing his thoughts out carefully. He didn't want to appear flip or insincere. Or to leave anything out. "Though lately, I guess it's been pride. And perhaps even envy."

Rachel eyed him confusedly then, realizing it was her turn to talk, blurted out a shrill peal of laughter over which she managed, "looks like you're just missing the lust!"

Morris wondered whether, during the lull that inflated the next few seconds, the dotty figurine before him might replay the tape and second guess her remark. Probably not.

"Well, I'm not particularly vengeful either. Or greedy, for that matter."

"Oh, don't worry about that," she assured him with a hearty wave, as if these mere deficiencies could be corrected without too much coaching. "The main thing is you're here and we need someone right away. Everything else you can pick up on the job. Plus, you've got a fun accent. Joni said it was cute, but in the fun kind of foreigner way. Not the other kind..." she trailed off. "Well, you know."

Morris didn't. But the following Monday he had a phone, a desk and the all the cubicle inches a rat race aspirant could ever want. He could hardly wait to share the news.

#

The office building was actually an old carriage house, converted by the owners of the attached mansion (and others) into a new kind of draft horse, one that better served the peculiar economics of a new and accelerating American century. Gone were the coaches and anvils and hones, the smell of iron and warm strop leather. In their place, rayon pleats and coffee capsules and all-purpose disinfectant. And the indifferent, omnipresent flood of blue-white fluorescent lighting. Unimaginable discoveries in processes and technology had come to both liberate a nation from the drudgery of the menial and, somehow, tether its emancipated masses to a new and shinier oar. In ergonomic swivel chairs a fleshier army rowed ceaselessly toward an unseen point on the horizon, its gaze, as ever, cast firmly on the shoulders of the man in front.

His own corner, ground floor desk afforded Morris a near uninterrupted view onto the adjacent alleyway. Occasionally, a bum would enter the frame. He (invariably *he*) would pick through the trashcans or slump next to the smoothed red bricks for an indeterminate spell, then saunter off down the line. Mostly, though, the laneway was empty, save for a few paper bags blowing in the wind.

Though he spent a good deal of his working day staring out the window, Morris didn't see much beyond the glass. The little red light on his desk phone flashed without remission. On the other end of the line, piped in from homes around the country, familiar strangers waited to tell their story.

[FLASH...FLASH...FLASH]

"Yes, Ed Robertson here. Look, I been on this call damn'd near twen'y minutes. What kina operation you folks runnin' there? Any longer here n' imma forget whate'er it was I called you fo' in the first place..."

"Certainly, Mr. Robertson. I'll be glad to help you out. Tell me, where are you calling from today?"

"Why, I'm in Conway, Arkansas. 'Bout an hour's north-a Little Rock, if ya ever been there. But it don't sound like you woulda. Now where are y'all located? I though' you was in Bal-a-more? Sounds like you got an accent though..."

"Indeed sir, I do. I'm from Australia."

"Whoa! This call ain't gonna cost me inner-national rates now, is it?"

"No sir, I'm right here in 'Mary Land.' But tell me, how's everything in Conway today? I'm just looking at it on the map now. You're right, I've never been, but I would love to visit sometime. I don't believe we have much in the way of Arkansas back in Australia..."

"That so, eh? Well, the first thing you've gotta know is..."

[FLASH...FLASH...FLASH]

"Betty Parker, from Florida. I phoned last week."

"Of course, Mrs. Parker. Where in Florida exactly did you say..."

"Sebring. Why, I phoned in just last week. Friday, it was. Or Thursday. Anyway, I'm still waiting on my newsletter. It's been almost a month and I still haven't..."

"I can certainly assist you with that, Mrs. Parker. Now, I don't know exactly where Sebring is, having not been there myself, but a month seems like an awfully long time for a package not to have arrived."

"Never been to Sebring? Well, most people haven't, to tell the truth. Unless they're passing through. The 'City on the Circle,' they call the place. Nothing much going on if you ask me."

"Now, I'm sure it's a lovely place to live."

"You're kind to say so but, between you and me, I wouldn't be here if it weren't for my in-laws. They up 'n died a few months back. My poor Bobby is trying to sort out their estate. They left it in a right mess. No surprise there, though. If you'd only known 'em. Anyway, it's too humid for me here. I'm from Oregon, originally. Just down from Portland..."

"No kidding? I spoke with a reader from Salem just this morning. Tell me, what's it like up there?"

"Oh, it's just like home to me. We had a big ol' weatherboard house on top of a little hill. Guttering would leak when it rained, which was practically all the time. And the floorboards needed some work. But it was home. Sometimes, when I'm having trouble sleeping, I just imagine the rain coming down off the roof. Whoosh! ..."

[FLASH...FLASH...FLASH]

"[*Now just wait a moment, Hal. I've got 'em on the phone now.*] Hello? Are you there?"

"Yes ma'am. How can I help."

"[*Don't press that. We've already pressed that and it didn't do nothing good.*] Hello? Yes, well...we've forgotten my password. [*OK, then. I've* forgotten my password.*]"

"I'll be happy to get that straightened out for you ma'am. Where are you calling from today?"

"[*Where are we calling from, he wants to know.*] We're here in Springfield..."

"Near Columbus?"

"[*Near Columbus, he says.*] No, not near Columbus. Near Boston. And thank God, too!"

"Ah, sorry about that. Still learning my U.S. geography."

"Where are you from? You sound British? [*He sounds British.*]"

"Australia, ma'am."

"[*Australia he says, Hal. Wasn't that where the Nortons went last fall, to see Clarence and Mikey?*] Our friends went to Australia last fall, to see their boys. Someplace near Sydney. Or was it Mel-born? [*Was it Mel-born, Hal?*] Mel-born, says Hal."
[FLASH...FLASH...FLASH...]

Occasionally a reader would call in from over the border, from Ottawa or Toronto or, if it was late enough in the day, Vancouver, where the sun was just peaking over the North Shore Mountains and spilling into the harbour (with a "u") below. Mostly, though, they came from across the States.

Morris relished these discussions, many of which turned into regular, sometimes daily, correspondences. He got to know, for example, Mr. March in Chicago and Mr. & Mrs. Patch in New York City. More than once he spoke to Mr. Joad and Mr. Trask in Tulsa and the Salinas Valley, respectively, and even came to friendly terms with the Kowolski's, forever bickering with one another down the line, who phoned in from their little love nest down on the Louisiana bayou. In the short time he worked in the carriage house, Morris never heard anyone call in from Maycomb County, but he could imagine it just the same. He was getting to know the country, one customer service call at a time.

#

Though the proximity of their office buildings meant Morris saw more of Ben, and occasionally Christine, after work, he only encountered Joni once during that period, and then by accident.

They were standing in parallel lines at an unpopular beanery on Calvert Street. Morris, himself given to roaming lunchtime walkabouts, was surprised to see her so far downtown. At first, she didn't recognize him. His thrift store shirt sleeves and ill-fitting slacks must have affected a significant departure from the usual corduroy and cardigan ensemble. Plus, his hair, ordinarily a bird's nest of healthy neglect was, if not quite styled, at least partially tamed. Morris espied her first.

Joni appeared as always; chipper, vibrant, with a floral print neckerchief befitting the season. (She always dressed for the day.) Though alone, she seemed to be smiling to herself, as if she were staring at her pretty reflection in a grand oval mirror housed in a mansion she'd just purchased for cash. Morris, holding the door open for a pair of exiting teens, who were oblivious to his service anyway, caught her on her way out.

"Ah, Morris!" she startled at his greeting, but continued, coffee tray and takeaway bag in hand, out onto the sidewalk. "I'm just... how are you? What are you doing here in... wait, you're all dressed up?"

She was simultaneously churning through the contents of her handbag and juggling a tray of hot coffees.

"Sorry, Joni. Didn't mean to scare you. I was just strolling around during my lunch break."

Morris noticed her searching expression. "I'm working..."

"Yes, yes. Of course," she cut in. "Rachel mentioned. And Ben too, obviously. He told me all about it. That's great, Morris. Really, it is. Something solid for you. Something permanent."

"Well, it's really just..."

"I'm so sorry, Morris, but I'm super late. I'm supposed to be in a meeting already and I haven't even..." she glanced at her watch. "Oh God! I *am* late! Tell Katelyn we have to catch up soon for that glass of wine. I want to hear all about her acting and the play and, well, the whole thing!"

Morris watched her frantic half climb, half tumble into a passing taxi. He thought how oddly she had behaved as he watched her yellow checker cab bound unsteadily on down the street.

#

In the kitchen early one morning, he readying for Calls across America, she standing over the coffeepot in pale chemise and odd socks, Morris and Katelyn exchanged a rare snippet.

"Anyway, enough about practice," she redirected the spotlight. "What about your job, Morris?"

He could not help notice the platonic tone with which she lately imbued his name.

"It's not a job, really," he shrugged. "I just talk to people on the phone all day, everyday people from all over the country."

"And they pay you to do that?" she smiled, recalling his happy-go-lucky attitude from when they first met.

Again, he shrugged. "Well, they do for now."

"OK. So, that's good, right? I mean, don't you like the work?"

"Sure I do. I'm not exactly skilled at it, though. The others get through hundreds of calls a day. I take maybe a dozen."

"Talking too much?"

"Listening, mostly." Morris drifted off into habitual reverie. "People have fascinating stories to tell. I spoke to a man the other day who 'hobos' for fun. That is, he works a normal job, like normal people, but in his spare time he breaks into freight yards and jumps trains, like a hobo. He rides them all over the country. People do weird and wonderful things to escape monotony. Anyway, it could be

106

worse. I could be really good at a job I absolutely loathe. Imagine the feeling of obligation."

"Yeah, imagine."

They talked some more, about this and that, then it was time to get on with the day at hand; he with his, she with hers.

#

One night late in April's closing week, Morris and Ben found their separate ways to the Owl for what had more or less become a routine session. Perched high on their barstools, or slouched low in a booth, the two young men would tackle public dilemmas and bare private grievances with equal vim.

Sometimes the discussion took the form of an alternative history. What might the present political landscape resemble if, say, the last presidential election had been decided by the popular vote, rather than the uniquely American Electoral College system? Would New Order (the band) have formed as a side project, even if Ian Curtis hadn't watched Herzog's *Stroszek* and decided to hang himself that night, thereby ending Joy Division's nascent ride? (The conversation became especially granular when English music and American whisky were involved.) Once or twice, the reconstructed narratives ventured into the personal.

"What if you'd been off shift that day?" Ben imbued his question with the undisguised tone of a friendly challenge. "Say you'd gone off to Manchester on one of your bus trips, or to Cheshire to visit Curtis' grave? You'd never have met Katelyn."

"It's true," Morris conceded at once.

"Well, then what? Would you still have come to America? To Baltimore? You might never have set foot in

107

this place in your whole life." Ben was probing, but something else seemed to be clouding his mind, as if his offense was playing defense.

"That's possible," Morris mused. "Maybe even probable. But what's absolutely certain is that I am not sitting in a thousand other bars right now. I'm not drinking soju at some dinky little shack down a Taipei backstreet, hitting on the owner's embarrassed daughter as she brings me sweet shrimp and cold beer. I'm also not bartering over handcrafted loafers in Ancona, Italy, where they make for pennies the footwear on which you spent a sizeable chunk of your last paycheck. You're right. And I'm not toking hashish with the new hippies on the Annapurna Range or scuba diving the islands off Nha Trang or living a million other random lives. These tracts, and plenty more besides, Ben, are simply…"

But Morris broke off when he saw the blood draining from his friend's face. He thought of summoning the proverbial ghost when Ben, looking right through Morris, blurted, "Joni is seeing someone else."

Immediately, a sense of guilt and complicity flared up in Morris' veins. Her image from the parking lot of the bagel shop struck him still on his stool, but now it had taken on a sick and sinister tone. Her clumsy embrace became an evasive maneuver, her silence in the line a roaring cacophony of lies by omission. He smelled her hair again and sensed the vile stench of deception, the thrill and sweat and bitter sin of other people's beds. He wanted to protest, to summon a defiant "Nonsense!" but he knew it was useless.

"How did you…? But, did she…?" he stammered, his words falling like stones into empty tin buckets.

"She told me," Ben announced, clenching the warble in his voice between his molars. "Actually, she told me because she thought it would be better coming from her than from you."

"From me?" Morris' guilt stirred to a panic, which his expression evidently betrayed.

"Don't worry, Morris. I know you didn't know anything at the time. Joni said she saw you at some cafe or something downtown and that…"

"Max's Deli, down on Calvert," Morris interjected, as if offering up trivial details now could possibly offset the damage done.

"At first she told me she thought you were drunk, but she soon abandoned that narrative. It was 10am, after all, too early even for you, Morris." Ben took a full swig of his own whisky. "Then she tried to say you were acting weird and asked whether had you mentioned anything to me. That's when I caught on; she'd moved herself into check. Maybe by accident. Maybe, subconsciously, on purpose.

"I asked her, 'Why would he mention anything to me?' Two moves later and she was in pieces, blurting out all kinds of things between sobs, treating our kitchen like a goddam confessional. It was pitiful, Morris. It made me wish I'd never found out. For her sake as much as mine. Of course, I suspected something was wrong. I think I aided her deception. She's too good, too virtuous to have gone so long lying without my help."

The two men sat in silence for a long time. Morris wondered what Joni had said to Katelyn, if anything. He wondered, tangentially, why he had never told Katelyn about his birthday. It was an unrelated point, but he felt the guilt re-injecting itself into his bloodstream.

"What are you going to do about it?" he probed, at length.

"Nothing," Ben sighed deeply and took a long drink from his glass. He saw the look on Morris' face. "Look, I'm disappointed. Obviously. But what can I do? I can't leave Joni. She made a mistake. And maybe she'll make another. But I can't just stop loving her. To suddenly unlove her. And to expect flawlessness is just childish. We all have shortcomings."

"Ben, infidelity is no mere peccadillo." With some difficulty, Morris held his tone in check. "She lied to you."

"Yes, but then she told the truth," Ben stiffened. "And she was truly sorry about it. Morris, you should have seen her, sobbing on the tiles like a broken child. What am I supposed to do, abandon her in her moment of need?"

"What about your needs, Ben? What about your need for a trusting, honest relationship? Don't you even deserve that much?"

"And what does she deserve? Someone who walks out on her the moment she stumbles?" He shook his head, as if cementing his own point inside of it. "No. I can't be that person. It's not my way. To err is human, after all."

Morris felt the guilt in his blood begin to boil off, leaving a thicker, virulent anger coursing through him, a primitive, sanguinary concoction. Taking a long breath through his nose, Morris surveyed his friend, small, pitiful, broken, yet defiant. What could he, Morris, a practicing non-believer, say to this man about sin, about moral righteousness? It was Ben's cheek to turn, wasn't it? His pious impulses, the martyr role, the desire to take another's sins upon one's shoulders in the hope of somehow sanctifying them, washing the cloth clean, anew; it was his prerogative, his right to choose, to accept, maybe even invite, this approach to life. Morris always found such self-abnegation incompatible with the moral experience. But what good would it do to say as much to Ben, particularly now, when he was fortifying himself against the hurt and loss the only way he knew how?

"How about your story, then?" Morris returned to the realm of the hypothetical. "What if you had never met Joni, never known her goodness, as you say, her pure heart. What then?"

Ben smiled at Morris. He didn't need to think of a response. It was right there for him, seared into his very soul.

"I'd be forgiving someone else, I expect. And hoping they'd do the same for me when my turn came to fall."

Walking back to Katelyn's couch a few hours later, Morris tried to picture Joni and Ben as he'd first met them, she hanging off his every word, he in puppy dog awe of her thrilling beauty. How true and together, how utterly indissoluble they had seemed. For blocks he searched his memory, but he still couldn't conjure their image.

#

Of the myriad office inanities punctuating his otherwise informative and constructive telephone conversations, the "Weekly Bulletin" was, to Morris' mind, in meaningful competition for the most obnoxious. Thus, the chance was an outside one that, on the morning he was to be fired, he should have been perusing the very same communique's self-aggrandizing column inches. Among notifications of charity balls (always named for their conspicuous benefactor), pending holiday raffles and social "get togethers," Morris discovered that the editors of the various magazines and newsletters to which his callers subscribed were due in town that day for some kind of mucky-muck confab. Skimming the details, his mind was engrossed in formulating mock dialogue with these men and women when an unfamiliar voice wrenched him from composition.

"Morris? Is there a Morris somewhere here?" the voice repeated.

"OK."

"Well, is that you?" angrier this time.

"It is me, yes. And who are you?"

The picture of indignation: "That's not important right now."

"It might be."

Morris wasn't entirely sure this was the manner in which the stroppy, charcoal pinstripe standing over his desk was used to being addressed, but he was sure of his own ambivalence regarding the matter.

"Look, I had a lot of things to do this morning that didn't include coming to tell you that you field one tenth the volume of customer service calls our second worst account manager...manages."

The man-child was visibly irritated. Irritated to the point of repeating himself. He seemed to be both leaning in toward the desk, as if creating a special privacy zone, but also raising his voice, presumably with the opposite intention. Morris waited for him to finish his point, then realized he had done so already.

"Well?" the voice boomed, standing back upright.

"Oh, I didn't realize there was a question outstanding."

"Look, Morris. I don't know what you think we do around here, but we sure as hell don't pay people like you to sit around here and waste everyone else's time..."

"...around here?"

"What?"

"It's not important."

"No, I suppose it wasn't. What is important now, is that you're now going to go and see Rachel in HR after lunch about your position here at the company." He turned to walk out the door.

"Jimmy Something-or-other, right?" Morris said without looking up.

"That's Mr. Benson, thank you."

"No, no. No need for thanks."

#

Morris didn't call by Rachel's office that afternoon but, instead, proceeded directly from a wet and unhurried lunch at the Owl bar to an old brownstone mansion near the carriage house. He remembered the details from that morning's "Bulletin."

Monthly Ed. Meeting: Engineer's Club, Mt. Vernon Square. First Thursday, 1:00pm. Sharp.

The brass intercom hiccuped as the lock inside the wooden door clicked open and Morris, feeling as though no moment of particular importance was upon him, entered the foyer. In the corner, a maître d'hôtel stand half concealed an elegant, middle-aged woman with smooth, ebony skin.

"Good afternoon, dear." Her voice was sweet and kindly and immediately put him at ease. "Can I get your name?"

"Morris, ma'am." He bowed his head slightly. "I'm probably not on the list, but I'm here for the editorial meeting."

"And where're you from, Morris?"

"Well, Australia...but I came by way of London."

She looked at him with an ancient patience.

"The London office, you say? Well, we wouldn't have your name down here. These are interoffice printouts, see. Baltimore buildings only." Her manner was smooth, her voice like a slow-moving molasses. "But never you mind, dear. We'll get you seated."

A group of men buzzed in through the door behind Morris just as he was receiving the last of his directions. "And it'll be a right at the end of the hall," she nodded, adding, for effect, a long and audible, "Sir."

Mouthing silently the exaggerated noun, Morris followed the oak-paneled hallways and gilded moldings through a series of doorways and arches. His steps echoed on the hardwood flooring, an intricate parquetry of maple and oak. The ceilings were double, sometimes triple overhead, giving an enormous sense of room. From lonely corners and atop lofty pedestals, statues of Old World marble glared into deep space with a mythological intensity. Morris didn't notice their concave pupils on his brow, inspecting the irremediable scuff of his seasoned brogues, the disorderly crease of his off-white collar, his thrift store tie in schoolboy green and hasty half-Windsor. Approaching the end of the instructions, Morris slowed his pace, instinctively, almost to a creeping halt. Then he stopped. Silence. It seemed for a moment as if he was the only figure in the entire building not made of stone.

"The meeting is about to start," a male voice accosted the quiet from around the corner. Morris couldn't tell whether the announcement was directed toward him or not, until a few seconds later when the author poked his ruddy, box-shaped head around the corner and repeated it with evident indignation.

"That means now," he added through bushy, raised eyebrows and the resentful grin of an under-tipped usher. Morris made a decision there and then to dislike this person, whoever he was and whatever his station in this life.

Without looking at the man, Morris strode past him, through a set of heavy, cream-colored French doors, and into what he assumed must be the meeting room. Like the other spaces in the building, this one was ornately decorated with thick-framed oil paintings and heavy velvet drapery. A giant chandelier, more like a glass castle, hung from the double overhead ceiling. Its soft yellow light shot through the dust as it billowed in gentle swirls and plumes, kicked up by the rowdy interlopers below. In the center of the room there rested an enormous oval table, around which were seated a dozen or so men, each seemingly following a dress code entirely distinct from one and other. Morris surveyed the scene.

At one end of the table, a middle-aged man with silver hair and a glen plaid sport coat in salmon and grey was gesticulating wildly to two younger men, one in solid purple shirt sleeves, the other in a hoodie, jeans and, bizarrely, a short capped woolen hat. (It must've been 25 degrees out, Morris thought...or whatever that was in Fahrenheit.)

Across from these three, a huddle of jacketed men was contesting a point of evident importance, their voices rising sharply at moments of opposition and falling again when passing over common ground. A thin-faced man in a pale blue guayabera took notes by their side, his pencil darting furiously about under the conversation so as not to allow a single precious word safe passage to the ground. The remainder of the inner oval group, some in spectacles, others wearing beards of varying length and style, either chatted absently or sat in calm, expectant silence.

One man, a heavy-set individual who seemed not to have registered anyone else's arrival, remained absorbed in a paperback sci-fi novel, the kind typically purchased in airport news agencies and gladly left on the plane. He mouthed the words as he read them, occasionally stopping to underline a particularly poignant line or to make a careful annotation in the margin. He might have been on a beach, Morris thought, or the Enoch Pratt library down on Cathedral St., where the studious and eccentric converged to mingle, doze or otherwise seek shelter.

Around those seated at the table, a secondary, concentric oval congregated, numbering maybe twelve or fifteen. This group appeared conspicuously less critical to whatever was about to take place in the center. Morris made his way silently past them and took a position in the only vacant chair, next to the sci-fi enthusiast. At length, the meeting commenced.

"I see a lot of new faces in the room this month," a handsome, goateed man in his mid-forties spoke clearly and with ready confidence from the head of the table. He wore a light grey, faintly pinstriped jacket over a crisp white shirt, open at the collar. "If we've not formerly met, my name is Aubrey Fields and I'll be chairing the meeting."

The silence in the room seemed to wait exclusively on Aubrey, though he showed no urge to hurry it from his shoulders. Looking once around the table, he made some notes on a yellow writing pad. A slow half minute passed before he glanced up again and addressed the group with a wry smile.

"To those of you familiar with the procedure," he interlocked his fingers and leaned back in his chair, his jacket riding up on his arms to reveal twin onyx cufflinks, "I trust you've all brought your Big Ideas."

#

Cranks, quacks, gurus, bona fide geniuses and wide-eyed oddballs. Morris listened, intrigued, as one by one, counterclockwise around the grand oak table, a parade of characters presented their views of the American Dream and how, for a modest subscription fee, you too could achieve it (and fast!).

Some sang to the tune of financial independence. They spun tales of vast, untapped riches buried deep in the heart of the Dark Continent, junior mining operations that were about to strike it big in Botswana or Malawi or some other hellish backwater. Or they touted proprietary trading systems, secrets used only by the "pros" to compound investment returns. Or they nodded to impeccable track records, polished plaques showing market-trouncing results, always with the whispered caveat, "past performance is no guarantee of future success."

Others promised readers eternal youth and beauty, ways to escape the elite's rigged system, a lifestyle afforded only by the rich and famous. Cutting edge biotech companies on the verge of solving the aging "disease," ways to get off the grid, secret coastlines where readers could retire in beachfront luxury for pennies on the dollar.

It was all there: a better, richer, freer life...all for $39 a year or $69 for two years, auto-renew billing optional. American Dreams, on sale for a limited time. (Hurry now! Offer closes midnight tonight!)

This was the retail newsletter business, a crude register of the nation's hopes and dreams and expectations, boiled into a lukewarm broth of sales copy and breathless editorial. And behind it all, a marketing machine that promised spiritual deliverance, one issue at a time.

Morris, sweating a little around the collar, found himself utterly in thrall to the unfolding spectacle. Opposite him, a heavy-set man in faded seersucker gesticulated en-thusiastically through the back half of his presentation.

"This is a real game changer," the man panted. "I mean, if you imagine one of these boxes in every garage, just as, say, you have a computer in every home office today... Why, there's no reason we couldn't do away with the decaying, centralized power grid entirely. And, as the price of this technology continues to come down (laser pointer loops around dotted "projection" line on chart), we can expect to hit a critical mass in most mid- to high density suburban areas sometime in the next 12-18 months."

The man's research assistant, a disheveled crumple of unironed shirtsleeves and curly hair seated at his left, nodded automatically over his own notes.

"What happens to the company's top line revenue when, as you predict, the price comes down?" a voice from the outside oval challenged Senator Seersucker.

"We've calculated profitability all the way down to $150 per unit," he responded. "Currently, as you can see here (laser hovers over current date), they're selling for more than twice that amount. Plenty of insulation there."

"Protective moat around the product?" another voice shot out from the crowd. "What's to stop the Chinese from ripping off the technology and just mass producing them over there for a fraction of the cost?"

"They'd still have to get them back here in order to impact our market directly. This is a domestic story, remember. Focused on our own backyards. Besides, this company is light-years ahead of the competition for that to be a worry right now. By the time the Chinese have a chance to unpack the tech involved with this, we're already onto the next generation."

"So, what's the angle?" Aubrey's voice carried down from the end of the table. All heads turned in his direction. "What's in it for the reader, aside from just another promissory tech story?"

"For the reader? Well, we recommend they buy the company up to this range (laser hovers over y-axis, price). And for our premium members, we can outline a more complex options strategy."

There followed some table discussion concerning the financial particulars of the company that Morris didn't quite follow. Price-to-book ratios and equations mapping various scenarios concerning future earnings. Finally, the group hit on a soft consensus regarding entry and target price for the recommendation. Once settled, the room fell quiet again, patiently awaiting Aubrey's signal. He filled his yellow pad with unhurried notes.

"Alright everyone," he looked up at last pressing his fingertips together. "Sound work, by and large. Chris, Dan, your ideas were excellent, as usual. And James, I think the Chilean bond story has some legs, if you can find a way to sex it up a bit. I'll have individual feedback to you all by week's end. Now, before we break for informal discussion, I want you to take a look at these."

Standing, Aubrey fanned out a stack of magazines.

"A selection of weeklies from the past month," he handed them to the editor in glen plaid at his left. "If you would pass them around please, Charlie. These have been sitting in doctors' waiting rooms, on friend's coffee tables, in lawyer's lobbies and company lunchrooms around America for weeks now. If you can find your idea for this month somewhere in the pile, it's already too old."

Morris saw the man in Seersucker whisper something to his assistant who, in turn, shook his head defensively. Aubrey continued, pacing behind the seated editors.

"The Do-It-Yourself dot com idea? That was a good one...if this was a Time Magazine meeting and it was still snowing outside. They carried it on the cover of their March 27 issue. Same deal with the piece on racing to decode the genome. Interesting story, except that Newsweek led with it in their April 10 run. In this room, we discuss the ideas the mainstream press won't publish, at least not for six months or a year, when our predictions become impossible to ignore."

Aubrey paused to look around the room. He looked at the chandelier, as if noticing something about it for the first time then, nodding to himself, made his way back to the head of the table. There he stood behind his chair, blue grey eyes surveying the room from the olive setting of his face. "OK, I don't think anything else needs be said about timeliness. On the matter of voice and style. Last month's work was better, on the whole."

Morris noted the way Aubrey dealt only in facts, even - and sometimes especially - when it came to the subjective. Something was better, or worse, because that was his opinion on the matter. It wasn't arrogant, just...so.

"What is it our readers desire from us?" he continued, opening the question to the floor. "Why do they pay a premium for our ideas over, say, those published by any of these other magazines? Ideas? Anyone?"

A youngish man with dark curly hair and a fat, moon face interrupted the silence. He was perspiring slightly, but spoke with a measure of self-assuredness. "They read us because they want us to tell them the other side of the story," he began. "We represent the contrarian view, something they can't find elsewhere, in these pubs."

Around the table, the others shifted in their seats, feeling the need to say something, but not quite settling on what it was they ought to say. At last, the man seated next to Morris placed his paperback on the table and leaned in.

"That's true enough, sure," he began tentatively, then quickly gained momentum. "But they don't just want us to be contrarian for contrarian's sake. We don't contend that two plus two is five, just because the mainstream says it's four. Readers want us to tell them the truth, whatever that may be. Sometimes it's contrarian, sometimes not. Our position should depend on the facts. Not who agrees or disagrees with them."

"Right," the curly haired man replied, "Fortunately for us, it just so happens that the mainstream media get the facts wrong a reliable amount of the time."

The group laughed, then, seeing that their chairman was also smiling, laughed harder. Aubrey began packing his yellow notepads and pencils when he said in an off the cuff manner, "And what about you, young man, next to Nester," he looked directly at Morris. All eyes followed.

"Morris," Morris managed. "I, ah... I work in customer service. At least, I used to..."

"Nice to meet you Morris, from customer service." Aubrey continued in much the same tone as before, no kinder, no more hostile. "Well then," he looked up from his papers. "What do you think the reader wants us to tell him?"

The eyeballs around the room seared into his unblinking expression. Morris fought hard to suppress a nervous smile.

"Nothing," he replied, more quickly than he would have planned. "I mean, he doesn't want you to *tell* him anything. He wants you to *show* him. He wants you to show him how he can be the hero of his own story, how he can live the adventures you're all here talking about, even if only vicariously."

Two-dozen incredulous, waxen faces stared at him with an unflinching mixture of confusion and indignation. Morris searched for the correct wording. "I believe your reader wants a conversation, not a lecture. That, he can get anywhere. This relationship is different. It has to be personal."

The flabby faced man snorted from across the table, "You believe that, do you?" his curls jolted spasmodically, ridiculously. "And how, if you don't mind my asking, would you know what my reader wants?"

"Because he told me," Morris replied. "I talk with him every day, after all."

#

Morris was making his way across the lobby of the Belvedere Hotel, toward his barstool at the Owl, when Aubrey espied him. It was nearing five o'clock, the time Morris would ordinarily have left the office. Outside in the tepid afternoon air, up Charles Street and down St. Paul, the traffic had already begun its quotidian creep. Aubrey strolled over to Morris and held out his hand.

"We weren't properly introduced earlier," he said. Always facts, thought Morris. "I'm Aubrey Teller."

His handshake was firm and easy. Up close, Morris noticed for the first time the soft, downward sloping grooves at the corners of Aubrey's eyes. They gathered when he spoke, especially when he smiled, as he did readily. Outside the meeting room, Aubrey appeared visibly relaxed, as if having slipped into his customary disposition.

"A few of the editors meet for cocktails upstairs in about half an hour," he raised an eyebrow. "You're welcome to join us, if you like."

"Thirteenth floor?"

"That's it. Not the worst sunset view in the city."

"Thanks. I'll be there."

#

Through the eyes of a western foreigner, weaned on American sitcoms and second-hand culture, the view south from the corner of One East Chase Street is a view over Any city America. The colossal Doric column in the foreground, pinned on rusted bands of red brick and flat lead roofs, the ascending skyscrapers in crude, jigsaw cutout looming from behind, Old Glory, proud, aware, inevitable, atop the highest peak. And a million stories in black and white unfolding in between. On stoops. In parks. Seated in groups at diners and cafes and taprooms with peanut shells underfoot. Waiting in line at the bank and the drugstore and the bus stop. Smoking and braiding and whistling. Busy living. Busy dying. All held in place by myth and tradition and the feeling of belonging to something unseen, unexplainable, more profound even than the mystery attending the immediate.

Morris heard Aubrey's voice before he saw him. Turning from the window, he saw him standing the bar. He had changed from his early clothes and now wore casual attire, mauve slacks and eggshell shirtsleeves, open at the collar. On his feet, plain brown drivers. He was somehow thinner than Morris recalled. Or taller. Or both.

He acknowledged Morris with a polite nod then, receiving his cocktail from a flirty blonde tending the bar, made his way toward the window where he stood.

"Gibson," he answered the question on Morris' face. "I drank them for years with olives before making the switch. It was not a move I made without careful consideration."

Morris had the distinct impression that Aubrey undertook precious few things in life without careful consideration.

"I didn't know they had a different name for it."

"They have a different name for everything. All marketing, of course." Aubrey rose his glass in salutation.

"Cheers," said Morris.

"Cheers it is."

The light below was beginning to fade from the city, receding into the crepuscular abyss. One window at a time, the buildings came to life, garments of flickering yellow and fluorescent white studs draped over their angular frames.

"You mentioned you work in customer service," Aubrey recalled, without turning from the glazed panorama. "How do you enjoy that?"

"It's fine," replied Morris. "Talking to the readers and all that. But I don't exactly fit the bill. Quota wise, I mean. I might have been fired today, as a matter of fact. I didn't show up at the HR office to find out."

"But you're not concerned."

Aubrey's remark wasn't a question. Morris wondered why.

"No," he realized, aloud. "I guess I'm not."

The pair looked out the window for a long time.

"Ever wonder how many conversations are going on down there right now?" this time it was a question. From the corner of his eye, Morris could see Aubrey lean toward the window, as if to press his nose to the glass, to inhale the view, as he might a good wine.

"It's all I think about when I look out there," Morris replied. "The lives, the narratives, the conversations."

A moment passed before Aubrey turned again to Morris. He spoke clearly, but kindly.

"Morris, there's a position available I'd like you to consider. It's an editorial position, of sorts." He watched the moment reflected in Morris' expression before continuing. "It's something you might enjoy. Something you could do very well at, given the right environment."

Morris barely noticed himself nodding, stupidly. "Yes! Of course! I mean... yes. Just... just tell me where and when."

"Very good." Aubrey smiled again. "I'm pleased you agree. The position begins as soon as you're ready. The earlier the better, of course," he paused to take the last sip of his Gibson. "Oh, and you'll be working directly with me. From my office. In New York City." He held his emptied martini glass aloft. "But we can run over the details later. For now, let's have another drink. A quiet celebration, before the rest arrive."

As Aubrey made for the bar, Morris turned south to meet the view down Charles Street, toward the Inner Harbor and beyond. The city was faintly backlit now, a soft fugue retreating endlessly over the horizon.

PART II

Chapter VI

Penn to Penn (Again)

Morris awoke on the floor. His face pressed hard against the parquetry, acquiring an epidermal imprint of its intricate geometry, a temporary copy of work done long ago. The space was cool and a soft morning light filtered in from somewhere above. He looked out across the squares and triangles and lozenges in coffee and tawny browns, focusing... blinking... focusing. The reflective surface appeared as a petrified expanse of dust and specks and fuzzy, indifferent particles. Exhaling through his mouth, he watched the Martian landscape violently disturbed, his fierce tornado roaring across the plane. Destroyer of worlds, he thought to himself, closing his eyes again and feeling the light filter through his lids.

In a single empty room, on a lowly fifth floor, in the middle of New York City, lay Morris, alive.

As it did daily for the opening stanza of his waking consciousness, Morris' mind returned to the girl he met in London. He saw again with a wave of unease her sweet green eyes filling with tears. They swelled to beyond full, wet like oceans in the rain, when he delivered the news, when he gave voice to what they recognized as inevitable.

"And so just like that," she sobbed gently, "you're gone from my life?"

Katelyn's words were clear and resonant in his ears, a recollection of painfully crisp fidelity. Morris rolled onto his back and let the feeling sink deep into his chest. He tried to define it, to give it shape and form and reason. But it wouldn't be moved or dictated to. So it sat, a great obsidian mass, square and resolute on his sternum.

Morris reached to his side, between objects strewn from an opened duffel, and drew the only remaining cigarette from the packet. Even the smoke reminded him of her, he recalled her form as he felt the familiar scent filling his lungs. Though hurtful, it was impossible not to replay their last days together. He had to resurrect them, to lash himself with her warm, silken tears, to revive her pitifulness, her rawness, her honesty. The final scene he reran each morning, frame by frame, a penance for her sorrow. He saw her there, in guiltless lilac dress, leaning against the kitchen bench, staring confusedly somewhere beyond the windowpane, out into the unanswering evening.

"I thought we'd go away," she had spoken in unordered, half soliloquizing bursts. "That after the season ended... That we could... Oh, I don't know." With an agitated brush she dismissed a tear from her cheek. "What were we even doing, Morris? It was stupid to think anything was ever going to come of this, I realize that well enough now... But at the time, and I see that's passed now too, it just seemed so... "

Her waves, blonder now in the ripening dog days, were tied back in a rose ribbon. It seemed to Morris a needless constraint. A sudden urge came over him to cut the flimsy binding, to free her, to tell her something true and calming and real. Then he imagined the fabric tearing and her hair cascading onto the kitchen tiles, the scissors clasped tight in his own frenzied grip. He felt his blood begin to thin and his heart, struggling to maintain pressure, suddenly quicken. Then she was speaking again.

"Morris, I knew we were impossible," her composure fought back under a pale, analytical expression, "but I guess

I thought that was part of our narrative, that there was some kind of romance and poetry in our defying the impossible, in doing it together. But now...now that it's falling apart, we're just another moment in this universe that no longer exists. A tremendous nothing where love might have been. A cipher. Another hopeless scream into the abyss."

He thought of their letters and postcards, a trans-Atlantic scaffold of paper promises. He watched their commingled smoke rise against the Cambridge sky, felt her tears on his lips in the spring rain, and saw the fire's flickering light throwing late night shadows across the walls of her great front room.

"Katelyn..." he began, but there were no words to soothe. All his excuses fell flat before they made it to his lips, harsh mockeries of their own emptiness. A wasteland of specks and dust and useless particles.

"I'm sorry, Katelyn," he managed at length. "I hope one day you look at our time together as something more than nothing." He watched her eyes as they filled again with tears. "For me, every minute was real."

Her hands trembled as she stole a cigarette from the counter and placed it slowly, automatically between her lips. Morris watched as she hesitated for a second over some unspoken point, let it dangle for a delicate eternity, then shook her head and, with familiar movement, lit the match in one strike. Heavily she exhaled out the kitchen window, her unspoken words billowing into the night sky.

Laying there now, on the wooden floor, a few hundred miles and a million lives away, Morris wanted desperately to ask her what it was that had given her pause, to hear her answer in rounded consonants and rich, deliberate diphthongs, to wade through her playful, unguarded voice, her luxuriant tones and ready laughter, to ponder her thoughts once more as they crystallized elegantly into form and shape and meaning. Again he closed his eyes and cleared his mind. The silence was painful because, trapped in the moment, it was permanent.

Gingerly, Morris climbed to his feet and shuffled across the maple boards. Foam filter pinched between his teeth, he used both hands to guide the windowpane up along its warped grooves. The room's stale air rushed out from behind him with jubilant exhalation and the city flowed in to replace it in hot, summer waves. It was early, but already the traffic was building. A parking lot across the street bulged helplessly against its chain link fence, cars and minivans packed in tightly against one and other. Morris saw a scrawny man by the boom gesticulating indignantly to the driver's side of a white Cadillac wagon with tinted windows. Horns sounded off behind the bottleneck and down the line into a stream of welded metal congestion. Morris followed the scramble down the cobble-stoned street, across the East River bikeway and into the murky waters beyond, where the black- eyed angels swam.

#

Though the immediate past was still too raw to the touch, the train ride north between Penn Stations afforded Morris time to consider what had come to pass since he first arrived in these states during the frosted winter months. The new landscape rushed by his window in verdant greens, each shade adding depth and vitality to the unfolding panorama before him. Over bridges and through valleys the train sped, carrying with it a mishmash of regional accents and expectations and hopes for the future. The car, Morris looked around, was mostly filled with business types. Not the kind that made the Acela run from the nation's thirsty capital to her money spigots on Wall Street, but the mid-level salesmen type, associate badges with years of commuting ahead of them before the miles accrued and the bosses' shoes were satisfactorily shined. Morris caught snatches of conversation between passengers both present and on trains of their own.

A male voice from the row behind him said, *"We're on track for fifteen percent... And the guys last year thought ten was killing it! Even if we drop a few points next quarter, we're still gold... Hey, did I tell you? Kristy and I are buying another apartment? Yeah, going in with her brother. He's got three already, but he's older, in his mid-forties. Real douche..."*

Spoke another, older male, into a cell phone he evidently mistook for a megaphone, *"It's not like the nineties anymore, Dan... Times were, academics got paid zillions for hoodwinking investors with their fuzzy math and magic models. But this technology is real, my friend, not bogus balance sheet shuffling... Believe me, it's going to change the game, big time. I'm all in, Dan, and frankly, anyone who isn't is only going to wish they were..."*

And from a bubbly female, somewhere across the aisle, *"It's something we've wanted to do for a while anyway, and now that Jason's firm is investing for him in this employee partnership program, we decided it's time for me to quit the whole rat race thing and really concentrate on building a family. Jason wants to start right away, as soon as we're back from Europe. I'm like, um...let's do it already!"*

On the seat next to Morris lay a discarded copy of the day's Grey Lady. He thumbed through the various sections, skimming the headlines and leaders as he went.

Stock markets were lately rebounding on what the press boldly termed "cautious optimism"...

A centennial music retrospective that began with Enrico Caruso's "disembodied voice" ended with Nirvana's "roaring ambivalence"...

And Gerald J. Whitrow, a "mathematician and philosopher who devoted much of his life to pondering the nature of time," died in London. He was 87...

According to the printed narrative, the new American century had begun well enough. A time for good, honest work, for entrepreneurialism and innovation, but also for inward reflection. To begin with, there was to be no more nation building. On this even the presidential candidates were agreed. Let the Arabs fight their own damned wars. They'd been at it long enough and could continue without America's sons and daughters getting blood and sand in their jackboots. The press mostly concurred. America had work to do closer to shore, business to conduct, its own national interests to tend to and nurture. First and foremost, she needed to be strong at home. If the Asians or the Russians were going to suffer another currency crisis, it would be their problem, contained meltdowns in far-off cities impacting distant populations. Not something that sent the American indexes into a tailspin. Such financial imbroglios belonged to the past. The future pointed to big picture ideas and the technology that would drive them, conceived in American think tanks and overseen by American boardrooms. We'll think, went the cry, let them sweat. Europeans stand united in diversity. America stands alone.

Hurtling anonymously along the northeastern corridor, Morris marveled at the great machine at work around him, working, churning, driving. Trains collapsing the distance between cities, building contiguous office space in forty-eight states, hulking Mac convoys carrying goods across the vast Interstate grid, thousands of planes overhead, transporting passengers and services and expertise from here to there, contrails crosshatching against the thinning atmosphere above.

Lost in thought, Morris almost didn't notice the woman who sat down opposite him. Only when she responded to the conductor, who approached in jolly tones to punch her ticket, did he fully register her appearance. She had dark, even skin and greying hair, cropped short. Straight-backed in a canary yellow blazer and teal stole, she sat with hands in her lap, a picture of immaculate patience. In profile, with an elongated neck and sharp jawline, she held a staid, dignified presence. Front on, the severity yielded to a softer edge. Her broad nose bore subtle freckles, the kind that always lends a childlike innocence to otherwise serious expressions. Examining her in the window's reflection, Morris guessed her age to be somewhere in the late fifties. Only when she spoke, did he realized she had left those years behind a long time ago.

"Punched ma ticket every Frid'y af'ernoon f'r near on twenty years that boy." She nodded in the ticketmaster's direction. "Still asks to see 'em jus' the same, bless 'im. Reckon 'e mus' be special."

Morris recalled anew the paunchy man's whistle, fading now down the aisle and into the next carriage. The tune was simple, short and repeated with unquestioning joviality. Morris smiled.

"Didn't recognize me either," he shrugged. "But then, this is only my second time riding the train. First in this direction."

"I coulda guessed at that, way you're lookin' out the window all serious like, contemplatin' time or bein' or some other such profundity," her voice had a soft warble to it, as if played over a victrola. Morris remembered the "Musical Century" article from the *Times*. Armstrong, Holiday,

Ellington. He wondered if she'd seen any of them in the flesh, known them, even.

"Just thinking, I guess." The phrase struck him suddenly as absurd.

"Not enough a that nowadays, not near half," she remarked, without bitterness. "How far you goin'?"

"Began in Penn Station." He reconstructed the grand building in his mind. "And that's where I'm headed."

"We all goin' back to the start," she half smiled with a shrewd self-awareness. "Some folks get there quickly. Others," she nodded fondly to the conductor who was passing back through their carriage, "they take a little longer."

Morris delighted. "And here I thought you said I was the one contemplating profundities."

"Ah, you got me there, young man. Philosophizin', 'n caught red handed at it," her laugh was inviting, open.

"Morris." He held out his hand.

"Eleanor," she replied. Her skin, smoothed by time, felt like suede in his grasp. "Now tell me, young man, what does Morris plan to do when he finally arrives, after all this time, back at the beginning, in ol' New York City."

Morris thought for a moment before answering. "I'm almost certain he doesn't know, ma'am."

"That sounds like a pleasant way to travel."

"In blissful ignorance, you mean?"

She shook her head in kind reproach. "Oh, you know enough to know that ain't so. I mean, in good *faith*."

"Right. Well, I guess I know it'll be something new, something I can't foresee."

"True enough. You got anyone in the city? It's a big place, I reckon you woulda heard that much."

"One fellow. He offered me work on a kind of newspaper. More like a news*letter*, really." Whether because of her auntie-like disposition, her restful, unjudging gaze, or simply her near-complete anonymity, Morris felt as though he could say just about anything to this woman, this *Eleanor*.

"I've only met him a few of times, actually. First at a meeting, back in Baltimore a couple of weeks ago. Then when he offered me the job, shortly afterward, that afternoon, in fact." Morris sensed her welcoming silence. He continued, "It was a surprise, I'll confess. Of course, I asked him why he chose me, of all the people at the meeting. Certainly I was - well...I *am* - the least qualified for the position. I'd only been at the company for a short time, maybe a month. I had absolutely no experience. And I didn't even work in the editorial department. He said they were three good reasons to choose me. Some, they would require too much 'untraining,' as he put it. Others, they all have lives, pets, home loans, various personal commitments..." he trailed off.

"And you?" Her questions were calm, unobtrusive.

Morris shook his head, letting the conspicuous gap in his narrative drop like a stone into an empty well.

"Well, that's all very exciting," she moved on, politely. "The beginning of a new and thrilling chapter in your life, Morris."

The train rocked through a longish tunnel, perforating their conversation. Morris looked at the window, at once opaque, the passenger's watercolor reflections whet against the rich, immovable blackness. The car fell into a boneyard silence as if, abandoned by the light, the characters became suddenly inanimate, confined to their own private thoughts. Of a sudden, from a tiny distant pinpoint, then in a desperate rush, the summer afternoon rushed in and engulfed the carriage once again.

"Do you know the Seaport area well?" Morris felt he could have asked about any part of the city to more than satisfactory response.

Eleanor shrugged nonchalantly. "South Street Seaport? Where the Brooklyn Bridge stomps firm on Manhattan rock, where Fulton crawls down to the East River and Water turns into Pearl?" she was clearly enjoying this and made no attempt to hide the fact. "You mean the Seaport with the little Browne Printers museum, with the Paris Cafe, in yellow and white, right across from the old fish market? Sure, I've heard of it. That where you're gonna be stayin', eh?"

Morris nodded.

"Mmm, hmm. It's changin' down there. Gettin' real trendy." She made the whistling sound that older people make when referring to areas in their home cities under the pall of gentrification.

"I'm going to share a place with two others," Morris continued. "Aubrey, the one who offered me the job, he'll be there, on and off. Apparently, he lives upstate most of the time. Anyway, he'll take one of the rooms, the biggest, I guess. And there's another guy, who I haven't met. Some friend of Aubrey's."

Morris was not quite sure why or how these details were relevant, but it felt good to hear them for the first time, coming from his own lips. Eleanor seemed to enjoy the conversational texture just the same, so he continued.

"Supposedly there's a kind of terrace with views of the river and the bridge. And it's not far from the office. I'll probably just walk home in the afternoons. You know, take my time, even call into that Paris Cafe of yours and order a cocktail, like a real regular. Maybe they'll get to know me and I'll just say, 'the usual, thanks, Freddy' and he'll know exactly what I mean."

Hearing himself now, Morris began to realize what a tremendous opportunity lay before him. This was not merely a serendipitous turn, a lucky longshot paid off. This was a moment in time that might forever shape who he would become, a front row seat to watch America make for itself a new a bursting century, to witness the opening act of the greatest show on earth. And yet, it was not something he had foreseen or earned in any meaningful sense of the word. A stab of guilt punctured his side and Katelyn's image began to form in his mind, but an announcement promptly arrested him from the scene.

"Next stop, Penn Station!"

The summoned passengers surged forward in a jostle of limb and luggage, pulling heavy cases down from the racks overhead into the crowding aisles. Morris and Eleanor made no rush.

"Can I get your bags for you?"

"Oh, that won't be necessary, Morris. But thank you jus' the same." Eleanor gave Morris a look that suggested she took a great deal of pride in making this trip all on her own.

He nodded and held out his hand once more. "Well, it was a real pleasure meeting you, Eleanor. Thanks for the company."

"Welcome back to the Big Apple, Morris, where all great tales commence."

"At the beginning?"

She squinted, her eyes a soft, milky white. "Yes Morris," a wry smile drew across her face. "At the beginning."

Once on the platform, Morris realized he knew nothing about his kindly interlocutor. Suddenly he had the urge to ask Eleanor about her story, her life in twentieth century America. Not just the big stuff, Ali and the Viet Cong, MLK's "dream" speech and moving to the front of the bus, rather the little things, too. The details. Where had she grown up? What were her parents' names? How had she come to know about the little cafe down by the Seaport? And did she really know The Duke, had she heard his orchestral magic ring through the smokey Harlem Cotton Club, perhaps even met the man himself?

Riding up the escalator, duffel slung over his shoulder, Morris looked back across the liquid hum of commuters funneling into the chute below, hoping to catch her canary blazer, but she was already gone.

#

The Seaport apartment, spacious enough in its own design, was even larger without the furniture. The plush, crimson couch, soft linen bulging with goose down and dappled in cream and russet throws; the round hickory table, sturdy against the bay window; the chess set and the slender blue vase atop the writing desk off to the corner, illuminated late at night by a green banker's lamp, hosting neat piles of modern correspondence; bills, postcards, specialty subscription magazines. All that and more would accumulate over the coming weeks and months. For the moment, it had to be imagined.

There was one piece of furniture, or rather, installation-cum-decoration. Propped against the lounge room's wall, the one dividing a capacious common area from the galley-style kitchen, stood an enormous framed canvas, taller than Morris' own six feet and wider than his wingspan by half again. Captured in thick, liberal brushstrokes, was a corporeal soup of elongated limbs and torso, a Picassoesque abstraction of fleshy pinks and blossoming orange against a twilight blue background. The figure, contorted and reimagined through the prism of a clearly deranged mind, appeared as part human, part serpent. Following the

138

movement of the piece from the upper left corner, where one of the creature's hooved hind legs kicked and bucked at the border, down through the chaotic, disfigured body of the canvas and back to the upper right quadrant, which housed the beast's ghastly, pockmarked head, Morris felt as though he were being pulled into a moulin, a portal swirling into a dark and terrifying Underworld. Indeed, the creature appeared to have some kind of coin or token in its mouth, ensnarled among wicked, yellowish fangs. Morris stood in bedclothes and bare feet, transfixed and wondering, in order, who would paint, purchase and display such a disturbing image. At that moment, down the length of the hallway, the sound of jangling keys cut the silence. Footsteps quickly followed.

"Charon's obol," a loud, grey haired man announced in emphatic tones as he bowled headlong into the open space in khakis and rolled-up shirtsleeves. He carried a brown paper grocery bag in one arm and sweated slightly at the brow. Looking straight past Morris with fervent, blue-grey eyes, he turned his attention to the serpent man. "The coin, here in our friend's handsome mouth," he pointed at the gnashing oral wreckage. "It's a bribe for the ferryman. *Viaticum.* A little something to convey this wretched soul over the rivers Styx and Acheron, from the world of the living to the realm of the dead." He stopped, as if momentarily suspended between the two himself, then continued. "Worth very little in monetary terms, really. The Greeks sometimes used gold and silver coins, the Romans mostly bronze or copper. Of course, those who couldn't afford to pay were condemned to roam the murky shores for a hundred years, or risked losing their memories trying to swim the distance. Either that, or Charon would simply beat them to a pulp with his great oar. Grizzly business, Hades. But then, what are you gonna do? Gotta pay the ferryman."

The unofficial guide considered the painting and shook his head, stroking grey stubble with his free hand. Then, without stopping to look at Morris, he strode off around the corner and into the kitchen. Morris heard bottles clinking and the fridge door slam. Within a minute, the man was back, this time carrying a pair of glasses brimming with thick red liquid.

"Saturday morning tradition," he handed one of the concoctions to Morris. "Bloody Marys with extra measures of celery salt and Worcestershire. Any decent shelf vodka will do, by the way. No sense wasting the good stuff when you're mixing it up like this. Save that for the martinis and the like. But we'll get to that in due course. Well," he raised his glass to Morris' and, not lingering a single unnecessary second, downed half his drink in one thirsty gulp. "I hope you like 'em spicy."

Morris surveyed his expression. He appeared more than just satisfied, like a man standing at the edge of a desert with a freshwater canister in hand.

Morris took a healthy swig of his own and offered an honestly approving nod. "I'm Morris."

"I know," the man confirmed with a reserved smile. "I'm the guy who covers the other half of Aubrey's rent here. But you can just call me Virgil."

"You mean," Morris looked at the painting before them, "Virgil as in...?"

But he had already started off down the hall.

"C'mon, Morris," he called over his shoulder. "The movers will be here any second and I'm double-parked downstairs with a trunk full of furniture, some of it for you. Aubrey will be over later this afternoon to sign the last of the papers and take us to a decent dinner."

"Right, I'll just..." Morris' voice strained through the tabasco's blaze. "I'll... be right with you."

But Virgil was already out the door.

#

The "little terrace" turned out to be the entire seventh floor rooftop and, though the building itself could have disappeared unnoticed in the vast canyons of the Financial District immediately to the south, or in the looming shadows of the Midtown giants, it was so situated, vis-à-vis the river, that it enjoyed uninterrupted views of the Brooklyn Bridge and the timeless currents swirling beneath it. Theoretically shared by all the building's denizens, only a couple of fashionable Latin men from the third floor and a spritely old lady from the fourth, who never went anywhere without her perfectly groomed chihuahua and a homemade frown of perennial disapproval, made use of the space at all. For the rest of the time, especially the cocktail hours stitching together late afternoon and early evening, it belonged to the unlikely trio residing in apartment 5A. And, of course, their immediate guests.

"Well, I'm off downstairs for another one," declared Virgil as he lifted a dangerously near-empty tumbler aloft as evidence for the cause. He considered Morris' own vessel with a frown. "Better fix you one too," he said as he sauntered off. "Oh, and Aubrey should be along shortly. In the meantime, why don't you just try to relax and enjoy the view up here for a bit."

Virgil always delivered deadpan and, as a consequence, Morris could never quite be sure if his remarks were cautiously sincere or mildly reproachful. Standing on the roof of his brand-new address that first Saturday afternoon, the fading sun at his back and the city lights beginning to flicker before him, the youthful newcomer was sure he didn't care one way or the other. If he were cast out onto the street there and then it would have been worth the ride. Instead, he stood still in his place as a soft breeze blew in across the river, carrying with it the smell of rust and wet leather and slow, distant traffic. Downtown had emptied out, the pulse and fervor of the city having decamped the office grounds for either the theaters and glitzy nightlife further uptown, or the cooling shores of Fitzgerald's Long Island haunts along the sound. Reluctantly at first, Morris allowed his gaze to turn northward, to become lost in the jumbled heap of murky buildings between the Seaport and Central Park. He remembered his last visit to the city, that dizzying whorl of poetry and drunken romance. Suddenly it seemed strange to be on the rooftop alone, exiled among the masses.

"O Solitude! if I must with thee dwell." Keats's words and Katelyn's lily pond eyes combined to arrest his breath from the descending twilight. The collusion quieted him, stalled his mind in a moment unexpectedly recaptured. Then, as from another realm, the sound of elevator doors opening delivered him back to the present.

By Aubrey's side, a slender woman flowed in a billowing white A-line skirt and sheer, flesh-colored blouse, an enamel red clutch the only spill of color providing solidity to her ephemeral form. Her shiny, metallic black hair reflected the dying light from a half dozen paces away. At the small of her back hovered Aubrey's hand, guiding her across the space as one might guide a butterfly toward an open window, marveling at its form but happily aware that it will, someday, naturally flitter away. The pair approached in step, but only Aubrey met Morris' eyes. The woman's attention followed the skyline over his shoulder, across the brown bridge, on to Brooklyn Heights and beyond. She maintained a look of silent approval.

"Morris!" Aubrey appeared unreservedly glad to see him. "This here is Celine," he smiled, allowing her beauty to do what beauty invariably does to a young man. She turned to him and permitted herself a thin smile. "And I imagine you've already met Richard?"

"Er...Richard?" Morris' vacant expression inspired in Aubrey a chuckle of realization.

"Ah, I see. Well then... He didn't ask you to call him Gautama, did he? Or Socrates? Or, humbly enough, The Nazarene?"

Morris nodded under a flush of embarrassment. "He told me to call him... Virgil."

Aubrey laughed again, this time more heartily even than before. Morris had not yet seen this sense of joviality in him. Celine, in contrast, appeared unmoved, which both relieved and bothered Morris in roughly equal measure.

"Well, his mother won't mind if you call him Richard," Aubrey offered. "Though he'll probably object to the common diminutive. Fair warning."

"Didn't you see him on the way up?" inquired Morris, the blush finally fading from his cheeks. "He's making drinks down in the apartment."

"Sidecars, I suspect," Aubrey nodded at Celine. "The 'Saturday evening tradition,' you'll no doubt remember?"

She chortled behind a white handkerchief which she had seemingly procured for just this occasion, as if she expected Aubrey to coax a gleeful display from her at any moment and needed always to be on guard. Seeing that a vocal reply would be welcomed, she added, in an unassimilated Parisian accent, "Yes, I suspect so."

"You can sub in triple sec for Cointreau if you absolutely must," Richard called from across the terrace. He had in one hand a fistful of cocktail glasses, bunched at the stems, and in the other an orange canvas tote, which clinked with bottles and various metal instruments as he strode confidently nearer. Setting his objects on the table adjacent without salutation or, even, interruption to his own sentence, he continued, "...and in a pinch, brandy will stand in for your preferred cognac. But absolutely," finally he looked each of the gathered bystanders in the eye, "*absolutely*, a sidecar must be made with fresh lemon juice." Here he held the perfectly formed fruit up for examination.

Across the terrace a quiet breeze blew. The vista sank itself into its beholders.

A silent minute passed before Richard, with some finesse, lined the glasses along the terrace rail. Giving the shaker one last blast, he filled each to within a perfect eighth-inch from the lip. A teetering foam meniscus rose to fill the void. Morris was about to reach for one of the magnificent creations when he noticed a conspicuous restraint from the others. Aubrey shot him a patient grin that seemed to say, "don't worry, you'll get used to him." A second later, the earnest barkeep returned from the prep table with a small plate and a set of ice tongs. Into each glass cone he sent splashing a spiral of xanthous lemon zest. Only then did the hands festively grab.

"To an old tradition," he motioned familiarly to Aubrey and Celine before rounding to Morris, "in new and, Zeus willing, propitious settings."

#

A brisk, quarter-hour stroll south of the apartment there was located, on the thirty third floor of a much taller building overlooking Wall and Broad Streets, the office in which Aubrey, Richard and, lately, Morris spent the bulk of their weekdays. The older friends, as Morris came to learn, were partnered in various entrepreneurial capacities, merging expertise and research to manage funds for wealthy, unseen clients scattered across the country. In addition to their common projects, each consulted for their own unending rolodex of brokers, traders and money men around town, arrangements that often necessitated long and unhurried lunches with clients, contacts and "old friends." The environment was frenetic and, in their own ways, the two men worked the energy to their advantage.

Richard, in particular, flourished when the conversation called for fast-talking financial jargon, a verbal soup of acronyms and abbreviations designed to render the field utterly impenetrable to the non-professional. Aubrey, meanwhile, seemed content to remain silent during these rapid-fire interchanges, except when some detail or strategy needed his astute correction or refinement.

Beyond the purely financial arena, there was the newsletter publishing business, the editorial department of which Aubrey oversaw. To this area Richard occasionally lent opinion while Morris began, in earnest, to learn all he could from scratch. Often the subject matter had an overtly financial aspect to it, research highlighting a particular trend in the markets, for example, or a certain stock or option. Other times, the content was of a purely socio-economic nature, or aimed at geopolitical interest. The all-terrain subject matter provided ample stimulation for Morris, who drank it in with growing vigor and an appreciation for all he had yet to discover. The atmosphere was congenial and warm to new ideas and theories, provided they were well researched, non-intuitive and, as a pass-fail proposition, had not already appeared in one of the dozens of weeklies scattered around the office to which Aubrey subscribed and read, leader to final word.

Despite its imposing address, and the impressive view from the southwesterly corner aspect, the space itself was rather modest, at least compared to the lavishly decorated suites inhabited by some of the town's glitzier firms and

145

personalities. The furniture, dull and practical, was selected purely for function. A jumble of desks crowded the center of the room, around which the men sat in black swivel chairs on a moat of blue-grey carpet, cut and unfurled, Morris guessed, sometime in the late eighties. In the corner of the room farthest from the glass door entrance, a stack of a half dozen unpacked boxes, crammed with documents and manila folders, leaned ominously over a worn, tobacco-brown Chesterfield. With space enough for three, the room felt suddenly crowded when the occasional visitor dropped by to deliver a message or see Aubrey or Richard about some detail regarding the tenancy. Nobody ever called on Morris, a fact he was not in the slightest displeased about.

A rogue shop of sorts, there was little in the way of personal items on display. Except, that is, for one humble keepsake. On the rectangular side table next to the couch was a single, silver framed photograph showing Aubrey as a boy of eleven or twelve, vacationing somewhere tropical. His hair was a childish blonde and his squinting expression somewhat awkward but, leaning casually against the rear of the wood paneled, family wagon, his repose was unmistakably Aubrey. In cheerful company with the young boy were, to his left, older sister and mother, both in knee length, floral print dresses and with matching bouffants, sculpted to frame wide and pleasant faces and, to his right, with an affectionate hand on his son's shoulder, the father Aubrey would come uncannily to resemble. A curlicue engraving in the bottom corner of the frame memorialized the happy occasion as "Summer, '65." To Morris, the sepia print captured more than merely a moment in his new friend's past. It spoke of a Wonder Years America, a period of sweetness when the brash, teenage empire had yet to realize the full weight of its capability on the global stage, an era of

146

cultural upheaval that produced Marvel superheroes and moon landings and mighty sluggers. And men like Aubrey.

Most weeks, Aubrey spent four days in the office. The remaining Monday or Friday he worked from his home in Westchester County, where he enjoyed long weekends from which he always returned to the city relaxed and revitalized. Morris tried to imagine Aubrey's house in detail, the setting, the yard, the photos in silver frames on the walls, but he could never quite get past the vision of a Rockwellian Thanksgiving.

Though his approach to mentorship was one of determinedly unfettered laissez-faire, Aubrey led by exacting personal example. At times, his commitment to his own, often peculiar regimen bordered on the compulsive. Where the rest of "The Street" arrived at work anytime between five and seven thirty in the morning, Aubrey appeared at eight. Exactly. Every day. Sometimes he would even wait outside the elevator in the building lobby, imbibing the first in a slew of morning *dopios* or taking notes on a legal pad in a sweeping scrawl legible only to its author, before making his precisely-timed ascent. He worked public holidays, sometimes forgetting about them entirely, but always took off for his own birthday. To seemingly inane editorial detail he paid terrific focus, often reworking a single paragraph of prose a dozen or more times before he was satisfied. And yet, watching a stock soar or plummet to the tune of millions of dollars, he would merely shrug, acknowledging the spontaneous order of the marketplace as something to be humbly observed as much as actively, arrogantly managed. And though his investing track record was among the best of his peers, he refused to take the kind of workload that might necessitate any compromise of his finely tuned daily schedule.

Regarding Morris' own position, expectations were made clear from the beginning.

"There are no rules here," Aubrey had explained on Day One, "except to prosper and flourish in your own estimation."

"But what if my own estimation is different than everyone else's?" inquired Morris

"In that case," replied Aubrey, "you'll know you're really onto something."

#

Chapter VII

Away by the Sea

Over the summer months, the Seaport apartment played setting for an endless calendar of multicourse dinner parties, chance get-togethers, hotly-anticipated reunions, lavish cocktail hours and spontaneous gatherings of characters both likely and, to Morris' mind, utterly unpredictable. Looking back on it much later, he often wondered whether half of Manhattan, and her terrific roster of visitors, hadn't somehow filtered through the revolving door in the building's marbled lobby. Sometimes the cast would be drawn from the professional world, financiers in town on business who owed Aubrey or Richard a favor, fund managers seeking advice or, not uncommonly, capital placement. Or they were editors of various special interest magazines to whom Aubrey occasionally gave audience or interview. Other times the crowd would be purely social, old childhood friends or classmates who came for a quick aperitif and ended up sleeping on the couch or watching the sunrise from the rooftop terrace. Very occasionally, an ex-girlfriend would swing through, invariably with an amenable accomplice at her wing. Some came to reignite ancient passions, others to flaunt, in strategic bursts of flirtation and guile, what once was and would never be again.

Most of the socialite crowd, and all of the snuffed flame contingent, owed their debt of invitation to Richard. In fact, Aubrey seldom made lengthy appearances at events numbering more than a dozen or so guests, except to offer his apology for having some prior engagement up or across town. When the predictable, inevitable protests came from the goading stayers, he would simply nod in Celine's direction as if to say, "You appreciate my bind, no doubt; if I am to stay here with you, I should have to pass on a date with her." This gesture the men took with desirous acknowledgement. The women, ill-disposed to admit that a single representative of their species, however dazzling her plumage, could outrank their combined efforts, would shimmy over to Celine with make-peace invitations and flutes of kir royal and little plates of brightly colored hors d'oeuvres.

They also plied Aubrey.

"Oh, but you can't leave yet," the skein would revolt in a sudden flight of complement and conspicuous hospitality. "We haven't had your darling lady a moment to ourselves."

Then they would descend on the unwitting object of their attention, each more inclined to furnish praise than the last, as if by doing so they were somehow demonstrating a confidence in their own poise and grace, a self-assuredness that had no need to cower in the presence of beauty but, rather, shimmered all the more for its proximate luminescence.

Ever the obliging pair, Aubrey and Celine would sometimes settle in for another glass of champagne or a slice of prosciutto and ripe melon then, when the conversation ebbed back toward the center of the room, typically occupied by Richard and whoever was co-narrating the nostalgic recollection with him, they would slip quietly out the door. Upon later realizing the fast maneuver, the remaining women would playfully bemoan what they were privately relieved to discover. Celine was gone. Gaze and attention were again freed to turn in their direction and a layer of familiarity would settle like a blanket on the group.

One such evening, while a dozen present were snacking on deviled eggs, champagne punch and prepared witticism, Aubrey and Celine began their familiar circling pattern, drifting from one pair to the next in a circuitous though determined route for the egress. In French cuffs and midnight silk chiffon, the pair was subtly overdressed for the occasion. A touch of finery – a pocketed bow tie or corsage, her red lipstick applied in the back of the town car – would easily bridge the gap between semi-formal cocktail party and box seat-appropriate. Morris watched as they glided effortlessly through the motions; a little bow here, a faint touch of the elbow there, a smile that implied, "Yes of course, but we really couldn't. Next time, certainly." Then, with the hallway at their backs, framing their intentions, the attire revealed for the calculated understatement it had intended to convey, Aubrey bid the group a collective adieu and escorted his elusive Venus off into the New York City night.

The party fell in on the pair's departure like teenagers waiting for the sound of their parent's car to round the corner at the bottom of the street. Richard, too, became somehow softer, easier going. Sensing the mood afoot, he promptly substituted Chet Baker's non-vocal efforts for an eclectic Mediterranean mix he infrequently played but always enjoyed explaining.

"The musicality of a place like Italy is much underappreciated here in the U.S." Morris caught the familiar snippet served up to a couple of youngish ladies he hadn't seen before, both in fashionably cut dresses. They appeared to swoon at their gentleman host's every word. Richard pressed his home advantage. "People think the Italians are all *Turandot* and buxom sopranos wailing from the balcony. Not at all. What they understand about music and love, and love of music, is more culturally embedded. Certainly you won't find it on any billboard top 100 single here." Then, as if the thought had just occurred to him, "Say, have you spent much time on the Riviera? I know a fabulous little place…"

Perching himself nearer the bay window, Morris watched from across the room as Richard delighted his company. The two women before him, all bouncing tresses and spaghetti straps, couldn't have been thirty years old apiece while he, Richard, was swimming in the deep end of the following decade. And yet, from beneath his greying hair and sun weathered skin, he conveyed a confidence that at one disarmed and intrigued. His audience let free another peal of girlish laughter as one of the pair, slightly the prettier, held out her hand for Richard to kiss, which he did only after taking a knee. Though he was beyond earshot, Morris knew exactly the lines Richard had just delivered.

"I don't know how you live with that thing," a pale brunette woman in a charcoal chemise had sidled up to Morris. "I would have nightmares."

"Oh, Richard? He's alright," quipped Morris, pretending not to notice that she was referring to the serpent-man painting, looming large and grotesque on the wall opposite where they stood.

"Well, I guess the forked tongue is not something you have to worry about," she shot back to their mutual laughter. "Or the bucking hooves."

They made their introductions. Forgetting her name immediately, Morris tried to recall whether he'd seen her smoking on the terrace earlier that evening. He sought to fill in some outlines.

"Am I to take it you two used to be an item, then?" The champagne had loosened whatever level of decorum he might have considered affecting.

"Not quite so formal as that," she demurred. "But yes, I've known Rich for a long, long time. Aubrey too, though not as well."

She had the air of someone for whom soirees of this kind were invented and an expression that told him she knew as much. Morris wondered how many such evenings had passed in a *long, long time*.

"We all went to college together, UCLA, class of..." she trailed off, suddenly examining Morris with a skeptical eye. "Well, never mind when. All that seems like another lifetime anyway. So many moons ago."

She took a slow sip of champagne and directly changed the subject. "What about you? Richard tells me you're working with Aubrey."

"That's a bit generous. Learning from him, more like it. And Richard too, I guess."

She let out a chuckle. "Goodness! What those two boys don't know about this town," his eyes widened at the prospect, "Well, it probably isn't worth your knowing, let me just say that."

Morris tried to imagine what the woman wouldn't say. A silence grew between them as her attention became focused beyond a fixed point in the crowd. It seemed as though a follow-up question was in order, but when he turned to her again, she was already making her way across the room in Richard's direction. Seeing her come into his vision, a slow grin formed at the edges of his mouth. Instinctively, the younger women found reason to be elsewhere.

The festivities continued until the morning hours with a small group rounding out the soiree on the rooftop. Though Morris had no reliable memory of how exactly it ended, he was quite certain he was the only representative from the apartment present for the closing.

#

Restaurant... Cafe... Laundromat... Bar... Diner... Gym... Pizza... Cold Beer...

Once a city grows beyond a certain size, it quickly becomes superfluous to give its essential building blocks a name beyond the immediate goods and services in which they deal. Anything more is regarded as either a pretentious distraction or belonging to that strata of swankier, non-essential enterprises whose logos and storefronts can afford to deal in adverbs and alliterative flourishes and "established in year 19..." vanities.

It was behind one of the former signs, a humble "Diner" in neon blue, that Morris and Richard sought to allay the effects of their latest evening's festivities.

"So you got to meet Abby last night," Richard managed between mouthfuls of strong black coffee and spoonsful of medicinal corned beef and hash. His eyes were a Tabasco red. The young man opposite him showed no signs of recognition.

"Pretty brunette, grey dress. Shapely..." He used both hands to indicate where and how.

"Ah yes, Abby. Right." Morris was still coming to.

Another bite and then, with a tentativeness rarely displayed on Richard's face, "She eh... she mention anything about me?"

Morris drained his coffee and, motioning to the young waitress by the window, recalled the devilish line. "Only that you have a forked tongue and bucking hooves."

For an uneasy second Morris thought he might have to administer the Heimlich maneuver, but the older man's convulsions soon gave way to a hearty laughter.

"She's one to talk!" he sat upright at last. "What that woman doesn't know about..."

"Ain't worth knowing?" Morris interrupted, hoping to ward off any carnal imagery that might attach itself to the dangling, unspoken intimation.

"Touché." The lines on Richard's forehead relaxed as he recalled all that was worth knowing about Abby. He and Morris retreated for a moment to the comforts of greasy fried potatoes and unrushed silence.

Just then the waitress returned with the necessary elixirs and the specially requested bottle of Worcestershire sauce. Morris watched her as she placed them on the table automatically, one by one, her mind clearly elsewhere. She was pretty, if a little bedraggled, and probably not feeling altogether unlike the very customers before her. Even so, she moved with purpose, poise. An aspiring dancer, perhaps? Morris imagined what her own kitchen might look like, a row of single white plates drying on the rack, checkered linoleum underfoot, threadbare orange tablecloth spread beneath an empty vase. And beside the toaster over, an unopened recipe book, a gift from mother. *("You take care of yourself while you're in the City, sweetie. Too many girls die skinny trying to make it big.")* She scooped up Morris' absent gaze in her deep brown eyes. Caught still, he quickly looked away.

"Well, it's not exactly the homemade recipe," Richard announced, raising his plastic diner tumbler, "but a Saturday tradition is a Saturday tradition."

The two men drank healthily. Morris followed the waitress as she shot something in Spanish to the line cooks and disappeared out a door marked "Fire Exit."

"What about you, then?" Richard examined him carefully. Morris knew exactly where this was heading.

"What about me?" he took a bite, playing for time.

"Well, I assume you didn't go to Baltimore because it leads the nation in murders per capita and crack cocaine addiction."

"Don't forget syphilis," added Morris, matter-of-factly.

"Wasn't that what did old Edgar Allen in?"

"They don't know," Morris assured his friend with all the certainty of someone who had "lived" there. "Apparently the medical records were all lost. There's plenty of conjecture, though. Newspapers reported 'cerebral inflammation' and 'congestion of the brain,' both acceptable euphemisms for other, disreputable causes."

"Like death by dissipation," Richard raised his tumbler once more.

"Could've been the *tremens*. Folks reckoned everything from rabies to epilepsy. Even cooping, bizarrely enough."

"As in, he was killed by a mob of voting fraudsters?"

"Well, I wasn't there."

"Right, but you were in Baltimore, which is what we're talking about here," Richard smiled his toothy, post-Bloody Mary smile. "Don't think I don't know diversion when I hear it, young Morris. I'll bet you followed your heart to Baltimore. Charmed all the way down to Charm City."

Morris raised his hands, assuming the universal "you got me" pose.

"Question is," Richard continued his mock inquisition, "what kind of woman does it take to lure our good friend Morris here all the way from the sunny shores of Australia to the rust and squalor of syphilitic Baltimore."

"Actually, I came by way of London," Morris began his familiar defense, in vain.

"Irrelevant, Your Honor!" Richard lowered his plastic gavel against the table, ruffling slightly a nervy couple in the adjacent booth. "The prosecution wishes to know about the caliber of woman required to capture the witness' heart. Whether he hails from Canary Wharf or Fisherman's Wharf is hardly the matter at hand."

"You do realize the witness is also the defendant," retorted one and the same.

"A circumstance not without precedent," Richard proceeded.

"Then I guess I'll just have to plead the fifth," ventured Morris, unsteadily weighing his options.

"Ah, but who said anything about self-incrimination?"

"We're talking about matters of the heart, aren't we? What else is there *but* self-incrimination?"

"Ladies and gentlemen of the jury," Richard motioned again to the waitress, who had just returned to the floor, "you heard the defendant here in his own words. A textbook case of premature cynicism. Now, before reaching your verdict, I want you to ask yourself, is this the kind of specimen you want roaming the streets of New York City, a menace to our dear and pure female citizens? And armed with a foreign accent too. No doubt just the kind for which our fair women swoon? What good can come of it, I beg you?"

With a faint smell of tobacco about her, the waitress leaned in over the table to collect their empty plates, her sheer white blouse stretching against her form. Morris leaned back in his chair, averting his eyes.

"Your honor," Richard addressed the young woman in an exaggerated, lawyerly tone. "Against this man before you the state seeks the maximum allowable penalty."

"And what is the poor boy looking at here?" she winced coyly in Morris' direction. He could see she was enjoying the attention.

"Another round of these God-awful concoctions for a start," the prosecutor gulped down the last of his own.

"What, to be shared in conversation with you?" She was fast. "What on earth did he do to deserve such a hefty penalty?"

"Now, now," Richard grinned back. "That information I cannot divulge. But if you wish to show mercy on his wretched, abandoned soul, you might find yourself inclined to write your telephone number on the back of the check."

She blushed ever so slightly, despite herself.

"If you do," concluded Richard, "Morris here might actually pick one up. A check, that is."

#

Notwithstanding Richard's occasional ribbing, money, as a subject, was rarely discussed in the apartment, except for in purely abstract terms. Even so, it was to his private relief that Morris discovered the living arrangement was not quite how "Virgil" had first communicated it to him. Rather, it was the publishing company that floated Morris' obol, if somewhat indirectly. As Aubrey explained it on the terrace one afternoon, shortly after unmasking the Ferryman for the Richard he really was, it was to the company's advantage to maintain a visible presence in the City. If they were going to cover the financial markets, among other topics, with any credibility, they'd better do it from where the action was taking place.

"Perception counts," Aubrey affirmed in the characteristic, matter-of-fact tone he employed when discussing all things work-related. "People don't want to read about what's happening on Wall Street from some guy living and working on Main Street. There's no magic in that. No story."

"He already knows the Main Street mentality..." guessed Morris.

"Because it's his own," Aubrey finished the thought. "But all this," he gestured over his shoulder toward the silhouetted giants downtown, "all this is something very different, almost beyond imagination. When tourists come to the City, they go to Midtown. They see the Lion King and walk around Central Park and take a photo in Times Square. Then they stand on the eighty-sixth floor of the Empire State Building and look vaguely south, wondering what mysterious activity goes on in the fast-talking world of high finance."

Morris thought of the icy winter's afternoon when he and Katelyn had visited the observation deck, how he had wondered at the unknown lives and stories developing between West 33rd and the jumble of towers crowding the island's tip. A great biomass lurching forward atop a tectonic plate of birthday candles and business socks and Metrocards and Chinese takeout boxes and disappointing bank statements. All drifting...somewhere.

"Thing is," Aubrey, too, had become suddenly pensive, "most people who come to work in these buildings don't know what's going on either. Ask the guy in that office, way up there, second from the top." He pointed to a fluorescent postage stamp on a mountain of glass and steel. "Now, he'll be there until midnight tonight. Maybe later. And if he doesn't sleep there, he'll be back first thing in the morning, freshly shaven and ready to throw another sixteen or eighteen hours at his work... And you know what? That work never, ever goes away. In fact, the better he is at the job the more it grows. As Sisyphus learns to master his rock, the hills grow commensurately higher."

"I imagine he gets paid fairly handsomely, though." Morris squinted to make out more clearly the tiny figure hunched at his desk. "You know, as far as boulder rollers go."

"Corner office? Second top floor? That *particular* building?" Aubrey ballparked a figure.

"That's..." Morris tried to compute the amount, to give it some day-to-day context, to quantify it in terms of bar tabs or steak dinners or plane tickets. "That's..."

"Before bonus," Aubrey filled the amazed silence. "Which, in a good year, could be just as much again. Or more."

"OK, OK." Morris did some calculations of his own. "So you do that for a year or two, stuff the coffers, then you pack up and begin living the life you want. You never have to worry about money again."

"Those guys don't have to worry about money," Aubrey laughed, but not in a mean-spirited or dismissive way. He, too, was looking in on a world not his own. "At least, not from a pure survival standpoint. Folks making a tenth what they do could never spend it all. But it's not that, for them. They need money like blue whales need buckets of water. A gallon might hold a dozen goldfish, but it can hardly sustain their voracious need."

He paused, resting a hand on the concrete ledge. Then he turned to Morris. "I remember hearing a story when I was a boy, growing up on the west coast. A man in New York City made a million-dollar bonus in a single year. Next day, he jumped right out of his office window."

"What?" Morris was suddenly aware of the height of the buildings looming around them. "Nothing more to achieve in this world?"

"No. He just couldn't bear to face his colleagues, who had all made two million."

Morris looked up at the tiny fluorescent light and considered once more the hunched man's enormous sum. He

160

multiplied it by the number of postage stamps that could be glued to the side of a mountain, one mountain in a range, one range in a world where barely a single natural surface is absolutely, perfectly flat. Not even the liquid ones, under which sometimes great creatures dwell.

"Of course, it's just a unit of account," Aubrey said at last, addressing the source of Morris' reverie. "A simple way for us to keep track of who owns what. Nobody cares about actual money itself, except for that bizarre clutch we call numismatists, who spend all day in library corners fussing over pieces of defunct fiat paper and crude metal discs. The vast majority of folk only care, and reasonably enough, about what can be done with it, what end it serves. A fancier mansion. Food for the kids. Something to win a wife...or keep one. Like all inanimate objects, money requires the human mind to imagine it into life, to imbue it with value based on its usefulness to us. Money itself is just a tool. It's human behavior that really counts.

Morris found himself nodding along. The idea of money as the root of all evil had always struck him as a strange shirking of mankind's duties. After all, if the root of all money is human, whence cometh evil?

"Richard asked me how much I'd need, you know, to just quit everything and do whatever I wanted with my life."

"Oh?" Aubrey was genuinely interested.

"He called it..."

"Yes, I've heard the term," he cut in with a cocked eyebrow. "Vintage Richard. What did you tell him?

"I told him I've already quit everything to do whatever I want. And I did it with virtually no money at all."

"And what is it you want to do?"

Morris surveyed the skyline, a glittering worldly reflection of the star strewn expanse above. To exist here was almost too much for his imagination, such that it often seemed both real and unreal at once. At last, he shrugged. "Right now, I want to do just what I am doing."

He let a moment pass before rephrasing the question for Aubrey. "So, you wouldn't want to do what that guy does? Work eighteen-hour days to make more money than God? That wouldn't satisfy you on some level?"

"We all have our Egos," Aubrey mused. "Mine feeds elsewhere."

Morris considered this carefully. Deriving a sense of self-worth from money, which really derived its value from us, was axiomatically absurd, an ouroboros-like proposition that fed on itself until there was nothing left to measure. Aubrey was right, it was human behavior that mattered. Money was merely the pool in which our intentions and actions, both base and pure, were reflected. Self-worth needed to come from somewhere else. From within.

Aubrey looked at the time and, seeing they had a few minutes before guests were expected to arrive, redirected the conversation.

"Now what about your lady, in Baltimore?"

"Ah, so Richard told you." Morris felt more embarrassed for not having mentioned anything to Aubrey than he was upset at Richard.

"Actually, no. You did."

"I did?" Morris tried to recall the relevant conversation, until Aubrey gave him a look that said, "you told me, *just now*."

"You'll find no shortage of distraction here in New York, if you want to take your mind off things, that is. It's true what they say, this place never sleeps. I sometimes feel like time goes by faster in the City, maybe because so many people are living it all at once..." Aubrey broke off, his attention arrested by some broken fragment of his own history.

162

Around them the great glass canyons settled into the night. And within their walls of steel and rock, the millions of discrete lives that went into making up the whole.

Morris recalled Donne's famous poem. *"If a clod be washed away by the sea..."* Then, without consciously summoning the thought, he wondered what promontory Katelyn had been to him? What part of his continent? His main? And, not as an afterthought, what had he been to her? There would be plenty of time to consider all the pieces, he reasoned, after the waves had washed over them all.

When they reentered 5A, Beiderbecke had already yielded the floor to a livelier Mingus and a handful of guests were in cheerful orbit around one of Richard's tales. He saluted from the middle of the crowd, motioning for them to retrieve a cup of punch from the sideboard.

"I thought we'd go to *Les Halles* tonight," Aubrey announced from the periphery. "We can walk over from here, if that plan suits everyone. I've reserved a table for eight, on the chance that it does."

A nodding quorum affirmed the motion.

#

The party, counting four men and three ladies, actually numbered seven, but just as he never extended invitations in even numbers, not even to couples, Aubrey never booked tables for odd numbers. Another quirk.

"We keep a standing reservation for the unexpected," he once explained to a guest who, as it so happened, had arrived barely announced and only moments before the gazpacho.

In addition to the names on the Seaport door were seated, [from Aubrey's right], the immaculately attired Celine in a slate grey dress with a simple, bateau neckline; Richard's artist friend, Colm, in green pencil stripe shirt with flecks of

163

dried paint at the cuffs, [Richard, in nothing unusual], Abby and her guest Sarah in slight variations of the same "LBD," the former actually a dark blue [and, at Aubrey's left, Morris]. The table was in the rear of the restaurant, slightly raised on a corner platform, so that guests facing outward, in this case Aubrey, Celine and Morris, were awarded a view across the floor and on toward the bar. A constellation of candles lit the dinners' scattered faces, while softly dimmed lights overhead allowed the darkness to fill the space into which conversation spilled. The room was without an empty table.

From somewhere within that murmuring colloquium, painted thick with baritone and splashes of girlish laughter, a thin male server in black bistro apron and dark, slicked back hair emerged with a look of slight impatience and a stack of leather menus. He handed them first to the ladies, then the gentlemen, instinctively pairing the wine list with Aubrey's.

"Champagne to start?" Richard looked around the table and found it free of objection. "Six to a bottle..." he scratched his grey stubble with the metal bracket at the corner of his menu then, turning to the unmoving server added, "Better make it two. Perrier-Jouët. The rosé, if you have it."

Colm shuffled his bulky frame conspicuously. "Nutin' a wee but stiffa far we out a townas then, eh?" he ventured. Under his patchy, Irish-red beard, he was already growing ruddy about the cheeks.

Richard feigned offense at the mere suggestion he might under-serve his guests. He turned back to the waiter, who was patiently doing just that. "As I was *about* to say, anything else these fine people might care to order, *a la carte*. But since my dear friend from across the pond here insists on moving the issue up the agenda, I'll take the liberty of ordering for him, *un perroquet*." Then, as the server was

164

finally about to turn, Richard added "Wait. Better make that... *deux*."

"Oui monsieur," replied the thin man, his left eyebrow having forced its way a quarter inch up the furrowed terrain of his impressive forehead. He motioned with upturned nose around the table before adding, somewhat under his breath, "Comme tu veux, grand homme."

"Certains perroquets sont plus lourds que d'autres," Aubrey smiled at the waiter, who promptly blushed into Celine's unguarded laughter. The others merely smiled the way all people do when a punchline lingers beyond the frontier of translation.

"Very well," the waiter switched to a heavily accented English. "I will re-turn presently wis your *apéritifs* and se daily especiales. Everysing on se menu is available to-night."

"Mer-ci *bow-coop*," blurted Colm, ridiculously.

When it came time to order food, Morris followed Aubrey and Celine through the *foie gras* and *salade frisée aux lardons,* but left them, respectively, at their *confit de canard* (served with the traditional *pommes de terre sarladaises*) and *coq au vin* (which, in the end, went largely untouched), to savor his own favorite, *steak tartare*. The others, swept away by either conversation or inebriation, or both, blithely waved through the *salade de laitue et de noix* followed by, per the waiter's supercilious advice *l'entrecôte* ("*Saignant!*").

As typically happens in groups of such a size, the quadrants quickly partitioned in such a way as each individual was privy only to direct conversation with the party immediately on either side of him. Except, of course, when the table was silenced for a sort of collected storytelling, the kind that the Richards and Irishmen of the world very much like to narrate.

165

"Tell them about the time you decided to quit drinking," Richard rallied an audience for his friend, who shook his bristles in a manly show of deep, retrospective disgust.

"Naw, never agen with dat," he began in lyrical tones. "Gawd's honest trewt. Longest afternoon a me life, 'twas!"

The sympathetic gallery, itself half-pickled, chuckled in unison. Richard, now a similar hue to Colm, picked up the thread.

"I asked him a week or so later how it was all going. I said, 'How is it you come home from a hard day's work and don't feel like a cold beer?' Know what he says to me?" here Richard affected an Irish accent worse even than his French one. "'Oh,' he says, the picture of surprise, "I still 'ave a few cawld beers in the afta-noon. Sometimes wit' lunch too. I've awnly quit *drinking*, don' cha know.'"

More laughter before Richard rounded it out. "Apparently in Ireland the verb '*to drink*' only pertains to whisky and paint thinner!"

Another round of merriment followed. Only Celine, who excused herself presently for a cigarette, maintained composure, though even she smiled when Richard raised his glass and toasted his friend, "To abstinence, the Irish way."

Conversation flowed easily with the wine. Sarah, who had been rather timid earlier but who now had the wind firmly in her sails, piped up. "I don't know how y'all do it. Doesn't it take a mighty toll on your body?" She had a charming southern drawl that was beginning to tire at the edges.

"Ya know," Colm leaned unsteadily over the table, his chin tucked into his neck, "I daw't usually go aquotin' Englishmen, but I make an exception far Mr. George Orwell, who once said tat 'at fifty, ev-ury man has tha face he de-surves.'"

"You realize Orwell died at forty-six," Morris heard the words before he realized they had passed his lips.

"Ah, ma point exactly!" exclaimed Colm, and everyone laughed, though nobody quite knew why.

#

Somewhere along the wobbly, post dinner stroll back to the apartment it was decided that the group would take a nightcap on the terrace. It was a fine night for it, and Colm had brought a special bottle of Irish whisky for Richard, who insisted on sharing it with "whoever needs some hairs on, or against, their chest." Aubrey alone declined the invitation. He had an early flight he couldn't reschedule leaving from JFK the following morning.

"You go on ahead," he leaned over the elevator's threshold and kissed Celine on the forehead. "Henry Downe's famous #9 whisky is not to be missed. I insist."

Morris rode in silence while he pretended to listen to one of Abby's stories, something about a party Richard had thrown back in their college days that necessitated "more police than I think I'd ever seen on campus. And the K-9 unit, for obvious reasons."

Celine wasn't paying attention either. Morris watched her from the corner of his eye. The skin of her cheeks, ordinarily a soft, almost translucent gypsum, had borrowed a tinge of rose from the champagne. The effect, rendered in high definition under the elevator light, was to somehow marbleize her ethereality, to capture and solidify her person, to cast her in the moment. He wondered whether she was aware of this sudden metamorphosis or if, as is so often the case when one thing becomes another, the transformation was only visible from the outside. He glanced furtively in the mirror to ensure no such alteration had taken place on his own face. To his unexpected disappointment, he saw that it had not.

"The apothecary prescribes one fluid dram before bedtime," Richard was in high spirits as the elevator spilled its human contents out onto the terrace. "Two or more if symptoms persist."

The sky was pregnant with rain, or perhaps hail. It seemed to hang perilously low over the city, as if any one of the myriad needlepoints might puncture its sump, unleashing a flash deluge onto the abandoned streets below. Lighting his cigarette, Morris imagined the plump summer drops hitting the warm concrete underfoot, the splashing torrents sending the crowd running. He would stay and finish his cigarette, he determined, come rain, come hail.

"May I?" He hadn't noticed Celine by his side. Was she closer, he tried to recall, than she had ever been to him? He struck a match and held it to within a few inches of her lips. She stared at him directly as she drew the flame alight then, turning her gaze heavenward, released the purple-blue plume into the ether.

"Aubrey hates it," she confessed, holding her cigarette at the top of a slender arm bent at the elbow.

"I thought I'd seen him smoke with you sometimes... After lunch, or dinner?"

"He's a perfect gentleman." Somehow it sounded like an accusation. "He would never say anything, of course. But I know him."

Unsure of what exactly to say, Morris took another drag of his own. Her eyes, he noticed for the first time, were the same slate grey as her dress. He was thinking of Athena when a shriek of laughter from across the terrace stole them from the moment.

"Morris! Morris, come on over here," Sarah's drawl had unraveled with the whisky so that a rasp now ran through her voice whenever it rose above a certain register. "Here," she enjoined him, "Have your dram. The apocath... apocath..." She abandoned her attempt to another peal of laughter. The others, save for Celine, who Morris sensed by his side, joined in. Caught in her own hysterics, Sarah didn't notice much beyond the lip of her cup.

"Look. Hey!" Colm interjected. "We're loike the Unoited Nations 'ere," his eyes were wide and vacant, like windows on an abandoned school bus. "I'm from Oi-reland, the Emerald Oisle fa you Yankees. And young Morris 'ere, 'e's from Australia. Ah was it New Zealand." He broke off into a private chortle before rejoining his own thread. "And Christine, she's from... We're are you from, darlin', Canada or France? I mean, I know you ware speaking French at dinner 'n' all, but I 'aven't tahk'd ta you much yet."

"*Celine* is from France," Richard tossed a glowing, fluorescent lifeline in an attempt to rescue his man.

"Paris," corrected the lady in grey.

Richard looked at her with a mixture of embarrassment and apology on behalf of his wayward friend. Seemingly satisfied with his propitiation, the only person who could properly relieve the tension did so.

"But my accent is not so purely Parisian now, since I'm living in the U.S. almost two years."

"Ah, that's it. *Celine*." Colm helped himself to another generous dram. "Helps with tha memory, uf I ramember correctly."

"I'd love to visit *Pa-ree*," Sarah was almost as drunk as Colm, but less able to pretend she wasn't. "Say, why do they call it 'gay' Paree?"

"You'll have to excuse we Americans at the table," Abby put her arm around her unsteady friend, whose heels appeared taller every time she shifted her weight. "Apparently we don't get out much."

Sarah moved to say something, but thought better of it and took her dram instead, leaving the floor to the boisterous Colm.

"I fuget the statustic," he began, "but sometin' like ninety-eight percent of Americans don't even 'ave passports. I was well shocked when I 'eard that," he shook his head in earnest reproach, "but ya know, it just goes to show..."

"Goes to show what, exactly?" Morris felt himself strangely emboldened. "I've heard that statistic too. We all have. But I think there's a lot more to the story than what that one figure seems to suggest."

"What?" Colm tucked his chin into his neck again. "Is it that it suggests Americans are unward looking? That the average American - and I'm not talking aboot anyone 'ere, *ob*-viously - but the *average* American is ugnorant. I'm talking about *average*, mind you. And it's worse when you think that 'alf the population is even stupider than that!" he broke into laughter again, before adding, somewhat disingenuously, "I'm teasin' a-course. Jus' *teasin'*."

Morris felt his nerves tighten. "I don't mean to be a stickler," he began, "but that's not quite how averages work."

"You don't have to stand up for us, Morris," Sarah laughed, her bowlegs almost deserting her in the process. "We're not your fault."

"It's not that," he adopted a less personal tone in an effort to remove any heat from the table. "It's just, this... this running down America. I hear it all the time, usually from people who haven't spent much time here. It's so... beyond fashionable. So... *passé*. Everyone wants to hate on the Top Dog. I get that. And I don't know why it grates on me, but it just does. Look," he found his thoughts crystallizing, "the *average* American gets two weeks vacation per year. This is an enormous country, the size of Europe and then some. You could drop some European countries into Texas a dozen times and still raise enough cattle on the remaining land to feed a nation. It's a lot to explore a couple of weeks at a time. And it's diverse, too. Culturally. Racially. Linguistically. Socially...

"Moreover," he was gathering an unseen momentum, "unlike on the continent, you don't need a passport to travel ten minutes in any given direction. You don't even need a passport to go to Canada. Or Mexico! That's the whole of North America, a continent in itself, from Spanish-speaking Baja California to the French-speaking province of Quebec; an area far greater than the *average* world citizen will properly cover in ten lifetimes. And yet, Americans get a bad rap for being poorly traveled. Aside from the obvious problems with creating a monolith out of three hundred million people, the basic assumption itself is just not correct. It's...lazy." Looking at his silent audience, Morris took his dram from Colm's still hand and drained it in one. "Lazy and...trite."

An expectant silence followed, the kind that is unsure whether the orator is done with his drunken sermon or just beginning. Morris began to feel his own cheeks flush. Unexpectedly, it was Celine who broke the stillness.

"Well you know," she took a long, almost permanent drag on her cigarette, "what they speak in Quebec [theatrical exhalation], that's not *really* French."

The collective laughter relieved the mood and again the revelers dissolved into smaller conversations. A soft mist began to appear in the air, a prelude to something more torrential. Colm and Sarah ambled to the nearby railing, the preceding conversation a distant memory to be foggily recalled another time. Pointing at some vague object uptown, the swaying shadow placed his free arm casually across

Sarah's shoulders. She did not flinch, but instead leaned in toward his much larger frame.

"Well, well! Wasn't that a spirited defense of our poor and parochial peoples!" Richard topped off Morris' glass. "Now have your medicine, young man. Oh, and try not pick fights with drunken Irishmen." He winked merrily and turned to escort Abbey to a couple of lounge chairs at the far end of the terrace. Morris was suddenly aware of the pairings.

"You really like this country, yes?" Celine trained a pair of deep grey eyes on him. He saw in them the skyline reflected, a display of tremendous power and beauty at once.

"It's been very gracious to me," he hesitated, before adding, "Yes, I like it here very much."

"Like," she raised a pencil thin eyebrow, challenging him beyond the subject at hand. "Or love?"

"I'm not really sure yet. We'll have to wait and see."

#

Chapter VIII

A Pretty Illusion

"If I am out of my mind," Morris reread Bellow's masterly opener with a naked, sinking awe, "it's all right with me." There it was. Uneditable. Unimprovable. And, from the moment it was committed to press, unavailable. Along with "Call me Ishmael" and "It was the best of times," Herzog's deranged soliloquy surely ranked among the greatest inceptions of all time. And so it would stand, vaunted and unparalleled in Morris' mind. Until, of course, the budding bibliophile read another classic and was thus compelled to add a new line to the scrawled, pocket-ridden list he carried with him in and out of the city's rambling, weekend hours.

Morris wondered how much stock the truly gifted artists, the savants, the Nabokovian synesthetes, put into those initial words. ("...light of my life, fire of my loins," he recalled the delicious fruit of that other towering literary trunk.) Were they cast and recast, then smashed into a million pieces, only to be reworked time and again? Were they agonized over, mentally penned in showers and at bus stops and during intercourse and, perhaps the purest infidelity of all, while composing other, peacefully oblivious prose? Or did they flow easily, forming the naturally unexamined sequent to the series of thoughts immediately preceding them, the only line the writer *could* conceive, the best (and worst) of one possible world? He considered the cadence, the tone, the movement, the elegance and euphony demanded of that single sentence, that unrepeatable first impression. A novel may well end with an arrow shot boldly into the vast philosophical beyond, Morris thought to himself, but it had to begin with a particle of poetry. It had to carry with it the precise embryonic structure from which life itself could proceed.

The procrastinating, would-be author smiled. This useless cerebral abstraction was exactly the kind of thing he liked to reckon through on a rainy Saturday afternoon in The Strand bookstore, the one just off Union Square, near the old Regal Stadium movie theatre. There he sat, cross-legged at the end of no particular row and with a half-dozen books at either knee, the clouds outside spilling their unending greyness onto the world. Some of the books were opened, dogeared, their ancient pages thumbed like brail on bronze; others still held their secret delights, their own introductions and parting thoughts and all the wondrous, imagined realities in between.

If well-written, and granted by the universe no small measure of luck and favorable circumstance, a book had the potential to long outlive its author. Even if underappreciated during its creator's waking hours, the spark of chance was ignited so that it might someday be recognized as a work of importance. Morris read sideways the names around him, eighteen miles of alphabetically ordered spines, each yearning for a glimpse beyond the shelf, into the stampeding global consciousness presently mapping history onto the streets and avenues outside. He imagined the island, pelted by wind and rain, from its huddled tip to the point at which Broadway switched tracks, on through the verdant midst to where its slender northern finger pointed up the Hudson. Therein-lay generations of collected knowledge and experience, bound in dusty sleeves and grooved in shellac and polyvinyl chloride. Millions of stories sung in chorus, sometimes in harmony, mostly not. And the Strand's iconic red awning, with its own colossal catalogue, just one stop along the way. This is how Morris learned the city, piece by piece.

When not gazing out across the swarm of concrete obelisks converging on mighty Wall and Broad or connecting the hazy, nighttime dewdrops suspended across the Brooklyn Bridge, Morris would often drift aimlessly further uptown. More often than not, he began these little adventures with no set destination in mind, content to saunter from cafe to diner, bookstore to music shop, along wide, spinal avenues and down sharp lateral side streets. An anonymous flaneur with no direction, he roamed among the busy multitudes, people with places to go and to be, faces to meet and placate and demean and praise, and Morris, with no call to answer, no clock to check, and nobody to notice if he turned to water and washed with the leaves into the foul and fathomless rivers.

Sometimes, during these escapist jaunts, his mind would fixate on the city's myriad and often peculiar details, a corner plaque commemorating the (since demolished) First Presidential Mansion on Pearl and Cherry, say, or the one bolted to the Radiowave building at 27th and Broadway, where once lived Nikola Tesla, "The great Yugoslav-American scientist-inventor, whose discoveries [...] contributed to the advancement of the United States and the rest of the world," or the white marble stone in Samuel Paley Park, near the MoMA, which humbly urged that the space be set aside in the man's memory (1875-1963) "for the enjoyment of the public."

New York City swells with such markers, from solemn decrees cast in bronze to quiet etchings on lonely barroom tables; tomorrow's ancients scratching Sator squares into time's shifting dunes.

Emerging from the Strand's paper trenches into the clearing afternoon weather, Morris pondered the sheer volume of recorded language swirling around him, more than could ever be humanly ingested. And yet, here they were; customers, readers, hungry brains stubbornly scouring the discount shelves for plot and character, love and mystery, eroticism and poetry and inside tips from chisel-jawed, flat-abbed self-help gurus. They were well-dressed, these insatiable word seekers, and shabbily attired too. And everything in between. The man closest to Morris, a tall, mustachioed fellow with a bright red scarf and black T over jeans, thumbed a weighty astrophysics text. The copy looked a decade old, or more. Ample time for a single scientific breakthrough, a lone Copernicus, to turn the universe inside out. To his left, within range of the flapping scarlet neckwear, a Latin woman with a hooked nose and pirate-like earrings puzzled over a paperback fiction, then added it to a bundle of similar titles already firmly underarm. And by her side, a hunched Asian lady in her late grey seasons shouldered a tote so full of books Morris worried whether she would really have time to read them all. He marveled as she hauled her load over to the checkout and slowly, deliberately, began piling them on top of the counter with the happy nonchalance of a beaver building a damn.

When Morris stepped out onto East 12th Street, he discovered the world still very much turning beneath his feet.

#

Somewhere between Houston and Canal Streets - on Wooster, perhaps, or Lafayette - Morris noticed a spatter of pedestrians gathered on the sidewalk. The collective gaze directed his own attention to the external fire escape of a five-story building in red brick and green-grey window frames. Placing the modest stack of books on the concrete step beside him, the newest observer took a seat among the onlookers and, lighting a cigarette, waited unhurriedly for the next act.

A sudden gasp swept through the audience as Morris saw at once what it was that had arrested their murmuring concentration. From high above his own head, a caped man shot between the buildings on a high wire, landing squarely and with a loud clang on the adjacent metal platform. There he remained, poised on bended knee for a solitary second, before a woman's scream pierced the scene. Emerging from the window on the floor below, in a shock of blonde frizz and torn animal print, the voice's owner shrieked her casting best. Another second of silence followed then, a man perched on a giant crane, one that had somehow eluded Morris' notice, cried out "cut!"

On hearing this direction, presumably not for the first time that day, the caped figure exclaimed something incomprehensible into a gust of wind and, struggling to liberate himself from his harness, finally gave up and sat down, cross legged in defeat, on the iron grate. The woman below, meanwhile, had more luck removing her wig and, throwing it dramatically over the edge, yelled something very comprehensible at the man on the crane.

The crowd, unsure as to whether this might be part of the script, merely looked on, unmoved. A few surreptitious whispers could be heard, but mostly they just stared. Morris got the impression that the woman could have thrown herself over the edge and the onlookers would have remained just so, perfectly indifferent. The responding ambulance men, roping off the scene and covering the body with a white sheet, would have no end of trouble convincing the mob that this was, in fact, a serious accident. A tragedy, even.

"So... you're quite sure it's *not* part of the movie?" someone in the crowd would finally insist.

"I'm afraid not," the solemn, official response.

Only then would the hordes disperse, disappointed that the veil had been lifted and their pretty illusion spoiled.

#

Returning from his afternoon outing, the heavens already washed clean from the gutters, Morris was greeted by Jerome, the cheery, Jamaican-born doorman who covered the Saturday afternoon shift.

"A note fa ya t'day, meesta Morris," he passed an unsealed envelope across the desk. "A young man, 'bout ya age, came by jus' afta ya left."

The two men, not so different in age and stature, exchanged a few friendly, if desultory remarks - something about the storm, about the forecast for the coming weekend, and about the lady from the fourth floor, with the chihuahua, who had mentioned again the "situation" regarding stray cigarette butts on the terrace. Morris assured the smiling attendant that he knew nothing about this most serious of crimes but that, if he caught anyone discarding butts improperly, he would call first to the front desk and second to the city's police commissioner.

"Don' faget da FBI, man," Jerome nodded gravely. "Dey be wantin' ta know dees tings too, ya know."

Morris held the envelope to his forehead in military salute as the elevator doors closed between them. The note inside he read on the ride up.

Called by 10am. In town until Monday afternoon. Will be at the old ale house down on Front if you want to beer later. Ben.

The signoff was superfluous, of course. Who else, besides those actually residing in or having recently visited apartment 5A, even knew where he lived? Ben was always going to drop by one day, probably unannounced. Morris knew that instinctively, but for some reason he couldn't quite explain, he still felt vaguely unnerved at the prospect of seeing his old friend. They had only known each other a short time, but that was not it. Had he been remiss in not writing or calling? The months had dashed by so quickly. He tried to picture the conversation. Would it be just like old times at The Owl? And what about Katelyn? Was he ready to hear about her life, unfolding in all the ways he had been careful not to imagine? Bad news on that front would be almost unbearable. But good news might be even worse.

Morris changed shirts and washed his face in the *en suite* basin. To his mind, the geography between the South Street Seaport and Mt. Vernon might have stretched on for a million light-years. With Ben's visit, that space and time quietly collapsed into nothing, the past pressing urgently up against the present moment, mocking his attempts to modularize personal history, to break it off into discrete, disinterested fragments. The mirror showed a tired but persistent expression warming on his face. Examining the faint, blonde stubble, the weary eyes, the sandy hair still unkempt but acceptably so, Morris wondered if he looked very different from his Baltimore days. So much had happened in such a short time, he could scarcely imagine himself from last week. Leaning closer to his reflection, he saw a man still young in years, though nevertheless coarsened by the hours and minutes and seconds of each passing day. With a deep exhalation, he dried his hands through his hair and made his way downstairs once again.

The only ale house Ben's note could have indicated was not at all what Morris might have expected. He had walked by the joint dozens of times and never once been tempted to enter, its dank atmosphere as much a deterrent as the stripe of patron often seen loitering, Styrofoam cup in hand, on the little deck off the front door. It was the kind of place where misogynists didn't need to look over their shoulder before telling a joke, where cops threw bachelor parties, where the floor was better hosed than swept.

Approaching him under the dim lights, Morris noticed his friend had grown sallow about the cheeks. His eyes, though they sprang to a nervous life when Morris came into view, appeared slightly sunken, as if they were retreating from view.

"Hey man," Ben's voice was disarmingly familiar and for a second Morris forgot their grimy surroundings. "I hope this isn't your local."

"First time in here, actually. Watcha drinking?"

"Why, you buying?"

"Certainly not." Suddenly aware that he was the only one in the bar with a collar, Morris rolled his shirtsleeves up to the elbows. "Do you know what rent costs in this city?"

"Somehow I think you're getting by just fine," Ben raised his glass and two fingers to the bartender. "I went by your place earlier. A friendly guy, Rastafarian, I think, said you'd just stepped out."

Morris nodded, strangely relieved. "Jerome, yeah. He's a funny soul. I'd never met a Jamaican before him. He talks about it sometimes. His family and stuff. Growing up in Kingston. He actually lives over in Brooklyn. Bedford, I think. Or Bushwick. Anyway, he comes in for the Saturday shift."

Morris wondered if Ben sensed the unease in his conversation. He took cover in a fresh round of unnecessary detail.

"He's one of three doorman who work in the building. If you came by an hour earlier, you would've met Steve, old Italian guy. Kinda moody..."

"If I'd come by an hour earlier," Ben cut in, "I would have met you." Though colored by unsteady laughter, his statement sounded more like an accusation than probably intended.

"Yes, well," Morris puzzled. "That too. Eh... sorry?"

"Hey, I didn't mean that," Ben's tone softened. His eyes, mildly furtive, looked down over his ruddy brown cheeks. "Look, I only found out I was coming up here two days ago. They sent a sales team for some conference in Midtown. I decided to spend the weekend on a whim. Thought I'd look my estranged Aussie mate up while I was here."

Morris detected a distant uncertainty in his friend's ordinarily cast-iron tone. They sat in silence for a minute or two, each feigning sudden interest in the late innings of a ball game neither of them cared about. Morris was about to break the silence when Ben blurted out his confession.

"That's the good thing about singledom, I guess. Not having to ask permission to just up and go."

Morris felt the anvil drop. Ben looked directly at him, smiling the dumb smile of the truly heartbroken. Then he turned once more to the uncaring refuge circling the bottom of the 8th. It was clear from his posture, his timbre, his sunken cheeks and disheveled appearance, that the breakup wasn't his decision. Morris thought to say something of comfort, but again came up empty.

"Ah, geez. You'll be alright, mate," was all he could manage before, "Maybe it's better this way?"

Ben's facial expression performed the equivalent of a standing backflip, his mood switching entirely from uneasy distance to the kind of unguarded optimism that's almost always empty of content.

"Of course it's better this way," he cheered. "You were always trying to warn me about Joni and her... ways. You know better than anyone, this is the best possible outcome. Only, I should have been the one to leave her."

"I'm sorry, Ben," Morris offered. There seemed to be little else to say. "How are you doing?"

What began in considered, if not contemplative tones soon unraveled into bitterness and despondency as Ben relayed the story of he and Joni's fallout. He had forgiven her cheating, yes, but what he regarded as a show of moral strength, of character and fortitude, she had taken as condescension, as a display of his own perceived superiority. His capitulation ("Her word, I still prefer forgiveness") was, to her, nothing of the sort. Rather, it was marshalled as evidence that either a) he didn't care for her in a truly deep and meaningful way in the first place, or, more likely, b) that he couldn't or *wouldn't* hold her to the standards she herself wished to be held. It was the type of logical contortionism specifically designed to trace the breakdown of human relationships. And to drive those in the crashing vehicle to all manner of abuse and self-loathing.

It was some ales later when Ben clapped both hands down on the bar and proclaimed his case utterly lost.

"Turns out there are no grand narratives, Morris. No whole answer. No *holy* answer." He took a sip of his beer and let out a long sigh intended to convey satisfaction, but which actually betrayed only pain and inner turmoil. Settling on the only conclusion at hand, he shook his head. "There's no explanation worth the struggle."

"I know you cared about her deeply," Morris was growing wary of his friend's detachment. "And it's likely you still do. It can't be easy to let that go. It hurts. But that's the part that makes it all human."

"What? I *feel* therefore I am? Something like that?" Ben's laughter had a distinctly cynical note to it. "You're right, it hurts. But not because I didn't get something I really wanted. It's more than that. It's a practical failure of my basic, core ideas about what it means to do good, to *be* good, in an evil world. So my little experiment in love didn't work the way I thought it ought to. It didn't accord with my own laws and assumptions. So what? Well, for me, the breakdown has existential implications, it challenges my whole framework, throws my position into complete disarray. It's like if you dropped a stone from a cliff and it didn't drop, just levitated." He snapped his fingers to underscore the moment.

"Poof! There goes gravity. Now what?" The question lingered, gathering dust and dim light.

"Now you have to question everything. Ugh, you watch," he cringed visibly, "now I'm going to have to embrace some kooky postmodern philosophy, like a self-referential character in a book written to look and feel as if it was set before all the kooky, postmodern philosophy came along, a grand narrative but with no ultimate redemption. I'll be just another narcissistic barfly, tottering from one taproom to the next, floating my sad story to anyone who'll listen. The whole 'Woe is me in a world made for you!' spiel."

"I wouldn't worry so much about that," Morris patted his friend on the shoulder. "There's redemption here, mate...even if you can't quite see it yet."

#

Morris welcomed the distraction brought by Ben's impromptu visit, even if his friend's state of mind gave him cause for increasing concern. At least he had something upon which to focus his own scattered thoughts, a problem in the immediate that could occupy his drifting mind.

During this time, Morris thought more and more about that night on the rooftop with Celine. In his recollection, they had passed it more or less alone. Now, with Aubrey out of town on business until later in the week, Celine had no ostensible reason to visit the Seaport apartment and so remained, safely ensconced in the mysterious circumstances of her own life, further uptown. Morris was only vaguely aware of her coordinates, a studio apartment somewhere on the windy streets of the Upper West Side. He tried not to imagine the space into life, to see her walls with black and white prints of little-known Parisian streets misted in spring rain, to fill the wine rack with Pomerols and Pauillacs, to notice the Penhaligon's candles in Lily of the Valley or Samarkand by the clawfoot tub, to imagine...

No, he snatched his reverie from the scent of vanilla melting into clove and the feel of the deep porcelain slipper against his spine. He would concentrate on the task at hand; huevos rancheros and too many margaritas with his bedraggled friend somewhere in the Village. Horchata, perhaps, or Dos Caminos. Somewhere safe, far away from sophistication and French accents and thoughts of betrayal.

Ben was there already, the rock salt on his glass licked clean in nervous anticipation of the next round. A glasshouse of honey-colored tequila bottles backlit his eager frame. Over the thin but livening brunch crowd could be heard a vintage mariachi ensemble, their melodic strings and jousting trumpets cutting in and out of conversation. Ben greeted Morris with a bear hug, an act of affection he seldom performed before 11pm, when the liquor was well and truly in his veins.

"We're going to talk about you today, my Antipodean matey," he began eagerly then, to Morris' private relief, promptly switched subjects.

"This city is wild," he gushed. "When I left you last night, I told the taxi to take me for a nightcap, something nearby my hotel. Well, he dropped me out front of a secret cocktail bar he knew in, where was it," he scratched the thinning hair on his scalp to attention, "ABC City? Alphabet City, that sound right?"

"Alphabet City, in the East Village?" exclaimed Morris in cheerful bemusement. "I thought you said you were staying somewhere up in Midtown?"

"I am, I am," Ben brushed this observation off as a mere detail. He slapped Morris on the knee in another rare display, this one of delight, and rushed on with the narrative.

"*Now* I see why you moved here! *Now* I see the genius of that cool and calculating mind of yours." He tapped a shaky index finger against his temple. "This place, Morris, a little cocktail bar with a secret entrance...what was it called? Don't Tell Me, or Do Tell You, or something like that... Well, whatever. Morris, it was absolutely teeming with women. And I'm not talking about your average, run-of-the-mill college girls. I mean *women*, Morris. Sirens. Sultry goddesses calling my poor, rudderless vessel ashore.

The difference in Ben's mien was more than just attitudinal. It was biological, too. He seemed, within the course of 24 hours, to have grown into a new skin, undergone some kind of full-body, metabolic reconstruction. Even his sullen cheeks appeared fuller, more vital. It was as if his drunken, nocturnal adventures had reenergized rather than depleted him. He talked on, charged by that heady mixture of enthusiasm and machismo familiar to all men who are called, unexpectedly, to indulge in matters of the flesh.

"I swear, I must've spoken to more beautiful women last night than I did in the whole five years I spent with Joni."

Morris considered him skeptically. Pure, unadulterated concupiscence, this new and liberated Ben.

"Well this is a change from yesterday." He pointed at the runny eggs swimming in *salsa verde* at the table beside them, to which Ben nodded in unreserved approval. "You were like a ghost at that alehouse. I was honestly worried for you when you got in the taxi. I thought maybe you'd tell the driver to take you right back down I-95, all the way to Joni's doorstep."

"I actually thought about it," Ben became grave for an instant. "I mean, I thought about asking him to take me to the train station. But it was late and I didn't feel like sleeping on some concrete bench until the first ride. Something in the coldness repelled me, physically. I literally felt the hard surface against the back of my head. That's when I decided to just say, 'To hell with all that! I've got life in me yet, even if I don't know what it means and where it's taking me. I've got life in me, New York City.'" He let forth a melodious laugh. "You know, I might have even yelled something to that effect out the taxi window. Anyway, I told the driver I wanted a place to forget my old life. I said I didn't want to know about the past anymore, and I didn't want the past knowing about me."

The slow crawl of realization came over his face. "Ah ha! That must've been why he took me to the speakeasy joint, the 'Don't Tell Them,' or whatever it was. Ha!" he let out another yelp of delight. "What terrific luck!"

Morris listened as Ben recounted the evening in a rapid-fire series of hazy, half-finished vignettes.

"Some kind of rambling boustrophedon, Morris... A, B, C... C, B, A... crisscrossing the Avenues like a wine-maddened, Dionysian poet..."

"But you repeat yourself..."

"If it bears repeating, yes. Then, now listen Morris, then enters this raven beauty, all Italian eyes and deep olive skin and legs like you wouldn't believe. Muscular. Sculpted. Like she's been hiking the *cinque terre* her whole life..."

"Not to stereotype or anything..."

"Of course, not to stereotype or anything, Morris. Geez! Well, listen, she suggests I join her friends and we head over the bridge, back to Williamsburg, where there's some band playing..."

"And one of them knows the singer..."

"Drummer, actually. How'd you know?"

Morris shrugged.

"Well, we head over," continued Ben, "losing half the stragglers along the way, but it takes us so long that by the time we arrive, the band has already finished. 'Nevermind,' they say, 'there's another act about to start...'"

"But your olive skin raven has grown tired..."

"She was tired, Morris! You're right!"

"And since her apartment was just around the corner..."

"Yes, it *was* around the corner!"

Ben gave Morris a look as if he had just discovered something that he preferred people thought he discovered long ago. He fumbled through the next couple of verses, another "rambling boustrophedon," then arrived on surer ground with the punchline section.

"Of course, I didn't realize it was shared" His eyes widened. "So imagine my surprise when I come out of the bathroom this very morning... with nothing to cover myself but a towel... only to see three complete strangers playing Boggle at the kitchen table!"

187

"Boggle, as in..."

"As in the hilariously entertaining 16-letter word game of near infinite anagrammatic delight?" he monotoned the delivery. "Yes, Morris. That one. Luckily for me the lexical combatants were in hysterics about one find or another and I was able to slip down the hall without their notice and, with a burst I was out, into this glorious, brand new day."

"After returning your towel, of course?"

"After bidding my raven beauty adieu, Morris. And yes, after returning the towel."

By the second or third margarita, the pair had found their old groove. They remarked covertly on the passersby, constructed for them elaborate backgrounds brimming with cheap liaisons, moral intrigue and ludicrous psychological aberrations.

Morris: Red flannelette and lumberjack beard... six o'clock. Wife divorced him on account of getting too 'intimate' with his patients. Lost everything. House. Car... Taxidermy practice.

They ventriloquized strings of clichés on behalf of the muted T.V. sportsmen during their pre- and post-game interviews...

Ben: We're here to give the fans something special... full confidence in coach Johnson... very happy with the preparation... firing on all pistons...

Morris: We gave it 110% out there today... had a lot of open looks at the basket... we're down but not out... all a matter of going back to the drawing board...

And in unison: "Offense wins games, defense wins championships."

Morris delighted in Ben's company and, for a brief moment, weighed asking whether he would ever consider moving to New York City. Then, for some reason he couldn't quite grasp, he caught himself mid-thought and decided to hold the balance in reserve. Fitting the past into the future seemed somehow to corrupt them both. Morris realized closure was at hand, that the other cliché, about change being the only constant, was true too. He let his mind rest on Baltimore again, on the time he had spent there and the people with whom he had briefly shared it. And, of course, he thought of sweet, green-eyed Katelyn.

"You know, you can ask me about her," Ben said at last.

"It was that obvious?"

Ben sighed. "The couple in matching Che Guevara t-shirts has been standing in your line of sight for nearly half an hour and you haven't said a thing. You're a good sport, Morris. But I know when your mind is elsewhere."

"Well?"

"She's good, man. She's...good."

"What did she say about you and Joan?" Morris diverted the momentum of the incoming information. He needed it delivered piecemeal, buttressed by extraneous context and tangential detail.

"She was hard on Joni," Ben replied. His tone had become impossibly sober. Reverent, even. "Maybe even harder than I was."

A group of kids sat down at a table near them. They seemed young, too young to be ordering pitchers of margarita and relaying cigarette breaks and bemoaning the problems of the world. Ben let them settle in before continuing the conversation.

"Look, a lot of stuff happened after you left, Morris. With Katey. With all of us, I guess." He shook his head and took a bracing gulp. "Look, I don't know if I should be the one to tell you this, but I think it's probably better if I do..."

Morris sensed the inebriation of a month's worth of cocktails rushing to his forehead. He willed his legs to carry him from the barstool and across the floor toward the gents, but they remained stolidly uncooperative. Of a sudden his body became clammy and leaden, as though he were filled with a molten metal, then rapidly cooled to room temperature. He waited, involuntarily, for Ben's next words.

"Morris," a whoosh of silence filled the vacuum before, "Katelyn is engaged."

#

What remained of the weekend passed for Morris like a slow rolling fog. Snatches of sporadic clarity occasionally rent themselves from the haze, only to recede again as quickly and unexpectedly as they had appeared. During those flickering moments of lucidity, he was able to observe clearly his own body, though as if from a third person perspective. He watched the uninhabited form as it muddled through conversation, nodded in dissembled response to remarks unheard and made loose, disconnected gestures at more or less appropriate times. But for the most part, he was at sea, breathing beneath an endless sky emptied of the luminous constellations by which others found their way.

Ben's visit had been like a bizarre anachronism, their presence together borrowed from another time and place. Morris wondered what, if anything, was left to fill the vacuum on the other side. Did anybody notice a Ben-shaped void on some foreign plane of existence, an unanswered roll call, a reservation for two filled by one, a ghostly apparition in the back row of a since forgotten photograph? There were too many questions for him to process. What if Ben hadn't stolen away from that distant reality, if he hadn't brought news from Baltimore, if he hadn't lodged in Morris' brain the irreducibly dense kernel of information that weighed on his neck, his shoulders, his entire, inescapable being? And yet, there it was. Katelyn's exclusive entity, her con-

190

tinuation, aloof and beyond his reach. He ran the words over and again through his mind, trying to rearrange the simple sentence so that it might carry some alternative meaning. But the phrase was mercilessly devoid of ambiguity.

"Katelyn is engaged."

He couldn't bring himself to say it out loud, to pass the words across his lips and into the present, objective world of substance and truth. Of course, the fact had been there all along, even if the revelation lagged; a tree long fallen in some strange woods, out of Morris' earshot. Perhaps it had been there before he even encountered her, dancing merrily in the indifferent future of that slate grey London day.

Sometime after the margaritas and the huevos rancheros, after the seismic force of Ben's disclosure had rippled through his flesh, Morris accompanied his friend to Penn Station. They vowed to keep in better touch, though Morris sensed in the lingering handshake that it would likely be their last. Ben had brought with him a perforation in time. It would be some years before Morris could cross that line in what he, himself, might term a healthy, conscious state. Even then, the waters would be turbulent.

#

Though he slept little and restlessly the following nights, Morris dreamt with a furious energy. Like seeds fallen on stony ground, the images came to him in bursts of straining vividity then, lacking depth of soil, withered and perished in an instant. Some of the dreams were incomprehensible abstractions; flashes of color or sound, vast expanses of coastline, windswept and stormy, the sound and *feel* of heavy machinery. Others were more lifelike, parties and gatherings populated by half-obscured faces or figures he

191

had somewhere encountered. The last in this series of dreams was the most brilliant, the most intense of them all.

It began with Morris waking into the middle of the scene, acutely aware that it was a dream, yet resigned that it must be lived out just the same. A crowd was gathered in a large and ornately decorated atrium, somewhere in Europe; the hushed murmurings carried on Latin tongues. The women, every one of them dressed in white, toted little parasols and folding fans of intricately embroidered paper and silk. On their heads they wore great decorative plumage, coiled swans' necks and speechless snowy owls, Yeats' white birds on the foam of the sea. The menfolk, as far as he could tell they were men at all, were robed in abayas of a shadowless, midnight black. They crawled, beastlike, on all fours, faces pressed to the earth; an oil slick seeping beneath the airy spume.

Through the glass roof a crepuscular light spilled in silver streams. It fell on Morris, too, who saw himself now in his naked form. In his hand he carried a roughed, leather riding crop. By his side lay a great Friesian warhorse. It's slow breathing strained against deep lacerations to its crest and withers. Leaning close so that his reflection swam into the creature's eye, Morris saw that it was bleeding from the nostrils, its life draining into a pool of magnificent black liquid shimmering in the twilight.

Detaching itself violently from the periphery, a silhouetted figure let out a piercing scream that shook the tiles from the walls and shattered the atrium glass overhead. Amidst the hailing shards, a million white birds came suddenly to screeching life, their wings spiriting the female figures through the light and into the invisible air beyond.

Morris felt his exposed back and shoulders lashed by the falling shrapnel, his skin splitting and tearing in waves of hot, excruciating pain. Beside him, the horse let out a final, choking bray, then sunk, thrashing, into the gleaming black pool. Petrified in terror, Morris tried to call out but found himself mute, his voice engulfed by the relentless howl emanating from the strange figure now moving desperately, fiendishly toward him.

Shivering and breathless in perspiration, Morris awoke with a startle to find Celine's ethereal form directly over him.

#

Chapter IX

On Here and Now

He could see her lips moving, the tiny veins in the whites of her eyes straining like time cracking marble, but for an instant that seemed long enough that the stone might just break, Morris heard nothing of Celine's frantic cries. Then the volume hit him in a sudden rush of panic and excitement. Pushing past her shuddering frame, he processed her words as they faded into an abandoned sobbing down the hall behind him...

"Just collapsed... not breathing... everything was fine..."

In rapid, shortening strides, Morris rounded the corner that opened onto the living room. At first he could see nothing departed from the ordinary; the soft light thrown forth from the bankers lamp on the corner davenport; a dozen chess pieces frozen, to Aubrey's advantage, on the far window sill; and Astrud Gilberto's vocals wrapped in sweetwater lyrics, lulling the scene into the evening's promised serenity...

> *Eu nunca fiz coisa tão certa*
> *Entrei pra escola do perdão*
> *A minha casa vive aberta*
> *Abre todas as portas do coração!*

Then, one wretched, sinister detail at a time, a pall descended on the moment. First the long green stems of the

194

Blue-Eyed Grass and Boneset, upturned and left helpless on the coffee table in a bath of shattered crystal. Then the growing pool of red wine running freely across the parquetry, seeping unchecked into the silk rug. And finally, Aubrey's legs from the knee down, motionless, leather slippers pointed toward the ceiling, protruding from behind the great Bergere chair.

"Just collapsed... not breathing... everything was fine..."

Morris stood in his pajama pants, stunned, the slowing drip from the granulated vase and the thunderous beating of his own heart the only movements in the room. He swayed absently as their rhythms overlapped, hummed, then began to diverge. Before they caught each other again he was summoned violently to attention.

"Did you call nine-one-one yet?" Richard was shaking him by the shoulders in a barely-controlled panic of his own. They were standing by the Bergere chair now, Aubrey's curiously serene expression at their feet.

"Morris! Listen to me! The ambulance, the medics. Is anyone on the way?"

How long had Richard been in the room? Time seemed to be gaining speed, events unfolding in a quickening confusion.

"I, I..." Morris grasped at a moment that existed somewhere beyond the image of Aubrey's inanimate corpus, lying stone-idle on the floor. He shook the vision loose from its moorings and, exhaling fully, breathed life into his own thoughts. "Richard. Look, I don't think anyone's coming. Celine, she... she ran straight into my room to tell me. Said he'd just collapsed, that he wasn't breathing. She's in some kind of shock, I think."

"OK," Richard was marshalling his own thoughts, breaking the situation down into manageable segments, turning a monolithic catastrophe into solvable, bite-sized action points. He looked sharply at Morris. "Do you know CPR?"

Morris nodded, unsure as to why that which now seemed obvious had not occurred to him earlier. "I have my Bronze Medallion."

"Your what?"

"I have... never mind." He grabbed composure by the throat. "I know CPR."

Richard stared at some unseen spot between them for a second, then muttered something to himself and rushed from the room, presumably to fetch help. Morris and Aubrey were left alone in the trailing silence, on the brink of this world and the next.

Surveying the scene, Morris saw around him a wide and sandy beach...

From across the grassy dunes, a warm breeze blows, gathering heat before sweeping out across the breakers. In the distance, a lush headland painted in bottle green slopes gently into the water, its volcanic bulk in the shape of a long-slumbering giant. And in front of a young and attentive group, a muscular man with wraparound sunglasses and zinc painted across his nose and lower lip gives instructions in broad, Australian English.

"First you're gonna wanna make sure the immediate area is free from danger, both to you and the patient. No electrical cables or stinger tentacles or anything of that sort laying around, righto?"

The gathered children, in every shade of blonde, nod in unison.

"Then it's time to check for response." The man considered his crowd. "Now, how do we do that?'

Half a dozen tiny hands shoot up.

"Yes, Suzanne?"

"Give the patient a gentle shake of the shoulders, ask him for his name and... and..."

"And?"

"And squeeze their hand and ask them to blink their eyes," leaps an interruption from the fringe.

"Thank you Gavin, but we'll give the other kids a chance to finish off their answers before butting in next time, won't we?"

Following a quick speech about "dee-fibs," "oxies" and "pistol grips," the time finally comes to revive the patient.

"Who'd like to go first?" The man stands tall, arms folded on his great barrel chest.

The same half dozen hands scratch eagerly at the clouds.

"How about someone different." Again the wraparound shades scan the group. "Morris, you wanna come up here and show us all how it's done?"

Morris looks at Suzanne, then at the other children's squinting faces. Approaching the scene of the accident, he runs through all that he and his persistent father practiced that same morning. He locates the sternum with sunburned hands, moves an inch down the mannequin's blue rubber singlet, looks to the instructor and, with life-giving oxygen filling his own thirsty lungs, begins compressions.

"Counting out loud please, Morris. C'mon kids, let's help him now. Everyone counting!"

"...thirteen... fourteen... fifteen... sixteen..." they chorus.

"That's good, Morris. Keep it going now. Ok then, another cycle. And another."

Morris felt the hot sun on his back and the skin on his shoulders burning in the climbing summer heat. The mannequin was still to his touch.

"C'mon, Morris. This man needs your help now. Push! Push!"

The young boy's arms tremble in agony, every exertion a triumph over the growing fatigue flooding his muscles.

From somewhere in the distance, Richard's voice beat instructions into the telephone receiver.

"Yes, we need an ambulance right away... Male, 48 years old... a heart attack, maybe. Or a stroke.... Look, I don't know... When? Just now... A minute ago, I guess... Less than five."

He called Celine in a voice that strained and cracked with urgency. Then he stated into the telephone receiver, in icily clear diction, the Seaport address under their feet, under Aubrey's back.

The directions rang out in Morris' ears as he counted his compressions.

"...twenty-eight... twenty-nine... thirty..."

[BREATHE! BREATHE!]

The cycle drained into an endless loop until the paramedics arrived and cloaked the room in navy uniform and military efficiency.

Morris lay exhausted on the beach, the sound of the crashing waves lapping gently in his ears. The repetition rings out, circling the clouds overhead.

Breathe... Breathe... Breathe...

#

Morris couldn't remember how he came to arrive at the hospital waiting room, nor how Richard and Celine came to be pacing the vinyl floor in front of him. Noticing them, finally, he attempted to read any clues that might tell him what was happening in this foreign world of beeping machines and anguished expressions and rushing orderlies. And, it occurred to him in a sudden, rousing waft, the choking smell of disinfectant.

Richard's aspect was like that of an athlete midway through a particularly grueling section of an already difficult race. Any expression beyond the potent tonic of pain and determination was accidental, an involuntary bodily function. From time to time, he stopped in his tracks, as if some far-off thought had leapt into the forefront of his mind. Then he would shake his head in bewilderment, run his fingers through his hair or expel an irritated exclamation of some kind.

"Aaahh..."

"Uuugghhhh..."

"MMmmmm..."

Whenever someone in a doctor's uniform pushed through the swinging doors marked, in bold red letters, [EMERGENCY], he leapt toward them like a predator made skittish by the ravages of hunger and doubt. Morris had no idea for how long Richard had been accosting these stethoscoped, white-robed impalas of the corridors. Minutes seemed to him as good a guess as weeks.

Celine's air, in marked contrast to Richard's overwrought demeanor, had about it a gloomy, even morose bearing. Her face wore an expression of sadness, almost guilt. It was as if she, herself, were about to deliver to those gathered under fluorescent tubing some irrevocable, heartbreaking news. Morris considered her lithe figure as it moved under the grey of her sheer, cloudlike dress. Even for Celine, Athena-eyed Celine, her form seemed weightless, otherworldly, as though she had accepted news of the worst and was already in transitional mode, floating for a final breath on the threshold between this realm and the next.

Considering the unthinkable himself, Morris had the immediate urge to storm through the emergency doors and into the swirling labyrinth of morphine and syringes and clipboards beyond. He wanted to find Aubrey, to see that he was still there, alive, that doctors were monitoring him, invigilating his every breath and heartbeat, noting the tiniest, barely perceptible signals with an unwavering consensus of crescive optimism.

Seeing Richard, however, his eyes reddened by fatigue and the worry that comes when fate tests long years of happy, fond acquaintance, he knew instinctively that the role of protective, surrogate brother belonged fairly to him. And to Celine, mournful and resigned to the least favorable conditions even before they prevailed, the responsibility of maintaining the gravity of the situation itself had fallen. Morris wondered what other roles the various characters in Aubrey's life had come to play at one time or another. He saw, clear as if he were holding it in his own hands, the silver framed photograph from "Summer, '65." What of Aubrey's sister and mother, with their matching bouffants and floral print dresses? Where were they now, and were they aware of the situation at hand? Morris felt the warm, tropical breeze rustling through their memories as they received the news.

Then there was Aubrey's father, his kind eyes squinting over his son's matted straw hair, a tender hand rested on his shoulder. Morris couldn't recall if the old man, who would have to be well into his octogenarian chapter, was still among the living. Aubrey so seldom spoke of personal matters, believing them to be inevitable to the point of utter banality. Where ideas illuminated his presence and sharpened his mind like a blade, he found in gossip only permission for his attention to take leave, to roam the lusher fields and distant horizons of his own consciousness. Perhaps that was a characteristic painted with his father's brush.

There were other characters along the way, too. People Morris would never meet who had impacted Aubrey in ways he could not comprehend, in times and places he would never visit. There were favorite teachers and arch-nemeses and women named Betsy and Lou and Mary-Ann. And men, too. Men who had inspired in a young Aubrey thoughts and notions that would carry him away from the crowd and set him on a course he would call his own. The words of writers, philosophers, comedians carried with him his whole life, until this moment. Along with his worldly flesh, the experiences of Aubrey's unique history also hung in the balance; incalculable connections tethering him firmly to this world, else delivering him in fans of gentle memory to the next.

Lost in reverie, Morris hardly noticed the tattoo of leather soles on linoleum that trooped through the EMERGENCY doors under a billow of starched white lab coat. Richard, who had momentarily abandoned his own impotent marching, leapt to his feet once more and approached the team of three. Celine peeled herself from the wall and, with pleading apprehension, convinced her legs to transport her to the center of the conversation. Morris heard their words, confided in hushed, respectful tones, as he approached...

"...to the nature of the heart attack and the fact that the paramedics were able to respond so quickly, we expect Mr. Fields to make a full recovery."

Richard pinched the bridge of his nose between thumb and forefinger and, exhaling deeply, allowed his shoulders to slacken back into something like their natural position. Closing his eyes as he filled his lungs with renewed breath, he wrapped his free arm, then both, around Celine, whose silent figure was already collapsing into his embrace. Morris moved alongside the pair and, not sure exactly what to do, shook the doctor's hand in unreserved gratitude.

"He'll need to spend a few nights here so we can monitor his condition," the man was saying, "but our initial tests show no signs of permanent damage. Your friend was incredibly lucky."

"Our friend was saved," Richard remarked, looking directly at Morris, "by the actions of this young man." It was the first time Morris saw in Richard's face, heard in his words, an unguarded, unalloyed sincerity. The intensity of the gesture took him slightly aback.

There were some other details, mostly regarding visiting hours, recovery time, what to expect over the coming weeks and months. Then the doctor left them in the hall, with nothing more save the wholly-sufficient knowledge that Aubrey's heart beat steadily a few rooms away.

Morris surveyed the other faces gathered; downcast, apprehensive, doubtful. Unmistakably human. For some present, the date would be recalled with solemn observances, moments of silence, an unending parade of ritual and ceremony and fading memory. Outside the grey concrete walls, beyond the land of the stricken and infirm, the trucks and delivery vehicles were beginning to burn their gas and sound their horns. The city jerked restlessly under her night covers. Morning was nigh.

#

Despite his otherwise upbeat prognosis, the doctor had insisted on just one visit that first day. "He's remarkably strong, considering what he's been through. But let's not leave anything to chance."

Richard and Morris insisted, to Celine's feeble protest and, later, unrestrained tears of joy, that she be the one to welcome Aubrey back to the folds of familiar company. After she left, the pair moped around their own separate quarters of the Seaport apartment, each pretending to busy himself in the pages of weekly magazines or old newspapers and avoiding, at all costs, the grim task of cleaning the living room. In his own room, Morris began an inspired feature story about a boy in some Central American village who had built an entire art studio out of discarded plastic bottles...but abandoned it after his attention wandered from the fourth or fifth attempt. He could hear the television in Richard's room blaring down the hall.

Morris was glad that Celine had acquiesced to their suggestion that she be the first to see Aubrey. In the frailty of the moment surrounding his brush with darkness, and in the young aftermath filling the atmosphere, Morris sensed an unspoken accord forming between himself and Celine. No doubt she had been aware of his affections for her. Perhaps she had even courted them in a casual, playful way, her ego nourishing itself on the harmless, blithe nature of his boyish infatuations. And yet, to indulge in such behavior now, with all that had passed, would be beyond insensitive; it would be impossible. The nature of the equation had changed forever, a prime no two factors could reach, save one and itself.

At last Morris heard the weight of the front door close behind Celine's footsteps. He waited for her to strike up a conversation with Richard, whose room was nearer the apartment's entrance, then, hearing their mingled voices, made his way with some reticence down the hall.

With a sigh of relief, she exclaimed his name. "Morris!" Then, scattering his uncertainty with a sincere, un-ambiguously platonic embrace, she allowed herself to be held. Drawing away, finally, she retained his gaze and silently confirmed the sense he had entertained moments earlier. Friends, then.

"He's going to be fine, Morris. And you saved him. I'll never..." she put her hand on Richard's shoulder, "*we'll* never forget that."

A lifetime of conversation passed in a second of silence.

"And here I was certain it was my friendly reminder call to the paramedics that did the job in the end," quipped Richard, unable to resist. It was clear he had already donated more naked emotion to the episode than he cared to add to. His Cheshire grin conveyed a welcomed feeling of normalcy on the situation.

"*Reminder* call?" Morris shook his head in confusion.

"Well, Celine here beat me to the punch," said Richard, feigning indignation, "but only with the unfair advantage of having been seated next to our dear friend when he decided on this little stunt."

"So you both called?"

Both nodded, then Celine, raising her eyebrows delivered the verdict they'd been skirting around. "It was a minor heart attack. But the doctors say he's strong, unusually so. Like an ox, they said, or a bull. I can't remember. Anyway, there's no reason to think he won't make a full recovery."

The men were nodding, beckoning forth the good news.

"How're his spirits?" Morris was eager to hear of the man's state in his own, irreplaceable words. "Did he say how he's feeling?"

Celine permitted a plucky smile to cross her lips. "He's...Aubrey." Her eyes misted for a fine instant. "He told me to tell you both to 'get out of town.' I think that was the expression," she let out a girlish laugh, recalling his message alive and well in her ears. "He said he didn't want you two here all 'long in the jaw,' is that it? I should have written it down. Anyway, he said you should go on to Sid's place, as agreed earlier, before," she cast Richard a playful reproach, "before his 'little stunt.'"

Richard made to protest, but was immediately shuttered by the addendum Aubrey had carefully, expectedly pinned to his message. Celine shook her head for the veto. "He said he simply won't take 'No' for an answer, that knowing you're here in the city, while Sid's End of Summer Party rolled on in our absence, would cause him just the kind of unnecessary stress his doctors are cautioning him to avoid. He said, 'Tell them to go and if...no, *when* they protest, insist they enjoy themselves, as though... as though it were a matter of life and death.'"

"Who's Sid?" Morris gave voice to his confusion once more.

Richard answered, "A spineless little toadie whose very existence enervates culture and taste and civilized discourse. Also, my brother-in-law." He looked at Celine, then back to Morris. "My disgustingly, obscenely, repulsively well-heeled brother-in-law... who likes to compensate for his miserable life and character by throwing an annual summer party on his disgustingly, obscenely, repulsively colossal estate in Southampton."

"I see," mused Morris in deadpan consternation. "Well, if it's a matter of life or death..."

#

The drive out began with the usual choke and smoke and smog of the city boroughs. Ike's mighty Interstate heaved with the traffic of a million impatient commuters, each vying for pole position in a race that, at times, could have been won by a rock on the side of the road. Gradually, though, the city peeled away and the great buildings sank down from the skies to take more earthly dimensions. Once they got out past Queens and Old Westbury Gardens, Richard turned his slick German automobile off the Long Island Expressway and took a slow road south. Comfortable then on the Southern State Parkway, he lowered the windows, opened the gas and let the European engineering do what it was designed to do.

The rushing wind, warm and salty, filled their noses and blew their hair clean back. By the time they hit the Sunrise Highway, it had carried their troubles and preoccupations out to sea.

They spoke little on the trip, content to let the scenery occupy the silence. Occasionally Richard would underscore some point of historical interest; so-and-so writer lived here, for instance, or this-and-that actor had a house by the beach, over yonder dunes. When they were close to their destination, Richard pulled the car into a gas station.

"I intend to maintain a blood-alcohol level significantly exceeding the legal driving limit during the next few days," he declared, removing the nozzle from the pump. "If you want anything... cigarettes, aspirin, prophylactics... now's your chance."

Stepping outside onto the oil-marked asphalt, Morris went through a handful of stretches, feeling his elongating muscles warm into the afternoon temperature. Inside the convenience store, he purchased a bag of jerky and three boxes of Camel Lights. At the last minute, he added an economical fifth of scotch to the take.

"You know we're going to a multi-millionaire's party, right?" Richard chided him back in the car. "They don't expect you to get yourself drunk. That's the host's job. Or their server's, at least."

"Should we bring them something?" asked a sheepish Morris. "You know, flowers or a bottle of wine? What does your sister like?"

"My sister likes money," Richard laughed. "On a scale beyond what you or I could possibly tender." He turned the key in the ignition and gave the engine a couple of short, firm revs.

"Besides," he continued once they were back to cruising speed, "they have a cellar large enough to resurrect the

Festival of Dionysus and an orchidarium my sister cares for more than she does her own husband. What she wants, desperately, is acceptance from her peers or, rather, Sid's peers. But it's not forthcoming. His family bears a tenuous connection to some Old-World title. Second cousin to a baroness, or a viscount or something. There's a village in their name somewhere in Belgium. Anyway, it doesn't matter. To them, Rachel will always reek of the unwashed New World and its brash, uncivilized ways. Still, she persists. It's sad to see, really. The way he takes her for granted. But like I said, the cellar is enormous. I take my revenge out on his *grand crus*."

#

A twice overhead privet hedge separated the poor and unfortunate world outside "The Dunes" from all the rich vacuousness that existed within. The iconic barrier was studded at the driveway by an imposing wrought iron gate, the center apex of which alone peered over the turfed dune immediately behind it, so that the would-be gawker was left only to imagine at the unattainable wealth that lay beyond the overlapping panels of leaf and lawn. Inside the gate, a little white guard house provided shelter and a few radio channels for a rotation of gruff men, each equally capable of deferential hospitality as indifferent refusal. They wore dull, grey uniforms, as befitted their professional demeanor. For those whose surnames had, by whatever means necessary, landed on the guard's sacred lists, a slow bending driveway in the shape of a giant keyhole led them up to the primary building's main entrance. There, the head valet made busy notes of plate numbers and guest names and ordered his scurrying minions to deposit their respective vehicles in an adjacent lot. A pair of footmen heaved open the front doors and, even before the guest could begin to take in the spectacular scene before him, a servant had in his hand a fresh-squeezed seasonal fruit cocktail (before 1pm) or flute of champagne (anytime thereafter).

The main entertaining room was sunken from the landing, so that newcomers to any gathering were put immediately on show for those already mingling on the floor below. But arriving guests seldom noticed the glittering stemware or colorful dresses or, depending on the time of day, bronzed swimsuit bodies and eggshell linen for, over their bobbing, conversating heads, a thirty-foot wall of sliding glass doors gave way to an uninterrupted panorama of the windswept Atlantic Ocean. Only the most fragile egos, those belonging to creatures who lived perennially in the shadows of others people's' opinions, bothered concealing their awe.

There were two, maybe three dozen people melting from group to group, wall painting to statue, divan to bookshelf, when Morris and Richard clinked their own welcome glasses on the landing. Guests wore poolside attire, mostly, which meant silk wraps and heels for those ladies who could manage them, and brightly colored trunks under polos and guayaberas for the men. A few wore hats; broad and floppy for the ladies, trilby straw and panama atop the gents. Few deviated from the general style such that, it might have been a kind of themed party, except for the fact that this set always dressed in unison, moving through the catalogues as fast as the retailers could mail them. The mood was chatty, refulgent. The rich irony of Don Cherry's Band of Gold piped in through the speakers...

I've never wanted wealth untold
My life has one design

A simple little band of gold
To prove that you are mine

Going by the verve and volume on the ballroom floor, it was evident the bubbles had been flowing for some time.

Richard had just begun sharing with Morris some preliminary notes regarding what he referred to as the "seasonal Hamptons fauna" on display before them, when the brightly plumaged hostess caught their presence. She waved an enthusiastic, bejeweled arm at her brother, who poked Morris in the ribs and spoke in low tones from behind unmoving teeth, "I believe you call them 'maggies' in your part of the world, Morris; short for magpie, as in, birds that collect shiny stuff to feather their nests. Generally of a mischievous nature and better avoided." He drew a breath and straightened his shoulders. "Oh look! Here she comes."

"You're quite the colloquialist, *mate*," Morris broadened his own accent, relishing for a second Richard's conspicuous unease.

"We all collect something," he sighed, bracing for his sibling's loud and imminent approach.

"Darling Richard," she craned her neck forward, presenting one, then the other powdered cheek in clumsy, faux-Euro style. "It's been so long. How wonderful you could come. And I see you've brought a friend. I'm Rachel," she turned a birdlike face to the young foreigner, "Richard's only and favorite sister."

She was tall and rail thin, a combination that betrayed in her manner a desperate longing. Morris accepted her limp fingers into his, unsure as to whether he was expected to shake the hand to which they were attached or drop to his knees and kiss it. He lingered half way between the two actions when he was rescued from decision.

"This is Morris," Richard returned the introduction. "He's working with Aubrey who, I regret to inform our Dear Hostess, is unable to make it this year. Prior commitments. He sends his regards."

Rachel appeared momentarily wounded by this apparent snub. Unable, or unwilling, to conceive that any social event could surpass her own fete's allure, she placed the blame for Aubrey's absence where it seemed to her more likely to fit.

"Oh, such a shame." A bejeweled hand drifted to her forehead. "You know, it's my opinion that some people simply work too hard. Chained to the office like he is. He really must get out and live a little." She took a lazy sip from her champagne flute, her thin red lips assuming the shape of the glass to give a kind of suffocating goldfish effect. "I guess that means his wondrous French *beauté* won't be joining us either. What a catch that one is, even for Aubrey!'

"Alas, she'll remain in the city, too," replied Richard, who had earlier informed Morris just how little Celine cared for Rachel's pompous affectations, though the latter had always assumed the opposite was true.

"Well, you'll give them our best, won't you," she remarked at last in clipped words. "Sid will be disappointed they couldn't make it, of course. Speaking of the old boy, I'm just out to see him by the pool. He wants to show some cousins of his the new statue we had brought in just last month. I think it looks hideous, but he insisted. Anyway, Richard, you know your way around. As for rooms, you're in *Gengen-Wer*, as always. Morris can take *Khonsu*, given that Aubrey won't be making it along. Excuse me a second..."

In a flurry of "*Darlings!*" and a swoop of her silk-wrapped wings, she was off to meet a handsome young couple in matching salmon Bermuda shorts who had just crested the landing.

"She also collects useless degrees," Richard rolled his eyes. "You may thank her fleeting infatuation with Egyptology for being allocated the room of the Moon God."

"So, what's Gengen-Wer?"

"Why, the Goose God, of course." Rachel's little brother almost spat his laughter.

"A senile, long forgotten fragment of their much-celebrated mythology."

"I see," Morris chuckled. "And what did she name the master bedroom?"

"She'd never forgive me if I told you this." Richard motioned to a passing waiter that another round was due. "But there are two master suites, a 'his' and 'hers,' if you like."

Morris shook his head, bewildered by the pretension of it all.

"Amun doesn't lie with Amunet," Richard continued. "I wouldn't be surprised if she kept the little wastrel's organ in a canopic jar beneath her bed."

"So all this," Morris swept his arm around the room, "It's...it's all for show?"

"And what a show it is," remarked the doddering Goose God, scooping up a pair of golden flutes as the waiter swept by. "One great, diamond-studded declaration that, whatever people may say about an Afterlife, it's the Here and Now they really care about."

Morris thought of saluting the 'Here and Now,' but something belonging to his surroundings, something written on the faces of the squawking attendees, woven into their carefree expressions and easy laughter, stayed his hand.

#

His bags safely deposited under Khonsu's watchful eye, Morris, with no particular place to be and plenty of time to get there, wandered by the poolside area in a cool, half daze. The afternoon light faded among the thinning crowd as guests retired to their rooms, alone and in pairs, to groom and preen their pretty faces for the evening's big soiree. In light brown cotton slacks and a blue collared shirt, unbuttoned at the neck and rolled at the sleeves, Morris had done all the grooming and preening that he was determined to do. Nevertheless, he was later relieved to see that Richard's own attire was of similar formality to his own, even if the rest of the gents posed and postured in sports jackets and colorful suede loafers and ridiculously over-festive bow ties.

Drifting between the postprandial stragglers, Morris made his way to where the deck dropped over white and blue painted balustrades onto the rolling sand dunes below

The storied Atlantic, brave and cold even in the late summer months, clawed at the shoreline some fifty paces away. A thin strip of pale blue separated the horizon from the gathering clouds above. Down the beach a little ways, a young family was packing up its folding chairs and umbrellas and many-sized totes. The children, a handful in all, chased each other in circles around the encampment, their yelps and squeals of delight carried by little eddies along the shore. His back to America, Morris could hear the congregating guests beginning to echo around the great marble caverns over his shoulder. Their conversations he caught, in snippets and snatches, as he meandered back through their real estate...

"The Peruvian shamans have been performing these rituals for decades, maybe centuries," enthused one wild-eyed man, a glen plaid sport coat slung lackadaisically over his shoulder, chest puffed toward his all-male audience.

212

"Though of course they don't register time in the same fashion as we do. They have their own means and ways. Like this medication I'm telling you about. As my own guide emphasized, the ayahuasca drug itself is only part of the experience. Poorly administered, it can lead to one hell of a trip. But taken properly, under careful guidance, the journey to our deeper self, a universal connectivity, can be truly life-altering."

The congress nodded in silent agreement, each making mental notes so as to properly convey the anecdote to their own audience when they returned to work the following week. Morris moved on through the crowd, dallying for a moment by a group of sniggering ladies.

"But he's such a *boooore*," sniped one of them in haughty tones.

"I'll say!" confirmed another. "He sure is slow getting to the point."

"Slow?" quipped a third in rehearsed indifference. "Why, the man turns a phrase like an ocean liner rounding to pick up a man overboard."

"Yeah, a man already perished in the icy waters," added another, to the group's renewed laughter. "By the time he's got to the punchline, the thing's dead as Jack Dawson."

"Well, he may not be the wittiest conversationalist," followed a slightly older voice. "But he does throw an incredible bash."

"Speaking of which," the first woman snapped her fingers to a young Latin boy who scampered over, "fetch my dear lady friends and I here another round of these delicious Bellinis, won't you?"

The waiter bowed in silence and, catching Morris' sympathetic expression, rolled his eyes almost imperceptibly, before disappearing into the kitchen quarters.

Morris was glad when, circling the periphery, he caught the familiar tones of Richard's narrator's voice.

"The amount of history being lived right now," he was expounding on a theory Morris had heard him develop over many dinner parties in the Seaport pad. "We almost certainly have a Mozart in our midst. A Shakespeare too. It just happens that they're buried under a thousand ton of plastic pellets in a Bombay slum or distracted by the imposition of some compulsory secondary school curriculum, designed to magnify their averages and suppress the diamond within..."

The gathered feathers neither nodded, nor offered signs of rebuttal. Unfazed by the lifeless reception, Richard carried on with his musings as if he were sorting through his thoughts in the privacy of his morning shower.

"History is speeding up, you see, because the lives in existence at present, stacked end-to-end, has never been greater. Humans are registering more words and impressions and images and information than ever before, both collectively, as a species, and on an individual basis. And it's not just technology, though that's one of progress' obvious co-pilots. Think of the biological world, the amount of evolution under way this very second, bursting forth in fits and starts, reams of mistaken genetic code discarded before this sentence has time to make you think, before you finish your glass and snap your fingers for another..."

Reminded of the vessel in his own hand, he took a nourishing quaff.

"Time was when precious life was lived more or less end-to-end, one miserable, wretched generation following another, if all went well. Now, history is experienced side-by-side, six billion pairs of shoulders shuffling forward into the expanding unknown. The long rope of human history has...Ah, there he is!" he broke off to make way for his friend.

"This here is Morris. Morris, I'd like you to meet," he paused, evidently at a loss for a single name, "well, everyone you need to know at a party like this."

The surrounding faces smiled in oblivious gratitude, the backhanded compliment having landing exactly as Richard intended it to.

"Ah, you're the young Briton, then?" said one of the men, adding, in an affected cockney accent, "awright then, Guvna?"

Animated by a joke within their reach, the others sprang suddenly to life.

"Say something British," pleaded one of the women. Morris recognized her from earlier in the day, when he'd seen her swaying, tipsily, by the main staircase, threatening endless conversation to anyone who ventured nearby. Her sun-blushed cheeks bunched under glazed eyes as she spoke. "Something, *Brut-ish! Please, sir... can I have another.*"

"'Some *more*,'" corrected Richard.

"Yes, yes," the woman chorused gleefully, "some more *Brut-ish*, Morris."

"Well," began the dancing monkey, addressing himself to the rosy woman, "If I was British, I'd probably say something like, [clearing his throat] 'My dear, I must say, you're doing a positively *marvelous* job in that dress. Green is such a difficult color to wear, after all. And yet, here you are, managing to the very *best* of your abilities. It's *inspiring*, really. Jolly good for you!"

He raised his glass as, slowly and unsurely, the others followed.

"To you, my dear, and," he nodded, ever-so-seriously, "in the face of it all, your *irrepressible* sense of self-confidence."

"Here, here!" Richard steered them toward the home straight. "Now, if you ladies and gentlemen don't mind..."

215

"Hold on a second," a portly man standing beside the green dress felt the sudden urge of relevance. "He said, '*if* I was British.'"

"Yes," replied the non-Brit.

"So then, you're not?"

"'fraid not..."

"But if you're not from Britain," demanded the woman, perplexed, "where are you from?"

"At a party like this" Morris began, capturing the grandeur of the surroundings in a sweeping gesture, "and with guests such as yourselves," here he bowed, "I'm not sure such a trivial detail really matters."

"He's right!" the fat man agreed at last. "A toast!" he panted, raising his own glass, "to trivial details."

They all joined in the splashing of champagne, but only Morris felt a sense of melancholy about it. Was this the noose at the end of history's long rope? Civilization saluted with a toast to the meaningless?

#

As twilight's tepid breeze dropped between the grassy dunes and a mild, expectant air filled the space behind, the tempo of Sid's End of Summer Fete began to gather in speed and energy. Cocktail dresses swirled across the dance floor, suitors became ever bolder in their propositions and revelers dropped the weight and pretense of serious conversation in favor of hollow chitchat and airy, idiomatic flatteries. Against a throbbing crowd, waiters held aloft their shiny silver disks, on which bubbly golden trophies huddled against groping hands. The British monkey was frequently among the grasping hordes. The champagne washed over his recent past, over Katelyn's sea green eyes and Aubrey's

216

arrested heartbeat, over Ben's existential reconfiguration and Celine's exhaling smoke.

His brain buzzing like a snare, Morris gave in to oblivion with happy release. He welcomed the familiar lightness of being, the easy laughter, the painless introductions to equally tranquilized personalities. Even Sid seemed affable enough at first, when Morris finally did meet him.

"I want you to try one of these chocolate truffles, Morris," enthused the little man, a walking absurdity in yellow seersucker and a candy stripe bow tie. From his breast pocket a polka dot kerchief wilted.

At first Morris couldn't recall how he and the cartoon host came to be in the center of a circle of onlookers. He thought of something witty to say, something about lions and circuses and barber poles, then lost it all in a fog of competing metaphors.

"They're from Belgium," Sid was giggling, his oily moustache twitching with excitement. He looked to Morris like giant otter. "We don't add edible gold or put Swarovski ornaments on our boxes, either. No tricks or novelties. Just pure, Belgian perfection," he turned to the audience. "My family has known the chocolatiers for generations. Every year, on my great grandfather's birthday..."

"Tastes like," Morris sputtered, interjecting, "like dusty chocolate. But with old nuts, or something. Old boy," Morris wondered why his accent suddenly sounded like that of an actual British monkey ("but wait, do monkeys have accents?"). "Why, I do say, I think your famous chocolate mates are giving you a jolly good runaround!"

The crowd roared with mirth, at least one member spilling the remainder of a pink martini over an immediately ruined crepe skirt. Indeed Sid, who loathed being interrupted in his most patient of moods, much less so when the story at hand was woven from the golden threads of his vaunted genealogy, burst into rapturous convulsions.

Stumbling from the group, Morris waved down a waiter and, scooping up a handful of sloshing flutes, left the circus behind in favor of the outside air. As he lurched toward the enormous glass doors, he noticed a slender figure in a kimono of whirling fuchsias and seafoam greens leaning against a giant Japanese vase. Steadying himself, Morris prepared to proffer one of the stems in hand but, before he could attract the woman's gaze, she flittered off. With some confusion, he followed her colorful image as it multiplied itself across the reflective, concertina panels, then disappeared into the crowd. Morris cursed, to nobody in particular. Stringing his steps together with evident effort, he made his way toward the outside pool and came to uneasy rest on one of the wicker loungers. His head felt heavy on his shoulders. A gentle breeze rustled through the leaves of the potted figs. From the near distance came cosmic musings on Julie London's lips...

Fly me to the moon
Let me play among the stars
Let me see what spring is like on
On Jupiter and Mars
In other words, hold my hand
In other words, darling, kiss me

Morris felt his eyes begin to close when he heard a vaguely familiar voice distinguish itself from the lulling soundscape.

"You too, eh?"

Morris turned to find the young waiter to whom he'd tossed a sympathetic glance earlier in the evening. He was smoking a hand rolled cigarette, purposefully exhaling its pungent aroma into the violet sky. Off in the distance, a girlish laughter escaped beyond its intended volume, then slipped back under cover of night. A glass fell to marble somewhere in the main house, inspiring shrieks of laughter.

"How do these people stomach each other?" Morris at last wondered aloud. It was more of a statement than a question. The waiter simply shrugged, indifferent to the passing spectacle. He wore a simple, contented expression. Morris had the idea that the kid might be a hundred years old, or not yet twenty. But nothing in between.

"Would you care for one?" he asked, holding out another bullet-rolled cigarette. Taking one, Morris leaned in toward the flame, eventually catching its energy with the end of the twisted paper. It crackled at the touch, then burned a slow and crimson red. The silent glow filled his body and Morris sank back into the curvature of the chair. Overhead, the celestial canopy dazzled and glittered.

"The distant past," Morris heard the immortal man whisper, "lies immediately before us. All we see in the heavens has by now come and gone, a million light-years passing between us and the sublime. Here we bask in the light of astral eternity, beckoned to blissful Elysian Fields, yet anchored to our perception of life on a rock."

"And..." Morris mouthed the word in silence...

"Prostrated on Virgil's fertile plains, forehead to earthen soil do we beseech, 'Bachus and fostering Ceres, for your needful succour do we sing.' And into transcendental realms, bounding in numinous beneficence, into your mighty embrace do we swim."

Rising to his feet, Morris made to thank the waiter, but discovered he was already gone. He drifted along the deck toward the shore until he espied a red-tailed hawk, perched proudly on the balustrade. Mounting the railing, the damp wood groaning and knotting between his toes, Morris moved slowly, steadily toward the bird. The creature rested calmly, as if inviting the approach. When he was near enough to touch its burnt sienna plumage, Morris noticed for the first time a snake writhing in its beak, its reptilian scales set aglow in the night, a thousand interlocked diamond mirrors reflecting the outer reaches of the seraphic marquee overhead. Of a sudden, the bird cocked its head, angling its black, opalesque eye so as to catch the moonlight in its iris. With a raspy, shrill cry it alighted, gliding between the shifting dunes and out across the lapping breakers. Morris rose to his full human height and stood, poised for a breathless moment, then, aiming himself toward the stellar atrium overhead he leapt, hyperextended, into the cold, dark Atlantic.

#

Plantation shutters cut the morning light across Morris' face like sunshine through a cell block window. Awakening to a distant rumble, he felt the pillow damp beneath his head. His clothes were soaked, with sweat or what, he could not tell. A rank, mangrove odor filled his nostrils, raising the bile in his sandpaper throat. To his temples raced a pulsing throb, like mercury shooting up a melting glass tube.

"Wakey, wakey," Richard's tone sliced deeper than the light. "We're heading back in fifteen. Celine left a message to say we're needed back in the City. ASAP. Wouldn't say why. Sounded urgent…"

Morris lost an involuntary wince.

#

220

Chapter X

Elysian Fields

Death rode with them all the way back to the Seaport. She was calm, silent and, after her own peculiar fashion, unnervingly patient. Though neither Morris nor Richard addressed her directly, fearing, perhaps, that mere recognition of her presence might somehow stir her to unwanted action, they nevertheless felt her icy breath against their napes. Richard drove deliberately, linking up with the 495 just out of Westhampton to ensure the fastest route. Questions regarding Aubrey's condition hung, unasked and unanswered, in the rushing Fall wind.

Morris replayed the near fateful scene in the apartment. The shattered vase, the dripping, bloodred wine, the upturned shoes, pointed at the heavens in defiant, eternal accusation. "There's the culprit! Look, look to the skies! There one common, unavoidable destiny awaits us all."

He slung his cheek in the seatbelt and turned his face to the window. The whole ordeal had impacted him in ways he couldn't adequately comprehend. Kneeling in the sand of his childhood beach, fighting back Death with every exhalation, he could feel her black-eyed gaze fix itself upon him, peering placidly through a dozen children's eyes. Friends, acquaintances, enemies. Wild huntress, she might snatch this body, or the next, at a whim. What then of earthly philosophizing, rationalizing, moralizing? What of the unspent desires and vaulted savings, of plans for the future and calendar appointments, of certificates of deposit and accruing air miles and reading lists? What of it all, when existence could be snuffed out in a single, unannounced instant, time arrested for the best of men just as easily as for the very worst among us?

The explanation for such apparently indiscriminate slaughter was almost worse than the crime itself. Nothing. A deafening, universal yawn. A glaring, cosmic indifference. A silent scream into everlasting meaningless. When all was said and done, even the stars were liars, the light and heat of the long dead majesties indistinguishable from those still reigning. In what, then, to trust?

Tall and ominous, the City loomed in the fast-approaching distance. Morris felt his heart pounding in his chest, so much so that he looked down to see if the palpitations were visible under his shirt. Manhattan's serrated skyline presented itself like a hot knife resting against his jugular. He thought of asking Richard if he would drive him somewhere else, someplace high, where the smell of death and hospital disinfectant and city garbage could not reach. But where? He had no place to go. Nowhere to be. Nothing but his own wet socks into which to slowly sink.

Richard's own silence did little to assuage Morris of his anxieties though, to be fair, he didn't exactly appear to be in too great a shape himself. Morris noticed his hands trembling whenever he took them from the wheel. When he last saw him at the party, Richard was tossing chocolate truffles at the feet of Hebes, the dust melting into the nectar and ambrosia spilling from her golden jug.

"Decadence in the fountain of youth!" he was laughing maniacally. "Lo, good citizens of Southampton! Lo! The Wild Goose is on the warpath!"

"Wait?" Morris recalled the drunken scene. "Was Richard alone in his attack? Didn't I, also...?" Once again, shame and worriment stormed through his conscious mind like that Olympian's army sweeping through an unguarded village. He felt himself unraveling, unable to hold his center together. Had he, too, desecrated the Gods? And had he fare for the passage that awaited?

As they drew nearer the city's throbbing heart, Richard shifted down through the gears, slowing the car into the hardened asphalt shadows. Morris surveyed the bustling sidewalks, the crowded bus stops, the subway entrances swallowing the multitudes in great, serpentine gulps. He studied the pedestrians as they passed by the window, trying to decide if they were alive or, like so many distant suns before them, already turned to dust. Daylight clouded over and tiny streams began to appear on the glass, blurring the expressions on expressionless faces. Then the rivulets turned to an ocean and the scuttled hordes were drowned in one.

#

When at last they saw Aubrey, seated upright in the Bergere chair and scrawling notes keenly into the margins of a clothbound book, Richard and Morris couldn't help but give a sigh of relief. Looking up from the page, Aubrey's expression was one of genuine delight.

Morris couldn't tell if he appeared slightly thinner, especially about the cheeks, or whether the features on his face were simply more pronounced for their unexpected vitality. The rain was coming down harder now such that, even though it was close to noon, the skies over Manhattan were splashed a dark green-grey. Aglow in the reading lamp's amber embrace, his hair combed neatly back and to one side, navy woolen cardigan pressed at the shoulders, Aubrey seemed as though he had not a trouble in the world.

"You two look like death," he stated, matter-of-factly, as they entered the room. He surveyed his friends gravely, then a warm smile rose to his lips and he welcomed them back home with familiar kindness. "You'll forgive me if I don't leap to my feet."

Richard dropped his overnight bag, then his weary body, onto the sofa. "Actually, I was going to see if you wouldn't unpack these clothes for me," he smiled at Aubrey. "Maybe skip down to Gene's and get Morris here and I some bagels and coffee, too. We've been drinking for ten men, I'll have you know."

"Oh, I'm well aware of that," Aubrey raised his book to conceal what Morris hoped was his customary wry smile. "Sid telephoned this morning. Wanted to make sure you arrived safely back to the city."

"Such a considerate host, that Sid," scoffed Richard.

"Yes, he filled me in on the predictable antics of the Wild Goose. Also remarked what a tremendous swimmer you are," Aubrey nodded in Morris' direction. "Especially given the unseasonably brisk water temperatures they've had this year."

Morris felt the blood rush to his face. He recalled only the vaguest details of the event. A raspy bird... the oily, moonlit breakers... someone - was it Richard? Or maybe Rachael? - calling him back to shore and pressing a towel on his shivering frame. Muddy footprints on the guesthouse carpet. Waking, after a spell, amidst a steaming shower. Had all that really happened?

"Yes, well," Richard groaned to his feet and hoisted his bag over his shoulder, "of the aforementioned ten men, our amphibious antipodean here must've imbibed for seven, maybe eight."

"A sensible course of action, no doubt," Aubrey lowered his book. "And how did you enjoy your first edition of Sid's End of Summer Soiree, Morris?"

"I have a sense it may be my last," he replied, sheepishly.

"I'll leave you to fill in the details," Richard patted his comrade on the back and disappeared down the hall and into his room.

"I wasn't going to tell him that Celine's already gone to grab breakfast," Aubrey confessed when Richard was out of earshot. "Doppios and Gene's Everything Bagels should be here any moment."

Morris nodded, feeling revived by the mere expectation of caffeine. "Thank you."

"No, Morris," Aubrey was suddenly very serious. "Thank *you*."

They nodded together, allowing the gravity of the situation to rest squarely between them. Morris was glad to see his friend back up on the chair, reading, pondering... *being*. At last, the silence got to him.

"How do you feel?" It seemed a weak question, but he could think of none more important.

Aubrey set the book down atop a short stack on the side table and interlaced his fingers on his lap. He looked at the painting above Morris' head.

"You know," he began after a short pause. "I never much liked that piece. Richard's friend painted it. You remember Colm. He gave it to Richard as a present some years back, for what I don't recall. It's hung in every one of Richard's apartments since, and always in some unfortunately prominent spot. He likes it, I guess. It always made me squeamish."

Morris turned to view the thing for the thousandth time. It was not a scene easily forgotten. The creature's penetrating eyes looked down from its hideous head. He could virtually hear the teeth gnashing, smell the rancid breath.

"Charon's Obol," Morris recalled Richard's classical observation.

"Yes, but how did this demonic creature come to procure that particular token?" Aubrey ran his fingers over his smoothed chin, "From what poor, human soul did he thieve it and, assuming that he did, what foul beast steals a man's fare from the world of the living to the realm of the dead? Condemns his soul to wander the shore for a hundred years, else be flogged by the mighty oarsman himself?"

"Maybe he won it on a bet," Morris ventured, absently, "or in some kind of bargain?"

"A drunken Irishman's modern rendition of Mephistopheles?" Aubrey cocked his head and squinted his eyes. "Perhaps, though he's usually depicted with horns, appendages I can't imagine Colm omitting if he saw an opportunity to paint them. He's a devil himself, that one. No, I think this creature represents something more sinister. Something that feasts on the virtue of man, robs him of his own safe passage, enervates his vigor, his life force."

Aubrey took a deep breath and, steadying himself with both hands on the armrests, leaned back into his chair. His eyes were clear, like those of a man who has seen more than he can describe or even comprehend. A man driven to calm by wild things.

"It was the last thing I remember seeing before I fell to the floor. As I felt my endurance wane, the motion melt away from my arms. They felt stiff by my side. I tried to hold onto an image in my mind, something sweet and everlasting, from my childhood. I felt my father's heart in my own, my mother's lungs in my chest, the sinew of ancestry coursing through my veins, this helpless vessel, on loan from the past and fast depleting of future," he paused to allow himself a perplexed laugh. "Then I felt a sense of serenity like I've never known. Not like the asomatous experiences you sometimes hear of, flying up to the light, that sort of thing. Nothing incorporeal. Just a complete absence of fear and hate and urgency and boredom and pain and doubt," he stopped for a second and shrugged. "An unending moment of transcendence."

In no rush to escape the afterglow of this recollection, Aubrey closed his eyes and filled his vessel with oxygen. Morris saw his chest rise and fall, the heart beating again within it, the life force restored.

"It sounds..." the younger man began, but he could think of no words to add.

"Yes, exactly," replied Aubrey, seeing the look on Morris' face. "And then I felt something familiar taking over, the vision from my childhood, but authentic, palpable, like a dream so vivid you continue living it forever when you wake, something so real it takes over reality itself." He leaned forward on the chair once more, enthused by the image before him. Slowly, dreamily he spoke, painting the scene with carefully chosen words.

"I was sitting in the back seat of my parents' car, next to my sister. She was asleep, her peaceful countenance accentuated by the sun pouring in through the window. The red vinyl bench seat was cracked and faded at the corners, near the head rests. Outside the maples and alder and birch trees blazed in Technicolor streaks. My mother and father were talking over the radio up front, discussing which route to take. I could hear their conversation between the dancing melody. They always spoke in affectionate, amiable tones. Never once fought in front of us kids. Anyway, Mom wanted to take the scenic passage. She had an idea we could stop in a small town and grab ice cream and maybe take a walk around. I had the sense she wanted to discover something there, an antique, perhaps, some remnant of her past. Her voice carried in it something forlorn, as though she were expecting Dad's answer. Of course, he was all for staying on the Interstate. We were making good time, he reasoned. If we pressed on for a couple more hours, we could be at our destination in time for dinner. He was always so eager to get to where we were going. People who knew him well complained that he was always 'busy,' rushing here and there. Well, Mom made to say something, then let the moment pass, like she always did."

Aubrey sank back into the chair, a wistful look on his face. "I wonder what it was she wanted to find, in that small town in the middle of nowhere..."

Outside, the rain pelted away at the windows. Occasionally the slow roll of distant thunder would mute the lower register coming from the traffic below. Morris was glad to be inside, listening to his friend.

"Well, Celine will be back shortly," Aubrey came to, patting his knee. He seemed almost embarrassed that he had spoken so personally.

"You were in New England?" Morris asked.

"New England?" Aubrey puzzled as he returned to the scene. "Oh, yes. The ride. The maples and birch. Right. We used to take road trips all the time. And all over the country, too. Dad was always fixated on the destinations, but Mom made sure we saw plenty of beauty, too. The Kancamangus up in New Hampshire... One-O-One, between Port Orford and Brookings along the North West coast. The Lehmi Pass out in Big Sky country. There's a lot to see here," Aubrey paused, noting his listener's captivated expression. "America is not a country, Morris. It's a world. Henry James said that."

228

Morris was silent, his imagination roaming the myriad trails and drives and ridges branching out across the world at his feet.

"So," Aubrey continued, as if to change the subject, "I'm going to be taking it easy for the next few weeks. Plodding around the apartment. Convalescing. Following doctor's orders and so forth."

"Now *that's* a sensible course of action," agreed Morris.

Aubrey grinned. "Well, for the most part the office will be closed. So, there's not going to be a lot of work for you here in the City. I'm wondering if perhaps you'd like to head up to my home in Westchester for a while. Water the plants. Collect the mail. Say 'G'day' to the neighbors. That kind of thing. I won't be able to get up there, obviously, so the place will be all yours," he reflected somewhat before adding, "You would be doing me a big favor."

Just then the front door opened down the hall and Celine's voice raced the aroma of her offerings into the living room, "Bagels and cafe for all," she cried. "Gene's special!"

Morris smiled when she threw a happy, wide-eyed greeting around the corner. Then he turned to Aubrey, who seemed restful, contented. "Of course, Aubrey. I'd love to."

"Very good," he replied, evidently pleased with his plan. "You'll like it up there. Very relaxing. It's where I go to think. To reconnect."

Surely, he meant to say 'disconnect,' thought Morris, but he let the moment pass. Celine was relaying to and from the kitchen, laying out the breakfast spread on the coffee table. Aubrey watched her move, his splendid Parisian butterfly. Finally, he turned to Morris, and to the painting over his head.

"You know," he nodded pensively, "I think I'm going to ask Richard to get rid of this awful thing. It's time for something beautiful."

The storm grew until it stretched over the whole of the afternoon. After an unhurried brunch with the others, where in contrast to the raging weather outside the mood was light and cheerful, Morris retired to the privacy of his own room. Absently, he ran his fingers along the spines of the books collected on his shelves. With tapping forefinger, he drew them out at random and, peeling the pages back, read a line or two aloud...

"This is a delicious evening, when the whole body is one sense, and imbibes delight through every pore..."

"It was a deluge of winter in the Salinas Valley, wet and wonderful. The rains fell gently and soaked in and did not freshet..."

"The funeral games were over. Men dispersed And turned their thoughts to supper in their quarters, Then to the boon of slumber..."

...and replaced them as one might glass ornaments on a wealthy host's armoire. After a while, he plonked himself on the bed and listened to the sky as it emptied onto the sidewalks and parking lots and harried black umbrellas, jousting on the streets below. He really should begin work on his own book, the thought occurred to him, at least formulating ideas and developing the characters who would carry them through the pages. Maybe he would use the time in Westchester to go over what he had begun in Baltimore, see if there was something in his scattered notes, a flicker, a spark with which he could ignite and new and exciting narrative.

He would begin the story, as he had always planned to, by delving into the mind of a young, displaced writer. Someone who, not unlike himself, had far more questions than answers, who needed guidance as much as freedom, whose perspective of the constantly changing world around him was occasionally open to interpretation and always susceptible to influence. His thoughts glided over the myriad possible settings for his tale, through epic cities and bucolic towns, over expansive bridges and down winding country roads, in and out of glitzy hotel bars and beneath fiery sunsets collapsing into vast, rolling pastures. He saw stretched out before him a map of the world, then he narrowed in on the area north of the great metropolis where he lay, followed a path through a yellow wood and, finally, felt the autumnal foliage crackling softly under his boots.

The next morning, after a long and fitful night's slumber, Morris boarded the MetroNorth train bound for Westchester.

#

Alighting from his carriage, Morris fell in with a thin procession of trench coats and Sunday editions and damp shoes as it shuffled along the platform. The smell of wet leather and brake fluid filled the atmosphere, then dissipated in the first gush of cool, fall air. Feeling the blood rush to his legs, Morris lit a cigarette and pulled a light jacket over his shoulders.

Any lingering sense of urgency held over from the city had faded into the train's gentle lulling. With an unhurried gait he followed the passengers through the station and out to the parking lot, where he espied, as per Aubrey's instructions, an old green Jeep at the far end of the lot.

For a long time, Morris sat motionless at the wheel, keys in the ignition, watching the other cars as they idled at the gate and then, exhaust blending into the surrounding mist, inched out onto open roads. He fidgeted with the stereo until an unfamiliar female voice finally sang it to life...

> *When morning comes to Morgantown*
> *The merchants roll their awnings down*
> *The milk trucks make their morning rounds*
> *In morning, Morgantown...*

In the glove compartment he found a heavily creased map and, matching its spindly roads up with the instructions in hand, set it down on the passenger side seat. Adjusting the rearview mirrors, he watched the station shrink into the distance; once a point of arrival and, now, of departure. The road ahead passed beneath the green hood more or less without interruption and, in the time it took to familiarize himself with the vehicle's idiosyncrasies (and driving on the "wrong"/right side of the road), Morris was out of the immediate area and into less constricted spaces. The house was a half hour drive if he drove there directly, which he had no intention of doing.

Aubrey had given him a few points of interest; the closest gas station, drugstore and food market, the name of a few nearby cafes and one decent restaurant, a general store at the bottom of the hill where he could stock up on essentials ("But please, don't buy any wine or liquor. You'll find plenty of bottles under the stairs...") and a hardware store, should he need it. They hadn't discussed specific timeframes for the stay, though it would hardly have impacted Morris' planning. Into his duffle bag he had stuffed a half dozen button down shirts, a couple of pairs of pants, underwear, a notepad, three or four books he hadn't yet read and one he planned on rereading, and a toothbrush, which needed replacing in any case. Supplies enough for a weekend, or a year.

With nothing but time and space before him, Morris guided the Jeep slowly through the countryside, occasionally pulling over to the shoulder of the road to allow purpose-bound drivers the right of passage. On a ridge that overlooked an empty sports field in the valley just below, he got out of the car and stood a while in the cooling breeze, sensing its movement as it felt its way through the dappled canopy. The leaves, emitting vitality from yellow to orange to red and, finally, indifferent brown, were beginning to gather in loose little piles at the bases of trees and fence posts. The rock underfoot, he noticed, was of the same grey schist on which Manhattan was founded, that broke through the fields in Central Park and pinned the great city to the ocean's floor. He butted his cigarette on an exposed crag, watching the sparks extinguish fully before returning to the road.

Immersed in reverie, he almost missed the turnoff leading up to Aubrey's house. His host's generous offer notwithstanding, Morris called into the general store at the bottom of the hill just the same, determined to at least leave the liquor cabinet in the state he found it. Besides, he needed cigarettes.

A doorbell, trembling on the end of its curved brass handle, announced Morris to the shopkeeper as he entered. In no particular hurry, a grey-haired figure in denim and flannelette emerged from behind a stack of boxes. He had a box cutter in hand, which he set down casually on the counter as he approached it.

"What can I do ya for this fine day," he inquired in friendly, small town tones.

"Ah, well...just the staples, I think," replied Morris, squinting as his eyes adjusted to the store's dim, dusted light.

The man pointed as he spoke. "Sodas and mixers in the fridges by the back wall; jerky, nuts, assorted snacks over by the window; liquor and cigarettes, they're back here, behind the counter."

Morris fingered the keys in his palm. It struck him that he had no name here, in this place, this street, this store in which he had never before stood. He might be Jim or Greg or Buddy. He smiled awkwardly at the waiting attendant.

"In that case, I guess I'll start at the back and work my way forward," Morris tipped an imaginary hat. "Thank you, sir."

An assortment of the aforementioned staples in brown paper bags on the back seat, Morris stared out the windscreen at the little shop in front of him. The kindly man was back to work, stacking boxes, cutting tape, shelving inventory. Morris thought of the vacant horizon that was his own afternoon. He had only one item on his agenda - to arrive at Aubrey's house - with no particular time affixed to its execution. Suddenly he had a near overwhelming desire to scrap even that modest plan, to simply drop the car at the bottom of the driveway, thumb it to the next town and see what happened. Maybe he could find work stacking boxes and cutting tape, or rewinding and renting out old videos, or threshing cereal with a worn-down flail.

Across the street he noticed an elderly man attempting to deposit a package in a blue U.S. Postal mailbox. It must have been right on the dimension limit, as he was having some difficulty fitting it through the slot. Morris reached for the door handle, imagining himself the good Samaritan approaching the struggling fellow, waving, helping him hoist the twine-tied package to just the angle that would see it smoothly through the metal aperture when, to his slight disappointment, the man managed to deposit the parcel with one, hefty, last-ditch effort.

Morris sat back in his seat and surveyed the area. He waited a minute... then five... then ten. Seeing no other scenario during that time in which he could imagine himself helpful, he proceeded up the hill to Aubrey's house where, to his disproportionate relief, he found no small pleasure in ticking off the lonesome item on his to-do list.

#

The gabled roof, set amidst climbing, uneven columns of oak and birch, was barely visible from the road. So too were the neighboring houses tucked roughly into the bristled hillside, resulting in a seclusion that gave the whole area a sense of quiet and solitude. Behind the brown, split-rail fence set back from the roadside, a meandering driveway led from the fissured asphalt up a fairly steep incline and, skirting around rocky outcroppings and the occasional tree stump, arrived to a double garage of white doors and grey shingled siding.

The main house, adjacent and of identical tone and material, was spacious enough, though far from opulent. Set over two levels - the lower featuring the main entertaining areas, including an expansive, open plan kitchen which looked directly down the front yard; the upper reserved for living quarters and an office with views over the hillside across the larger, rear of the property - it was not at all as Morris had pictured it. For some reason he had in his mind a sort of cottage retreat, something on a lake, perhaps, with a smoking chimney and a jetty leading off the front porch, a fishing line or two cast out from the landing into the rippling, silvery surface below. Something like Thoreau's Walden, only with less vegetable patch and more than three chairs "for society." He was alternately disappointed then delighted to discover in the place all the modern comforts of American living. After all, he told himself as he loaded the fridge doors with ale and bock, not everyone finds Zen in the middle of a hand-hewn log cabin.

After an hour or less spent wandering around outside, smoking, soliloquizing, poking anthills and scattered bark and wild tussocks with a branch, Morris headed back to the house. There he sat on the porch for a while, drinking a bottle of beer and listening to the birds in the trees and the occasional vehicle winding through the pass below. The afternoon grew still around him, a soft light painting the trunks and shingle siding and spilling over onto the rugged earth squeezing the driveway. From somewhere down the hill came the faint aroma of country cooking, pumpkin pie and cornbread and gravy. They brought Aubrey's instructions to mind and, locating the freezer in the garage, Morris took out meat enough for the next few days. Steaks, sausages, a pork shoulder. Then, going through the fridge and pantry, he made a mental list of fresh ingredients he would need from the market. He drank another beer on the porch, pacing its length and kicking a rock along the rough wooden boards. Following the clump of earth off the end of the porch, he noticed a ruby-throated hummingbird had come to hover by a feeder near the far railing. It dipped its needle beak a few times but, finding no fresh nectar, soon darted off between the shrubs and tree stumps. Morris followed it out of view, then went back inside and checked the clock. He had been at the house less than two hours.

Back on the porch, with one of Aubrey's records playing out through the opened kitchen windows, Morris began to think of the land and people around him. No doubt the area was home to a good many commuters who worked in the city but, like Aubrey, kept a place, a retreat, within reach where they could go to relax and unwind. They were said to be *in* the area, but not *of* it. Then there would be others, he assumed, whose parents had grown up here, maybe even their parents' parents, too. And so on down the line. These were the locals who watched the seasons pass and measured the years with the turning of the leaves and the coming and going of the migratory birds. They would recognize familiar faces in the main town, at the grocer's, the post office, the bakery. They would call the Little League coach by first name when they ran into him at the store, remembering fondly his guidance at some crucial point of a long distant game, perhaps even one from their own childhood in which they hit the winning run or mitted the winning catch. They would pass by trees with memories etched in the bark and feel a pang of jealousy when espying an ex-flame across a restaurant years later, her kindly aged face set aglow by the eternal, unyielding company of her loving and devoted husband. They would each bow their heads in discreet, respectful recognition, then return to their own conversations, their own dreams and lives and responsibilities. Familiarity and fraternity and frailty. And family. There were counties and communities like this across the country, of course. And abroad, too. Villages and hamlets and parishes with roots all the way to the center of the earth.

A distant vehicle shifted gears as it climbed through the pass and over the ridge. Following the fading motor beyond the hills, imagining for its churning cogs and firing pistons both a driver and a destination, Morris considered the nature of personal journey, of individual motivation. Unmistakably, there were those drawn to breadth of experience, whose humming engines drove them to far-off lands, who sought trial and adventure and ordeal on unfamiliar shores and with persons unknown. They worked with broad brushstrokes, painterly in style, loose and free flowing. Essentially impressionist, their canvasses conveyed as much through the light and space between the subjects as from the form and composition itself. To this group Morris assigned the itinerants, flaneurs, treasure hunters, artists and assorted other peripatetic intellectuals. Also the drifters, hobos and buskers, the tramps and weirdos and the roaming, socio-anthropological cartographers. The dreamers.

Under a second subheading, marked "Depth," he listed doctor, shopkeeper, police officer, schoolteacher, accountant, lawyer, minister, mayor, post office worker...but all that was largely irrelevant. Importantly, what defined this group was not the title of their vocation. More than doctor, shopkeeper, police officer, etc., these people were father, mother, friend, coach, mentor, big sister, little brother, confidante, drinking buddy, and plenty more besides. They were "around" such that they got to know a limited place, and its inhabitants, in depth. Likewise did their (relatively) intimate community come to know a little something about them, too. Mention of their name around the barbecue or children's soccer game or school play evoked certain adjectives; dependable, honest, reliable...scoundrel. For better or worse, they were *of* their area, inseparable from their natural habitat. Unlike their footloose, impressionistic counterparts, these folks worked slowly, methodically, affording every detail its proper attention. They were linear painters who focused on a much smaller surface area, more concerned with getting it right than trying it over, anew.

Morris thought of the different people in his own life and what category they best suited. Some craved a little of a lot, others a lot of a little. It all came down to personal preference, of course. And who was he, one man, alone on a hill, to judge any life but his own?

Morris felt the afternoon sun warming his face. He dozed a while and woke again, peacefully, when the cool breeze returned just on dusk. Inside, the record spun silently on its turntable, a soundtrack to his suspended consciousness. Tallying the emptied bottles on the kitchen counter, he decided it was probably better he didn't drive all the way back into town to visit the market, if it was even open at this hour. Rather, he would have a quiet dinner at the little restaurant Aubrey recommended, which, according to the map, was less than half way down the hill. He waited until ten minutes before opening time, then shouldered his jacket and stepped out into the ebbing twilight. Moments later, the old green Jeep was swerving and rolling gently down the slope, the quiet of night following closely behind.

#

Most of the clientele, Morris noted between measured sips of his house-red-by-the-glass, came in elderly pairs through the side door, from the adjoining bed and breakfast. As if by some unwritten agreement, the male partners wore dress pants in uniform browns and beiges, hitched high on the waist, and dinner jackets which, better suited to later in the season, were soon slung over the backs of the chairs. The women, likewise in accord regarding dinner appropriate attire, came in a series of floral blouses, silver brooches and knee-length skirts or dresses that neither offended taste nor excited sensibility. Only those who entered through the front doors, the locals whose SUVs and pickups filled the gravel parking lot outside, wore jeans and shirt sleeves rolled to the elbows. These men and women alike waved in friendly gestures toward the bar and called to "Betz" by her diminutive.

Morris ordered from the daily specials board - seasonal vegetable soup with ale and cheddar biscuits followed by lamb chops with new potatoes - and allowed Betty to talk

239

him into trying a cabernet franc from somewhere upstate at no additional cost.

"Trust me," smiled the lean, middle-aged woman as she poured his glass with a free and happy wrist, "If you really don' like it, 'n I mean absolutely hate it, I'll give you the resta' the bottle, on the house."

"By why would I want..." Morris caught the joke before he could rewind his reply.

Betty laughed easily, the soft creases at the corners of her eyes deepening along familiar, upturned grooves. She and her husband, A.J., the cook, had been there so long the locals couldn't envision the place without their handwriting on the chalkboard menu. "Why, we've been here since, since..."

"Since before my folks' folks been coming here!" an ancient man seated next to Morris at the bar exclaimed, seemingly out of nowhere. Morris did a double take. No way that adds up, he reasoned. Betty couldn't be too far into her fifties. This fellow was clearly much older than that. His grandparents, they must have been... Again the locals laughed, signaling to Morris that there was no harm in their playful banter. When he was full of dinner and wine, he ordered a port wine and settled into his new surroundings.

Apart from a few stragglers and a conspicuously affectionate couple in a booth by the rear, much younger in manner and years than the since-retired early birds, the place had all but emptied out. Morris watched the amorous duo from the corner of his eye. He tried not to think of the big, empty house back up the hill.

"You headed far tonight, young man?" He turned to find Betty eyeing him carefully. Her look was kind, maternal, rather than reproving.

"Just up the hill, ma'am," he assured her. "I'm house sitting a little while for a friend."

"Wouldn't be Aubrey Fields's place, would it?" the old man beside him broke in again.

"Yes, as a matter of fact." Morris nodded. "How'd you know?"

"There's only six houses up the hill," Betty explained with the aid of five fingers and a fork, "four of 'em inhabited by folks even older'n Georgey Boy here. The fifth of 'em being his own handsome dwelling. And the last," here she was down to the utensil, "well, that one's belongin' to Aubrey."

Arm in arm, the young lovebirds made their way past the bar and, in a series of bashful mutterings, said their goodbyes as they stumbled through the side door to their waiting upstairs room. Morris winced, then immediately regretted his envy. Betty threw George a look as if to say, "Kids these days!" but he missed it and turned instead to the young man at the bar beside him.

"Say, we haven't seen Aubrey in for a while. Everything alright with him?" There was a hint of concern in his voice, such as conveyed by widows and widowers when asking after good friends they haven't seen for a while. "I know he works an awful lot," he assuaged his own doubts, before doubling back to them. "Not too much though, I hope..."

Morris noticed Betty leaning in for his response, idly polishing the same square foot of counter over and again. He settled the words in his throat before answering.

"Fine, yes. Excellent, in fact." Then, not wanting to oversell the statement, he added, with a disapproving shake of the head, "Of course, he does work an awful lot. But he's learning to relax, to stop and appreciate the...the beauty in life."

"He's a good boy, that Aubrey," George nodded, affirming his own judgment. Then his look turned to one of measured consternation, "But just like his father, he's always busy. Busy, busy, busy."

"You know Aubrey's father?" Morris caught Betty's downcast look the moment the inquiry escaped his lips.

"I knew both his parents," said George. "If only briefly..."

Morris felt the atmosphere tighten. The last of the cars could be heard leaving the parking lot outside. Betty and George exchanged furtive glances before, finally, she broke the silence.

"They came out here in, goodness, it musta been the fall of '75. Real nice folk. Honest folk. Not flashy, know-it-alls like some West Coast types I've known. Well..." she looked to George for assistance.

"They'd been here a few months, hardly more." The old man blinked over cloudy, pale eyes. "I guess they weren't real familiar with the weather an' the roads an'... Well, it weren't nobody's fault, mind. The road just iced over the night b'fore. Happened not too far from here, on the ridge over by the Simmons' place. They just..." he looked up at Betz, who lowered her shaking head and let out a sorrowful sigh.

"Well, it was instant. Both of 'em, gone from this world together."

Morris mouthed something he couldn't remember. His mind turned immediately to the photograph in Aubrey's office, the fatherly hand resting on his son's shoulder, unconcerned for the immediate future; the daughter cut from her mother's fresh, optimistic look. They would have been young, those new orphans, in their mid-twenties and with nobody running between them and the long relay into the ground.

"Aubrey came out a short while later to take care of the family affairs." The kindly woman concentrated her focus on the cloth as she pushed it along the wooden bar. "We saw the sister - what was her name? Melanie? Melissa? Anyway... - she came out a few times at first, then not at all. Pretty much it's been Aubrey keeping the place up since. Of course, he has his own life in the city. It's been a burden, I guess. All those years. Still, we love to see him when he makes it out, don't we, George?"

"Such a good boy." The old man stared vacantly into his own memory, deep and detailed. "Busy boys. Busy, busy, busy."

#

Aubrey's parents visited Morris more than once over the following days and weeks. Sometimes they appeared in the front yard while he stared through the kitchen window, washing the dishes or cutting vegetables. Other times they joined in the reverie of his afternoon walks around the back of the property or came to him on the porch as he dozed after reading or writing a few pages, an empty beer bottle in hand. He thought about the short time they spent there, far from their roots back west. In new, unbroken boots they would have cleared away the brush, split firewood and made hopeful plans for the future. Morris read them in the books on the shelves and heard them singing gaily along with the same old records Aubrey must have played a thousand times, over and again, year after sorrowful year.

It was hardly surprising, given that the family was never too far from mind, that when the son arrived at the driveway late one afternoon, alighting from a black Lincoln Towncar, Morris at first wondered if he had lost his mind completely. After all, he was older now, wider in breadth, if not depth, of experience. Even the self he knew from a year ago was no longer familiar, automatic. He wondered to what extent he could safely trust his own senses. For some reason he thought of Keats, dead at tender twenty-five. A treachery of youth. Did he go mad first? Morris wondered. Did it matter?

"Ah, nice and relaxed." Aubrey waved from the driveway as the Town Car slid off down the hillside behind him. Just as I'd hoped to find you. Only, I trust you didn't buy that wine."

Morris remembered the half-emptied cabernet franc beside him. A gift from Betty. "I saved you a glass," was all he could think to say.

For a long while they sat on the porch. They talked a little about Richard and Celine, about Baltimore and New York, about various experiences, deep and wide. But mostly, they talked not at all. Aubrey slowed easily to the pace of the surroundings, his mood settling into its familiar grooves.

"You've made a friend," he observed, noticing the red-gorgeted visitor hovering by the end of the porch.

"I bought the nectar from Joe, down at the general store," replied Morris, admiring the bird's natural instinct. "He said to replace it every three to five days. So far, so good. This little fellow returns around the same time every afternoon. He dips his beak a few times, then he flitters off down the hill, probably to some other feeder."

"And what about you?" Aubrey cast an un-characteristically vague question.

Morris thought a while before answering, unhurried by the moment. "I'm relaxed," he said at last. "You were right, of course; the time out here has done me good. It's a great place to think. And yet," he hesitated for a second, unsure quite how to express a feeling that had been welling inside of him for some time, maybe forever, "there's a certain anxiety. That's not the right word but... I feel like there's something more to do, like I'm on the precipice of something important, something meaningful and defining that will only be obvious in retrospect."

Aubrey split the remainder of the bottle between their two glasses, then reposed in patient silence. Morris searched the landscape, the same landscape he had pondered and probed, more or less in solitude, for the past few weeks. High along the ridge, the trees yielded their leaves to a restless wind blowing in from the north. The air was fresh, much cooler than when he arrived. Of a sudden he felt the wine, warm and easy in his head.

"All growth is a leap in the dark," said Aubrey at last. "A spontaneous, unpremeditated act without benefit of experience." He turned to Morris. "Henry Miller said that."

The pair sat in quietude a while longer, light dissolving from the great empty dome overhead.

"Do you ever think of leaving, Aubrey?" Morris shifted uneasily in his chair. "I mean, going someplace...else? You know, away from..."

"From the past?" Aubrey filled in the void with a respectful nod into the middle distance. He looked up at the darkness and let his shoulders sink under a deep sigh.

"Well, that's what I've come here to do, actually." He looked out at the winter-tinged gusts swirling between the branches. A peaceful expression came over his being.

"After all these years, I'm finally going home. I've only come to say, 'goodbye.'"

#

The early bird brigade had long since retired and whatever might be called the "dinner rush" of a Thursday night at Betty and A.J.'s little restaurant on the hill had slowed to a few satisfied tables. In twos and fours they lingered, conversing over coffees infused with Italian liqueurs and slices of fresh pecan pie and the sweet, viscous generosity of last harvest grapes. By the bar, a tall, smartly dressed man, equal parts *in* and *of* the town, made his toast to a gathering of familiar faces.

"I've been saving this particular case for a long time," he began, meeting each of the faces around him with a sincere expression of gratitude and warmth. "My parents, whom most of you knew, used to visit the vineyard out in Napa where this wine was produced - is still produced, actually. Mom and Dad would spend a week up there every harvest season, winding their way around the area, dropping into tasting rooms where and when the mood struck them. Thinking about it now," he raised an eyebrow, "it was probably the only week of the year I think she could get him to slow down and really appreciate his surroundings."

A respectful laughter rustled through the crowd like an eddy through fallen leaves. Heads nodded. A few eyes watered. Aubrey went on, "Oddly enough, I've never actually been to the Chateau, which is one of the oldest in the region, but for the longest time I felt like I knew the place just the same. You see, along with cases and cases of this very wine, enough to last us all a lifetime, no doubt, my parents would return with rich tales from their romantic, annual sojourns. And Mel and I would sit at the dining table, transfixed, as Mom described the rolling hillsides and the electric sunsets and Dad would talk about masonry and coopering and how they 'sure don't make things like they used to do.'

"Here! Here! to that," someone called from the periphery to a muffled chuckle.

"Well," he continued, "they truly loved it there and, I think, were it not for this place, where they'd always dreamed of owning a little patch of land and retiring, they might have made a home for themselves out west. I sometimes think of them there still, driving around in their old Town & Country wagon, eternally young at heart, sipping great vintages and generally enjoying life."

Aubrey swished the rich cabernet around his glass, then raised his head and held the vessel up to catch the light. The legs ran long and slow and ruby red.

"It's been almost a quarter of a century since they passed away, together. And there's not a day goes by when they're not on my mind. At first, I used to imagine what might have been, if they had taken a house in Napa instead, for example, or simply decided not to go out that one, particular day..." He shook his head, as if emptying the unanswered questions from his conscious mind.

"Now, I don't know if it's just me or it's part of getting older, but lately I've come to shift my perspective somewhat, to focus more on what might be, rather than what might have been. You all have been like a second family to me. George," he nodded in the old timer's direction, "Betty, A.J. All of you here, in your way, are my family. But the time has come for me to leave, to move on. And to tell you all to come visit me in California, where we'll share many more great vintages together."

He raised his glass and proclaimed, with unreserved emotion, "So a toast... To family. To friends. And to the road ahead."

The surrounding tables, having eavesdropped in on the speech, joined in the applause. Some of them stood. More than one wiped dry an unexpected tear. In blithe pronouncement, Betty invited them one and all for a glass of the house cabernet franc, saving Aubrey's case for a close and emotional circle.

"And here I never thought we'd get rid of you," George approached slowly and rested his hand on Aubrey's shoulder. The veins in his wiry arms were a purple-blue, his fingers crooked and weathered by time. But he clasped on tightly.

"Well, you know I've always been slow at taking hints," replied Aubrey then, placing his own hand on the older man's frail shoulder, he added, "Thank you, George. For everything." The men embraced and again the crowd applauded and brought their glasses together.

The revelry reached into the early morning, long after Betty closed the doors behind the last of the well-wishing strangers. The remaining friends, family now in the welling of the moment, exchanged anecdotes and fond memories, each suitably embellished through the prism of time and wine and good cheer. Morris watched in silence, nodding occasionally and fielding a question or two, but mostly listening to the recent history of a small-town community and their prodigal, if adopted, son.

#

Later that week, Aubrey signed over the title to his parent's property and, the very next morning, he and Morris were in the old green Jeep, headed toward the train station.

"What will you do with all your stuff?" Morris asked absently, his hands now comfortable on the wheel.

"I was thinking of paying a mover to haul it cross country," replied Aubrey, his attention seemingly occupied elsewhere. "But I'm starting to think that's not such a good idea."

"Oh, no?"

"Well, a lot of the furniture was there when my parents took the place, so it's not like I'm all that attached to it. There are a few items of sentimental value, books and records and the like, but I can have them shipped priority, or just pack them myself. The rest of it is just, as you said, 'stuff.' It seems silly to cart it around."

"And this ol' girl?" Morris said, tapping the dashboard.

"Well, I thought about that, too," Aubrey focused on the passenger side rearview mirror, a quarter of a century fast fading in its reflection. "I was actually hoping to find someone who might drive it out there for me. You know, someone who wouldn't mind taking the scenic route, seeing a bit of the country, maybe writing a page or two about his journey."

"I see," Morris laughed, acknowledging that plans were already afoot. "And how long were you thinking such a trip might take?"

"Well, I'll have to find an office out there, set it all up, maybe rent a small place by the beach," he struck a pensive expression. "Could take a while."

The autumnal scene peeled back over the windows in a flurry of oranges and reds, the season changing even as they drove on through it.

"As it so happens," Morris replied, seeing the road stretch out in front of him, "that's just how long I have."

#

249

PART III

Chapter XI

Enter, America

The air rushed by the windows, brisk and fresh, as Morris guided the old green jeep through the Lincoln Tunnel and over the imagined state line buried somewhere deep within the Hudson's cleaving gorge. Emerging from the darkness and into the rusted morning light, he adjusted the rearview mirror to deflect the glare, New York City's now-familiar skyline shrinking in its jolting reflection. Fall was in firm control of the atmosphere now, summer having surrendered its annual bid to merge the days into a single, blistering eternity. Before long the trees would appear bare against the slate-grey skies, Schiele's sickly distorted limbs climbing into the emptying heavens above.

Morris recalled the morning he came to New York, to America, in a trance. The gritty snow. His breath heavy in the air. The commuters hustling along well-worn routes. He remembered the taxi ride uptown, his jetlagged mind wandering though the cafes and laundromats and dive bars dotting the island's broad avenues, the mile-high buildings preserving a cacophony of life and energy and irrepressible vitality from the wintry sea of blacks and greys and dirty whites outside. And against that monochromatic scene, the green-eyed girl who had brought him there, seated across from him, her emerald gaze directed through the cab window, the skin on the back of her hand close enough to touch, to kiss... Many months had since passed by, he mused to himself as he steered the vehicle onto the new and unfamiliar road ahead.

Not for the first time Morris felt a peculiar surge of kinetic energy propelling him onward, the sense of movement swelling within his being, the world revolving beneath his feet, catapulting him across the arcs and slopes and ravines of her teaming continents and beyond the vast, melancholic oceans surging between. He thought of the moment at his fingertips, buzzing with imprisoned lightning. Behind him, the beacon-hand that had welcomed him to her sea-washed, sunset shores; before him the expanse of an idea, a particular notion of liberty and the waves of huddled masses that had spilled in earnest, tired and afraid and hopeful, over the harsh, untamed lands. In one way or another, all of humanity had found its way here, flailing, yearning, stumbling and rising again to determined knee. They came from lands holy and desecrated, some in shackles with the smell of death rancid in their nostrils, others in first class cabins with fat cigars between clenched teeth. They came for succor, for opportunity, for escape and to discover the unknown frontiers beyond their own lands and within their own hearts.

Brimming with nervous excitement, Morris followed the signs northwest along the 280, toward Eisenhower's grand Interstate. Though he had no intention of seeing the country from the concrete stretches of its primary arteries, he did feel an acute motivation to put some distance between himself and his immediate point of departure. It occurred to him that, until this moment, his journey had been guided, to varying degree, by a relay of co-pilots. First Katelyn, then Aubrey and, to a lesser extent Ben and Richard. Even Celine, in her own, unspoken way. All these characters had impacted his trajectory, though for better or worse he could not definitively say. With the wheel now firmly in his own two hands, reverberating with anticipation, he felt a supreme sense of relief.

There are precious few moments in life so free, so liberated, that even death herself cannot touch them. For Morris, this was one such moment. He tapped his fingers along with the beat of a vaguely familiar tune and considered the horizon opening before him. Beyond the first few turns, he had no specific route in mind. No fixed schedule. A man shot from a cannon, with no predetermined ballistics. And no possession he need turn back for if a sudden gust blew it out the Jeep's rear window. Even the car itself he could ditch, if absolutely necessary.

"It's not like I'm going to report it stolen," he recalled Aubrey's words from when he left the apartment that same morning. "Take your time and end up where you end up. And if that's not where I end up, you can owe me one old, albeit reliable, clunker. 'No worries,' as your countrymen would say."

Morris again considered his co-pilots and the impact they each had made on him.

"For better," he thought to himself as he opened the gas along the conquering Spaniard's namesake trail. Looking first over his shoulder, he pulled out around a merging truck and cruised past its shiny silver siding. The driver returned his salute as he crossed in front.

"Whatever confluence of events, of characters, has brought me to this moment, it has surely been for the better."

The sun rising at his back, Morris drove on for a spell, daydreaming across the burned hillsides and flicking through the local radio stations, from country to talk back to bible verses read in quavering voices by earnest, morally territorial men. The morning was dry and crisp and cool when the windows were lowered. A featureless sky stretched out above.

Cresting a red-blanketed ridge after a long, straight valley run, Morris saw on the other side a small town huddled against the banks of a nameless river. Without notice, an irrepressible urge overtook him. He dropped the vehicle into neutral and let it roll on under his feet, veering to the right as it slowed onto the side ramp. Soon the town was all around him; pretty, quaint. Any other day he might have found a spot to park, taken a stroll around the square, up and down the main street, in and out of bric-a-brac shops and the inevitable general store. Not this day. Spurred by an automatic focus, he proceeded directly to the riverside, where he parked on the grass under the spindly branches of a black cherry tree. Without looking around, he stripped down to his underwear and waded into the waters, the time-smoothed pebbles sifting themselves into new shapes under his step. When he was submerged to his waist, he raised his hands above his head, lengthening his neck and allowing his jaw to fall open, as if to catch unseen rain. The water, fresh and clear, shifted his weight on the rocks. Lungs full of chaste country air, he drew his arms akimbo and dove, headlong, into the current. For a second all was silent, except for the sound of the water rushing over his body, over the riverbed, over the country beneath him.

He swam until the water was no longer cold, alternating between the different strokes recalled from childhood, feeling his muscles stretch and his bare skin warm in the sun's lengthening rays. He felt his heart beat strong and young, the rich, oxygenated blood flowing into his hands, his feet, his temples. He dove again, this time keeping his eyes open. The crystal liquid washed the rust from his shoulders, washed clean his eyes, washed a thousand lifetimes from the fore of his mind. With smooth strokes he cut through the water, his elongated torso pulling and rotating along his spine, arms plunging into the depths, wrist to elbow to shoulder, feeling the full power and leverage of his body. Then he was still, calm. He floated, face down, watching the riverbed pass beneath him at alternating depths. After a while the air in his lungs grew tight. Still he waited, allowing the pressure to build inside him. When at last he was on the verge of a final, involuntary gasp, he let forth in a barrage of froth and aqueous tumult a submerged below from the absolute pit of his soul.

In soft, concentric circles, the ripples flowed outward from their source before drowning on the long journey to shore. The surface soon returned to calm, bathed once more in the stillness of a late fall morning.

Drying his body in the sunshine, Morris at last pulled on his clothes and climbed back into the Jeep. A few moments later he crossed the concrete bridge headed west, the droplets drying in his hair and the light still playing on the racing current below.

#

The sun was high in a cloudless sky when Morris pulled into a gas station in midway Pennsylvania. He checked the time. For nearly three hours he had driven practically dead straight, the impatience of man and his inbuilt imperative to domesticate nature seeing to it that not one unnecessary inch lay between him and the precise spot at which he presently stood.

"Just the water, thanks." He placed the bottles on the bench in front of him. A woman with matchbox red hair, perhaps in her mid-thirties but with older, hard pressed features, surveyed him with a mixture of suspicion and ambivalence. In the end, the latter won out and she transacted the purchase without further interrogation. Only when he reached the door did she call after him.

"You need a lottery ticket, too?"

He looked around and saw there was nobody else in the store. "I beg your pardon?" The door wheezed shut behind him.

"A lottery ticket." Somehow the woman managed simultaneously to scowl and smile. Morris couldn't decide which was the dominant aspect.

"This Thursday's the big draw. Jackpot's set for twenty million. That's a record. Well, is for this state anyway." She took another look at him and the angle of her brow made Morris think the earlier expression was majority scowl. "Where you from?" She looked down a long, steep nose.

"Outta state," came the reply in an accent she hadn't before heard.

A few partisan talkback segments later, the water long since emptied and the lottery ticket flapping in the breeze on the passenger side seat, Morris began to regret not having purchased anything to eat. There were fast food outlets dotted at various intervals along the highway, but somehow their appeal diminished in direct proportion to their repetition. Eventually he decided it was time to stray from the Spaniard's trail and, eschewing the familiar logos perched high above familiar roofs along familiar strip malls, he steered the Jeep off the highway and onto a smaller route. He happily hummed an impromptu ditty as he folded the roadmap along its worn crease and buried it in the glove compartment. Within a half hour he was downtown somewhere, passing streets known to all American communities of a certain size; Elm, Fairview, Market, Front...and the rest. With no guidance save for the gnawing severity of his own hunger, he pulled into the gravel parking lot of the first beanery he found. A sign above the front door read, simply, "Sal's."

Taking a seat at the short length of a long, L-shaped bar, Morris surveyed the hardscrabble men seated in their customary, well known positions down the line. One or two turned their heads when he ordered a beer. The others registered his presence in automatic silence. They had been there forever, these men, in trucker caps and uniforms of denim and flannel and three-day beards. In comfortable quietude they passed their lunch hours and happy hours and closing hours. And all the hours in between. The days had settled deep into their brows, Appalachian and Alleghany and Pocono ranges cut to the consternation and resignation of a greying cohort of working, grinding lifetimes.

These men drank black Folgers in the morning and Yuengling & Sons after lunch and smoked Marlboro Reds all day long. They ate their bacon undercooked from a cast iron skillet and, when the winter was hard and the income scant, took oatmeal instead for breakfast without complaint. Or nothing at all. They distrusted lattes and craft brews and Chinese food, though they ate the latter just the same. They loved and would defend with sudden, coiled reflex the lofty idea of the American dream, only vaguely aware that it had long passed them by, the capital and rewards of their industries having accrued to anonymous men in shiny suits on Wall Street and Madison Avenue.

At home, their wives despaired of the great men they had lost, to depression, to drink, to boredom and withdrawal and the attrition of one disappointment following another to the point of utter banality. Occasionally, they saw a glint in the eye; when sons brought grandchildren to the family home; when a football team completed a vintage play; when a passing politician made townhall promises to bring back their jobs and reinstall a sense of purpose, dignity, self-sufficiency.

"We ain't lookin' fer no handouts," they'd chime at the bar afterward. "Jus' the chance to do an hones' day's work fer an hones' day's pay is all."

But these moments of optimism were fleeting, even under the magnifying vigilance of loving, misty-eyed wives. The team's form varied from season to season, but the game they played had fundamentally changed. New tactics, new rules, new drugs and technologies and new brash, showy personalities. New ways of making complicated even the simplest of pleasures.

The politicians, by contrast, were reliably, universally cut from the same cloth. Through the years the weight of their heartfelt pledges became less and less, so that even the slickest, most earnest, most carefully manufactured remarks barely raised a pulse. The men simply nodded, raised their glasses to "change" at Sal's after the meetings, and bid each other farewell until tomorrow, when everything would be the same as it ever was.

Still, the future had a way of getting out from under them too. Visiting sons returned from coastal cities with kids and ideas and theories of their own. They had bachelor's degrees and hybrid cars and pretty wives who weren't afraid to dive into the deep end of the dining table conversation. Their hands were smooth, their outlook certain, as if forged in the crucible of years beyond their own.

"It just doesn't work like that anymore, pops," they'd say, softening the sharp end of a point just won. "Anyway, we'll try and make it out again in the summer, when the kids are off school and work eases up some. You take care of mom now, and yourself."

Morris ordered a second beer and the same daily special that had been on the board for as long as anyone there could remember. He considered what it might mean to enjoy a sense of comfort, then to have that comfort disrupted either by sudden impact, by some unseen, cataclysmic event, or by the gradual abrading processes of time and nature itself. He tried to imagine all the ways America was in the youth of the present men, how their daily lives were filled with warmth and health and the nourishing sense of usefulness, and how that had all come to pass in the shadow of fear and uncertainty and looming obsolescence.

Man, empire, constellations, all these things would eventually return whence they came, their dying light screaming down the darkening hall of subsequent generations, beyond the reimagined borders of nascent, breakaway states and inchoate economic models, across the light-years inflating between one galaxy and the next, accelerating towards the final frontiers of time and space, bound for the ultimate source, an ageless, everlasting origin. Shot from and destined for apeiron.

Morris finished his pint and motioned for the check. Off to the side of the bar, above a cigarette machine with an "Out of Order" sign peeling off its coin slot, a television buzzed with the weather forecast. A cold front was due in from the northwest later that week. Rain and falling temperatures were expected to follow.

He looked out across the straight cut states, blue and red arrows indicating the climatological patterns swirling overhead, uncountable atoms in perpetual flux. Tomorrow he would be in another town, another state. As for next week, next month...

Upon the counter Morris left a fair tip and a claim on that Thursday's record setting jackpot.

#

That first day Morris drove on until the sun overtook him and, teetering for an uncertain moment, disappeared beyond the fast-cooling horizon. His toe resting on the gas, he didn't stop in towns like Claysburg and Johnstown and Latrobe. Nor did he then, or ever after, visit Monroesville or Bethel Park or Prosperity. Signs to those towns and many besides passed him by while his mind drifted between other matters. He thought for a long time about the men in Sal's bar and the fading light in their eyes. He thought about communities torn asunder or wrenched apart, clinging to rusted industries standing proud and vacant and useless in the evening air.

It was a curious thing, Morris reckoned as he watched the light recede over a parade of gas stations and into the distance, to watch a man age before his time, to see the long dormant process accelerate suddenly, the slow climb to middle age an eternity compared with the sharp descent of the back slope. Avoiding the rearview mirror, Morris wondered what he, himself, might look like given the passage of time that had washed over these men.

As always, he was unable to form a definite picture in his mind, not of the person he might become, nor where and with whom he might spend his dwindling, unrepeatable days. Conversely, he could, without any difficulty at all, imagine an infinite number of possible futures for those around him. He practiced this little thought experiment from time to time. For friends. For loose acquaintances. For random people he saw seated at bars and in cafes and stranded at cold, windy bus stops. Sometimes his foretellings were of a propitious nature; other times they involved scenes and circumstances decidedly more macabre. An oncoming truck veering off the shoulder, crashing over the matchstick guardrails and into the gaping ravine below. Or an elevator snapped free from its cables, plummeting down a dark and unforgiving shaft. It was at these times he was glad that reality was not subject to the whimsy of idle imaginations and that, however vivid or conceivable they might be, his reveries were in no way predictive.

Life may be something lived in the moment, he thought to himself as a passing tanker truck did not swerve across the island and engulf the parallel line of traffic in a monstrous fireball, but it was a phenomenon constantly imagined into existence, one thought following another, one white line bleeding into the next, a series of reflections angling eagerly toward the future.

His thoughts drifted on aimlessly until the onset of fatigue shook him alert. He checked the highway signs and discovered himself careening across West Virginia's northernmost isthmus, a tiny needle bounded by Pennsylvania to the east and Ohio dead ahead. Willing himself on toward the frontier river, he cruised past sleepy Bethlehem and down the Appalachian foothills into Wheeling. There, the friendly proprietor of a roadside motel outlined the details of a continental breakfast (served daily in the hall between seven and nine A.M.) and handed him a map, through which Morris politely thumbed before, what seemed like seconds later, collapsing onto the blanket of a double bed in a single room. He felt himself falling over the guardrails, off the bridge, into the darkness below. Sleep overtook him instantly.

#

The following morning the air was fresh and dry and clear enough that the sunlight, pouring down the golden hillsides and into the Ohio River below, appeared as a wildfire sweeping across the land. On the water it sparkled in brilliant white glare, before dissipating among the fields and planes of the great earthen mass beyond. The blunt hum of traffic occupied the lower registers, punctuated occasionally, irreverently by a whooping bird or an impatient driver.

Bleary-eyed, Morris emerged from his room shortly after daybreak to find a half- dozen bikers inspecting their steeds in the parking lot. They conversed in furtive, almost conspiratorial tones, as if they were planning a surprise raid on a nearby village. After some final points of stratagem, discussed over a large map unfolded on the hood of someone else's SUV, they roared off down the way, over the old suspension bridge and into the distance. Morris finished his cigarette then made his way, book in hand, in the direction of drip coffee, plastic wrapped muffins and stale cereal held captive in little glass silos.

Clad in retrograde orange and lime greens, the breakfast room itself was uninspired, though not altogether uninspiring. A few early risers milled around the coffee pots and chatted at their tables in hushed, morning voices. Morris took a table by the window and, looking through the glass and down over the red brick houses dotting the hillside, promptly lost himself somewhere beyond the middle distance.

Who were these people, living in these houses, commuting along these roads, pushing their children on these swings and kissing under these trees? What stories were told of their lives and experiences, what lies shared and rumors spread, what blissful beginnings and quaint coincidences and good intentions lay among them?

Morris recalled a scene from his own childhood. He was running down a hill out back of his primary school. The turf was sparse upon the hard, dry earth and his legs jolted with the impact of every step, sending warm shocks through his body as he careened toward the field below. Someone was chasing him, a friend, perhaps, or a teammate. Probably he was playing a game of some kind; red rover or bull rush or whatever they called it that semester to skirt the teacher's rules. The hill was long and uneven in sporadic shade, with bumps and bulges and lots of places to trip and fall. Great eucalyptus and flimsy melaleuca raced by his periphery in a parade of peeling whites and greens and twisted, thirsty browns. Bounding by their painted trunks, he skipped over gnarled roots as he sped down the hillside. The summer air rushed against his face, full of the fragrant gum. After a while, he forgot entirely about the reason he was running. All he could see was the vast yellow field below, stretching out beyond the barbed wire fence at the bottom of the hill and across the valley to the darkened copse at the bottom of the next rise. The familiar blue haze draped itself carelessly across the canopy.

Arms flailing like windmill blades, he slowed to a panting halt. High above, a breeze rustled through the leaves and the giant gums bent and groaned beneath fearsome azure skies. The crows were squawking off in the distance. Morris let his breath catch up. He had never before been all the way to the bottom of the hill. He took the fence wire in his hand, releasing it quickly when he felt the metal begin to burn his skin. The boundary line extended all the way along the field, at the end of which there stood a small wood shed, said by all who knew about such things to be haunted. He wandered along the frontier, alone on the edge of the school's property and the dreaded "out of bounds" line.

Coming upon the weathered structure, clearly uninhabited and with weeds creeping between the gap-toothed paneling, he noticed a small yard cordoned off to the side. The grass there was overgrown and restless against the wind. Looking around to make double sure nobody was watching, he crawled under the wire fence and waded through the whispering blades. In the middle he found a clearing of no more than a few square yards. At the head of the rectangular space, a pair of granite tombstones leaned in toward one and other. Morris approached them from the side, so as not to walk directly over what must lay beneath. He read the engraving to himself. Husband and wife, he supposed. The latter had died less than two years after her partner. Both perished young and in lean years, many summers ago. He thought of their life here, amid the swaying melaleuca trees, the murderous crows sounding off in the stark, unending afternoons. Did they have children, this pair, or was this the end of their line, two lifeless stones in an unvisited clod of red clay. A wave of sadness welled inside him, but he could not be moved to cry.

Under the metal-hot Australian sun, the young, sandy-haired boy, out of bounds and face to face with death, whispered the names of the fallen into the breeze, then vowed in silence never to speak of them to anyone, and never to die in his own backyard.

#

During the following days, or perhaps it was weeks, Morris circled Mariettas and Maysvilles, Richmonds and Jacksons, Springfields and Bloomingtons, an unfurling scroll of college towns and downtowns, beltways and Interstate loops and railroad yards, of strip malls on repeat and postcard skylines glimmering in the hazy twilight of rush hour pollution. There were suburban sprawls, too, and heartland expanses wide enough for silent tornados to pass cleanly through, unimpeded by what was unquestioningly regarded as "human progress." Around him the foliage curled at the edges and the cooling winds blew the fallen leaves across the ground. Overhead, he heard the conversations from his telephone calls across America, buzzing down the wires...

264

[FLASH FLASH]

"*[Never mind all that, Neville. They already said they're not coming until... Oh, wait! I've got someone on the line.]* Yes, howdy? Hello?"

"Good afternoon, ma'am."

"Yes, afternoon it certainly is! But let me tell you, I've been on hold since morning."

"*This* morning, ma'am?"

"I beg your pardon?"

"Well, we're a bit understaffed at the moment. Some of our Dear Readers have been on hold for *many* mornings."

"Many mornings, you say?"

"A week's worth, in one regrettable case. Poor fellow out in Norman..."

"Norman, Oklahoma?"

"Arizona, ma'am. Longest suffering case I've heard of in my time here, though some of the old timers recall folks waiting a month or longer to get a human on the line."

"A month or longer, you say? *[Longer 'an a month, he says, Neville. Can you believe that?]*"

"Say, you're not in Norman yourself, are you?"

"Norman, Oklahoma?"

"Or Arizona, for that matter..."

"Neither, it turns out. Neville and I are here in Lincoln... *Nebraska*, before you ask."

"Of course, ma'am. Nebraska. And how is it there in Lincoln, Nebraska, this afternoon?"

"*This* afternoon?"

"Well, any afternoon, really. Let's just say, 'in general.'"

"Well, 'in general' it's very good."

"But...?"

"But this afternoon I've been on hold since morning!"

"That's *this* morning, just to be sure...?"

[FLASH FLASH]

"Johnston, with a 'T'. Fresno, California."

"Got it. And the publication to which you were referring just now?"

"Oh, I can't remember. I've got so many of the darned things. The investment one, I guess. Profits Digest Something-or-Other..."

"Platinum Profits Monthly?"

"That sounds like the one..."

"Or Peak Profits Weekly?"

"Hmm..."

"We have a number of similar sounding publications, I'm afraid. Do you happen to remember the analyst's name, Sir?"

"Hmm... Could have been a Steve. Do you have a Steve on staff?"

"Regrettably, Sir, we have several."

"I see. Well, any of them on the Profits side?"

"Not currently."

"Hmm..."

"Perhaps you recall the specific recommendation?"

"Let's see here. *[Shuffles paper.]* I think it was Teletronics Something-or-Other. Some initials in there, maybe? I'm sure the price has spiked already, but I just wanted to see if I still had time to get in before the *real* run-up."

"Could have been J&J Telemetrics, Sir? Ticker symbol JTLX, listed on the NASDAQ?"

"Sounds familiar..."

"Right. Well, that recommendation was published in the May issue of our Pure Profits Briefing, a bi-weekly stock trading service run by Randall Stevenson, PhD."

"Yes! Yes, that's the one!"

"Ah, well... I'm afraid that particular trade has already expired, Sir."

"Hmm, I see. Did I miss much? You know, in the way of profits?"

"According to my records, Sir, that position was closed out just last week for a considerable loss."

"Considerable, eh?"

"Down eighty-six percent on some fraud news when Dr. Stevenson issued his sell recommendation."

"Eighty-six percent, you say?"

"Yes Sir."

"Why, that's terrific news!"

"A narrow miss for you, Sir."

"I'll say! Well, thank you very much, young man. You've just made my day."

"Glad to help, Sir. Call again with any inquiries regarding your services."

"Will do. Say, you don't sound like an American..."
[FLASH FLASH]

"It's like I told you last week, Morris. She simply doesn't want to go to any of the in-state colleges. Flat out refuses them, in fact."

"Uh-huh..."

"My husband just loved his time at UND. Recalls it fondly to this very day. And, if I may say so, I received a perfectly satisfactory education at NDSU."

"Of course."

"It's just hard not to take her decision personally. It's like she just wants to be as far away from her mom and dad as humanly possible. I mean, us... her *family*."

"Now, come. I'm sure it has nothing to do with you and Mr. Pitman."

"But what else on God's green earth could it be?"

"Well, where else has she applied?"

"Oh, all over. Colleges in Florida, California, Texas..."

"Hmm..."

"What? What is it, Morris?"

"I'd hate to overstep my mark here, Mrs. Pitman. I mean, I'm really just an account manager for your husband's..."

"Oh nonsense, Morris. You know more about Janey than most of my friends at this point."

"Well, and this is just a thought, mind... could the reason be... climactic?"

[From North Dakota: Silence.]

The late fall landscape speeding by his window, Morris marveled quietly at the country around him and the familiar, yet utterly unique, people who brought it to life, one experience at a time. By the time he reached Madison (the one in Illinois) he was ready to encounter just about anyone. And a good thing that was, too.

#

After a million bottomless cups in New York City, Morris had come to appreciate the unambitious drip coffee served in uniformed black handled, fishbowl pots across the nation's vast network of musty, roadside motels. He was gazing out the window of one such establishment, enjoying the familiar taste as it warmly ushered in the desired, morning effect, when an unexpected query brought his attention back suddenly to the dining hall.

"Don't you prefer eggs for breakfast?" Her voice had a calm directness to it that both alerted and disarmed him. Morris turned to discover a lithe figure seated two plastic chairs to his right, her long crossed legs extended out from under the tablecloth to reveal a pair of tanned suede, ankle-cut boots. They lingered in his periphery, even as he directed his rising attention toward the source of the question. She neither smiled nor frowned but looked at him serenely, expectantly, her light blue eyes unperturbed by the play of blonde tresses which teased and twirled beneath the ceiling fan.

Morris tried to locate her face in the immediate past. He couldn't recall whether she was present when he arrived or whether she had, by some incredible act of stealth, drifted past him unnoticed. Looking at her now, permanent against the fleeting morning light, that hardly seemed possible.

Oblivious to his unvoiced confusion, she went on in clear, easy tones. "I only ask because they don't serve them here. Not scrambled. Not benedict or poached or Florentine. Not over easy or over hard. Not over anything, in fact." She paused to consider her predicament. "I just hate that about these places. Don't you? Eggless breakfasts. That and their uniformly bad linens." She crossed her arms and rubbed both her elbows, as if she had spent the night sleeping on the cold gravel outside.

"Yes, well," he sifted through a dozen clichés before landing, disappointedly, on, "I guess we got what we paid for."

"I'd have an omelet, given the choice," she fantasized aloud, not so much ignoring his remark as giving him a pass for it. "Mushroom and bell pepper and spinach. Oh, and three types of cheese," she sighed and, throwing her head back, gave a look of exaggerated satisfaction, a simulacrum for something far more desirable.

"That's some omelet," nodded Morris in solemn agreement then, allowing a cautionary raise of his eyebrow, added, "Careful, though, or one of the ladies nearby is going to deploy the 'I'll have what she's having' line."

A flush of mischievous embarrassment filled her widening eyes and a naked hand flew to her mouth. "Now I really want that omelet!" Her laugh was childish, unabashed.

Happy that he'd brought her to such a state, Morris fought the urge to engage her again prematurely. Instead, he let a minute pass by the window, her boots tapping the linoleum floor in the corner of his eye. Years dragged on before, to his unending relief, she retired the silence with a bullseye guess.

"I've never been to Australia," she ventured as his expression confirmed her hunch. "I heard it's pretty, though, in a rough, rugged sort of way. So why are you here, in..." she looked around as if trying to remember where, in fact, they were, "in ..."

"Madison, I think."

"Yes, that's it. Madison. Of course. Well, what are you doing here in Madison, Mister Mystery Man from Down Under."

Once again, he marveled at her directness, which seemed to stow away in her remarks under cover of a refreshingly honest enthusiasm. It was as if she had known either too little or too much cynicism in her formative years and, as a result, decided it was incompatible with, even enervating of, real experience. Meeting her unflinching eyes, he tried once more in vain to ignore her physical appeal.

"It was love, wasn't it," she smiled generously, confirming her estimate in her own mind before he could marshal his facts. "Figures. Everyone is either moving toward or away from love, in one direction or another. I guess that's what distance is," her tone softened, as though she were inviting him into her own private meditations on the subject. "It's really just the space between us all, a convenient measurement between those of us coming and those going."

It seemed a fine enough observation to Morris, at least as far as breakfast chit-chat was concerned.

"So, what about you?" he probed, acknowledging immediately the contagious nature of her candor.

270

She replied without hesitation. "Me? Oh, I'm going, leaving just as fast as my legs will carry me." Then, as if the subject had simply run its course, she directed the flow of inquiry elsewhere, away from her sprightly limbs. "I saw you scribbling something earlier. In your notebook, there." She pointed to the cover splayed on his table. "You looked very concentrated. Are you studying or something?"

"Sure, I guess so." He remained pensive for a second and, when he spoke again, he did so without knowing exactly what form his thoughts would take. "I mean, I'm studying in the sense that we're all studying. Generally. Blindly. Not knowing whether I'm actually getting anywhere." He closed the book and, unconsciously, leaned in over the table between them.

"You know, sometimes I feel like there are little breakthroughs, incremental advances, that certain things are, really, within our grasp. Then, other times, I get the feeling I've missed the whole thrust of the equation, that the best I can hope for is to earn some partial points for at least showing my working. Like those little half-related sums you jot in the margin of the test paper when you don't really know what's going on."

For the first time since he could remember, the naked vagueness of his thoughts didn't leave him feeling vulnerable, as if even his fragmentary working might actually draw him nearer to some unseen truth.

"I like that," she said flatly, decisively, claiming absolute authority over her own opinion. "I think we need to feel like we're getting somewhere, making progress, even if it happens to be by way of our mistakes. Life's 'little sums,' as you called them just now. I like that turn."

"I'll be sure to write it down," Morris grinned. Stupidly, he thought. He waited to see if perhaps she knew where the conversation might go next, silently terrified she would simply smile, wish him a safe journey and stroll right out the door.

"We should go for breakfast," she said suddenly, rising from her chair as if they had made the plan together.

Morris wondered if it were possible that they had not.

#

"You always bring this much luggage to breakfast?" joked Morris before hoisting his passenger's twin suitcases into the back of the Jeep.

She climbed into the passenger side and called out over the bench seat, a mane of untamed blonde engulfing the scene as she burrowed into a comfortable position. "I figured we'd just continue on straight from the diner."

The word froze in his attention: *We'd.*

"Sure thing," Morris breathed. He settled himself behind the wheel and kicked the motor over once, twice, before the engine came to life. "Where are you headed next, anyway?"

Pulling down the visor, she surveyed herself a moment in the vanity mirror. "I'm not exactly sure yet," she said, producing from her handbag a pair of oversized sunglasses and a lip balm that smelled like butter, which she proceeded to smooth across her lips. "I guess I'll see when I get there."

He waited for more clarification, but soon abandoned the thought when it became apparent none was forthcoming. Instead, she smiled glossily at him and patted the dashboard. "This is going to be fun!"

They drove on through the usual numbered streets, past twin gas stations on diagonally opposing corners, a City Hall connected, seemingly as an afterthought, to the local Fire Station, big, flimsy houses next to breezy, vacant lots. All this under a sky that didn't quite fit the space available for it.

Eventually they came upon the Mississippi River and, bolted to either side, a steel truss bridge in three uncertain segments.

"People assume it was named after President William McKinley." She sounded as though she were reading from a pamphlet titled "Misnomers, Myths and Misconceptions on the Mississippi."

Morris looked at her, puzzled.

"It's a common enough mistake, just in case you're wondering. It was, in fact, named for the builder, William B. McKinley."

"Ah, the bridge," he realized aloud with an accompanying look that said, "and how exactly do you know this stuff?"

"Apparently it was quite a marvel in its day," she rose swiftly to the challenge of his unspoken incredulity, "The first alignment connecting Route 66 across the Mississippi, you know."

He peered at her again.

"Ok," she demurred. "So I heard it from a table behind us in the breakfast hall. The gentleman, in the olive sports jacket, if you'd noticed, seemed very enthusiastic." She rested her feet on the dash, apparently satisfied with her source. "I'd be inclined to go with his research."

"Well, it's never been more important to me than this very second," Morris said truthfully as they drove out along it, the only car in sight in the early morning. He tried not to imagine the aged steel buckling under them, the Jeep condemned to a wreckage site somewhere between Illinois and Missouri. The front page of the morrow's city paper flashed across his mind:

Locals Weep as States Lose Historical McKinley Landmark

(There would have to be an asterisk in there somewhere, of course: *not McKinley as in the president.) Then, in smaller font running along the side column inches:

Visitors Perish in Modern Day Mississippi Tragedy

Mentally editing the imaginary details buried in the "cont. overleaf" supplementary story, Morris realized he didn't even know his fellow victim's name. He thought to ask her but she interrupted his motion with the answer before he could get the words out.

"I'm June," she stated as if resting a case, a kind of *quod erat demonstrandum* to cap off a lifetime of inarguable, well researched points that led her to be, irrefutably, June.

"Morris," he replied, glad to be back on solid ground on the west side of the river. He watched for the familiar signs: Broadway, Jefferson, Montgomery, Spring. "Now that the formalities are out of the way, where's this diner of yours?"

She relaxed into the seat and, smiling broadly, pointed on down the road with her chin. Then she turned her attention out the window, resting her head to one side, and took in the passing landscape as someone might a place they are seeing for the first time, but which they never expect never to see again. Morris felt an infinite number of questions on the tip of his tongue, but none formed themselves fully in his mind, so they drove on in silence until, after a series of directional nods and gestures, she tapped him on the arm in time for him to pull into a diner off Compton and Park.

"How on earth did you find this place?" he asked, jokingly. "Eavesdrop on another octogenarian cross-country couple's to-do list?"

She shook her head and laughed, but offered nothing more by way of an answer.

Inside they ordered breakfast. Morris had steak and eggs, June an omelet with mushrooms and bell pepper and three types of cheese. The waitresses lingered over the refills, pretending not to listen in on the pair's strange conversation. Then, when the check came, June swooped it up. "I'll get this one," she assured him breezily. "Call it gas money."

"Well," he ventured, eying the bill, "That'll get you enough to last until just about lunchtime."

"When it'll be your turn to buy grits," she replied and, with a barely perceptible wink, "and mine to drive."

"Fair enough," he agreed. Shortly afterward they were back in the old green Jeep together, headed off along the open road.

#

Chapter XII

Nóstos Álgos

A conversation began just inside the St. Louis 270 beltway fared them well across the Show Me State, through Hermann and Jefferson City, past Eldon, Warsaw and Clinton, over the border dividing Merwin and Linn Valley, and into the waist high sorghum and overhead corn blanketing the endless stretch gathering itself before the mighty Rockies. Mirroring the landscape around them, their discussion was one of long, comfortable lulls, deep flatlands of absent reverie, straight lines bent in the distant haze of a never nearing horizon. And overhead a sky stretched so thin the blue appeared at times almost transparent, so that at any moment, the atmosphere might give way to reveal the naked vanities of the gods themselves.

When Topeka was not yet in sight, June wove another silken thread into their dialogue's growing orb. "Gunpowder or papermaking?" she mused aloud, her head cocked to one side behind the red, windowpane sunglasses.

"Thought you were sleeping." Morris took a long drink of water and wiped his mouth with his sleeve.

"I was." June cracked the window to a gust of country green air. Her distractingly lithe legs she crossed absentmindedly on the dashboard. "I mean, I am."

They rode on a dozen miles before passing a single vehicle, a bouncing jalopy loaded down with hay and workers, more or less in that order. Morris watched them turn off in the rearview mirror, disappearing into an unmarked break in the cornfields.

"So... Gunpowder or papermaking, then?" he mused.

"As in, China's greatest invention."

"Ah." He considered the long tail impacts of force versus persuasion in the Middle Kingdom while June fell back asleep in a field of Kansas sunflowers. Over her blonde-sheathed shoulder, a swab of storm clouds mopped the northern frontier. To the south there was nothing to see but space and all that lies beyond it. Morris watched the fields racing by in rich golden bursts, the drying husks thirsty for the promised showers. Then he saw the road ahead covered in virginal grassland, the Great Plains as they appeared to the pioneers who had marched west with soil in their fingernails and dirt etched into the creases of their hands, their temples, their coarsened knees and elbows. How they must have trembled, those proud men and women, pressed firm against the limits of their imagination, their capacity for awe and wonder finally unbounded beneath the endless skies.

For no reason other than that she was next to him, he began to wonder about June's own silent heritage. Had her forbearers toiled in these fields, leaned hard into the plow with blistered palms, sweat tracing rivulets down the contours of their aching, muscular backs? Or were her authors of the metropolitan type, better acquainted with war than with harrow, as Mr. Ford had once famously remarked? In the moment, he couldn't decide whether she was a girl lost in her country, or the other way around. What had brought her to this point, he wondered? And what mysterious gauntlet of events had drawn them together, funneled them into a single vehicle, hurtling across such improbably vast terrain?

Sifting through a series of mental snapshots, dating back to the breakfast room at an otherwise unremarkable Madison motel, Morris sketched out a portrait of the wispy stranger seated, reposed, beside him. At first, her features introduced themselves in an eastern European accent; high, broad cheekbones, wide-set eyes, narrow, though defined jawline. Then, in the slenderness of her nose, the white-on-white palette, that captivatingly pale ocular abyss, dispersed across quick and easy symmetry, the look yielded, in balance, to something more recalling Deniker's *nordique*.

Tracing a transatlantic line from the seat of Baltic monarchy to the promise of the New World, he considered again what single event, or series thereof, had drawn her lineage here? Public executions? Private retributions? The empty, scots pine whiff of the bark bread years? Had her family decamped to the similarly harsh northern reaches of this land, the windswept prairies of Wisconsin or Minnesota or (he remembered [FLASH... FLASH...] Mrs. Pitman's dilemma) the frigid Dakotas? Or perhaps she came down much later, with the bootleggers, passed through tender hands like a sacred package along the Midwestern lines, down through Racine and Kenosha and Evanston, hugged by frigid lakes, delivered alongside desperate Francophone relatives into the underbelly of Capone's seedy jazz town.

There were many routes to America...

Back on a long straight road, and well into the afternoon's trough, Morris returned to the question most immediately at hand. Discarding the choices on offer, he chartered a new course of possibility. "I thought most people were agreed on the compass," he remarked, at last.

Blonde, Teutonic June stirred in the receding sunlight. "Well, it wouldn't be a very useful tool if they didn't," she yawned.

"No, no. Not that," he reached for a cigarette. "I mean, as China's greatest invention. The compass."

She lowered her windowpanes over "I'm joking" eyes and they laughed about it then and twice again before Salina, where they called in for a late lunch and a change of shift. In the Heart of Dixie they ordered biscuits with gravy and bottomless coffee and, after agreeing there was enough road behind them for the day, whiskey sours and the check.

There was a motel back up the road a mile or so where they could watch the rains roll in.

An hour and several whiskies later they were seated on matching blue patio chairs, the paper-thin walls of their respective, adjacent rooms at their backs. Morris smoked a cigarette, exhaling between the swollen droplets that pelted the parking lot a few feet beyond their outstretched legs.

"How about nostalgia?" mused June in her characteristically open-ended manner. It occurred to Morris that she didn't so much ask questions as she did simply propose subjects.

"In the true, Odyssean manner, you mean?"

"How else?"

He drew long, the expressed smoke backlit by a distant flicker of lightning. "I think, generally, it's overrated."

She cocked an eyebrow.

"Sometimes I think about it. Sure," he conceded. "It's always there. Home, I mean. I can find it in the clap of thunder, for example, or that smell just before the rain breaks. I remember storms like this rolling in over the sugarcane farms on the northern beaches, not far from where I grew up. The farmers would set the crops alight at dusk and the smoke would rise up into the atmosphere, mingling with the thick green clouds overhead. You could smell the sweet air for miles, down valleys and over ridges. Then the rains would come, breaking the heat and drenching the fields."

She issued a long, permissive silence then motioned toward the packet resting at his arm. "May I?"

"I didn't know you smoked."

"I don't. But I like your story."

He handed her a cigarette and she took a drag, clean as though she had been smoking since before his narrative ever began. "Well?" her look seemed to say.

"Well, my friends and I used to drive down the coast on long weekends, and some short ones too. We would bunk at the surf clubs, right on the beach, and cook sausages on the public barbecues in the parks." He hesitated, "I realize this all sounds very cliché..."

"Does it?" her expression was, as always, free of irony.

"It used to be you'd have to detour a long way inland before joining up with the coastal road again," he drew a line on the concrete with his foot. "Behind a giant headland, like this. The route wound through pineapple plantations and the rolling sugarcane fields I told you about just now. It was only a couple of hours, but it seemed like a real journey at the time. Like we were actually going somewhere. I guess we were, in a way. We'd stop off on the side of the road, at rickety little stalls, and buy these giant bags of passion fruit and bananas for a couple of bucks. And, being students, we'd drink the cheapest beer we could find, whatever was on sale or cheaper bought warm."

Morris let out a laugh, which she joined easily, automatically. "Good times," she nodded, as if she had been there all along, her suede boots rested on the dashboard, blonde tresses blowing in the salty, coastal air.

He stubbed his cigarette under his heel. "Anyway, that was then. There's probably a highway blasted right through the headland now. Not that that's a bad thing, necessarily. It's just not..." he searched for the desired phrase...

"...as it was," she understood him, aloud.

Morris fell asleep to the sound of rain falling on the awning that night, recalling the days of his youth and wondering if, on the other side of the paper-thin wall, June might be doing the same.

She was perfectly, blissfully unconscious.

#

As usual, Morris was deep into his second cup of coffee when June, prettier at daybreak before makeup, sauntered into the breakfast room the following morning. And, just as usual, he didn't notice her come in until she was seated opposite him.

"So," she stirred a lump of sugar into the bottom half of his cup and took a long, two-handed sip, "what about this book, then?"

He watched as she shook her fingers through bedraggled locks. For a brief moment he even considered denying her (anyways correct) inference. She can't have failed to notice, in that innocent, childlike way she noticed everything around her, that he was working on something.

"It is a book, isn't it?" She frowned. "Or maybe it's a play. I couldn't quite decide."

As if it were up to her, Morris thought, not unkindly. "It's not much of anything at the moment," he shuffled the loose sheaf in from of him, folding the scrawled pages into his notepad. "Just some...ideas."

She cast him a look that said, "aren't they all?" then loosened him some slack. "OK then. Fiction or nonfiction?"

"Interesting dichotomy," he was glad for the widening generalization. "I've wondered for a long time if there really is such a difference."

"Oh, goodie," she smiled. "A.M. musings with Morris. You should grab yourself some coffee."

"You know, I'm not sure anyone really writes non-fiction," he began when he sat down again, "because it's always filtered through the mind of the author, crafted, metamorphosed, dragged into the alley and beaten senseless, then hoisted on a cross and worshipped or desecrated, if only by its creator. It's not immutable because it's human, and nothing about that state is certain or permanent."

She nodded him on, neither agreeing nor refuting, her pale eyes fixing on him over the rim of his original mug.

"Witness the so-called news," he continued, synapses in a frenzy. "Allegedly objective reporting of historical fact by imperfect mammalian transmitters. Measure these supposed truths against a glass of water or a mile of earth or a fast-falling apple. They melt away like so many miracles. You know," Morris recalled one of Aubrey's favorite quotations, "Fitzgerald called nonfiction a 'form of literature that lies halfway between fiction and fact.'"

Hearing himself say this, he gave a reverent laugh and recalled to mind the story, maybe apocryphal, about the modern author who had copied out The Great Gatsby, word for word, because he wanted to feel what it was like to "write perfect prose." How real was that?

"So too is our blessed fiction a myth in and of itself,' he carried on, "birthed by the great authors of every nation, every epoch. See if you can't tease out of their foamy dreamscapes a composite character wrenched from real life, render a subconscious acknowledgment to the concrete world, locate the seat of unalloyed anxiety or ambition or adulation, each as real an emotion as a piano falling on your head. Fiction springs from the world around and within us. We couldn't write the unreal because, the moment it's committed to the record, it becomes part of the cosmic firmament. It exists. Like its dubious cousin, pure fiction is therefore equally impossible, because it's irrevocably tinged with that experience, real and irreverent and iron clad in its impact on the psyche. It is *a* reality, undeniably that, but reimagined through the same warped filter which denies us pure non-fiction."

June smiled, first at Morris, then at the elderly couple seated two tables down from them who had, in the absence of anything else to say to one and other, been eavesdropping on this cheerful rant. She was prettier in profile, thought Morris, if that was even possible. In a drab little room, awash in molten morning light, her beauty seemed to be actively daring him to look away, challenging him to miss a moment of what might come next.

"Have you seen those experiments," she shocked the silence to life, "where a group of researchers basically dose up spiders and then watch them spin?"

"Huh?"

"They administer certain toxins," she pressed thumb and forefinger together in front of one pale blue eye to indicate "tiny, spider-sized doses. Then they observe them as they construct their webs." She took another, full-lipped sip. "Morris, you should see what they're capable of on caffeine. Some devastatingly beautiful creations. Haunting, really. Not at all symmetrical, intuitive, like what you'd imagine your run-of-the-mill Charlotte constructing. But not without their own special kind of logic."

"I think I see where you're going with this." Morris had become, if not enamored of, certainly intrigued by June's playful, tangential musings.

"They even took a pair into space," she continued, happily. "Named them Arabella and Anita."

"Wait... What on earth for?"

"Some kind of arachnid alliteration, I guess."

"No, I mean why did they take the spiders into space?"

"Right," she nodded, still grinning. "I guess they wanted to test A&A's orb weaving capability, you know, in a zero-gravity environment."

He stirred a lump into his own mug. "And?"

"They died, of course. Probably from dehydration." Came a flick of blonde, then the pivot: "So, what about this Great Australian novel of yours?"

"Ah, but we're all Americans now." Morris found himself answering before he realized they had circled back to the center of the subject. He rambled over his notes for a few minutes before concluding, "So yes, it's the next Great American novel..., as told, according to an old friend of mine, by an aspiring, non-American ingrate."

She gave a chuckle and then, as quickly as she had drawn him into the personal, she withdrew once more to the vastly general. "I wonder who it will belong to this century. If anyone."

"The novel, you mean?"

She nodded, barely, then swept the keys coolly off the table and stretched her arms overhead. "I'll take the first shift today," she half yawned. "You just think about the next great narrative and to whom the future belongs."

"Deal," he replied to the elderly couple beside him as his airy co-pilot drifted out the door.

#

They drove across Kansas as though passing through the eye of an America-sized hurricane, aware of but unconcerned by the centrifugal force blasting the world and everything it was said to contain into the vast oblivion east of Lawrence, west of Oakley, south of Wichita and north of Concordia. Tearing along the open routes, the old Jeep kicked up dust and stones and clods of sacred, mineral-rich earth. Morris watched in the side mirror, a distant sun reflecting on his concentration, as the tiny, broken planets disappeared into the storm wall and the gnashing rain bands beyond. Inside the cabin, while Patsy Cline fell delicately to pieces, all was tranquil and calm.

"It's like a scene from some other time," observed June, her gaze rested on the circular horizon, somewhere between Stockton and Hoxie. Then, before the Rockies had come into view, but long after their shadow had fallen on the ground ahead of them, she appended, "Only, I can't decide if it's a scene from the past or from the future."

Morris wiped the sleep from his eyes and sat up fully in the passenger seat. How long had she been driving for? He wondered. It seemed like an eternity.

"I thought about your question," he pointed to a yolky dust devil, spinning off over the cornfields in the northern distance. The dancing spiral reached high into the sky, a hundred feet or more, before dissipating in an instant, relegated to its own blink of the past.

"Oh," replied June, nodding to another captured spiral, already forming up on the plains ahead. "My question?"

"You know: Who will own the novel in the twenty-first century."

"Ah. And what does Mr. Morris have to say on the subject?"

They bantered for a while, playfully filing in the blanks in each other's patchy, literary history. The nineteenth century, they decided, was a three-way tie between the British, French and Russian heavyweights. The twentieth belonged mostly to the Americans, with a few early exceptions; Proust, Joyce, Wilde...perhaps even Woolf. Over the future they lingered, inferring, hypothesizing, ultimately unsure as to whether there would even be nation states standing at the end of another hundred years to claim the prize. It seemed such an unlikely proposition. The very notion of patriotism, they agreed, smacked of something bound to the bawling infancy of a species, not to its far reaching, full-height potential. Still, history was full of giant leaps backward. Maybe the future would see a rise of jingoism and small-mindedness, the collapse of culture, the death of art. In that case, maybe the future wouldn't even last another century. (At that point in the conversation, and on June's prodding, they had gone off on another tangent: Eliot's "whimper or a bang?" articulation.)

In any case, Morris was glad to enjoy his stranger's company. Even, perhaps especially, during the long silences that fell frequently between them. At times it felt like they drove for days without exchanging a single word, as if he really was alone on the journey, adrift in his own reverie, lost in the wonderment of his colossal surroundings. She seemed so ethereal there, dozing against the window or tapping her feet on the dashboard, meting out time with whatever song happened to be playing on the crackling stereo. Languid and flightless in the corner of his eye, she became a familiar, comforting part of the atmosphere, a point of eternal, unwavering reference. Then, just when his thoughts had carried him as far away from the old green Jeep as they could safely go, she would say something that brought him right back to the moment.

"What do you suppose lies beyond the Rockies, Morris?" They were coming upon them now, hazy but undeniable, immovable on the horizon.

"Don't you know?" he asked.

"I do, of course." They sped on for a long time, the majesty rearing itself quietly ahead. "But what do you *suppose*?"

"You mean, besides a Grand Junction and a Great Lake and a big, black Pyramid in the desert." He watched a smile tease at the corners of her mouth.

"Yes," she red-lipped a June grin, "but more than that..."

"More even than Death Valley and Hollywood stars and the endless, fathomless, dauntless Pacific Ocean beyond?"

"Yes, Morris." June raised her voice against the gusting breeze. "Something much, *much* more."

She looked ahead, the looming snow-capped peaks melting into her eyes and running down her face.

"There is always something more, June." Morris put his hand on her arm. He noticed she was shivering.

"Promise?" she ached.

But he couldn't be sure of his answer, so they rode on in silence once more, the quiet mountains rising to fill the darkening wine sky.

#

With shards of the primordial explosion scattered overhead, and the Interstate miles well-beaten into the panels of their trusty old steed, the weary ramblers veered off the road on the Rocky's eastern foothills, just outside Castle Rock. The evenings had a cool bite to them now and the thinning air, quick and light in their lungs, brought their dreams alive at night. They checked into a perfectly nondescript motel and were glad when the elderly proprietor said they could walk to the Mexican joint just down the ways without too much trouble.

"Only, stay good 'n' clear a' the road on your way back." He looked up over thick rimmed reading glasses, taped together on one side. "Gets mighty dark out here of an evenin'. Lotta drivers get to drinkin', think they know the roads better'n they do."

"We'll be careful, Mista," assured June adding, to the first of Morris' hearing, "Gotta be off in the morning anyhows. Expect us bright and early for that breakfast of yours."

The old man looked at Morris with an avuncular affection, the light from a side lamp flickering across his long face and onto the framed map hanging above the reception desk behind him. His brow was deeply creased, set after its owner's kind disposition. Morris liked that he smiled at the beginning and end of each sentence, a tick that inspired the same in those who came to see him; about a room, regarding directions to the nearest gas station or, on rare occasion, to hear tales about the local area for a school project or newspaper article or "frontiersman" lifestyle piece. The man was a certain brand of American, cut from the rock, unavailable anywhere else in the country or in the strange, unvisited lands outside it.

To the "young fellow" at his desk he handed a folded map and an assortment of proud pamphlets, "in case you wanna stop by them on your way out tomorrow. The ol' railway building is worth seeing down on Elbert, since you're in these parts anyhow. There's some nice gentle trails over by the ridgeline too, if you're interested. And the old rock itself, obviously. Gives you a view from Pikes Peak right down to Devil's Head."

Morris and June nodded in polite appreciation and, pulling their jackets on, started off along the doglegged road. The smell of crisp ponderosa and pinyon pines suffused the night air, tracing its falling temperature down the hillside.

"He's been there forever, that sweet man." June's voice suggested a passing melancholy. "His grandparents probably helped settle the place, lured by the prospect of gold or free land. Or maybe they worked on that railway depot."

Morris kicked a loose stone along the shoulder and watched it disappear behind a shadowy tuft of oak brush. "Takes many hands to make a country," he mused.

"In some places," June stretched out her arms and twirled on the spot, "places like this, those hands become part of the land, inseparable from it, from the shape it has become. In that way, just by mentioning a place, you also refer to the people who inhabit it, and to all those who ever did."

"How poetic we are tonight," Morris teased, then immediately regretted it.

"Witness the primordial shards, Morris, surreal and incandescent," she thrust her head backward, casting herself into the violet dome above. "Just like us."

They walked a ways in silence, each contemplating just how like the stars they really were; a mass of common elements hurtling through space, the great unknown still ahead.

Up the hillside a joyous music coiled in merry tones, reaching them even before they espied the restaurant's dimmed porch light off in the distance, obscured as it was by jutting rock and the shadows of clouds passing in front of the moon. Outside, under a sad duet of motionless ceiling fans, a few loose couples smoked and laughed and drank bottles of beer, which they balanced on the railings between sips. Inside there seemed to be more bodies than could possibly fit in such a modest shack, but everyone appeared comfortable and familiar and conversed in the easy tones of sleepy, mountainside towns. Noticing a pair of vintage pinball machines off to the side of the entrance, June quickly disappeared, leaving Morris to order and occupy space at the bar for two, which he did without complaint or much consideration. He often ate or drank alone when they were together.

From a well-bearded bartender in flannelette and tattoos he ordered twin margaritas and the combination dip.

"Bit early for the ski season, ain't ya?" the man observed in a hoarse but cordial voice. The blender drowned out Morris' reply.

"I don't mind you Aussies," he continued on his own. "Dated a couple of your ladies over the years. Nice gals, but they always return home, leave me here, sittin' on the edge of a mountain."

Morris got the impression this wasn't the first time the man had deployed this quip. Still, he seemed kind enough and keen for a fresh ear. He and Morris fell into the cheap, serviceable conversation plied by nomads and the barmen who have tended them since time immemorial.

"How long y'all in town for?"

"Just passing through, really..."

"That so? You travellin' alone or... I beg your pardon. My bad..."

"No harm done..."

"So, where're you off to next?"

"No real plans, as such. Just heading west, like so many before. City lights to City Lights and all..."

"Nothing wrong with that, man. I tell you somethin', I'd be up and joinin' ya tomorrow if I could..."

"Oh?"

"Used to do a fair bit of roving 'round myself, you know..."

"Yeah? Anywhere in particular?"

"Aw, here and there. Went to Nepal once. Man, I'd be back there in a flash, I would..."

"But...?"

"Well, I got a few things to take care of 'round here first. Gotta fix up the van, pay off a coupla loans. And this place'd fall apart if I didn't give her proper love 'n' care. Plus, my old lady, she don't much like travelin', all that time without a decent shower and a place to hang her pretty clothes. So, there's always that. But it's coming along alright, man. One day, though. One day real soon..."

Morris drank his margarita quota, then moved on to rye and water. Over the fuzzy conversation the band played on, transitioning from a handful of token numbers from south of the Rio Grande to a discordant mix of bluegrass and new wave rockabilly. June, meanwhile, flitted in and out, stealing a corn chip here and a highball there, before returning to "the pins," as she laughingly called them.

After a while, Morris noticed the colorful bulbs behind the bar, giving off lights in blue and red and yellow hues. He wondered if they had been there all along, buzzing, or if they had only appeared in the past few minutes, while he balanced on a suddenly uncomfortable stool, talking to... now, what was his name? He ordered another bastard rye and felt the grain burn his throat and warm his insides. The music rolled over him in waves. Blue, red, yellow. And dancing in his peripheral vision, on the edge of his imagination, sweet, sweet June, twirling in blonde and denim and someone else's quilted scarf.

Backlit by primary colors and waving gracelessly as he passed the pins, Morris made his way out onto the porch and lit... lit... lit a cigarette. "There it is," he thought out loud as the cool breeze washed his face anew. A young couple from neighboring Conifer (or was it Evergreen?) asked for a light, then cigarettes, and the threesome spoke excitedly for what could have been minutes or hours. There were others, too, as Morris later recalled. The chatty folk in from Seattle. A group of college friends from "back east." A band that played local bars and a select few restaurants in the area. And a burly, tattooed man who tended bar someplace nearby. Said he wanted to travel some...

Through the fogged porch window, Morris observed June swaying on the dance floor, her supple arms interlocked with those of a comely, brunette figure poured into sheepskin boots and a shoestring top. To the applause of a ramshackle crowd the pair spun and swung their bodies across the space, their molten forms overlapping for a few, tantalizing seconds before parting again to joyous cheers and howls. He minded again her glacial blue eyes, freed to stronger music and madder wine, adrift in another realm. Then came soft linens and down, loose stones underfoot, her steadying hand on his shoulder, and the darkest depths of sleep. But not in that order.

#

His head full of peat bog, Morris nevertheless made it down to breakfast in time to commandeer the lower half of June's second cup, which she yielded to him with an affectionate, knowing smile. A friendly, unspoken dialogue passed between them while June studied her nails and Morris pushed his eggs and beans around the plate. Within the hour they were packed and headed out across the ridge, Morris dutifully manning the passenger seat. By mid-morning, the brisk mountain air had filtered through his mind and he could foresee a time when thoughts and actions and emotions might once again communicate with one another, when he would be human again.

Without discussing the route, they traveled the road north, past signs to places like Deer Creek Canyon and Indian Hills and Lair O' the Bear Park. Then, when Hog Back Road linked up with the teaming Interstate strap, they took the hairpin west, past Buffalo Bill's Tombstone and on toward Saddleback Mountain, Silver Plume and Bard's Peak. The climb was steady and unrelenting, but the old Jeep kept steady pace with the bulk of the traffic as it marched through the passes, alongside fast running streams and on toward distant peaks that seemed to disappear into the clouds. Occasionally a sports car raced by, leaning dangerously into the curves, swerving between slower drivers. Lining the slow lane, a dreary procession of draft horse semitrailers, broken into packs, lurched ahead, their gears and cogs and pistons straining under their immense loads.

At the head of one such peloton, another green Jeep of the same model was tethered to a groaning U-Haul. Passing by the cabin, Morris peered over at the driver and his companion. A pair of unshaven young men, perhaps in their middle twenties, were singing and laughing, clearly unphased by the snaking line building long and slow behind in their wake. They wore dirty truckers' caps, the kind often for sale in gas stations, and from the wilds of their eyes looked as if they had never been to sleep. Morris turned his attention back to the road, wondering quietly what kind of lives these men led. Whence had they come? To where were they headed? And what grizzly tales of love and war and betrayal had they beat into the path between here and there, the path that so divided their experiences from his? He would never know.

Somewhere along the late afternoon's trail, after they had lingered over an unhurried lunch and moseyed through several roadside markets, June drew the Jeep up on the yellow, grassy shoulder of a descending slope. Without a word, she alighted. Morris hesitated a moment, then followed her steps over the narrow road and toward the edge of an unguarded mountainside. A sudden updraft blew her hair backward, the lashing blonde tresses ablaze atop her frail, purplish silhouette. Morris felt the scene pressing itself firmly into his chest, the expansiveness seemingly drawing the very breath from his lungs in an involuntary sigh of awe. Stretched out before them, a deep and jagged valley cut its way southwest, through sturdy mountain ridges and sheer, jutting cliff faces. Beneath the snowcapped apices that

293

rimmed the valley, rich bands of red and yellow aged the landscape like tree rings. Morris and June stood in silent veneration, shafts of cloud-filtered sunshine mottling the vista before them, the pallet of each passing moment rendered unrecognizable from the last. From somewhere behind them a stream came to life, rushed under the cold, dead asphalt at their feet, and disappeared into the boundless majesty below.

When she spoke, June did so in reverent tones, as if not to disrupt the birds circling overhead or the breeze folding itself coolly in and out of the frame.

"What about the end of all this, Morris?"

He was on the verge of taking up the subject, but something stalled the words in his throat. She opened her mouth and a minute later it all flowed out. Her incredible past. Her never-ending present. Her uncertain future.

"I've been running for so long, now. So long I can't remember a time when I ever stood still. Running over plains and mountains and valleys and oceans. Over weeks and years and more lifetimes than one person can ever possibly live. It all seems like eternity." She turned her face to his. It was almost translucent, a perfect reflection of the blazing, blue-white peaks around her.

"How does all this end, Morris?"

He stood still, shivering in the sun's generous rays, as he heard her walk slowly back to the Jeep. At the roadside, her footsteps hesitated for a second. Morris gazed out over the valley, deep and immense and full of nothing at all. In the distance he heard a truck careening around a corner, its gears crushing and grinding together, its full load pouring itself down the mountainside. Then he heard a noise louder than anything he could remember.

When he saw June's face again, pale as a memory, he couldn't tell if she was really standing there at all, or whether her ghostly white form had simply melted into the snow.

Chapter XIII

Citizens of the World

Flanked by gossamer-strewn peaks and threading an arc imagined by the sun's quotidian march, Morris guided the old green Jeep south across gulches and through valleys, past springs and villages and lonely groves, on toward Mexicos, old and New. For more than two thousand wandering miles he had followed the center of the solar system over the afternoon horizon, the earth turning away from its gilded flare, even as the wheels beneath him drove on toward it. Now it set at his shoulder, a celestial mystery disappearing behind the mountains and into the silent heavens beyond. As he steered on under lengthening shadows, Morris recalled the space stretching out behind him; the endless fields of sorghum and corn and sunflower; the red brick row houses lining Maple and Park and Main Streets in a dozen towns small and large; city skylines bended to star spangled pinnacles, their well-hustled corners squaring off below in a deep sea of enterprise and capital and tooth-and-claw competition. Big skies and big ideas and big dreams. He thought of the people, too, going about their business, living their lives in a million different ways, all imbued with a sense of what it means to be American, confident and tall and proud, and beaming at the cusp of a millennium fraught with the unknown. And he pondered the land on which these people made their homes, so full of promise and potential, so essential to their collective identity.

Streaming alongside the crooked route, the Arkansas River whispered an ancient wisdom, told of the long days before man and beast, before railroads and arrowheads and caravans and placer gold; before wagon wheels and Interstates and contrails tearing impossible holes in the scorched blue yonder. It spoke in rich, warm tones, sometimes gripped in a torrent of sudden excitement, other times suffused with gentle, timeless patience, but always honest and steady and true to its own form. Morris cut the radio between signals and held close to the river's tales. He was glad for its company until, somewhere around Nathrop, it too surged to the east, returning just once to gather up Shavano's streamlet, before continuing on its pilgrimage toward the mighty Mississippi-Missouri and its own place in America's vast and interwoven folkloric narrative.

Alone again with his thoughts, Morris watched as the faithless winds swept through the long, reedy grass blanketing the valley floor. High above on the mountain rim, the same winds were blowing clouds off some of the higher peaks.

He recalled with a chill June's open question, "What do you suppose is beyond them..."

He regretted not having answered her... or was it his not having an answer that really bothered him? He couldn't tell. For June, there seemed to be more fullness contained in a single supposition than in all the geology and cosmology and biology packed into the universe, as if the simple act of imagining could, indeed, shift the hulking mountains into the sea. He looked again toward the darkened ridge, tried to see through them to the other side, to summon an answer out of sheer force of thought, but he could not conjure it. They were real to him, solid, even in the dying light.

Morris drove on past lodges full of vacancy and empty cantinas and schools that looked like tiny white church buildings. And in between, mile after mile of silence and calm. It was almost dusk when he curled off the main route and into the quiet center of a sleepy little township. He surveyed the scene for a short while, then circled back to the first and only accommodation he remembered passing.

Outside in the evening's early chill, Morris smoked a cigarette and replayed the events of that afternoon. He had not, until that moment, noticed his hands trembling. Recalling the scene left behind him, he felt once again the cold wind rush by his body as the truck careened around the corner. He saw the valley stretched out at his fingertips and imagined June meandering breezily across the road, her face the picture of serenity, her steps calm and languid. And he heard the gears crunch and the brakes screech as they echoed out across the great expanse.

After a long while, he walked back to the car and opened the driver's side door.

"Hey," he announced to the figure, a thatch of blonde, slumped in the passenger's seat. "That's it for today. We're here."

#

The diner across the road was the only place still open when Morris and June sat down at a table for two near the window. They ordered something that went uneaten and a bottle of cheap wine.

"You know," Morris waited until the third glass had steadied his hands before broaching the subject, "I had a near death experience once,"

"Oh," she replied in invitation.

Strange, he thought, June's hands seemed not to quiver at all, not even in the miraculous minutes after she almost walked right through a truck. She simply climbed back into the Jeep and fell, almost instantly, into a long and deep slumber, her near-extinguished light still glowing fresh beneath her translucent skin.

Morris shook his head and recalled aloud his own almost-last story.

"I can't remember the year, exactly, but I do remember the ocean was incredibly rough. I was only young, maybe seven or eight, but I'd never seen swells that large before. Not by a long way. There must've been a cyclone off the north coast or something. They used to get battered up there. Still do, I guess," he paused over a sip of wine. "Anyway, my friends and I would go down to the beach in the morning, before school, and just watch these ferocious green giants rolling in, one set after another, each crashing onto the sand in huge bursts of dirty white foam.

"'Whoa!' we'd exclaim. 'Did you see that one?'

"It was thrilling just sitting there, to see nature whipped into such a frenzy like that. Nobody dared go out. Of course, there were rumors that some of the older kids skipped school to go surfing, but nobody really believed them. It was just too crazy. Too...raw.

"Well, we kept waiting for it to settle down, but the ocean only seemed to grow angrier and meaner. Day and night these enormous waves just pounded away at the sand.

We could actually hear them from our house, back across the coastal highway. I'd have these incredibly lucid dreams, these night terrors, really, where I was tumbling around beneath the waves, pinned to the ocean floor by their unrelenting power, unable to breath. And I'd wake up screaming in a cold sweat. Well, I remember lying there in the darkness one night, exhausted yet too afraid to sleep, and thinking to myself, 'If this keeps up, the ocean is going to wash away the whole town, the whole country by morning. We'll all just sink under the waves and be done for.' I was never so concerned with living on an island as I was at that very moment. Really, I was truly terrified." Morris laughed to himself. "Childhood naiveté, I guess."

"Gift of imagination." June smiled back. It seemed more of a general observation than a direct reply.

"Right," Morris nodded in slow agreement. "You're right. Anyway, I remember lying there thinking, 'If this is really it, if this crazy ocean really is going to wash over us and drown us all in our sleep, I'm not going to be having some horrible nightmare when it happens. I'm going to be wide awake, damn it. More awake than I've ever been. In fact, I'm going to be standing right there when it happens, on the shoreline.'"

Morris watched the whites of June's eyes grow as she anticipated the next move.

"So I got out of bed..."

"No!"

"I got out of bed and put on my board shorts and favorite T-shirt, a black 'Bad Billy's' shirt I'd just gotten for my birthday. I remember it now. Then I climbed right out my bedroom window and, in the dark of night, all of seven or eight years of age, I crossed the highway and marched right down to the beach to confront this mighty ocean."

June leaned in over the table, an attentive, captivated expression on her face. Morris thought he could hear her heartbeat quicken as he approached the water's edge. It was almost as if she didn't know how it ended but was waiting breathlessly to learn if he had actually survived.

"The air was still and warm and the booming sound of the waves carried easily across the night. I could hear it growing louder as I neared the end of the street. Then I saw them under the moonlight, these enormous white mountains moving across the black sea, through the howling darkness. The sound of them crashing was something unreal, otherworldly.

"BOOM! ... BOOM! ... BOOM!"

"I stood there, at the top of this rickety old wooden staircase that led down to where the sand used to be, where the currents were swirling, ripping the dunes back out to sea. I stood there for a long time thinking, 'This is it. It's all come to this. I'm going in.'"

"No..." June covered her mouth with both hands.

"So I took the stairs, one step at a time, feeling the turbulence rushing under me, hearing the water gurgling like a great big sink, then sweeping out to sea again. Well, I damn near had my foot in the water when I saw something, way out in the deep. It was like a... a kind of light. Don't ask me what it was. Probably a ship. Or a star. Or my own, seven-year-old's 'gift of imagination,' as you might say. But I saw it then and I believed it like I had never believed anything in my life. And I thought, maybe this isn't the end after all. Somewhere out there, over this giant black thrashing pool, there's another land, another shoreline. And if that's so, maybe there's another Morris, standing on that shoreline, staring out into his own abyss. Well, I thought, I have to go and see if he's there, this strange, foreign Morris, standing on that strange, foreign shore. I have to know if he's as real as I am...

Morris paused to properly relive the moment, one he hadn't summoned in this way since he was just a boy.

"Well," he returned to the present at last, "I guess I didn't really understand what I was thinking. Maybe I still don't. But I do remember grabbing onto that rail for dear life. I remember scrambling back up the stairs and running all the way home. And I remember listening to the giant waves crash until I fell asleep."

June appeared visibly relieved by this apparent revelation, as if only now could she go on talking with the Morris who had lived to narrate the tale.

"And you know the strangest thing of all?" he added, as if an afterthought. "The next morning, I walked down the beach, as usual, expecting to see the thrashing waves and churning currents... but there was nothing. No waves. No foaming geysers. No high-pitched shouts of 'Whoa!' from the other kids who had likewise gathered at the ends of the streets. Just a calm, serene ocean, blue and at peace with itself. It was actually kind of eerie. Like we had all witnessed something die."

"Come alive," she stated, fixing him with a penetrating gaze.

Again, he couldn't tell if it was a correction, an imperative or just another one of June's general observations.

#

So they drove on, Near Death in the rearview mirror, Uncertain Life out on the road ahead. Gradually the mountains yielded their space to the morning sky and the sleepy Colorado towns folded into the foothills behind them. Gone too, it seemed, were the Market and Elm and Front Streets of Middle America. The stark southwest landscape belonged instead to places with names like Tres Piedras, Sangre de Cristo and Ojos Calientes, strange words that rolled off the tongue, invited an accent, even from the occasional antipodean visitor. The transition was all around. In the juniper shrub, the undead cactus, the endless sandy plains, here was one country bleeding into the next, the love and wars of generations spilling out over the rough terrain and into the common arteries feeding a nation.

It takes a world to build an empire, thought Morris as he steered between a mountain pass on the way to New Mexico's capital pueblo. Just as June had said. They come from near and far, those who make this land. They are born and they die, they strive and they perish in the wind. How many stories, originating from the remotest parts of the planet, were somehow tied up here, in these shifting sands? And in unlikely combinations, too. He was trying to imagine what a ranch hand up in Los Alamos might have to say to a third generation Italian from East Harlem when June interrupted his meandering reverie.

"There used to be an unbeatable chili place just up ahead." She craned her lovely neck as if to get a view around the bend.

Morris was again made abruptly aware how little he knew about his pale eyed co-pilot. "I didn't know you'd been to Santa Fe before."

She smiled at him sweetly. "How would you?" The question didn't need asking.

Following her directions, Morris steered off Paseo de Peralta, down from North to South Guadalupe and on past the old Railyard Park to their destination. A simple, yellow structure in the pueblo architectural style, the place was unassuming enough from the outside. Morris was about to say something when June beat him to it.

"Ah!" she exclaimed, grinning like a schoolchild. "This is it!"

A matronly Hispanic woman in her middle years, with shiny olive skin and deep brown eyes, escorted her guests past a bar bedazzled with multicolored bottles and various religious paraphernalia; skulls, candles, painted masks, weeping statuettes and so forth. At June's request, she led them to a table in the patio area out back, where they took a table under the shade of an orange-red umbrella and a few sparsely leafed pines. A head high fence of cut spruces, strung together with wire, rimmed the tiny space and year-round Christmas lights, dimmed during the daytime, were draped carefully over the branches and through the umbrella spokes. All the furniture seemed to be made from local wood; perhaps, Morris guessed, crafted down the road by the owner's brother or son. Or maybe in his weekend hobby shed.

"You really should try the chiles rellenos," June read Morris' menu upside down from across the wobbly table. Hers remained unopened on the adjacent seat. "Or the sopaipilla," she added, "with pork adovada. Yeah, the sopaipilla for sure. Or the green chile stew."

Morris looked up from his menu. "And what are you going to order?"

"What, me?" She appeared honestly blindsided by the question. "No, no. I'm still full from breakfast. I'll probably just have a spiced coffee. With cinnamon and piloncillo. Or," she read the time off her naked wrist, "maybe a glass of sangria. They make crazy-good sangria here. With mezcal, in place of tequila. It's maybe the best in town."

Slowly at first, then in more enthusiastic numbers, the lunch crowd began to saunter in. With them they brought dust and conversation and the small-town life of the quiet capital. They came in wide brimmed hats and leather riding boots worn around the insteps; in blue jeans and band T-shirts and moppish college hairdos; in long floral dresses and ribboned curls and strappy sandals. Morris listened to the slow hum as it filled the patio, transforming it from a lonely little corral on the corner of nowhere in particular to a convivial meet-up where friends and neighbors traded tips of the hat and the kind of bare, honest chit chat that neither arouses suspicion nor indicts character.

Across from Morris and June, a brown-skinned couple sat with their three small children. They might have been from El Salvador or Guatemala or perhaps Old Mexico. Or, Morris reasoned, just up the bend. The father, a healthy ten years older than his pretty wife, wore deep laugh wrinkles around his eyes and slightly greying hair combed back at the wings. He was short but thick through the chest; powerful in stature, like an ox. He addressed his wife in Spanish and the children in English.

"And what about you, Clari?" he spoke to the youngest child, a girl, her mother's embodiment in miniature but with her father's kind, slightly glazed expression. "What did you study this morning?"

"Dad, you ask me the same every Wednesday," she complained without gusto or intent. "You know every Wednesday we have the same thing."

"And every Wednesday I want to know, guapa, what my beautiful girl has been learning in... now, let me see," he stroked his chin theatrically, "is it camel riding?"

"No!" she rolled her eyes and half moaned, half laughed.

"Oh, ok. Then, it must be...scuba diving?"

"No!" the mock annoyance gave way entirely to girlish laughter.

"Ok, ok , ok. In that case, it's most certainly... parachute jumping?"

"No!" the older brothers chorused their sister's protest.

"Geography and math, Pa," corrected the older boy, who couldn't have been much beyond ten years of age. "Clari has geography and math. Rafa has English and science and I have history and religion."

The father whispered something in Spanish to his wife who, raising her hand to a smiling mouth, let a honeyed laugh escape over a row of billboard white teeth.

"And tell me, Miguel," the father continued his gentle interrogation, "what did you learn in history this morning?"

The boy appeared flat-footed for a second, his mind clearly reshuffling some unseen events from that morning before a satisfactory response came to him. "Nothing you haven't taught me already, Pa."

The father said something else to the mother and this time the whole family began to laugh. Morris had the sudden urge to join in but realized how obviously inappropriate that would have seemed to do so. Instead, he turned to his right, where a group of a half dozen young men and women were pushing a row of tables together, evidently expecting more guests to join them. They were engrossed in two simultaneous conversations; one regarding the present state of American immigration policy, the other to do with some finer points on the works of Plutarch.

"College kids," whispered June, looking eagerly over Morris' shoulder and making no effort to conceal her attempts at eavesdropping.

"I'm not saying they're not vital to the economy, or even that they don't have a place in our society," a lanky ginger kid was lecturing anyone unfortunate enough to be caught within earshot. "Only that there's a right way to come to this country, and there's a wrong way. I'm for the right way. That's all."

"Andy, your family's Scottish for Chrissake!" one of the young ladies snapped back at him to the undisguised amusement of a few others in the group.

"Scotch-Irish, thank you. Presbyterian dissenters, actually, just as you're blaspheming right now," his protest

306

drew rolling eyes along his table. "And what of it? They came through the front door, didn't they?"

"Yes, when it was the size of a barn door," the young woman, a pert brunette character with flashing eyes and a red kerchief tied around her head, rejoined. She waited for the stragglers to seat themselves before she brought the rest of her point down.

"Your Cochrane folk re-emigrated from Ireland, correct? When the Church of England was laying down the law there."

His floundering silence was all the invitation she needed to plough ahead.

"So, when was it, eh? Eighteenth century? Nineteenth? Do you even know?"

"What does it matter 'when?'" the young man, who looked suddenly more like a boy now that he was seated, shook his orange head like he was making a cocktail inside of it. "They came legally. That's all I care about it."

"That's just it, Andy," the woman in the red kerchief lowered her voice which, oddly, seemed only to give more weight to her what she had to say. "Laws change, my fickle friend. Morality doesn't. I mean, it's not like your ancestors were somehow superior to the people trying to come here today, looking to start a better life. It's just that your lot got in before the loop closed. That's it. It's not about 'huddled masses yearning to breathe free' anymore. Times are different."

"Oh yeah?" Andy spat back, clearly annoyed. "And how do you know all that?"

One of the other students murmured something about the Immigration Act of 1907 and how the tougher parameters for 'feeble mindedness' might have made life difficult for the arriving Cochranes, when the rest of the group arrived in a cheer.

"And what are we arguing about today, my learned students?" An older man with a grey beard wrestled multiple pitchers of frothing ale onto the middle of the table as they were promptly, simultaneously emptied into outstretched glasses. He was maybe in his late fifties, reckoned Morris, and quite likely their professor.

"We were just saying that Socrates was not an Athenian or a Greek, Sir!" exclaimed someone from the other discussion group. "He was..." and here they all, even the simpering Andy Cochrane, raised their glasses in chorused unison, "...a Citizen of the World!"

A small army of busboys and waiters followed the professor with more pitchers of beer and tumblers of water and menus and bowls of tortilla chips with little ramekins of salsa verde and guacamole. They worked as one, darting under outstretched arms and wild gesticulations, laying a feast before the pliable, boisterous young minds.

It takes a world to build an empire, Morris repeated to himself. When he turned around, he saw June's sangria glass raised and a fresh smile spread wide across her face.

#

As the lunchtime rush subsided and the libations, poured at the feet of fragile yet determined inquiry, continued to flow at the students' table, the ebullient group came to occupy more and more of the patio's available volume. They rehashed and refined points, reworked angles of attack, redoubled positions of defense and reinvestigated suspect premises. The conversation was wide-ranging and cascaded easily and seamlessly from one subject to the net, oftentimes with little more than a common name or author or place to connect the oratory sinew. Occasionally the professor, for Morris had since discerned that he was, indeed, the custodian of these rambling, colliding cerebrums, would interject, but he did so only to act as guide, not judge or jury. His contributions, therefore, came mostly in the form of questions.

"And you, Jay," he addressed an affable character in a green trucker's cap, "would you likewise follow the opinion of the learned expert in the field, gymnastics in the case of the son of Melesias, or that of the majority?"

Searching the crowd for support, the young man scratched at his stubbly chin. "I'll go for the expert," he said at last. "I mean, right?"

"Because a good decision is based on knowledge, and not on numbers?" the professor encouraged.

"Right. Of course!"

"And so, in the case of democracy, is it not then fair to say..." and here the strand was lost amidst the general to and fro, only to be resolved in a burst of clapping and laughter. So it went, the atmosphere open and warm and convivial and, without being consciously so, inviting, too.

Morris could not define, nor later recall, the precise moment at which he and June became enveloped in the wider discourse, their own ideas and notions suffused with the prevailing current, only that it seemed improbable that they should ever have remained separate, discrete from its flow, their table a mere satellite to an investigation that had been carried on since the dawn of time. Indeed, it seemed perfectly reasonable to him, on deeper consideration, that they had all sat down together, taken up a set of founding principles at the inception of human consciousness and carried it over the very lip of the event horizon. So he thought to himself in a moment of perceived clarity, the mezcal now coursing happily through his temples, his veins glowing in the afternoon sun.

Enjoying the buzz of the blue agave nectar, Morris tuned in and dropped out of conversations as they flew by his earshot.

There was Orange Andy's fearful nativism...

"It comes down to respect for the law. I'm not talking about legal immigrants, you see. It's the illegals I'm concerned about. And not just me, either..."

"Tell me again," came a voice from the hidden corner of the crowd, "the difference between an immigrant, legal or illegal, and an expatriate?"

"What, like people who are no longer patriotic?"

"Hmm..." the collective hum.

Red Kerchief's bookish expositions...

"Literally, from the Latin, ex 'out of' and patria, 'fatherland' or 'country. But yes, you're right. The difference is mostly sociological. That we use 'immigrant' as a pejorative for relocating non-westerners and 'expat' as a friendly badge for the welcomed whites is one of many problems I have with the current dialogue."

"As for the term 'illegals'..." someone could not help but stoke the embers.

"Ah, don't get me started!"

And many more confused and cross fired snippets besides...

Morris was enjoying himself out on the little patio, with the homemade tables and the quenching sangria and the budding sophistry. So much so, in fact, that he didn't notice the escaping day until it had settled into the hillside. The professor, resisting fervent pleas to stay for another round, waved his students "and our new friends" goodbye and left the future at the bar. The next round came anyway.

It was June who drove them, Morris and an uncountable number of vaguely interchangeable characters, to someone's place in the foothills a while later. Functionally, the house was more tent than permanent abode, with people spilling out of every loose flap and panel. They wandering the halls, lazed on mismatched lawn chairs and, in the case of one conspicuously liberated threesome, sloshed around in a children's wading pool full of pink and blue suds. Drinking and smoking and talking in circles were students of the pre-, post- and non-graduating variety, plus random townsfolk, drifters, runaways, backpackers and at least one frustrated pizza delivery man who remained, despite having hounding everyone present, seventeen dollars short of the order in question. Surveying the freewheeling symposium of classicists and pseudo-intellectuals, wannabe musicians and trashcan percussionists, chess enthusiasts, neo-hippies, fire-twirlers, steam-punks, madmen and assorted other non-classifiable identities before him, Morris was at once enchanted. In his fractured, agave-doused state of mind, however, he had little at his disposal to separate the real from the unreal, the dialectician from the sophist, the concrete present from any other freely plucked moment in time. And so, resigned to a rather non-Socratic ignorance, he went happily, blissfully along for the ride just the same.

#

It was against this feverish backdrop that June came to Morris and, without disturbing the moment with a single word, took his hand in hers. Leaving the fire but not the wine behind, they climbed a slow rise in back of the house, edging higher and higher along the ridge until the music became a distant chant and the light could barely be seen through the smoke and the haze. After a while, they came to a clearing, off the rocky path, which afforded an uninterrupted view out over the bluish-purple darkness below. There they sat while

Morris gathered his breath. The heady elixir steeling his resolve, he leapt into the deep end of unanswered inquiry.

"Who are you, June?" He wanted her to start at the beginning, to reveal everything. "I mean, who are you, really?"

"But you already know, Morris," she demurred. "You've known since the beginning."

"I know, yes. I mean, I think I do. But I need you to tell me," he hesitated, faltered. "Does that make sense? Do you understand why?"

When she spoke again, after an infinite pause, Morris had a sense the stars themselves were listening in.

"As you have by now guessed, I came to this land from all across the known world. I am pilgrim and puritan from England, from Anglia and Sussex and Kent. I am Dutch platoon and barbarian of the Middle Rhine..."

She looked at him, unblinking in the moonlight. Her beauty seemed to have gathered a sudden agelessness, an elegance transcending time itself. Morris sat, wholly captivated.

"I hail from Ulster and Scotland. You see me scattered across the North East and settled up and down the Appalachian range.

"I trace from Spain, too, soldiered in the forts of Florida and here in Santa Fe, not far from where you sit.

"I am Isleño and Criollo, as well as Tejano and Californio and mestizo. I am Cajun, too. Brought down from Acadia."

Morris listened with intense concentration, June's words swimming through his consciousness. He felt a kind of fresh lucidity wash over him.

Freely, she continued. "I was born in conflict, Morris. In chains. A Protestant and a slave, a freeman and an indentured servant. I came in good health and poor, carrying smallpox, measles and plague, the seeds of destruction rooted deep within me, the knives at my brothers' and sisters' throats running through my veins, their whips in my hand and lashing my own back."

Her figure, lithe and ethereal, shimmered against the sky. Morris breathed her in.

"I am Deniker's Nordique and Ripley's teutonisch. That much you can tell from my skin and my bones, from my eyes here shining under our pale lunar guide. But I am also black as the night above; purple black and blue black and rich, red black like the iron soil under our feet.

"My blood is Kongo and Mbundu, of the north and the south. I am Ibibio and Bamileke, Tikar and Igbo, Mende and Mandinka, Fula and Akan and Yoruba too. I am more tribes than can ever be killed or displaced or forgotten.

"I am Macua and Malagasy.

"I am indigo and tobacco and rice. And later, cotton, too.

"I am death on the ocean and blindness in the field. I am rape and savagery in the barn. I am fear in the heart, piety in public, intolerance in the quietest soul. I am graven images and blasphemy in one. I am murder a million times over. I am screaming, howling silence.

"But I am also beacon-hand and worldwide welcome...

Morris closed his eyes, feeling the salty rivulets stream his face.

"I am Russian, of the Orthodox Church. I am the unslain children of Alix of Hesse, those who fled after the February Revolution.

"But I am also the Jews of Odessa, of Kiev and Warsaw, the ghastly pogroms ripping at my gut.

"I am Italian. I am Catholic. I am the starving emigres from the sunburned Mezzogiorno.

"I am the Christians of Lebanon and Syria. The Muslims and Druze, too.

"I am Filipino and Korean.

"I am the Chinese who came down through Canada, the Mexicans who crossed the Rio Grande, the Cubans who fled their pretty, impoverished island."

"I am Micks and Dagos, Polacks and Limeys, Niggers and Okies and Beaners. I am Japs and Chinks and Towelheads, too.

"I am the mighty put upon, the unbreakable oppressed, the enduring masses who hold together the history of our kind, of humankind."

Morris lay on his back, staring at the skies above. He imagined the stars, those abiding celestial bodies, migrating across the heavens on their endless march through time and space. When he felt June's lips pressed on his closing eyes, he saw the light run together in a flash.

"I am America," she declared at last. "The world inside a country...and far beyond it."

\#

Chapter XIV

Morris, Alive

Morris woke, alone on the side of a mountain, with the sun on his face and a crystalline image fixed at the fore of his mind. For the first time since his journey began, he knew exactly where he was going. Despite, or perhaps because of, the previous evening's activities, his head was free of noise, of clutter, the world around him rendered now in brilliant, high definition.

Stepping carefully down the hillside track, he noticed over by the drop-off, behind a mound of red dirt and rock, a magenta peony with a lush, cream-colored center. Against the harsh earth the flower expressed its full, magnificent bloom. Morris recalled, from some rainy afternoon session at The Strand on Broadway, the myth of Paeon, student of Asclepius, the Greek God of medicine. When Paeon began to overshadow his mentor's skills, the God became enraged with jealousy and threatened to have his pupil killed. At the last moment, Zeus himself intervened, saving Paeon from certain death by turning him into the perennial that flowered now, quite out of season, by Morris' feet. Smiling, the young man descended the remaining slope and made his way across the vacant yard to the old green Jeep.

There might have been tumbleweeds or unconscious revelers or a fiesta still in full, vibrant swing, but Morris could not have noticed any of it. Now that he had a clear idea of his destination, his attentions had begun to focus on that singular point out in the future. He walked with purpose, the dust kicked up by his heels relegated to the distant past of some bygone century.

On the passenger side dashboard he found a paper serviette, carefully folded into the shape of a swallowtail butterfly. The work of steady fingers and patient hands, its delicacy seemed unreal against the careless, windswept landscape swirling around outside.

Morris unfolded it gently; slow, reverse origami. On the opening side, in long, sloping cursive, was written:

Suppose we could see what lies beyond the mountains.

With Love ~ J

Her parting imperative. Or was it just a general observation? Arms resting on the wheel, Morris reread the words ten, twenty, fifty times over. He felt the paper in his hands, as if he were holding hers. Then, turning the note over, he read aloud the name of a roadside motel in Madison, where he had first encountered that true American Spirit. He wondered when she had written it, imagined her pale eyes on these same words, her fingers running along the precise, lepidopterous creases. Had she composed it during their time together on the road? A flight-filled expression inspired by all they had discovered and shared together? Or had it always been with her, part of her own peculiar story?

For a long time he sat motionless on the cracking leather then, instinctively, hopefully, even, he leaned back over the rear bench seat. Seeing his duffle bag was the only luggage in the car, he laughed, softly at first, then with profound, soul shaking abandon.

"Suppose we do," he declared aloud to himself, to the rolling wind sweeping ripples across the wading pool, to the defiant magenta perennial, in sweet, solitary blossom, high up on the hillside. "Suppose we do."

Finally, Morris put the Jeep in gear and, still laughing, drove off into the rising morning, alone at last and with his destination at hand.

#

At first, Morris barely noticed the racing scenery as he tore out across the vast, unwatered mass of rock and sand between the Cross of the Martyrs and all that lay to its bone dry, bloodshot west. Mesita, Thoreau and Gallup flew by his periphery in uniform signage before he even realized the state border was under his wheels and, scorched into dusty insignificance, fast disappearing behind him. Climbing over his shadow in the early morning air, he heard raspy whispers from the north and south, from the Navajo and Zuni reservations and those belonging to the Hopi and the Apache. Like cool breezes they rushed through the valley of his mind, indecipherable tales mounted on zephyr back, riding the winds of time across the ancient planes. In silent reverence he drove on, the parallel lines of the elsewhere beside him racing ahead to converge on a single, unseen point in the future.

Immersed in the excitement of flight, he almost forgot about the laws of physics underpinning his every moment. Were it not for a parched gas tank and a slow leak in his left rear tire, Morris might well have blown right through Flagstaff and headlong into a realm of suspended impossibility beyond. The final hiss brought him to within one hundred yards of a mechanic's shop just off Historic Route 66, where he deposited his trusty ride for the afternoon with a cheery old fellow in dungarees part denim, part grease.

"This one's not far-off done neither," the mechanic tapped his boot against the smoothed tread of the

317

corresponding rear tire. "And you'll want the front pair rotated too. You goin' much further?"

"Not far." Morris squinted into the high noon glare. "One more shift. Two, tops." The old man nodded at the wheezing radiator grill, "Ya mind?"

Morris stood back as the mechanic stepped around to the driver's side and, with blind familiarity, leaned in and popped the hood. The captured steam escaped with an audible rush.

"I could get to seein' 'bout this too," the old man offered from the corner of his mouth. A slow wince crawled across Morris' face in muted response.

"It's not critical, yet," the man conceded after poking around for a few minutes. "Coolant's pretty dry... but there doesn't appear to be any serious leaks. I wouldn't be pushin' my luck though. She ain't no young buck, not like you 'n me." He smiled and wiped his hands on the cleanest part of his dirty clothes. "Say, any reason you need to be drivin' this time-a day?"

"None at all," Morris seized on the chance of returning to his course.

"S'pose I get this turned around this afternoon," the man nodded, as if offering his side of a bargain. "You take that last shift of yours through the night. Ride slow. Take 'er nice n easy. Keep the heater on." He threw Morris a look, half puzzled, half cautionary. "Get's cold out here in the evenin', you know."

Morris looked at the old green Jeep, the state's miles flogged into its panels, the dirt and grit of an entire country splattered across its mud guards and windshield and caked onto its iconic name. He thought again about the wounded faces of rust belt America and wondered what might become of places like Toledo and Detroit and Pittsburgh and the men and women who built the factories that built a nation. What postindustrial fate awaited those graveyards of heavy machinery, those heaving, hardscrabble beacons of yesteryear? He thought of Baltimore, too, and the friends he had known there. Charm City's population had been in decline for half a century or more.

"She'll make it fine enough." He shook himself to. "Thank you, sir."

Having arranged to return later that afternoon, Morris struck a match and set off down the street, following the old man's directions to a local beanery where he might take a bite to eat and rest up for the night ahead. The air was cool, but not unpleasant, and he was glad to find himself among the noon pedestrians who, almost without exception, nodded in salutation as he passed them by. For a block or two he imagined himself painted into a similar background, a cabal of unseen centripetal forces bearing down on him from the distant corners of the known universe, conspiring to stay his wandering feet, to plant him in the familiar soil of Anytown, U.S.A. He pondered this new reality for a second, then a cooling gust blew by his feet, sweeping the leaves from the gutter and casting them off down the street. He watched them lifted into the air, cradled for a fleeting glimpse, then scattered across car roofs and alongside the multi-colored newspaper boxes that bordered the sidewalk. There they rested for a moment, before a relaying current whisked them on, further down the way. Morris lit another cigarette and resumed his pace, the breeze dancing happily at his back.

Shortly thereafter he came upon the red paneled wooden facade located, as promised, across the street from a rusted iron hotel sign that looked older than the sky against which it leaned and swayed. A bell above the door announced his entry to a small group of early bird drinkers. Morris took a menu and a seat at the bar.

"Getcha sumthin' a drink?" The barkeep didn't so much interrupt her work as she did simply intuit his need.

"Just a water, thanks," Morris heard himself reply, then quickly added, "I mean, for now."

From under straight cut brunette bangs, she gave him a suspicious eye. "Gotta range a house brews on tap," she nodded toward a glassed off area in the rear of the space, behind which an enormous, copper colored chemistry set, replete with hoses and gauges and various tanks and vats, was busily turning raw ingredients into boutique seasonal ales. He got the feeling they took their beer very seriously in this particular establishment.

"You know," smiled Mrs. Brunette Bangs, "for when you're ready."

Morris looked around him, at the old rail yard memorabilia hanging on the walls; the potbelly cast iron stove in the center of the dining room; the smoothed, black walnut countertop catching liquor-filtered light from behind the bar. There was a genuine respect for craftsmanship here, a kind of pioneering attitude toward the honesty and purity of manual labor, for bringing something forth from the elements and carving, boiling, staining, fermenting, augmenting its properties until it yielded to man's needs and desires. He was thinking about the early frontiersmen, their backs rigid against the fast-cooling days of a dawning winter, when from the end of the bar a husky baritone stole him from his reverie.

"Bar's a lonely place to be recording daydreams."

Morris looked down at the pad before him and the pen in his hand, then back in the direction of the remark. The voice belonged to a kindly looking gentleman, also seated by himself, elbows perched on the purple heartwood, flannelette sleeves rolled down weather-worn forearms, eyes keen and darting over an easy, preemptive smile. Depending on the angle of the light, dimmer at his end of the bar, the man appeared anywhere from middle thirties to late forties, perhaps even older. A shaft fell alternately on his high forehead and, when he leaned back, his own writing pad.

"Just a few ideas..." Morris shrugged off an affected apathy. "Notes and such."

"That's all any of 'em are, m' boy. Ideas." The man gave a hearty laugh, "especially the best ones."

"The best ones?"

"Oh, books, plays, poems," he held the yellow legal pad aloft, "scribbles on this and that."

Morris looked down at his own sheaf of ideas, his 'scribbles on this and that.' The pages, double sided, appeared suddenly innumerable, his messy scrawl cramping around the curled edges, clinging to the paltry margin space, squashing, concertina-style, against the indomitable right-side precipice, then U-turning sharply back, often with no apparent regard for gravity or direction or basic aesthetics. Here, in a three-inch-plus pile of letters and lines, dots and arcs, lay his freewheeling, roadside compendium, his insomniac's refuge, his first coffee treaty and last whisky dissertation, his solitary, passenger-side, window down confession. Here was London and New York, Baltimore and East Hampton, Westchester County and Wheeling and St. Louis and Castle Rock. And countless other pins on his mental map besides. Here, too, the Victoria-Cambridge coach ride, the flame-shadowed walls of a front room in Mt. Vernon, the connecting sinew between Penn and Penn Stations. Sunset on the Seaport terrace, the smell of iodine in the hospital hall, the taste of Belgian truffles and the "raspy, shrill cry" of a red-tailed hawk; it was all there in front of him.

"What about you?" Morris motioned to the pages between the older man's elbows. "What is it you're working on, besides ideas?"

"Oh, I'm jus' writin' the great American novel," his laughter came easily. "Again."

Morris motioned to the barkeep, who fulfilled his request for a single neat whisky with a certain amount of contentment. "And one for my friend here," he added, "for..."

"Never mind ol' Archer here," she shot an affectionate look down the countertop. "He can buy his own. And yours too, come to think of it."

"'t'll be my pleasure." Archer lowered his head into the dusted light, which fell on him like a spotlight in an empty theater. For the first time, Morris caught a straight look into his eyes, wide and open and knowing and, in some sense he couldn't quite figure, vaguely recognizable.

"A woman once asked me," Morris ventured, "'Who will own the novel in the coming century?'"

Archer rocked back on his stool and began slowly tapping his pen against his chin. For a long while he sat still, keeping steady time with his sword. Morris thought he saw him muttering something to himself but couldn't be sure. At last, the man named Archer interlaced his fingers and turned his heavy, squarish shoulders back to his younger interlocutor.

"And what did you tell her?"

"I didn't have an answer at the time..."

"...Ah," Archer swept into the gap, "but now you do. Or at least, you think you do." He let free another friendly laugh. "Let me see," he let out a long breath and began jotting something on the page before him. "First, you worked backward, avoiding the question at hand. You started with the centuries preceding this, our newest one. The Twentieth belonged to the Americans, you reasoned. Particularly the back half. Updike, Bellow, Roth, Pynchon, Mailer and the rest. Boy, that sure was a hard troop to best."

Morris began to envision a vast and towering library shelf, crammed with all the books he had not yet read.

"You could even throw Nabokov in there, though technically he was Russian-born. Still, he considered himself at least part American, and part Nabokov is more than the whole of most mortals." He leaned back again to drink in the light, then returned to his page, apparently possessed by the task at hand.

"Of course, there's Faulkner and Melville and Steinbeck, though I never much cared for that whole Sea of Cortez meandering... And there's..." he muttered a dozen or so names to himself, most of which Morris either didn't know or couldn't hear. Or both. Archer had swallowed the question whole, made it his own. "Then you peel back the cover of time a little further, follow the Americans abroad at the beginning of the century, the whole Lost Generation ensemble. So you have Hemingway and Fitzgerald and Miller, Dos Passos and Pound, even Stein herself, to a certain degree... And Cummings, too, most underrated as an artist. Most underrated. A real literary renaissance man, that one..."

And on he went, reeling off the names in clumps and clods, passing an occasional footnote or opinion along the journey. Nor did he slow down when the century ticked over.

"The nineteenth century is a bit trickier." He took another deep breath and a bracing sip of whisky, then steadied his pen.

"Most would call for a three-way tie. Yes, there's really no other way around it. Britain, of course, gave us Dickens and Austen and the Bronte sisters. To say nothing of Eliot and Hardy, Disraeli, Gaskell, Kipling...

Morris watched the bookshelf grow and grow.

"The French posted Balzac and Zola. Plus Hugo, Dumas, Flaubert..."

"Don't forget Proust," the bartender, looking up from beneath her bangs, threw another three thousand pages of staggering genius on the high piling stack. How many times had she heard this performance before, Morris wondered?

"Yes, yes. Of course. Proust. And the Russians, too! Perhaps the most important of the lot!"

The man's hand was trembling now, racing across the page...

"Dostoyevski, Puskin, Tolstoy... Yes, most obviously Tolstoy."

Morris sat, engrossed in the mental whirlpool spinning away before him, and sipped his whisky slowly, happily. Occasionally Archer would forget a name, then he would tap his pen against his chin and, summoning it from another realm, laugh it squarely into the line-up.

"And Gogol! Ha ha! Of course! Then there's Turgenev, Chekhov..."

So rose a giant edifice of literature, erected for the benefit of nobody in particular, a funeral pyre for the Gods of Letters, most of whom were long since deceased. Morris finished his drink and, without drawing the others' attention, tucked payment and tip for two under the bar top napkins.

"That's all very impressive," he interjected sometime later during a rare, multi-second lull in the list making. "Very impressive. But the question was regarding the future, about who will own the novel in the coming century."

Archer took on a solemn expression. He looked toward the barkeep and, seeing her back turned and elsewhere occupied, lowered his voice to a barely audible whisper.

Morris could not be sure, but thought he heard the man say, "The future has no content, not even for a young man such as yourself. It has only potential, the possibilities we must first imagine into existence."

He leaned back in his chair, the light bathing his forehead. Then he let out an almighty laugh and, with a furious gesture, ordered another round. Morris thanked him profusely, but by the time the drink arrived, he was out the door and into the fast-fading twilight.

#

When the city of Flagstaff was mostly asleep and the coolness of the night had crept into the Jeep's tired old panels, Morris straightened his seat to the familiar position and kicked the engine over once... twice... and a third time before it came to life. Leaving the silence behind, he steered his way due south, out of the downtown streets, over the old rail tracks and bound for the capital. It was some miles before his breath disappeared and the vehicle began to reach a comfortable temperature. Outside, everything was cloaked in darkness, the clouds overhead obscuring what light the celestial bodies cast their way. Only the earthly stars, tiny hillside clusters and sprawling valley constellations, filled the space around him.

Slowly he drove across the wine dark landscape, content to roll on the unseen waves, his confidence in the Fates sure and true. Once, outside of Phoenix, then again somewhere along Highway 8, he stopped for gas and coffee and to smoke a cigarette under the watchful sky. Otherwise, he carried on, neither pushing the vehicle or himself, rather maintaining a steady pace toward the break of morning.

Then, in the final hours of darkness, as he was running close along the Mexican border, the heavens cleared to reveal a blanket of deep-set light, called forth from the long extinct reaches of space. He pulled the Jeep over and lay on the roof for as long as he could bare, gazing into the past, until his desire for motion, for progress toward his destination, finally overcame him and flung him once more behind the wheel. Tracing the frontier under the infinite, flickering canopy, Morris imagined a symphony of humanity emanating from across the great southern horizon. Thoughts of what lay beyond the dotted line carried him forward until the faintest breath of morning delivered him to within reach of the ocean.

The sun had just expelled the light that would shortly fall on the west coast when Morris pulled the Jeep into a vacant parking lot in La Jolla, a few minutes north of San Diego. Without thinking to close the door behind him, he felt his way down a set of wooden stairs leading to the beach and, drawing the salt air deep into his lungs, alighted barefoot onto the sand. A few paces ahead, the edge of the ocean broke against a rock shelf, which extended like petrified fingers out into the lapping waves. Morris moved through the ancient grasp until he felt the water, cool and vital, rush over his feet. Behind him, the past laid itself out across a weary continent, the weight of the world heavy on her shoulders.

Gazing into the pre-dawn, where the whitecaps jostled for the coming rays, Morris thought he saw a light on the horizon, another figure, perhaps, standing at the edge of a strange and foreign shore.

THE END